# Aptitude
## J.S. Wik

JK Publishing

# Copyright

This book is a work of fiction, all characters names, places, and events are used fictitiously. Any resemblance is entirely coincidental.

Copyright © 2023 by J.S. Wik

As an independent author piracy can be extremely detrimental to my career. Please respect my copyright by not sharing, copying, or in any way using this file in a manner not intended.

Cover design by Sarah Kil Creative Studio
www.sarahkilcreativestudio.com

Please consider leaving a review to help other readers find this book.

# Contents

| | |
|---|---|
| Dedication | VII |
| Trigger Warnings | VIII |
| Newsletter Sign up | IX |
| 1. Inquietude | 1 |
| 2. Quietude | 5 |
| 3. Certitude | 14 |
| 4. Latitude | 24 |
| 5. Attitude | 30 |
| 6. Beatitude | 37 |
| 7. Turpitude | 42 |
| 8. Aptitude | 48 |
| 9. Plenitude | 53 |
| 10. Consuetude | 59 |
| 11. Vicissitude | 67 |
| 12. Gratitude | 72 |

| | | |
|---|---|---|
| 13. | Vastitude | 79 |
| 14. | Habitude | 87 |
| 15. | Certitude | 96 |
| 16. | Fortitude | 107 |
| 17. | Lassitude | 123 |
| 18. | Attitude | 131 |
| 19. | Definitude | 139 |
| 20. | Promptitude | 143 |
| 21. | Rectitude | 158 |
| 22. | Solicitude | 171 |
| 23. | Inaptitude | 175 |
| 24. | Gratitude | 180 |
| 25. | Beatitude | 187 |
| 26. | Plenitude | 197 |
| 27. | Pulchritude | 206 |
| 28. | Magnitude | 214 |
| 29. | Amplitude | 226 |
| 30. | Magnitude | 234 |
| 31. | Splenditude | 242 |
| 32. | Latitude | 247 |

| | | |
|---|---|---|
| 33. | Solitude | 254 |
| 34. | Finitude | 261 |
| 35. | Similitude | 273 |
| 36. | Multitude | 279 |
| 37. | Plentitude | 289 |
| 38. | Vicissitude | 298 |
| 39. | Amplitude | 307 |
| 40. | Inquietude | 314 |
| 41. | Lassitude | 319 |
| 42. | Plentitude | 326 |
| 43. | Rectitude | 334 |
| 44. | Certitude | 342 |
| 45. | Decrepitude | 350 |
| 46. | Attitude | 359 |
| 47. | Lentitude | 372 |
| 48. | Splenditude | 377 |
| 49. | Turpitude | 389 |
| 50. | Altitude | 393 |
| 51. | Pulchritude | 404 |
| 52. | Inquietude | 409 |

| | |
|---|---|
| Bonus Content | 418 |
| Newsletter Sign up | 419 |
| Also By J.S. Wik | 420 |
| About the Author | 421 |

# *Dedication*

Aptitude is dedicated to anyone and everyone that has ever doubted me and my choices. This life is mine to make the choices I decide to. If you find this uncomfortable or find yourself judging me in anyway, it is a reflection on yourself and is a mirror of where work needs to be done.

For anyone dealing with naysayers, doubters, and judgers, please ignore them and keep going! Whatever your dream is, it's in your heart for a reason! Prove them all wrong and do it anyway!

# Trigger Warnings

I would hate for my readers to come across triggering subjects that would be extremely emotionally difficult or potentially cause you harm. Read with caution if any of these are potential triggers for you. Your mental health matters!

- Date rape drug use

- Graphic violence/Murder (less than 15% of the book)

- Miscarriage (Infertility is a subject that will be included in the rest of the books in the series as well.)

# Newsletter Sign up

If you would like to be part of our Virtual Vacation Lovers community, and hear all about the incredible things J.S. Wik has coming up, simply go to the website below to sign up!
(You'll even get a free eBook out of it as a thank you!)

https://www.jswik.com

# Chapter 1

# Inquietude
Noun; disturbed state

*Present Day*

Faith finds it difficult to believe that waking up without Jonathan's kind eyes and sandy brown hair on the pillow next to hers will ever get easier. She misses the way he would look at her, the smile he would be wearing, and the way he always held her and pulled her in close. She felt completely safe in his arms, now she wonders how that could have possibly been true.

The mornings are almost worse than bedtime because some nights when she sleeps she's able to forget the nightmare she's currently living. Which means as she slowly wakes up, the realization leisurely comes to her like molasses pouring out of a spout. Other nights it's as if the nightmare just continues into her dreams; giving her no respite from it what-so-ever. Those are the mornings her overwhelming reality quickly slams into her like a freight train straight to her heart. The emotions of it all hit her before she even gets out of bed; making the rest of her day nearly impossible to go through in a normal manner.

She was able to get some sleep last night, however, the pillow beside her isn't empty this morning, but Jonathan's face isn't the one looking back at her, of course. The corners of Faith's mouth turn up slightly, she's feeling incredibly grateful for her best friend, especially in this moment. Jackie insisted on spending the night. It almost felt like the sleep overs they used to have when they were younger. The only exception being that this time there was a dark cloud looming overhead.

During the day she does what she can to keep her mind occupied on other things, but her husband's arrest and the consequent charges brought against him, always seem to barge their way through. Smiling is the most difficult it's ever been. Even with their infertility troubles and miscarriages through the years, she struggled, but somehow she still managed to hold onto a sliver of hope. There's not even a glimmer of it left for her now.

"How did you sleep?" Jackie's question pulls her out of her thoughts.

"It was better than most recent nights." She shrugs then continues, "Thank you for staying. I'm sure you being here is what made all the difference." She smiles at her reassuringly.

"You're welcome, Faith."

"What are you up to today?" She asks, not wanting to be a burden.

"I don't have anything going on. I was thinking we should go grab some breakfast. Get you out of the house and some food in you."

"OK. I can do that. Can we go somewhere that isn't in Luna Shores though? I don't want to feel like everyone's eyes are on me. Who knows what they're thinking." She looks down and says in a low voice, "Well, I'm pretty sure I know what they're thinking…"

"Anything you want. I'm not going to pretend to know what they're thinking, but I'm sure they're concerned for you."

"I'm not so sure about that." Faith shakes her head.

The news traveled fast, particularly since Jonathan's crimes took place in Caulfield; the city nearest Luna Shores. A restaurant in Sol Port may be an option, as the next town up the coast no one there would recognize Faith. Unlike in Luna Shores where everyone already knew her, especially now.

They climb out of bed and leisurely get ready to go to breakfast. Faith let's her beloved dog, Zeke, outside while she makes some coffee for her and Jackie.

"He's such a good dog." Jackie muses as she watches him run around the back yard.

Faith nods and thinks back to the night they found him. How little and vulnerable he was. Jonathan used to say he was a house warming gift from their new home since they were visiting the construction site the night he came into their lives. He was so dirty, matted, and starving, the poor little thing.

Faith has no idea what she would do without his comfort. His presence brings her a new level of peace. Especially right now.

# Chapter 2

# Quietude

Noun; *a quiet state, repose*

*Eight Years Ago*

Faith awoke on New Year's morning still Jonathan's girlfriend. He hadn't asked her to marry him. Not yet. The evening was special none the less. Dancing at their property with the moonlight glistening in the bay below was so romantic. She feels comfort in the fact that he has made it clear to her that a proposal will happen. Now, it's just a waiting game.

Jonathan sleepily rolls over, putting his arm around Faith's waist. She hadn't told him that she thought it might happen last night, and he didn't know that she had hidden her disappointment. She's thinking she should let some time pass before she shares those things with him, since they're feeling too raw right now.

Faith has the dinner shift at Love's café tonight. Her sister, Hope, will start coming back for short shifts a couple of days this week. Which will work out well since Faith has to return to her full time job as a teacher at Hilltop Elementary in a few days. Their parents, Frank and Diane, own the café. Frank has been running more of the day to day stuff ever since Hope's car accident on Christmas. Meanwhile, Diane has been taking care of Hope at their house.

Jonathan rolls over onto his back, taking his arm with him. Faith wonders if he will wake up soon. They didn't stay at their property much past midnight last night since it was getting cold. They did come home and make love and fall asleep in each other's arms shortly after, though.

Jonathan's deep breathing turns into a slightly shallower version. He rolls back over onto his side pulling Faith into him. She puts her arm around him.

Still half asleep, he kisses her on the lips. Then says, "Good morning, beautiful."

Faith smiles, "Good morning, handsome. How did you sleep?"

"I slept well. Why are you awake already? What time is it anyway?" He rolls away to check the time on the nightstand beside him.

"I just woke up. No real reason."

"OK. Did you want some breakfast?"

"Sure, I think I'm going to get in the shower first."

"I'd like to join you if that's OK?"

"Of course it is."

# APTITUDE

The two of them shower, Jonathan lets Faith finish on her own while he goes downstairs to the kitchen to start their breakfast. He takes the eggs and some bread out for French toast followed by maple flavored sausage. He's nearly finished when Faith emerges at the top of the stair case, her dark hair still wet. She's wearing comfy clothes and no makeup. Jonathan inhales deeply taking in the sight of her. He smiles.

From her vantage point she sees the furniture in the living room that they rearranged just a couple months before. Jonathan insisted on it as a way to help her feel like the condo is her home as well. She quickly notices Jonathan watching her. She starts down the stairs smiling right back at him.

As she approaches him in the kitchen, he points to the island counter, "I've made us mimosas."

"Thank you! What are we celebrating now?"

"Everything. We are celebrating everything. It is a new day, a new year and we are going to have the best year yet. Until next year that is."

"Yes we are." Faith grabs her glass and takes a sip. With a puzzled look on her face she asks, "What did you put in this?"

"I used pineapple juice instead of orange juice."

"It's delicious. Different, but delicious." She smiles graciously.

"Thank you. It seemed like a good idea."

"It was." She leans in and kisses him. He pulls her into him tight against his body.

"Last night was incredible. The best New Year's eve ever."

"Yes it was." She feels a slight sense of sadness come over her, but shoves it away before Jonathan can sense its presence.

"Is something wrong, Faith?"

"No, why do you ask?"

"It just seemed like something I said bothered you. Your energy shifted."

She wasn't fast enough. "I'm OK."

"You can tell me if something is bothering you. I'll do whatever I can to fix it."

"I know. Thank you. I'm fine, really. Last night was incredible," she gestures towards the stove and continues, "this breakfast is going to be amazing too."

"Yes it is. It's also almost done."

Jonathan puts their food on the plates as Faith grabs the utensils and glasses, then they walk to the dining room table and sit.

"This looks delicious Jonathan. Thank you so much." She says, grateful he hasn't tried to change the subject back to what might be bothering her.

"You know I enjoy cooking for you."

Taking another sip of her mimosa Faith says, "This was a nice touch too."

"Yeah, I've been planning these for a while." Jonathan takes a drink as well then continues, "I wasn't sure if you'd want to drink since you have to go into work at the café later."

"It'll be OK. I'll just have the one." She looks beyond the wall of windows beside them at Amethyst Bay. The sun has already risen into the clear sky. The bay is calm, reflecting the bright blue hue.

Jonathan follows her gaze. He reminds her, "Remember the view last night at our property? We're going to get that every day come summer."

"I can't wait. We got very lucky finding that piece of land."

"And so inexpensively."

"Well, considering that was nearly my entire house budget when I was looking to buy, it really depends on who you ask."

Jonathan smiles and says, "It is five acres, though."

"That is true." Faith side eyes Jonathan as she tries to stab a piece of sausage that keeps escaping her fork.

"Besides, that view is priceless."

"It definitely is!"

They both take bites of their breakfast. Jonathan laughs to himself, then says, "We do this a lot you know?"

Confused what he's referring to Faith asks, "What's that?"

"We talk too much and then our food gets cold."

"It's not too cold," Faith giggles and continues, "you're right though, we do this a lot."

"It's not a bad thing. I love talking to you. I think if you were the only person I could talk to for the rest of my life I would be content with that."

"Yeah? We would still have to eat though." She gestures to the food on their plates.

"We would." With that, Jonathan dips his French toast into his syrup before he takes another bite.

Once they finish eating breakfast they spend the rest of the day together, snuggling on the couch watching a movie and then making lunch. Faith wishes it could be like this all the time. Jonathan works so much she finds herself at home most weeknights alone at their condo.

So much has changed for them in the short span of the last few months. They bought property and started building their house, Faith has moved into Jonathan's condo and sold her house. She got a new car right after Christmas that Jonathan insisted on paying for, just like the house. Faith is definitely ready for them to get into more of a rhythm. Hopefully one that doesn't include Jonathan being at work so late most nights.

He's been very understanding and has even been bringing some work home with him some evenings. In an attempt at making it up to Faith, he also brings home flowers every Friday. She appreciates it very much, but she's also afraid it will lose all meaning. Having fresh flowers in the condo in the winter does bring some life to the place though.

Faith's evening shift at the café ends up being uneventful. They were not nearly as busy as they anticipated and Faith

# APTITUDE

was able to head home a little early. Even though Jonathan has to get up early tomorrow, he is still awake when she gets there.

"How was your day?" He asks as soon as she comes in the door.

"Long and slow. My feet are incredibly sore."

He gestures to the couch. "Come sit down and put those feet up."

She hangs her coat and purse up on the hooks in the entry. Slipping her shoes off, she slides them out of the way on the white stone floor. Then walks over to the couch to sit, the coolness of the stone feels refreshing on the soles of her feet.

Jonathan goes into the kitchen and grabs two glasses and opens a bottle of wine. He carries them into the living room, and sets them both down on the coffee table then he pours some wine in each glass and hands Faith hers.

Sitting beside her, he says, "Kick your feet up here." He gestures to his lap.

She does as he says and Jonathan takes one foot in both hands and begins rubbing, relieving the stress from the dinner shift.

As he rubs he asks, "Do you need some more comfortable shoes for when you work at the café?"

She sips from her wine glass then responds, "Once I get back to school, I won't be working there until summer again."

"Is Hope back full time yet?"

"I told my parents I would help out until I go back to work. I can't do both. Hope will be back full time soon enough. I'm sure she's going stir crazy at Mom and Dad's."

"Yeah, when I'd seen Hope and your mom at the café yesterday she was definitely antsy."

"I'm not sure how my mom has managed to keep her home this long, honestly."

"Well, I don't believe Hope has much of an option with not having a car to drive. She's reliant on your mom for rides."

"That reminds me, we need to take my old car over for her."

"Has the doctor cleared her for driving?"

"I don't think so."

"Do you think the temptation will be too much for her?"

"You have a point. We should wait until she's allowed to drive." Faith nods.

"Don't let her hear you say that." Jonathan chuckles.

"What, 'allowed'? Yeah, I know. She would absolutely hate it." Faith joins in his laughter.

"On second thought, I think maybe we should tell her. It'll be paybacks for nick-naming me 'Jonameister'."

"I'm pretty sure the way you let that one roll right off you got under her skin enough."

Jonathan laughs remembering the first time Hope had called him that. "You might be right," he agrees.

He sets down the foot he was rubbing and picks up the other.

# APTITUDE

"Thank you Jonathan. You're amazing."
"You're welcome. Is it helping?"
"Yes, it most definitely is. That feels incredible."
"You know I enjoy taking care of you."
"I appreciate you so much!"

# Chapter 3

# Certitude

*Noun; the state of being or feeling certain*

Faith's mom, Diane, brings Hope into the café the next day and Faith greets them as they walk through the door. The breakfast rush just finished. After she greets Faith, Diane walks back to the office to see Frank, Faith's dad. Faith and Hope catch up quickly.

"When is your next doctor's appointment?" Faith asks her.

"Tomorrow afternoon, why?"

"I was wondering when you might get cleared to drive."

"I'm hoping soon. Tell me what happened last night'?" Hope asks, staring at Faith's empty left hand ring finger.

Faith feels her cheeks get hot and says, "Not what you thought would happen." Quickly changing the subject, she continues, "I'm sure you are eager to get back to normal life, but that doesn't mean the doctor will agree. You had major surgery."

"It wasn't that serious." Hope pauses for a second realizing what Faith just said. She scrunches her eyebrows together and asks, "Wait…what? He didn't propose?"

"Hope, you were bleeding internally. They literally had to go inside you to fix it and no he didn't."

"It barely hurts now." Sensing Faith's reluctance in talking about the non-proposal, Hope decides to drop it altogether.

"You're on pain meds."

"That may be, but even when I'm not, it doesn't hurt that bad. I'm still trying to convince Mom that I'm OK to come back."

"Yeah, I know." Faith smiles at her, knowing how badly Hope wants to be independent again.

"I'm going to go check on things in the office." Hope walks back to the office finding her mom and dad talking about her return. She peeks into the door and says, "Am I interrupting something?"

Frank answers, "No. We were just talking about when you should be coming back."

"Well, I'm ready." She walks in and sits down at her desk.

"I don't think that you are fully ready. We need you cleared by your doctor for light duty at the very least before you come back."

"Light duty like sitting behind the desk all day?" She shoves some papers on her desk top to release some of her frustration.

Diane interjects, "Yes, exactly dear. You can't be stocking or waiting tables. Nothing on your feet for long periods of time. I don't want you to further injure yourself needlessly." The tone in her voice is bordering on pleading.

"Faith will be going back to school soon. We're going to be short staffed with me only doing half of my job and her back at her real job."

Frank says, "We've managed without her before and we will manage again. If anything I will try to find another waitress."

Diane looks at Frank and asks, "Has it been that busy?"

"Not really, but if it makes Hope feel more at ease…"

"Dad, if we don't need the help, don't hire anyone."

Frank's tone softens, "Honey, at the very least, you are going to have three more weeks of recovery. We don't want you to do anything to jeopardize that."

"I won't jeopardize my health, Dad. I'm doing well and I don't see the point of sitting at your house when I could be here working."

"We will know more after your appointment tomorrow."

Diane adds, "We want you to be happy, but we also have to protect you."

"I'm an adult. I can make my own choices."

Frank says in a more stern tone, "If you were working anywhere else they would require signed paperwork from your doctor with explicit limitations until you are fully released."

Hope is feeling a bit dejected and frustrated. "Why did that stupid truck have to blow that stop sign?" With her elbows resting on her desk she buries her face in her hands.

As reassuringly as she can Diane moves towards Hope, she puts a hand on her shoulder she says, "I don't know honey, but I'm sure glad you're alright and you weren't more seriously hurt."

Hope doesn't want to admit it, but her mom is right, "That is true. It definitely could have been worse."

"You've got this." Frank says smiling.

"Thanks Dad."

Faith pops her head in the doorway, immediately feeling like she's interrupting something, she says, "Oh, I'm sorry. I can come back."

"No, dear, this is family business. There's no need for you to feel like you shouldn't be here too. Did you need something?"

"Juan is here from the bakery with the pie delivery. He said he needed to speak with you."

"I'll be right there." Frank looks to Hope. "We will continue this discussion tomorrow after your appointment."

"I know, Daddy."

Frank follows Faith out and turns down the back hall towards where Juan is waiting. Faith heads back out into the main dining area, leaving Diane and Hope in the office.

Faith greets a gentleman at the pale blue counter that has been worn with age, "Good afternoon! What can I get you today?"

She watches his eyes as they look her up and down, which makes her feel the need to keep her guard up. He says in a deep southern accent, "Well, aren't you just a tall glass of sweet iced tea on a hot summer day?"

"Is that what you'd like to drink?"

His eyes widen a bit, then he retorts, "No, Darlin', I'll take a coke. Would you be able to sit and visit with me while I eat?" He pats the dark blue cushioned stool beside him.

"I have other tables." She replies with the straightest face she's probably ever made.

He smiles and says, "OK then," glancing at the menu he says, "I'll take the hot turkey sandwich with mashed potatoes."

"Coming up." She turns and fills a cup with soda before turning back around and setting it down in front of him.

"Can I get a straw please?"

"Yeah." She reaches under the counter and then places a wrapped straw down. They stopped automatically giving them to customers unless requested a few years ago.

Faith walks around the counter to go check her other tables, but she gets the sense that someone is watching her the entire time. As she walks back towards the counter to get a couple of drink refills she feels a hand on her ass. She spins around quickly and sees Hope tapping the man's shoulder.

As if in slow motion, Faith watches as the gentleman at the counter turns his head towards Hope, as Hope's arm swings through the air, her fist landing square on the man's jaw. His head falls back as his body slumps off the stool crashing onto the black and white tile floor.

# APTITUDE

Time quickly returns to normal as Faith's acute focus broadens noticing the other customers in the café all looking around trying to figure out what happened. Hope is holding her hand close to her chest. Frank comes running down the hallway as quickly as he can. Diane leans through the door of the office to see what the commotion is.

"What happened here?" Frank demands.

Faith answers, "A guy grabbed my butt as I was walking past."

Frank's face softens when looking at his daughters. As soon as the man on the floor begins to come to, his face hardens once again. Faith quickly walks to the soda machine on the back counter to get her sister some ice for her hand.

Frank crouches down so he can be eye level with the man. Placing his thumb and pointer finger on either side of the stranger's chin he tilts it up making sure the guy is looking him directly in his eyes.

Frank very sternly says, "Get the fuck out of my café and out of this town. If I ever see you around here again I won't be giving you the option to leave of your own free will."

Struggling to stand the man says, "What the fuck is that supposed to mean?"

"You felt it was OK to touch my daughter inappropriately." He gestures to Faith, then to Hope and continues, "My other daughter taught you a lesson you should have learned at least thirty years ago. Get the fuck out, now." Frank points to the door.

The man looks from Frank to Hope, then to Faith. Defiantly, he says, "Fuck all of you." Then as quickly as he can staggers out the swinging glass door.

Frank takes the baggie of ice from Faith and places it on Hope's hand.

Looking at Faith he asks, "Are you OK?"

"Yeah. It all happened so fast. I honestly had no idea what was going on until he was already on the floor."

Holding the ice on Hope's hand Frank turns to the customers still sitting in awe. Addressing them he says, "So sorry folks! Some people just don't understand bodily autonomy. Please! Don't let this incident curb your appetite!"

As if by command, everyone goes back to eating their lunch as they had been prior to the prick's unacceptable behavior. Frank walks Hope back to the office and Faith follows. Diane takes a few steps towards Hope replacing Frank's hand with hers. She begins to examine her hand, gently pulling the bag of ice away.

"Why don't we get into the office, dear. You'll be able to get a better look in there," Frank suggests.

"OK." She says, not letting go of Hope's hand.

In the office, Diane motions towards Hope's chair sitting beside her desk. Hope obeys without a word and sits down, setting her hand gently down. Diane takes it in her hand and moves it around, carefully inspecting it. She notices that Hope's knuckles have already begun to swell.

"What were you thinking?"

"Honestly, Mummy, I wasn't. I saw what the guy did as I was walking to the front and my hand was flying through the air before I could even try to stop it."

Frank's look of concern is very apparent on his face. He might look younger in the face than his actual age of fifty-three, but the grey hairs become more and more prominent every year. Hope more than likely being the main culprit.

"You're lucky you didn't hurt yourself more, sweetie."

"I know, Daddy. Nothing hurts at all right now though."

"That's the adrenaline." In what seems like a former life now, Diane had thought of going to school for nursing. Once she met Frank and they had the girls, she knew she couldn't make it a priority anymore.

Faith is just standing there staring. She feels both responsible and guilty. She should have been the one to punch that guy.

Frank breaks into her thoughts, "We should have called the cops."

She answers quickly, "No, we shouldn't have. Hope took care of him, and you finished the job." She smiles at him.

"No one touches my daughters without their consent."

Both Hope and Faith have heard this a time or two. Their parents were both adamant about bodily autonomy from the time they were young. Both of them were eternally grateful for all of the lessons their parents, bestowed, but especially this one.

With all the focus on Hope, no one notices Jonathan's presence. He stands leaning against the doorway, simply taking in the scene and trying to figure out what is happening for a second before he clears his throat. All four of them turn to look at him with slightly startled expressions.

"What's going on here?" His eyes landing on Hope's hand.

Faith walks over to him and explains, "Hope defended my honor."

"What do you mean?" His eyes narrow in on Faith.

"Well, a customer decided he could grab my ass which made Hope decide to use her devastating right hook."

Jonathan walks over to Hope and shakes her left hand awkwardly, saying, "Thank you Hope. I'm really wishing I'd gotten here a little sooner so I could have taken care of him myself." The tone in his voice is entirely serious.

Hope smiles and says, "I didn't do it for you, Jonameister."

"I am aware, but it is appreciated none the less. It sounds like that guy got exactly what was coming to him." He takes a closer look at her right hand and continues, "You should have a doctor look at that."

Diane smiles and asks, "Would you mind taking her to urgent care, Jonathan?"

"I wouldn't mind one bit."

"Thank you so much. Frank and I have some work to finish up here." She looks at Faith, "You don't mind do you?"

"No, of course not."

# APTITUDE

Jonathan goes back over to Faith, gives her a quick kiss on the lips and then escorts Hope to his Mercedes.

By the time they return it's nearly closing time for the café. As Hope walks through the back door she announces loudly, "Three broken knuckles." She waves her hand in the air with the new black brace the doctor gave her. She continues, knowing she has Frank and Diane's attention now, "Doctor said it was just like the boxers get, which means my punch was perfect!" Her pride is written all over her face.

# Chapter 4

# Latitude

*Noun; freedom of action or choice*

Faith arrives at the café early the next morning to find her mom and Hope already there in the office. Diane looks at her and shrugs her shoulders, nodding towards Hope. Faith walks over to her sister who is sitting at her desk desperately paging through a stack of papers.

Squatting down, so she is at eye level, she says, "Hope, I thought Mom and Dad told you that you needed to take things easy until you hear more from the doctor today."

"I'm fine. I really needed to come check on this." She holds up a couple of invoices. "Something isn't right here and I need to figure it out."

"OK. Can I help you?"

"I don't think so."

Faith looks at her mom, stands, and walks towards her. In a hushed voice she asks, "What time is her appointment?"

"Around eleven."

"Are you guys just going to stay here until then?"

# APTITUDE

"Yes. She insists on being here and I'm sure I won't be able to get her to leave until it's time for her appointment. Plus, I kind of figured if she could knock a guy out yesterday a few hours at her desk today would be no big deal." Diane shrugs.

"She can be very stubborn."

Before Diane can reply Hope says, "You know I can hear you guys, right?"

Faith holds her hand up to her mom, "I was hoping you could. You dragged mom out of bed and you won't let me help you."

"I don't need help. I got an email from Carl at the soda distributor about a discrepancy. I need to take care of it."

"That's fine, but at least accept some help."

"I've got it, Faith." Hope gives her a look that could kill.

"Ok, I'm going to go get the café ready to open."

Hope waves her off and buries her face back in the paperwork searching for the answer.

Diane excuses herself to help Faith up front. Grabbing the till for the register with cash in the slots she walks behind the counter and places it in the already open drawer. She watches as Faith wipes down all the tables and chairs and does a quick sweep. Some of the kitchen staff begin to come in and start getting food prepped for the breakfast rush.

"How are you doing, Faith? I feel like we haven't gotten to chat since Hope's accident."

"Things have been a little crazy," Faith agrees. "The house is well underway now and everything is going well."

"How's Jonathan doing?"

"He's good." Faith says a bit more sharply than she intended.

"OK…it sounds like there might be more to that. Care to elaborate?"

"It's just how much he's working."

Before she can continue Diane interjects, "You knew he worked a lot of hours when you guys started dating, right?"

"Yeah. I handled it better when we weren't living together. Which is weird." She realizes.

"It's not weird. It may have been easier when you were living at your own house because your lives were more separate. Now, your dinner times and so many other things are reliant on another person and their schedule."

"That makes sense." Faith nods.

"Your mom does have some wisdom up here, you know." Diane says as she taps her temple.

"Yeah, yeah." Faith smiles lovingly at her mom and then finishes sweeping and steps back to take a look at the café. "This place holds so many memories."

"Some of the best memories of our lives happened within these walls."

"I really like the outside seating and the changes you guys have made, but I wouldn't want it to change too much."

"Hope has explicit instructions not to renovate too much after we're gone."

"You guys aren't going anywhere any time soon."

# APTITUDE

"No, not for a long time. We have too much to do and see before then. Like our daughters getting married and our grandbabies being born."

"Well, you're clearly going to be waiting on all of those for a while, Mom." Faith lowers her eyes to the floor.

Sensing that something hit a nerve, Diane asks, "Do you not think Jonathan will ask?"

"He hasn't yet." Her eyes still aimed at the floor.

"Well dear, that doesn't mean he won't."

"No. It might not, but it sure feels like that in this moment at least."

"There is an old Buddhist saying, the exact words elude me at the moment, but the gist of it is that if you do not expect anything then you cannot be let down. Something like 'expectations are the thief of joy.' I think." Diane scratches her head deep in thought then continues, "Maybe that was Teddy Roosevelt. No matter who said it, they're right."

"So you're saying this is my fault because I expected him to propose to me?"

"No, no, not at all, honey. I'm saying that going forward it might be in your best interest, mentally and emotionally, to not have any expectations about when or how it might happen. He's told you he will and he has always kept his word to you, right?"

"Yes, he has." Faith churns everything her mom just said around in her mind.

Diane adds, "And besides, it hasn't even been a year yet. Maybe he's waiting until after that."

"That could be." Faith's mind is eased by her mother's reassurances as always. "Thank you, Mom."

"You're welcome, dear. Anytime." With that Diane walks back down the hallway into the office to check on Hope.

Faith pulls the chain for the 'Open' neon and flips the sign on the front door after unlocking it. The first customers begin trickling in for breakfast. Before too long the other waitress, Georgina, shows up to work her shift.

The breakfast rush makes the morning go by quickly. Before Faith knows it most of the customers have left. She takes a break in the office before Hope and her mom have to leave for Hope's appointment.

"Are you coming back here after your appointment?"

Diane gives Hope a look as she says, "It depends on what the doctor says. Especially with her new broken knuckles."

"Nothing hurts. I'm fine. I may need to come back if I don't find the right invoice in the next five minutes."

Faith asks, "Now will you let me help you?"

Looking up through her eyelashes Hope simply replies, "No."

"Well you haven't been here, if you tell me what you're looking for I might be able to find it. Maybe I was the one that put it in the wrong spot."

"Like where?"

"A file cabinet, maybe." Faith shrugs her shoulders.

Diane snickers a little until Hope shoots her a deadly glare. To which Diane replies, "You do realize you need a ride to this appointment, right?"

"Yes, Mummy. I'm sorry."

"It's OK. Just mind your manners, please."

"I think I'm stressing out about this discrepancy."

"So let Faith take care of it."

"I don't like doing that. This is my job."

Faith sees where Hope is going and interjects, "I don't want your job. I'm itching to get back to my students just as soon as holiday break is over."

"I know that." She practically spits the words at her as if the thought was preposterous.

Faith decides this isn't worth her break time and walks back out to the front.

# Chapter 5

# Attitude

*Noun; a negative or hostile state of mind*

Jonathan stops into the café on his lunch break. His attempt at showing her his devotion and desire to spend time with her is clearly seen by Faith. She appreciates it very much and knows that he is trying.

"How did Hope's appointment go?" He asks.

"They're not back quite yet. I'm sure they will be any minute now."

"OK. How was your morning?"

"It was OK. Busy as usual and then very slow until now."

"I can eat and get out of your hair then."

"No, it's OK. No need to rush. I love it when you come see me at work." She smiles.

"Yeah, I can't do this at school."

"No, you can't."

"Are you looking forward to being back?"

"Very much so." She gives Jonathan a smile and continues, "I miss those kiddos on long breaks. Especially this set since it's my second year teaching some of them."

"I'm sure they all appreciate how much you care about them."

Faith's eyes narrow, "Maybe not quite all of them."

As she finishes her sentence, Jonathan notices Diane and Hope enter through the back door. He nods in that direction to notify Faith.

Faith hears Diane in an exasperated and attempted hushed voice tell Hope, "Stop! You can't keep forcing your way. That isn't how this works." Then they both go into the office. Faith rushes down the back hall with Jonathan in tow.

When she gets to the door it's as if time has reversed six or seven years. Hope is sitting at her desk with her feet planted firmly on the ground. Her arms crossed tight across her chest and the most defiant look on her face.

Faith dare ask, "What's going on?"

Clearly frustrated Diane says, "She insisted on coming back here." She waves her arm in Hope's direction.

Faith looks from Hope to her mom and says, "You were driving, right? You could have just taken her home."

"I tried that. Don't you think I tried that? She wouldn't get out of the gall darn car!"

Meanwhile, Jonathan is watching from the doorway. He's barely peeking his head in, but he can feel the tension none-the-less. He's always seen them getting along, or at the very least playfully bickering a little, but never like this. Even in this moment of fighting, he's grateful for his place in this family.

After his parents died in the car accident when he was eight, he went to live with his Aunt Suz, which was nothing like a real family. There was no love there, there certainly were arguments, but it was never out of a desire to keep Jonathan safe. Aunt Suz was controlling and manipulative. She was also lost in grief and stuck with a kid she didn't want. He knows that now.

Shaking Jonathan from his thoughts he hears Frank get involved. "You three need to stop now." Looking up to Jonathan in the doorway he says, "Son, can you please close that? The customers don't need to be hearing all of this."

Jonathan does as he's told and Frank continues, "Hope, dear, what did the doctor say?"

"He said I could come back on light duty."

Diane interjects, "He said she could come back a couple of days a week for a few hours a day."

"Yeah, like I said, light duty."

Frank scratches his head. Once he has his words together he says, "OK. Then you can stay for a couple of hours, but you have to take tomorrow off. You can come back in on Thursday."

"OK."

It was as simple and as complicated as that. Faith smiled at her father seeing how he is truly the calm in the storm of the women he has lived with for twenty something years. She then notices Jonathan standing near the door and realizes he probably never had to deal with anything like this. With no siblings and what he's explained to Faith about his childhood after his parents died, this is all foreign territory to him.

She walks over to him, and puts her hand on his shoulder then she asks, "Are you doing OK?"

"Yeah, of course. Why wouldn't I be?" Faith gives him a look that he instantly understands. He continues, "I'm OK, really. This is good stuff for me to see. I'm taking notes from Frank for when we have arguing kids."

"Yeah, he's the best at calming the chaos."

"Seems like it."

Hope is back to rustling through the papers on her desk. Out of nowhere she bursts out, "I found it! I fucking found it! Finally!!"

Faith rushes over to see what it is that she's holding up. Hope compares the invoices she has in her hands. Diane smiles, knowing that's the real reason she insisted on coming back here after her appointment.

Hope points to the invoices explaining to Faith what the discrepancy was and how it may have happened. She gets Carl on the phone and they get everything fixed.

Faith walks over to Jonathan who motions towards the door and says, "I've really got to get back to work."

"OK, handsome. I should as well."

"I love you!"

"I love you too! I'll see you later."

"I shouldn't be too late tonight."

"OK, good to hear."

She walks back upfront to check on her tables.

Georgina, the other waitress working, says, "Isn't today your last day?"

"Yeah, but you know I'll never actually have a last day here. I'll be back to teaching tomorrow, though."

"Well, good for you honey. I love who I work for, but some of the customers can be something else."

Faith looks at Georgina, she's a fifty something year old single mother to a couple of grown boys. Her dark hair speckled with silver, but her bright blue eyes still shine with the feistiness she must have had when she was young. She is a damn good waitress and has worked at the café for as long as Faith can remember.

"It's sounding like you might be on your own for the most part since Hope is going to be stuck in the office."

"I'll be fine. Hope needs to recover and I hate seeing your mom waitress. She's better than this. So are you." She tucks her pen and paper into her apron, mindlessly wiping her hands on it after.

"Thank you Georgina."

"You're welcome honey. Now, do you mind covering my tables while I go grab a quick smoke break?"

"I'll cover your tables."

"Thank you."

"You're welcome."

# APTITUDE

By the end of her shift, Faith's feet are killing her. She still needs to prep her lesson plans for the week. That is what's on her mind as she drives home to the condo. The darkness gets thicker the further she gets from the lights that line Main Street.

Pulling in to park she doesn't see Jonathan's car in his parking spot. Although, she would have been surprised if he was home yet.

Faith walks through the door of the condo, slipping her shoes off in the entry. She hangs her coat on the hook by the door and slides her feet into a fuzzy pair of black slippers, giving them some cozy relief.

In the kitchen, she opens a cabinet door, then reaches up on her tippy toes to the top shelf, and she grabs a wine glass. She takes it over to the wine fridge and opens the door. Choosing a moscato, she opens the bottle and pours some into the glass.

She begins making dinner while slowly sipping her wine. Once the food is at a point that she can leave it for a few moments she runs to grab what she needs for her lesson plans. Laying everything on the island she multitasks dinner and prep for the week.

Jonathan comes home an hour or so later. Faith has already finished the bottle of wine and is feeling it. He makes a plate, grabs himself a glass for wine and a new bottle, and then brings them all to the island. He sits next to Faith.

"Hey Beautiful, how was your day?" He kisses the top of her head.

"It was OK. You were there for the most entertaining part of it. How was your day?"

"That I was. My day was pretty good, the best part of it was my lunch hour and now coming home to my beautiful girlfriend." He places his hand on top of hers on the counter, gently squeezing.

She gives him a half-drunken smile. Faith lets the word 'girlfriend' hang in the air a bit longer. It's sting a little less than it would have been that morning, possibly because of the conversation with her mom, but more than likely the moscato is the reason. Jonathan pours her a little more wine, then asks, "How's your prep coming?"

"I'm nearly finished."

Jonathan begins eating his dinner. Faith takes a sip of her wine and goes back to finishing her lesson plan.

# Chapter 6

# Beatitude

*Noun; a state of utmost bliss*

Faith takes another swig from her glass, looking over the rim to Jonathan who is sitting next to her at the kitchen island. He smiles, taking his last bite of the dinner she made. She's done with her prep work for the first few days of the week at least.

Jonathan stands, picking up his dirty dishes and his own empty wine glass. He walks over to the sink, rinses them and puts them in the dishwasher. Faith watches as he carefully places each one in the safety of the dishwasher rack. His hands are dripping from the water that rinsed them.

She slowly pushes her chair away from the island. Standing, she walks over to him and places her hand on his back. He stands and spins towards her in one fluid motion.

"Hey, beautiful."

"I was just sitting there, watching you and I couldn't help but notice how amazing your ass looks in those pants."

A smile spreads across Jonathan's face. He chuckles and then says, "Thank you. I'm so glad you noticed. It was hard work getting both cheeks into them."

Faith giggles, "I think they are a bit stifled in there." The wine has really set in.

"Yes. I think you might be right." Jonathan gently kicks the dishwasher door up and bumps it closed with his hip. He grabs Faith's hand and begins to lead her upstairs. He pauses for a second. Looking at the couch he says, "Unless you wanted me to bare my ass down here?" He gestures with the hand that isn't holding hers towards the couch.

"No, the bedroom sounds perfect!"

With that he swoops her up in his arms and carries her up the stairs. Once he reaches the bedroom he carefully places her down in their bed. In one swift motion, he is holding himself up over her looking directly into her eyes. He smiles and says, "I fucking love you, Faith."

Faith smiles, her head is swimming, and replies, "Jonathan, I fucking love you, so damn much."

He lowers his voice a bit, "So damn much." Then he kisses her fiercely.

Shifting his weight to kneel in between her legs, he sits up and begins to unbutton her white shirt. He moves slowly, with intention, taking in everything. He sees the way her chest rises and falls with every breath. Exposing her bra, he takes the sight of her in. Her soft skin glowing in the moonlight that is streaming in through the window he forgot to close. It cascades across Faith's breasts, the light accentuating her smooth skin.

Once he gets to the last button on her shirt he begins slowly kissing her skin that he's just revealed. He begins at her collarbone, working his way down to the top of her black pants. Goose bumps follow the trail his lips have blazed. When he reaches the seam of her waist band Faith's back arches to meet his lips.

Jonathan slides his hands under her back, feeling the goose bumps rise on her skin. He bites down on the fabric of her pants near the button, pulling them away from her body. He feels them release and then does the same thing with her zipper. He moves his whole body down, pulling the zipper in his teeth until it is completely undone.

Sliding his hands down her body he grasps the top of her pants pulling them down. He sees the seam of her panties peak out beneath them. Lowering his lips to her once again, he takes his time, worshiping the line where the black lace touches her supple skin.

Faith's breath quickens and Jonathan continues pulling her pants down. He removes them then places himself over her once again. He kisses her lips. Faith reaches up grasping his hair tightly in her hand, and pulls him into her. Jonathan's tongue quickly finds hers.

Faith moves her hands to the buttons on his shirt. She starts unbuttoning them as quickly as she can without ripping it off of him. Then she pulls the shirt over his strong shoulders. He moves to kneel once again and pulls the shirt off the rest of the way. Faith watches as Jonathan then pulls his T-shirt off as well. Her eyes fall on his pants. Just as he notices what she's looking at Faith's hands move to unfasten his dark grey dress pants.

She moves without hesitation or thought. Her fingers working the zipper and button with no issues. Once they're unfastened she loops her fingers in the waist band and pulls down. Jonathan moves to lay on his back and continues the removal of his pants while pulling down his boxer briefs at the same time. Faith takes in the sight of all that she is about to receive. His excitement very apparent.

Jonathan rolls to his side, placing his hand on her breast, gently rolling her nipple between his fingertips. A soft moan escapes her lips. He runs his fingers down her stomach, igniting her skin with every movement.

Jonathan's hand moves down to the band of her panties. He slips his hand inside finding the ample wetness he was hoping for. She moans once again. He pleases her a few moments longer before removing her panties.

Faith's body is aching for him and he knows it. Her hands are pulling him into her as hard as she can. He relents, pulling her on top of him. Her mouth opens allowing her audible ecstasy to be heard.

Jonathan enjoys the view of her body on top of his. Her movements giving pleasure to them both simultaneously. The grace in her sensuality brings him to the edge quickly. Too quickly.

Watching her face, he sees that she is nearing her breaking point as well. He thrusts, allowing her to ride as fast as she'd like. His excitement building exponentially. She leans forward her naked breasts resting against his bare chest. She places her lips to his, kissing him fiercely, giving him a glimpse of the passion she is feeling. He reciprocates, their tongues dancing.

Jonathan thrusts once more sending Faith over the edge, ecstasy washing over her. He feels her pleasure pulsating, making him unable to hold back his climax any longer.

Once the waves of pleasure subside, Faith collapses on top of him. Resting her head on his shoulder, he gently rubs his fingers along her shoulders. She shivers in response.

Wrapping his arms around her tightly Jonathan says, "I would love to have a lifetime of this."

"I would too." She fights allowing her mind to wander to the let down from New Year's Eve. She brings herself back to the moment by focusing on the way Jonathan is squeezing her tight. She can feel the depth of his love so intensely in this moment.

Jonathan holds her tightly to him a moment longer before she lays down beside him. He rolls to his side, facing her. He embraces her once more before sleep comes to them both with little hesitation.

# Chapter 7

## Turpitude
*Noun; a vile or depraved act*

The darkness envelopes the two figures, shielding them from sight. It's a typical Friday night and Jonathan has once again ventured into Caulfield to relieve his urge. His next unsuspecting victim is a young woman no older than Faith. Her name is Jana. Jonathan learned that and so much more at the bar he picked her up at, called The Blue Rooster. They're walking in the parking lot making their way to his car. She is still very much unsuspecting of any danger.

Typically, he rotates between locations, but The Blue Rooster has been quite a great spot for him over the years. Jana was an exceptionally easy target. Jonathan saw her for all of five minutes before knowing she would be his next. If he could predict them all with such ease this might lose its fun for him.

He has found that following the same plan nearly every time leaves nothing up to chance. It came as no surprise to Jonathan, that once he perfected this plan, as long as he chose the right women, they all make such similar choices in their moments of panic and fear. Jonathan quite enjoys the predictability of it, especially when it's proven to be so successful.

The women he chooses are always petite with long blonde hair, usually between twenty-one and thirty. He makes sure none of them are married or single mothers. This was never about making more orphans. He couldn't allow himself to be responsible for that.

They are of average or lesser intelligence and wouldn't have driven to the bar. That way their car isn't left in the parking lot causing suspicion. All of this information is easily found out just in asking the right questions as if he's trying to get to know them.

His targets' intoxication level and lack of friends at the bar are a prerequisite of his, also. If he studied the reasoning behind what started this it would most likely point to Aunt Suz. He did little reflection in this area, however. There was never a desire for him to psycho-analyze himself that way.

The urges seem to come in waves. There are times he can fight them off, but other times it is nearly impossible. Since living with Faith, he has found a new way of settling his urge just by going through the photos of past kills. It seems as though the urge is subsided for a short time before he needs to act on it.

These nights always start out the same. While driving into Caulfield Jonathan decides on the location for that evening. Once in the city, he drives to the warehouse where he has an unregistered vehicle parked and he switches cars. Once he's at the bar, he orders a drink, typically nonalcoholic in order to keep his mind sharp. He doesn't want to dull his senses.

While observing the room he takes note of any single women sitting alone at the bar with a partial drink left. He either has the bartender send them a drink or he moves to sit beside them, but doesn't acknowledge them for a time. He has found this will make them more eager for his attention.

Once he notices the signs of her wanting him to speak to her, he respectfully introduces himself, under a different name of course, and offers to buy her a drink.

After a lot of conversation and a few more drinks, she would almost always trust him enough to leave her drink at the bar or table while going to the bathroom. He then carefully slips a slow acting debilitating drug into the drink. Sometimes he would have to order her another while she was in the restroom. There was only one time a woman questioned it and he simply aborted the plan, playing it off as no big deal if she drank it or not. Luckily, he has a knack for making people feel comfortable.

The drug he gives them buys him another hour to get them out of the bar before they begin showing any major signs. These side effects are extremely similar to severe impairment from alcohol. Jonathan has found that it makes it easier to get her to his car if she can walk on her own.

Once in his car, he suggests he take her home. His favorite part is always enjoying the look on their faces at the very moment they realize he isn't taking them there at all. At that point, some would ask if he was taking them to his house instead. Sometimes he would answer yes, even though technically he wasn't.

He owns an old warehouse in a rundown area of Caulfield that is surrounded by other dilapidated buildings. He purchased the building under a business name with silent owners so that it would be difficult to trace back to him.

By the time they get to his building, most of the women are close to passing out. Sometimes he would have to carry them up the two flights of stairs. However, he could tell that their faculties were still there in some capacity because even behind the blank look in their eyes there is still a flash of recognition that danger is looming as soon as they see the dank, mostly empty living quarters he has set up.

Tonight things have, so far, gone as planned. They walk through the parking lot stopping at Jonathan's car. As he helps Jana get in the passenger seat she starts pushing her body up against his, sloppily trying to kiss him. This is something that always seems to happen. He isn't looking to hook up, but that is always their assumption. He plays into it as not to raise any suspicion, but if he is being honest it grosses him out. To most guys, these women are attractive, but not to Jonathan. To Jonathan they are simply a means to an end.

The drive to his building is pretty quiet this time around. Jana starts out by caressing his thigh. She moves her hand to his crotch. Jonathan gently places his hand over hers, grabbing it he moves it back to her lap.

"Let's hold off until we get there."

"But I want to please you, Jack." Every word a slur as it passes her lips.

"I know Jana. I can't wait for you to. You're so sexy." He says trying to be as convincing as possible.

Glancing over at her he notices her eyelids are beginning to droop. The drug is kicking in full force now. A sleepy drunk smile spreads across her face. The first floor of his building is still just an open area he uses for parking. Jonathan opens the overhead door and pulls in, parking the unregistered Lexus next to his Mercedes.

Jana looks a bit perplexed taking in the sight of the run down building. Barely understandably she asks, "Where are we?"

Jonathan laughs a bit, he's found this helps to soothe their initial panic. "We just parked. I'm going to help you get up to my living quarters. I'll get you some water. It's OK if you're not feeling like hooking up tonight."

"No, no, I want to." She slowly moves her hands up and down her body grabbing at her boobs and managing to lift her short skirt, exposing her neon pink panties. In some way this is supposed to prove to him that she is still very much interested.

He opens her door for her, holding his hand out for her to take. As he helps her to stand, she loses her balance for a second. Jonathan catches her and Jana places her arms around his neck while he supports her weight with his arm around her waist.

She smiles as big as she can, "My knight in shining armor. I want you to know, I never get this drunk." She points her finger trying to poke his nose, but narrowly misses it.

"Shh, it's OK. I can help you."

"You're such a gentleman." She says while slurring every word.

"Thank you."

They make their way up the cold metal steps to the door of his living room. Jana's eyes are all but closed. She hasn't noticed how run down the building is beyond the parking space. He opens the door and sets her down on the dirty green plaid couch that is sitting against the stained wall in the living room. The stains were from a number of things, some from water leaks over the years, others from people smoking, and yet others because of bugs and their feces. All the years of dirt and grime is collecting on the dingy wall paper that's peeling down at the edges and seams.

# Chapter 8

# Aptitude

Noun; a natural ability, talent

The abandoned warehouse he owns is simply a means to an end, literally. The means to ending lives of unsuspecting women in Caulfield. It doesn't have to be clean. In fact, the worse their reaction is to it, the more Jonathan revels in it.

He knows the dichotomy of his attire and the way he presents himself versus the appearance of the building gave these women the biggest clue that their demise was imminent.

The various blades he uses in the act are splayed out on the counter. You would think that would be a big giveaway, but most of his victims never even notice them. Tonight, Jana is no exception.

Jonathan changes into the clothes he keeps here especially for these nights. He slips on his blood splattered jeans and an old tattered grey T-shirt. The drug has progressed enough in Jana's system to paralyze her, he undresses her, then places her naked body in the grimy, soiled bath tub. What was once a shining white porcelain is now stained brown from rust. He takes his time in the beginning removing various appendages agonizingly slowly. Witnessing the blood drain from her body and the life from her eyes in such a leisurely way gives Jonathan a sense of power that is intoxicating and addictive as hell to him. He never wants to rush this level of satisfaction.

Jana struggles to scream with every cut of his knife, her body unable to do what her mind is fighting for. The sound coming from her throat is muffled. Jonathan doesn't even have to gag her. The drug is doing its job very well.

He enjoys hearing the strained guttural sound coming out of her mouth. She is more of a fighter than he thought she would be. He watches her face as he cuts a chunk of flesh from the inside of her thigh. The agony isn't apparent physically. Since her muscles are lifeless there is no kicking or thrashing about. Her eyes convey her pain, though.

Jonathan places his hand in the space where her flesh was just cut from, feeling her warm blood pulsate as it spurts. His hand now covered in crimson red. He grabs a small handheld tree pruner, and reaches down holding her big toe in one hand. The blade touches her skin with no physical reaction from her. She can't feel it. Once the blades get in to the little bit of meat and finally to the bone she most definitely feels it. However, she is unable to kick or move at all.

Once again, Jonathan watches her eyes. Tears and snot are freely flowing, there is no way for Jana to try to hold them back. Jonathan notices the bottom of the bathtub filling with blood. He puts his hand into the warm liquid and then closes his eyes. Wiggling his fingers in it, he feels the sticky fluid move between them.

Jana is watching him. Her mind is racing as fast as the drug will allow. Even with her body paralyzed she can still feel the immense levels of dread, panic, and fear deep within her. She, like so many others, begins to wonder what is in store, how long will this go on, and if there is any hope of escape.

Jonathan grabs his filet knife and goes back to cutting slices of flesh from her thighs. All of the pieces he removes, he places back into the bathtub. He will use an acid to help speed up the decomposition. With no one being in the building or even the vicinity he doesn't have to worry too much about the smell.

Jana passes out shortly thereafter. He relishes these moments. This is the indicator that the end is near. Her body and mind cannot take any more. Jonathan, however, is not even close to being done. He breathes in deeply, allowing the rush of the evening to wash over him. His urge has been satisfied.

The smaller the pieces he removes the faster they decay in the acid. With this in mind he keeps cutting away at her. He works quickly, thinking of Faith being home alone, all the while she's believing that he is working late.

# APTITUDE

The lies don't get easier, but this is what he needs to do to cope, at least that's what he tells himself. He has a great life now, but it wasn't always that way, especially not after his parents died. Aunt Suz was a strict woman with no motherly instincts. At times, Jonathan wondered if she knew how to love at all. He never felt that she loved him. He was a nuisance and a horrible reminder of her dead brother.

As he continues cutting, he thinks back to his first kill; a squirrel. He killed it behind the rundown shed in the backyard at Aunt Suz's house. The shed had been left there by the previous owners. Jonathan used it as a hideout when Aunt Suz was in one of her moods. That day though, it became so much more.

He watched the squirrel squirm and fight to try to get away as he squeezed the life out of it. Its beady little black eyes drained of life in just the few short moments after Jonathan had captured it. That incident awakened something within him that he hasn't been able to put to rest since. What began with that squirrel quickly turned into killing stray cats, then small dogs, and eventually people.

The blood coming from Jana's fresh wounds is freely bleeding less and less. What has already pooled in the bathtub is beginning to coagulate. Jonathan finishes removing her flesh quickly. He walks into the vile, cockroach infested kitchen and washes his hands. The water running brown at first before turning clear. Once they are dry he places them in thick black latex gloves. The powdered acid could cause horrific chemical burns if he got any on his skin.

Taking the five gallon bucket into the bathroom he douses what is left of Jana in the white powder. Totally covering her body in the bathtub, he ensures that there will be nothing left of it when he returns.

He carefully removes the gloves, washes his hands once more, and changes back into the clothes he wore that day. Washing his hands once again before he leaves.

His drive home to Faith is quiet. Jonathan doesn't turn the radio on. He silently replays the evening as if it were a movie engrained in his mind. The wave of peace washes over him all over again.

Jonathan understands that if Faith ever found out about this, their relationship would be over. There would be no forgiving him. He knows this. It's one of the reasons he was never this serious with anyone before her. His lifestyle wasn't conducive to a woman questioning his whereabouts and his intentions.

Most women in the past accused him of cheating on them. Even though he performs such vile acts, he is a one woman man. He's never hooked up with any of his victims, he's never even wanted to. That isn't where his satisfaction comes from.

# Chapter 9

## *Plenitude*

*Noun; the quality or state of being full, completeness*

Walking in the door of the condo, Jonathan sees that there are no lights left on. Faith must have gone to bed. He checks the time and sees that it is just after midnight. He knows how much she hates nights like this, but he also knows how he would be if he didn't fulfill his urge. He will make it up to her like he always does.

Quietly, he climbs the stairs to find Faith asleep on her side of the bed. Her back is turned to where Jonathan would be sleeping. The light from the full moon spills across the floor at the foot of the bed. It's illuminating just enough for Jonathan to be able to maneuver in the large primary bedroom. He walks to the bathroom, closing the door behind him, and gets in the shower.

When he climbs into bed he wraps his arms around Faith, hoping that might help her know how much he loves her.

Sleepily she pushes her body into his. That's the best sign he could have asked for. Sleep comes to him quickly.

When the sun rises Jonathan begins to stir, but is still too tired to wake. Faith feels him move beside her, relieved that he made it home safely last night. She rolls over to face him, barely opening her eyes. She hears him murmur, "Are you doing OK?"

"Yeah, just tired." She replies.

"Me too."

He rests his arm on her waist. Faith leans in and kisses him then says, "Let's go back to sleep then."

When the sun is higher over the bay Faith and Jonathan finally peal themselves out of bed. Both are still tired, but they don't want to waste their Saturday, even if it is one that ends up being on the lazier side.

Jonathan goes down into the kitchen to start on breakfast while Faith showers. He's finished when she comes down stairs. Two plates sit on the island, filled with fruit and scrambled eggs. Two coffee mugs are waiting as well. Faith smiles and sits next to Jonathan.

"Thank you. This looks absolutely delicious."

"It's the least I can do."

"So, what are you thinking we should do today?"

# APTITUDE

"I'd like to go check on the progress of the house. Does that sound good?"

"Yeah, it'll be good to see Michael."

"He and his crew at Amethyst Construction have done amazingly so far. I can't wait to see what they've managed to get done this week."

They each take bites of their eggs. Faith grabs her coffee mug and takes a long drink of the warm liquid, closing her eyes. There's something about a warm cup of coffee in the morning. Especially when you're able to take the time to enjoy it.

Jonathan notices Faith's slow sip and smiles. He places his arm around her, pulling her into him, then kisses the top of her head. Faith fills her fork with pieces of sliced bananas and strawberries, the sweetness ignites her taste buds.

"I could watch you eat all day."

"Lucky for us both, you don't have to."

"Ok, then. I'm lucky that I get to for as long as you'll have me."

Faith looks down at her plate, "Maybe it's for as long as you'll have me."

Without missing a beat Jonathan says, "I'm fairly certain that you'll out live me." He looks over to her, smiling.

She smiles at him, happy with his answer. She tells him, "Most likely."

He feigns surprise which makes Faith laugh.

Once they've both finished eating their breakfast, Jonathan takes the dishes to the sink. He doesn't allow Faith to do that ever since she dropped a wine glass and sliced her foot open. That evening wasn't a total loss though. As he thinks back to that moment, he remembers how he took care of her that evening.

Faith see's that he is deep in thought while holding an entirely rinsed plate under the running faucet for far too long.

She asks, "What are you thinking about?"

"The night you sliced your foot open."

Faith moves to stand next to him, barely noticeably with her body pressed against his.

In nearly a whisper she says, "Wouldn't you rather think of the morning after?"

A smile spreads across Jonathan's face as he thinks of how incredible the first time he made love to her was. In a quick motion he turns and puts his arms around Faith.

"That memory is one of the highlights of my entire life. Faith, you've given me so much more than you could ever know." He leans his head down placing his lips against her forehead and continues, "I love you so much."

Faith wants to mention marriage, but those feelings are still too raw. Instead, she simply says, "I love you so much, Jonathan."

"I'm so grateful to have you in my life."

"My life wouldn't be what it is right now if it weren't for you."

# APTITUDE

"I'm happy I'm able to enrich it." Jonathan pulls her in tight. Once their embrace releases he finishes placing the dishes in the dishwasher.

Once they're in the car, Jonathan drives his Mercedes up the coast to the land they purchased only a month and a half prior. The last time they were here was New Year's Eve when they danced under the moon light as the clock struck midnight.

They pull up the make-shift driveway and see contractor vehicles and heavy machinery. When they're closer to where those are parked, Jonathan see's Michael standing near where their front porch will be.

Michael notices their car and a huge smile fills his face. He grabs a couple of hard hats and starts towards them as they're getting out of the vehicle.

"It's so great to see you! I'm glad you came to look at the place today!" He says handing them the hard hats.

Curious, Jonathan asks, "Oh really, why is that?"

Michael turns and points to a crane. Following his finger with their eyes they see that all exterior walls have been put into place. The crane is hoisting a roof truss high into the air.

"It's roof day!" Michael says exuberantly.

"This came pretty quickly." Jonathan says.

"Yes. Building the shell doesn't take too long. It's the finishing touches that require more time and precision. What do you think of it so far?"

Faith answers, "It's absolutely amazing. The house looks huge!"

"No larger than the four thousand, seven hundred, seventy three square feet that the blue prints detail."

Jonathan smiles, "This home will be magnificent when everything is finished."

"It truly will be. Did you two come here for anything in particular? Or just to check on the progress."

Jonathan says, "Mostly to check on progress. We were here on New Year's Eve. You've gotten a lot done since then."

"My men certainly aren't sitting on their asses on the job." As soon as the word slips from his lips he looks at Faith. "Ma'am I'm so sorry. I shouldn't have sworn in the presence of a lady."

Faith chuckles, "Thank you Michael, that's very considerate of you."

His cheeks turn a slight shade of pink. "Working on construction sites can easily make a man forget his manners."

"You recovered quickly."

"My mother raised me right."

# Chapter 10

## Consuetude

*Noun; long-established practice considered as unwritten law, custom*

Sunday night dinners at Faith's parents' house have been tradition ever since the girls were in high school. Frank and Diane Brandt put it into place because they wanted to be sure that they were able to spend quality time together as a family. With the demands of running a business and the girls' schedule between school, sports, and helping out at the café, their lives had become hectic, to say the least.

As the girls grew older, went to college, and moved out of their home, they've still managed to keep the tradition alive. This Sunday is no different. All of them are gathered together, sitting around the table in the dining room of the light blue nineteen-fifties rambler to eat the delicious meal that Diane made. Hope takes a swig of her beer and her mom gives her a quick look.

"You probably shouldn't even be drinking that with the meds the doctor has you on." Diane tries to say gently, but it comes out a bit curter than she meant.

"It's one beer, Mummy. I'll be OK."

In an attempt to ease the tension, Faith looks to Hope and asks, "How has it been being back at the café?"

"It would be better if they would let me actually do something besides sit behind a desk for a couple of hours on the days I get to go in." She replies with a hint of disgust in her voice.

"At least you're able to get out of the house." Faith says optimistically.

"Yeah, but it wouldn't be so bad if I was at my place."

Diane interjects, "The doctor doesn't think it's best for you to go home and be by yourself for the majority of the day yet."

"I'm starting to think the doctor is just siding with you." She glares up at her mom through her eyelashes.

"That is not true, dear."

"I'm just calling it as I see it." Hope shrugs her shoulders.

Faith can feel Jonathan becoming more and more uncomfortable beside her. He isn't used to the bickering. She looks at her father, and gives him a look as if to say 'do something.'

He shrugs his shoulders, but then says, "OK, you two. Let's wait and have this conversation after we've eaten, when we have cooler heads and full bellies at least."

Hope rolls her eyes, but doesn't say another word. She finishes her meal in silence. Frank looks at Jonathan and asks, "How is the house coming?"

"All the exterior walls are up. They were actually installing the roof trusses while we were there yesterday."

Surprised, Diane says, "Wow that seems really fast."

Faith agrees, "I thought that too." She glances at her little sister to see her roll her eyes once more. Some things never change.

When they finish eating dinner Frank suggests they sit in the den. Instead, Hope goes to her bedroom, not wanting to be around anyone. If she could she would have simply gone home. She hasn't been able to drive since her accident on Christmas, and when she was released from the hospital they made sure she wasn't going home by herself. She has been struggling with the lack of freedom.

Faith helps her mom clean up in the kitchen while Jonathan and Frank go into the den and sit. Frank turns the television on as force of habit. The two men sit there in silence for a few moments as Frank flips through the channels.

Jonathan relaxes into the soft cushions of the oversized couch. He thinks to himself for a moment deciding if he wants to bring it up or not, eventually he looks at Frank and says, "It truly is remarkable how you handle these women."

"Oh, son, it has all been learned over many years. Early on, I would just ignore it. It didn't take long for Diane to become a little resentful that she was the only one dealing with their attitudes. I've since amended my ways and have been able to hone this skill. It doesn't work every time, but Diane can at least see that I'm trying."

"It's impressive. Just know that I'm taking notes. I feel like I'm a bit behind the curve since I never saw anything like that while I was growing up."

"Some lessons can be better learned later in life. Being a good husband and father will typically go hand in hand. They both require effort, but it won't feel like hard work. Not when you're doing it from a place of love."

"That is what it's all about right? That's one of the stark differences that I remember during my childhood. My parents did everything for me out of a place of love. When they were gone, Aunt Suz only took care of me out of obligation and even at the age of eight or nine, I could feel the difference. I felt that every day after until I left."

Just as Jonathan finishes his sentence Faith appears at the top of the steps that go into the sunken den. She catches the end of what he's saying, and senses the heaviness in the room. Quietly, she sits beside him.

Frank looks to Faith and says, "You've got a good one, Faith. He gets it."

Looking admirably at Jonathan she replies, "I sure do."

Jonathan leans down kissing her forehead. Then addressing Frank he says, "Thank you, Sir."

Diane walks in and sits down in the chair beside Frank, grabbing his hand as she does. She hadn't realized Hope

# APTITUDE

didn't come into the den with the guys and asks, "Where did Hope go?"

"Her room." Frank replies shortly.

"She's in another mood." Diane reasons.

Frank adds, "She's been in a mood since her accident. Maybe we should give her a little more freedom."

With a look of concern Diane says, "If it isn't cleared by the doctor, I don't want to take any chances."

"I know, dear. We need to think of her mental health just as much as her physical health."

Faith interjects, "I'll go talk to her." She promptly gets up and walks down the hall to Hope's childhood bedroom.

She knocks on the door and quickly hears Hope say, "Leave me alone."

"I just want to talk to you." She says, gently placing her forehead against the cold wooden door.

"You can't help. No one can. I'm stuck here and I can barely do anything at work, so unless you can make those things better then there's no helping me."

Faith tries to open the door by gently and quietly attempting to turn the door knob. Once she realizes it isn't locked she says, "I'm coming in. I can barely hear you through this thing."

She pushes the door open slowly to see Hope lying face down in bed under the blankets. No wonder she couldn't hear her well. Stepping into her room Faith walks over to the side of the bed, she gingerly sits down, attempting not to jostle Hope.

"I don't need a big sister talk right now."

"OK, then I can simply sit here with you."

An audible huff comes from Hope. Faith is trying very hard not to get frustrated with her little sister. She knows adding more frustration to the situation isn't going to help Hope at all.

Faith places her hand on Hope's back, gently moving it back and forth. Hope picks her head up from her pillow and says, "Sometimes, I just need to be sad." Then promptly places it back down.

"It's understandable. You were in an accident that was no fault of your own and it has altered your daily life to a point that you're unhappy with. I guess the thing you need to keep in mind is that this isn't permanent."

Turning her head, she says, "I know that."

"You might know that, but I don't think you are feeling that way."

"I'm definitely not."

"Jackie and I were planning on grabbing dinner and drinks sometime this week. Did you want to come with us? I think we need to get you out of this house."

A smirk starts before Hope asks, "Where were you guys thinking of going to dinner?"

"Probably Mama Garcia's."

Hope's smirk turns into a wide smile, "Mexican food and margaritas?"

"Yup. I take it you want to come with us?"

# APTITUDE

Her face lights up and she says, "I'd love that. Thank you, Faith."

Hope rolls over as quickly as she can, wrapping her arms around her big sister giving her a tight squeeze. Faith reciprocates gently, afraid to hurt her.

"You know, I'm not as fragile as mom makes me out to be."

"I know, but it's hard for me to get the image of my baby sister lying in a hospital bed out of my mind."

Hope backs away, moving to sit up straight on her bed, "I may not have seen myself, I did, however, see everyone's faces when they saw me. That is probably equally as traumatic. Let's not even talk about the trauma from the accident itself and now having to be reliant on everyone around me."

"That's understandable, though. We were all worried that day and now there are explicit orders from your doctor. You know that mom and dad, and all of us really are just trying to do what we've been told is best for you, right?"

"I know, it's just hard to accept. I don't like it. You know that I need my independence. It's not something I was or am in any way ready to give up."

"I know, and soon enough this will all be just a memory. You'll be back at your apartment and life will be back to normal."

"Hopefully very soon. Thank you for coming in and talking to me. I needed this, talking with Mom and Dad doesn't seem to help my mental state much."

"Try as they may, I don't think it's something they can understand. They're our parents and sometimes parents are too protective and loving to see what we actually need is some space."

"You're right. I've felt that a lot lately. Especially with mom."

"Try to remember that she is only doing what she thinks is best. She wants to keep you safe, her way of doing that is being overly involved. It's almost as if in her mind you've reverted back to being a toddler."

"That makes sense. I think that's why I've been feeling so stifled. She isn't controlling me, but it almost feels that way."

# Chapter 11

# Vicissitude

*Noun; the quality or state of being changeable, mutability*

Walking down the hallway together, Faith and Hope pass the living room, turning into the den where Jonathan and their parents are sitting. Faith sits down beside Jonathan. Hope sits in the chair across from her parents.

Diane smiles at Hope and says, "I'm glad you've joined us."

Faith looks at her mom and says, "We've made plans to have dinner with Jackie this week."

"That'll be nice."

"We thought so." She looks at Hope and continues, "You'll get to ride in my new car for the first time."

"I can't wait." Hope says, her voice dripping with sarcasm.

Jonathan laughs nervously then shrugs his shoulders as he says, "It is a very nice car."

"I'm sure it is. Just like the house will be a really nice house, and when you have kids they'll all be really nice, dressed in really nice clothes. Everything will be just perfect." She rolls her eyes.

Frank interjects, "Hope, that is uncalled for. Jonathan and Faith haven't done anything wrong. Just because you're unhappy with your life at the moment, doesn't mean you need to be so negative about the good things that are happening in other people's lives."

"You're right, Daddy." She looks at Faith, takes a deep breath and then says, "I'm sorry, Faith. Dad is right, you didn't deserve that."

"Jonathan doesn't either." Faith offers, nodding in Jonathan's directions. She doesn't want to make it seem like only her feelings matter.

"No, you're right." Hope continues, this time addressing Jonathan, "I'm sorry Jonameister. You've been so wonderful to my sister. I'm sorry I can be snarky towards you sometimes."

"Thank you for your apology. I do enjoy your sarcasm at times, so don't stop altogether."

"Oh, I could never!" Hope begins laughing then everyone else joins in.

When Jonathan and Faith get home to the condo he walks into the kitchen asks, "Would you like a glass of wine?"

"No, thank you." Faith goes into the living room and sits on the couch. Thinking about the great evening they just had at her parents' house makes her second guess what she's about to say. She can't wait any longer so she looks at Jonathan and pats the black seat cushion next to her. "Can we talk?"

A pit begins to form in Jonathan's stomach instantly. Trying to keep his voice calm he says, "Of course, Faith. Is something bothering you?" He moves to sit next to her, facing her, he places his arm behind her atop the back of the couch.

"Yes, and no. I know that doesn't help answer the question."

"No, but sometimes things aren't easily explained." He reaches for her hand. "Can you attempt to explain it to me? That's the only way I can try to fix it."

"There's nothing to fix really." She breathes in deeply. "I think that with how much we've been talking about the future I thought maybe you were going to propose on New Year's Eve."

The anxious feeling in Jonathan's stomach subsides a little. "I can see how you would have gotten that impression. I'm sorry it didn't work out that way." He nods his head.

"It's silly. I know that. I just thought that it was going to happen and I got my hopes up, and the rose petals and everything…it kind of made sense, but then you didn't do it. And that's fine. I'm not trying to say that you should have or that you were wrong for not doing it. I wanted to talk about it because it's been on my mind."

"This is what was bothering you on New Year's Day isn't it?"

"Yes. I was trying to deal with my feelings. Sometimes I eventually come to understand that my feelings were unwarranted or were stemming from something entirely unrelated."

"I get that. I'm sorry I didn't propose. I had thought of it, but I also thought that with everything going on it wouldn't be the best timing. Hope was just in the accident, we're building a house…I didn't want to add planning a wedding onto our plates."

"That's probably smart." Faith smiles sheepishly.

Jonathan's thumb caresses the top of her hand while the other twists her dark brown hair between his fingers mindlessly. "You know that you're my future, Faith. I fully intend on marrying you. I can't wait to be able to call you my wife, but I want to do it right. I want to ask your parent's permission and I want to plan something unforgettable." He looks deep in her eyes making sure she understands as he says, "I promise you that we will be married."

A tear forms in the corners of her eyes as she shakes her head and leans in to kiss him. Pulling back a little she says, "I love you."

"I love you, Faith. You're an incredible woman and I am so lucky to have you. I can't wait for everything our future has to offer!"

# APTITUDE

"Me either." She smiles as he leans in to kiss her again.

He pulls back, placing his forehead against hers as he says, "Thank you for talking to me about this. If something is bothering you I want you to share it with me so that we can at least come to a compromise."

She shakes her head against his. With half a laugh she says, "There's no compromise for this."

"No, but you have my word."

"I appreciate that so much more than you know."

Faith breathes in the faint mix of his cologne and soap grateful for his understanding and reassurance. She's glad she decided to mention it, as silly as she felt, it was only going to keep eating at her until they talked about it.

# Chapter 12

# *Gratitude*

### Noun; the state of being grateful, thankfulness

Jackie and Faith decide to go to Mama Garcia's Tuesday evening for their taco Tuesday margarita special. Faith picks Hope up right after she finishes grading papers after school lets out and then they meet Jackie at the restaurant.

"I took the liberty of ordering one for each of you." Jackie says as they approach the table she's seated at.

Seeing the three strawberry margaritas both Hope and Faith say, "Thank you!" in unison as they sit down.

Jackie laughs at them. "That reminds me so much of our childhood."

Hope protests while giving Jackie a sideways glance, "It didn't happen that often."

"I remember it frequently." Jackie giggles a little more.

Faith puts her hands up in surrender, "If you say so." Then takes a sip of her margarita.

Hope follows suit then says, "This is delicious."

# APTITUDE

The waitress comes by to take their order. After she walks away, Hope takes another long pull from her straw before saying, "Thank you guys for letting me come tonight. I really needed this."

Jackie shrugs her shoulders. "It's no big deal. I always enjoy having you around, even when we were kids." She hooks a finger towards Faith and adds, "It was this one that had an issue with it."

"I don't recall crashing your time together that much…"

Faith scrunches her forehead in a confused expression. "It was pretty much daily."

Jackie comes to Hope's defense. "It probably just seemed like it was that often to you."

"Who's best friend are you anyway?" Faith asks with a slight chuckle.

"Always yours, but I've known Hope just as long. Plus, I get to have a little sister vicariously through you."

The waitress brings the molcajete filled with guacamole and a bowl of homemade tortilla chips. She checks to be sure all three ladies are good with their drinks and then walks back towards the kitchen.

They each take turns putting some of the guac on their plate. With her eyes wide and mouth half full, Hope says, "This is amazing!"

Faith laughs at her, "It is, right!" She looks at Jackie, "I'd say it's a tie between the guac and the margaritas being the number one reason we come here."

"I'd agree with that. I sure as hell don't want to have to choose between the two!"

Hope takes another chip full and puts it in her mouth. Then takes a quick sip of her margarita. She grabs the drink menu to look at the other flavors they have available while putting another chip full in her mouth.

Jackie and Faith watch and smile to one another amused by Hope's enthusiasm.

"Have you ever been here before Hope?" Jackie asks.

"I haven't, but I've heard of the place."

"I guess you didn't know what you were missing."

"Not at all." Hope eats another chip full of guacamole.

Faith adds, "We've been coming here for a while now. Probably since before we could legally drink. We might have to bring you with more often. By the way, when does the doctor think you'll be released to drive?"

Hope rolls her eyes, "I could drive now, but my doctor seemed confident that I'll be cleared at my next appointment. He said I can't be on pain meds anymore. I'm barely taking them now as it is."

"Well, when you get cleared I can bring my old car over. Is that when you plan on going back to living at your place?"

"As long as mummy will let me." She rolls her eyes, then continues, "I know she's just trying to help. I also know that she's trying to do what she thinks is best for me, and I can appreciate that. But I would be fine to manage at home on my own. And thank you so much for letting me use your old car. I don't know what I would do without your help."

"Of course, you're welcome. Plus, I'm sure mom is going to want some reassurances from the doctor about you living on your own."

"Yeah, I know."

Just then the waitress brings their tacos, setting the plates down in front of each of the women.

Hope digs into her tacos taking a large bite, chewing, and then says, "These are incredible too!"

Jackie and Faith laugh again.

The conversation slows as the three of them eat. The waitress comes to check on how the food is and to see if anyone wants another drink. Hope orders a strawberry mango margarita. Jackie and Faith ask for strawberry margaritas.

"Have you guys tried the other flavors?"

Jackie says, "We have. I think we both like the simplicity of the strawberry."

"I had thought about trying something entirely different, but figured I couldn't go wrong with a slight change."

Faith remembers a conversation they had when Hope was in the hospital after her accident and asks her, "Have you started the process of suing Dalton Freight?"

"Yeah, I contacted the lawyer Jonathan suggested that handles all of Kansen Corps legal needs. She seemed to really know what she was talking about. I was impressed."

"Good. They should pay for what happened. More so than just for your car and hospital bills."

"I'm glad you and dad convinced me to go after them. When I was in the hospital it didn't seem like it was that big of a deal, and I wanted it to be over with. Now, though, I know how much it has affected my life and I deserve something for that."

Jackie smiles at Hope. "I'm glad you're getting better. When Faith told me about the accident on Christmas I was worried about you. I'm glad to hear you're sticking up for yourself. There's no reason that a professional truck driver should have blown a stop sign."

Hope rolls her eyes, "They literally get paid to drive."

The waitress comes back with their margaritas and begins taking their empty plates. "Is there anything else I can get you?"

"No, thank you though, Maria."

The waitress smiles then returns to the kitchen with the dirty plates. A few moments later she brings back their bill.

Jackie reaches for the small slip of paper first. Faith gives her a look.

"What? I've got this. Hope has enough to deal with and besides, we invited her. You can just consider this my congratulations for…well, everything."

Faith asks, "What do you mean everything?"

"Congratulations for moving up to first grade, for a new car, for the land and the house. You have so many good things going on in your life right now."

"Thank you Jackie. I meant to ask…how're you and Tom doing?"

"We're OK. He's still complaining about how much I'm doing between school and work. I can see the end in sight."

"Whoa." Hope says.

Faith gives her sister a sideways glance. "Hope, seriously. What the hell?"

"Oh, I'm sorry. I just wasn't expecting her to say that."

Jackie says, "It's OK, really."

Faith looks at Jackie. "Well, I'm sorry that he's not being better about it."

"It's not your fault. I've tried talking to him, he apparently doesn't think it's important for me to feel supported by my partner."

Hope leans in as if what she's going to say is a secret. "When are you going to do it?"

"I have no idea yet. It could still be months from now. Then again, it could be tomorrow." Jackie feigns a laugh.

Placing her hand on Jackie's shoulder Faith says, "I know you don't need me to tell you what to do, but maybe it would be better to do it sooner. That way you can start focusing on what you need and it isn't prolonging the inevitable."

"You might be right. It's hard because Tom is pretty great in most other respects. I can't keep dealing with this though. Right now it's not supporting me with school, but what happens when we get married or have kids? He's not going to help me with any of that either. I'd rather save my time and frustration."

"How long have you guys been together?" Hope asks

"Almost two years now."

"And you're not living together?"

"No. Thank goodness. That would make this so much more difficult."

Once they finish their margaritas the conversation continues as they're on their way out the door. Hope still wanting to make sure they know how much she appreciates this and also hoping they will invite her again says, "I know I already said this, but I'm glad you allowed me to come out with you ladies tonight. I really needed this."

"It was nice having you Hope. I'm glad we could help restore some of your sanity." Jackie gives a slight chuckle as she moves in for a hug. "It was so good to see you." Jackie squeezes her a little tighter, but is still gentle.

"It was good to see you too, Jackie. I may be over stepping, but you totally deserve someone better than Tom."

"Don't I know it! Thanks for reminding me!"

The embrace ends and Jackie and Faith say a quick good-bye. "See you tomorrow! Thanks for dinner!"

"You're welcome! See you tomorrow Faith!"

# Chapter 13

# Vastitude

*Noun; immensity, vastness*

With Faith's twenty-fourth birthday just a couple of weeks away, February is turning out to be a busy and short month. Jonathan is still bringing some work home, but a few late nights still can't be helped. Faith is looking forward to her birthday, especially since it's the first they'll celebrate together. Last year both of them celebrated their birthdays before they met at Jackie's birthday celebration in April.

Jonathan hasn't let on to any plans he may be making for her birthday. His lips are sealed. Faith was secretly hoping he may be working with Jackie to come up with something. If he is, Jackie is as quiet about it as he's been.

Going to visit their new home build is one of their favorite things to do. They try to make it out there a few times a week, even with the colder weather. Faith can see, even with only the bare bones of the house in place, how spectacular their new home will be.

Tonight they have plans to check on the construction of the house and then go out to dinner at Tollero's.

Faith is sitting at the dining room table when Jonathan gets home from work. She appears to be working on lesson plans. She looks up from her papers as soon as he rounds the corner of the entry way. A wide smile spreads across her face. This will never get old. He smiles right back, so happy to be home.

She gets up and starts walking towards him.

"How was your day, Faith?"

"It was good. These students are going to be hard to let go of at the end of the year."

"Maybe you should just follow them into second grade like you followed them into first." He laughs while he places his arms around her, pulling her into him. He inhales the scent of her hair.

"As tempting as that may be, I'm really enjoying first grade." She squeezes him tight, trying to make sure he knows how much she missed him.

"Is it just as you remembered it?"

"It's even better!"

Jonathan kisses the top of her head. "I'm glad you're happy with the change you made."

"Me too."

"Are we ready to head to the house yet?"

"I have about five minutes left." She nods her head towards the dining room table.

# APTITUDE

"OK." Jonathan follows her over to the table where there are papers strewn about. He smiles as she sits down, getting right back into her work. He motions towards the stairs and says, "I'll be down by the time you're done."

"Perfect."

Faith watches Jonathan as he heads up the open black stair case to their bedroom. She is slightly curious what he needs to do upstairs. For a brief moment she considers that he could be grabbing a little box with a ring in it, but she shakes the thought away. His stance on adding more to their plate at this point hasn't changed since their conversation about it last month. Although, Tollero's was the restaurant they went to for their first date.

Once she finishes her prep-work she starts up the stairs to grab a different pair of shoes. Jonathan is finishing up in the bathroom.

"I just wanted to freshen up a bit."

"OK." She gestures to the closet. "I'm grabbing some shoes."

"Make sure it's something warm. It's been pretty cold outside today."

"Yeah, and it isn't going to get warmer now that the sun has set."

"Not at all."

On the way to their property they spot a whitetail deer crossing the road just ahead of them. Jonathan slows down and they watch as it bounds up the tree filled hill on the left side of the road.

"I wonder if we'll see deer on our property someday." Faith asks.

"I'm sure we will. Especially with Silverwood State Park just on the other side of it."

"It's going to be beautiful, Jonathan." She breathes in deeply with the image of the finished house and landscaping in her mind giving her optimism for their future.

"Not as beautiful as you, Faith." Jonathan reaches for her hand. He squeezes it and then places it on top of the shifter resting it in his.

"Thank you." She smiles.

The crew is finishing up when they pull into the driveway. Michael greets them as they open the car doors.

"Today is a great day to come check the place out!"

Jonathan steps out of the Mercedes. The cold February air stinging his face. Michael outstretches his large hand.

"It's good to see you, Michael."

"It's wonderful to see you two as well! Come! Look at what we've got going on in here." He motions towards the front door. Jonathan and Faith follow behind him hand in hand. Faith's excitement is very apparent, she's practically skipping; her body simply can't contain her joy.

Faith tries to take in all of the changes since the last time they visited. She attempts to notice all the new details, but is quite overwhelmed in the best way possible. As they enter the structure that is to be their future home Faith's body is buzzing. She squeezes Jonathan's hand tightly.

# APTITUDE

The construction crew has been busy. All of the framing is finished. It makes it so much easier for them to clearly see where one room begins and the other ends. The sub floors are placed so you can easily walk through. There are makeshift stairs where their grand staircase will eventually be.

With all of these additions Faith must admit the house is beginning to feel slightly less enormous, but only slightly. It is still a massive house, especially in comparison to her old one or even the condo they're in now.

They visit the family room, dining room, and kitchen. Then they venture into the primary bedroom and en suite bathroom with dual walk-in closets. Seeing the placement of the doors and window openings, with the sheer size of the bedroom Faith starts trying to figure out how they should arrange the furniture.

Next, they go into the shared office. It is nearly as large as the primary bedroom. Faith is excited for the floor to ceiling built in book shelves in this room especially. It will be like her own personal library. Well, at least on her half of the room. Since Jonathan has been bringing more work home they thought having a shared office would be best.

"This is going to be amazing!" She squeezes Jonathan's arm against her body.

"It really is! I can't wait." He smiles broadly at her. Faith can see how much pride he takes in this house already and it isn't even finished yet.

As they head up the stairs Michael mentions, "The plumbers and electricians should be working next week to rough in. This is where it all gets exciting!"

"You really enjoy your job don't you?" Faith asks.

"I love what I do! I don't see it as a job, this is something I'm fortunate to be able to do! Plus, I get paid for it!"

Faith smiles, his excitement for his job and building their home brings her a sense of comfort.

In the first bedroom on the right up the stairs, Faith remembers the rendering that Stephen created for them in his office. This was the bedroom that was staged as a precious nursery with soft grey walls, built in bookshelves, and a circular crib. She can envision it even more easily now. Standing looking out the hole in the wall where the window will someday be, it will overlook the backyard and have an overhead view of the garden she hopes to have there.

They walk through the other four bedrooms and future bathrooms then see the rec room upstairs before heading back downstairs and then down another set of make-shift steps to the walk-out basement portion of the house. It is easy to see where their great room and kitchenette will placed. The huge hole in the wall shows exactly where the walk out part of it will be. Faith and Jonathan love the bi-fold glass doors that are in the condo so, they decided that is what they want to have here as well.

There's an additional full bathroom and guest bedroom on this level. They opted to add another bedroom in the basement bringing the house to six bedrooms. This flex room can be used as an in-law suite if ever necessary for Faith's parents. It could also be an older child's bedroom eventually.

Part of building the house means they can have whatever they want. This is the aspect that appealed to Jonathan the most. They have already made a couple of changes to help accommodate what they can really only speculate will be needs in the future. The two of them couldn't possibly know what lies ahead, but if they can avoid a remodel in the future, that's what they're going to try to do.

Back on the main floor, they walk to where the back patio door will eventually be and go outside. Jonathan asks Michael, "What size was the patio going to be again?"

"It will be the entire length of the house. That includes the pool area as well. So, approximately eighty by forty five. That's why the basement walkout actually goes to the side yard facing the woods."

Jonathan sees Faith's eyes get huge. "And will all of that be finished around the same time the house is?"

"That's our goal. We still need to meet with the pool builders to finalize the look you're going for and then we'll customize the rest of the patio around that." He gestures towards the expanse of yard in front of them.

"Perfect!"

Michael just now notices the stunned look on Faith's face. "Don't you worry, it'll be beautiful! We'll have different zones that will make it have a cozy feeling. And landscaping! Landscaping always helps!!"

"I'm sure it will be absolutely beautiful." Faith smiles, reassuring him.

"We were also talking about adding another seating area with a fire pit closer to the edge of the property facing Amethyst Bay." Jonathan says.

"That's a spectacular idea! We can do whatever you'd like and the budget allows."

"The budget will allow it." Jonathan smiles.

Faith says, "Thank you for walking around with us Michael. It was really good to see how much you guys have accomplished."

"We're working hard, but it's also fun! Being able to watch this piece of bare land become a home is like magic to me."

Faith swears she sees Michaels eyes get a little misty.

"I'm truly happy to have you as the project manager for our build. You've been so great throughout this whole process."

"Thank you! That makes me very happy to hear!"

Jonathan and Faith hand the hard hats back to Michael and start for the car.

"You're welcome, Michael. Thank you!"

"You two are so very welcome!"

# Chapter 14

## Habitude

*Noun; habitual disposition or mode of behavior or procedure*

The following night, while Faith and Jackie are having drinks at Lee's Pub, Jonathan has left work and drives straight to Caulfield. He hadn't planned to, but by lunch time the urge was grating on him. As far as Faith knows he's still at work. He also didn't have a hard time justifying going tonight since Faith isn't sitting at home waiting for him. The fact that she has something to do made it that much easier for him to go.

After switching vehicles at the dilapidated building, he drives to Duffy's Bar and Grill. He has had some luck at this bar in the past. Jonathan thinks back to the victims he's taken from here and recalls that one of his favorites came from this bar.

Thinking of that kill makes his whole body vibrate with anticipation. If the circumstances are right Jonathan could recreate that kill. He'd only have to find the right victim.

He remembers it clearly, if he had to speculate what made it so special it was more than likely a combination of the victim and timing. The victim had been a gamble. She wasn't meek or mousy like most he chooses. She didn't throw herself at him in an attempt to hook up. No, she had a high class air about her.

Her name was Erica, she was a very pretty girl, and as it turns out, a fighter. That was the part Jonathan loved most. He watched her fight the effects of the drug. He watched her attempt to fight him. The realization that something bad was going to happen was apparent in her eyes as soon as he pulled his car into the rundown building. He reveled in it until it was time to help her up the stairs.

Jonathan had started to wonder if the drug hadn't gone into full effect yet because she practically tried to throw herself out of his grip and back down the steps. He didn't understand where her strength came from.

The only conclusion he was ever able to ascertain was that she was special. Erica had an entirely different level of will to live. It didn't stop on those stairs either. It didn't stop in the living room when she managed to somehow roll off the dank pea green couch and then attempt to crawl to the door, failing miserably, but still trying. It did however end in that bathroom while lying in the bathtub where so many others had lost their will to live before her. *Yes, she was special.*

# APTITUDE

Meanwhile, in Luna Shores Faith and Jackie are dancing on the small dancefloor at Lee's Pub, shouting at one another over the DJ's remix. They're smiling, laughing, and having a blast together as always. When the song ends they breathlessly go to the bar together to order drinks, then they sit down at a high top table near the bathrooms and a pool table.

Sipping on the sweet concoction aptly named pineapple upside down cake, Faith giggles at Jackie as she makes a sour face.

"That is so sweet it's bordering on dessert!"

"I think it's delicious." Faith takes another long drink.

Jackie shrugs her shoulders and takes another pull on the straw. After she swallows she takes the straw between her fingers and stirs her drink. "That was all vodka!" A big smile spreads on her face and Faith tosses her head back in laughter.

Neither of them notice the stranger's dark eyes locked on them on the other side of the bar. Neither of them noticed while they were on the dance floor or when they sidled up next to the stranger at the bar when they ordered their drinks either.

A new song starts just as Jackie finishes her drink. She grabs Faith by the arm yanking her from her seat, pulling her back towards the dance floor.

"My feet are killing me!" Faith shouts in complaint.

"You only live once, Brandt! Let's go!" Jackie continues pulling her all while dancing her way out on the floor.

Faith can't help but appreciate Jackie's energy and zest for life. Jackie was always the one with the wild ideas and schemes that got them in a fair amount of trouble. It was never anything too serious. Jackie's parents didn't keep track of her much so she hardly ever got into trouble. Faith's parents on the other hand, kept very close tabs, so much so that she was rarely able to get away with anything.

Faith watches the smile on Jackie's face grow wider when she sees Faith dancing right alongside her. She's very proud to have such an amazing friend in Jackie.

When the song ends Faith insists on going back to the table and Jackie complies.

"Only for a minute! Then we're back on the dance floor!"

"Alright, alright." She laughs.

Faith grabs her glass and takes a quick refreshing sip. As soon as she does, Jackie's eyes go wide. She slaps the glass out of Faith's hands. Watered down pineapple upside down cake splashes onto the table ricocheting up back onto them. The glass shatters on the floor sending glass shards flying.

Faith starts, "What the fuck was that for?"

"Were you watching that the entire time we were on the dance floor?"

# APTITUDE

Faith realizes where Jackie is going with the question and answers, "No, I wasn't. I was thirsty and it was right here. I wasn't even thinking." She lowers her gaze somewhat ashamed of her lack of forethought.

"It's OK. I'm sure it's fine, but we definitely aren't taking any chances."

Just then the dark stranger comes walking up to their table. He's tall, muscular, with dark brown hair and dark brown eyes. He smiles at them both. In a southern drawl he says, "I couldn't help but notice your friend spilled your drink."

Both ladies notice the drinks he's carrying, one in each hand.

Jackie speaks up immediately holding her hand up, "No offense, but we won't be drinking those."

"None taken. I'm sorry, did I overstep?"

"We're both taken." Faith says flatly.

"Surely, you didn't think I was just comin' over to hit on yall?"

"Why else would you be bringing us drinks?" Jackie questions him.

For a quick second she notices his chivalrous façade drop. If it had been any quicker she would've missed it. Clearly being questioned isn't a thing he appreciates.

"I was just meanin' to make conversation with some beautiful ladies. I've been sittin' at the bar waiting on a friend who didn't show and I thought to myself that I either need to go home and call it a night, or try to turn this evenin' around."

"Maybe you should have gone with the first option." Jackie says matter-of-factly.

He isn't impressed with her forwardness, but persists trying to be as charming as possible. "I'm sorry, I never asked you ladies y'all's names. I'm Zander." He smiles.

"Hi, Zander. We're not at all interested." Jackie retorts.

Zander's eyes are locked on Faith now. Jackie notices how dark his eyes have gotten with his low gaze on her friend. A chill runs down her back as she realizes how quiet Faith has gotten. Jackie follows his gaze and sees that her eyes seem glassier than they had just a few moments before. Jackie reaches for Faith's arm to get her attention then she half whispers, half shouts, "Are you OK?"

Faith turns her head slightly to look at Jackie just as the realization sets in. "I…don't…think…ssso…"

Jackie's stomach drops as she hears the slur of Faith's words and then watches as her head slightly bobbles when she moves. She stands up getting nearly face to face with the stranger. "I don't know what kind of game you're playing, but you better not have been the one to slip something to my friend." If Faith wasn't spiraling fast she would have hit him.

He puts his hands up and says, "Darlin', I didn't do anythin' but try to bring y'all drinks."

"Get out of our way!" Jackie slips her arm around Faith and helps support her as they walk to the bar.

"Tracy, I can't prove it, but I'm pretty sure that man," She nods her head in Zander's direction, "just drugged Faith and then tried to drug us both. You should call the cops. I'm taking her to the hospital."

Tracy's eyes go wide and then she says, "OK, I'm on it! Please keep me informed!"

Jackie and Faith are already nearly to the door when Jackie shouts, "Will do!"

On the way to the hospital Jackie tries to call Jonathan. There's no answer. She then tries Faith's parents. Diane picks up.

"Hi Mrs. Brandt, its Jackie. I'm sorry to call this late. I don't want you to be alarmed, but Faith and I were out at Lee's pub and I'm almost certain she was drugged. She didn't drink much so I'm hoping that the affects won't be that bad."

Diane heard everything Jackie said, but it takes a minute for her to process. Finally she says, "OK. Thank you for calling us and letting us know."

Realizing she must have woke her up Jackie continues, "I'm taking her to the hospital. Do you guys want to meet us there?"

"Yes. Yes, we should do that." Diane's voice moves to the background as Jackie hears, "Frank. Wake up, Frank! We have to go to the hospital. Something has happened with Faith."

Jackie asks, "Do you want me to call Hope also?"

"That would be good. Thank you for being such a great friend to Faith, Jackie."

"She's the best, Mrs. Brandt. I'm going to call Hope now. I'll see you guys at the emergency room."

"OK."

Jackie hangs up and calls Hope right away. She answers on the third ring.

"Hello?"

Jackie says nearly the same thing to Hope and Hope agrees to meet them at the emergency room as well. Before they hang up Hope asks, "Were you able to get a hold of Jonathan?"

"No. I tried calling him first and there was no answer."

"OK. I'll try. You get my sister to the hospital. I'll see you there shortly."

Jackie hangs up the phone and glances at Faith.

"How are you doing, Faith?"

"Groggy…Hot." She manages to get the words out.

"It's going to be OK. We're almost to the hospital and they'll figure out what was in your drink."

Faith tries to reach for Jackie's arm, but it feels as though her arm is filled with wet sand. "Thank you…"

"You're welcome. Try to stay awake." Jackie rolls Faith's window down letting the cool February air into the cozy cabin of her SUV.

Faith seems to perk up a little. She says, "Jonathan?" One word responses are still better than nothing, even if they are slurred.

# APTITUDE

"Hope is trying to call him now. He didn't answer when I tried."

At that, Faith groans. Jackie glances at her. The street light illuminates the tears slowly trickling down her cheek.

She reaches for her friends hand, taking it she begins rubbing the top of it with her thumb. "It'll be OK. We're almost to the hospital now. I know I just said that, but it's only a couple more minutes."

Letting go of Faith's hand momentarily, she grabs her bottle of water. She opens it and tries handing it to Faith to drink. "Here, Faith. You have to drink this. It will help."

Faith doesn't move. Jackie can see that she's trying. There is determination on her face, but nothing is happening. Jackie presses down on the accelerator as she puts the water bottle back in the cup holder.

# Chapter 15

## *Certitude*

*Noun; the state of being or feeling certain*

Moments later, Jackie pulls up to the front doors of the emergency room. Leaving the engine running she rushes through the automatic doors, grabs a wheel chair, and brings it to the passenger side door. She slowly opens the door noticing Faith slumped against it.

"Faith, I need you to try to sit up. I have to unbuckle you and get you into the wheel chair, but I don't want you falling out of the car because, well, concrete is hard. We don't want you to get hurt."

She watches as Faith fights to move. Jackie helps her sit back and unbuckles her then swings her legs out the door before she puts her arms around her and lifts her up and out. Spinning around while holding Faith up is quite the maneuver, but she manages and then helps her sit down in the wheel chair.

# APTITUDE

Just as Jackie is turning the wheel chair around to wheel Faith through the emergency room doors she sees Faith's old crossover pull up right behind her SUV.

Hope steps out and sees her sister barely able to hold her head up on her own. Faith is half slumped over in the wheel chair. She tells Jackie, "Go! Take her in. I'll park both cars."

Jackie doesn't need any further instruction, she wheels Faith in and quickly walks up to the reception desk. Thankful there isn't a line, she goes straight to the lady behind the desk and says, "I think my best friend has been drugged. We were out at Lee's pub, dancing and then she took a small sip without thinking and now she's like that." She gestures towards Faith in the wheel chair.

"OK. We'll get her checked in, I'll just need some information. Then a nurse will be out shortly to bring you back to a room."

Jackie gives her the standard information then sits next to Faith in one of the chairs. She's never seen her friend like this and it's kind of freaking her out. Hope comes in just as the nurse walks through the double doors to take them back.

"Perfect timing." Hope says to Jackie.

"I guess so. Thanks for parking my car."

"No problem. Here're your keys." She holds them out, letting them dangle from her finger.

"Thanks." Jackie puts them in her purse then asks, "Were you able to get a hold of Jonathan?"

"Negative. I called at least half a dozen times. No answer to any of them."

"Weird."

"It is, but I know Faith has mentioned him working late on Fridays a lot, so maybe that's it."

"Maybe."

A CNA comes into the room to help the nurse get Faith out of the wheel chair and into the bed. Hope immediately recognizes them. She's unsure if she should say anything, though.

Her thoughts are interrupted by the nurse. "Hi, I'm Cassie, I'll be your friend's nurse practitioner tonight. I need all the information you can give me about what might have happened."

While Jackie gives Cassie more information about what happened at the bar, Andy says, "Hope, you look great!"

"Thank you! How have you been?"

"Good, mostly just working. It's really great to see you!"

"Yeah, it's great to see you too! Would be better under different circumstances." Hope smiles at them as she shrugs her shoulders.

"Definitely." Andy says as they walk out the door.

The nurse practitioner places Faith's IV which she uses to take blood for testing and then hooks up to fluids. Faith appears to be sleeping through it all. Thankfully the heartrate on the monitor above her head gives Jackie the peace of mind that she got her here in time.

# APTITUDE

"You said you alerted the bartender to the man you thought may have done this?" Cassie asks Jackie.

"Yes."

"OK. Good. I was wondering if we should be gearing up to see more of these tonight." The nurse practitioner rolls her eyes. "What people do to complete strangers is beyond me." She says half to herself as she enters some information into the computer. She looks at Jackie once again, "I have to ask this, do you know if Faith would have taken anything else?"

"No. We had two drinks each tops."

"OK. Like I said there are questions we just have to ask."

"I understand."

Frank and Diane are escorted into Faith's stark bright white room. They see her lying there and rush to the side of her bed. Hope stands and goes to them.

Jackie asks Cassie, "Do you have any more questions for me? I'm going to step out for a minute and try to contact her boyfriend, if that's alright." She gestures to the door.

"Sure, that's no problem. I'm almost done here."

Jackie leaves the Brandt family in the room and walks to the front doors trying to get reception. She dials and walks through the automatic doors into the chilly night air. This time it goes straight to voicemail. She hangs up. Under her breath she mutters, "What the hell?"

Jackie walks a little further down the sidewalk, the bright moon above is illuminating every step. She lights up the screen of her phone and calls Tom. He answers on the fourth ring. Sleepily he says, "Hello?"

"Hey, I wanted to let you know that I'm at the hospital with Faith. Someone drugged her. I'm fine. Don't worry. But I can't get a hold of Jonathan."

"Is Faith OK? And it's weird that he wouldn't answer."

"Yeah, I thought so too. She's pretty out of it, but seems to be sleeping right now. I was wondering if Jonathan was at work when you left?"

"Yeah, he's usually there pretty late on Fridays."

"OK. Is there any way for you to keep trying to get in touch with him so that I can go back in by Faith. The reception isn't working in the room. Her family is here, but that doesn't mean I want to be gone long."

"I can do that."

"Thanks, Tom."

"No problem. Do you want me to come up there?"

"Not really. The room is getting crowded. Just try to reach Jonathan and let him know what's going on, please."

She hangs up the phone and goes back inside and to Faith's room. As soon as she walks into the hospital room she's greeted by Frank. "Thank you so much for taking such good care of our girl." He embraces her.

"You're welcome, Mr. Brandt."

Diane adds, "Yeah, who knows what would have happened if you hadn't been there."

"Nothing good." Jackie lowers her eyes and thinks of the dark stranger, then continues. "I let the bartender know what was going on. Tracy should have called the police. I'm sure they'll be here to ask questions soon."

"Were you able to get a hold of Jonathan?" Hope asks Jackie.

"Still no. I wasn't sure what else to do so I called Tom to see if he can keep trying."

"That's a good idea." Hope looks down at her hands and says, "They better have caught this guy." With anger in her voice she continues, "How dare someone do this to my sister."

Diane goes to Hope, placing a hand on her shoulder reassuringly she says, "They'll catch him, dear. They have to."

"I'm sure Luna Shores PD isn't going to rest until they do. They don't want stuff like this happening here." Frank adds.

"No, they definitely don't. This is a safe little town."

Andy knocks softly on the door, then enters. They smile at Hope then say, "I need to get her vitals."

"No problem." Diane says.

Just as Andy hits the button to start the blood pressure cuff, Faith's body twitches ever so slightly. They all watch to see if she is going to come to. Faith lets out a quiet whimper, but her eyes stay closed.

"We're giving her a lot of fluids in an attempt to both keep her hydrated and pump the drugs out. She is doing well. I know this is scary and she doesn't seem like she's doing OK at all, but her vitals are really good, considering. Hopefully we'll have her test results back soon." Andy says as they walk towards the door. Then continues, "Cassie should be back in shortly."

"Thank you, Andy." Hope says truly grateful for their reassurance.

"You're welcome." Andy smiles.

Unsure of what to do with herself Jackie says, "I'm going to step out and try to contact Jonathan again. She's going to want him here when she wakes up."

As she walks towards the front doors again she tries calling Jonathan's cell phone, it simply goes straight to his voicemail. She leaves a non-descript voice message, but she knows as soon as he hears it he'll figure something is wrong.

Next, she calls Tom again to see if his luck has been any better, but isn't very hopeful.

"Hello?"

"Hi, Tom. Have you gotten a hold of Jonathan by any chance?"

"No. I called Kansen Corp and he isn't there. No one is left in the office. I did text a couple of people that I know who typically stay late, but they said he was still there when they left."

"But he's not there now?"

"No. I tried his office line and his cell phone. No answer on either one."

"I just tried his cell phone and it went straight to voicemail."

"I'm sorry, Jackie. I wish there was more I can do."

# APTITUDE

"It's not your fault, Tom. Faith was asking for him and I want him to be here for her when she wakes up."

"I'll keep trying."

"Thank you. I'm going to go back into the room now. Bye."

Cassie spots Jackie walking back down the hallway heading to Faith's room.

She stops her and says, "I just wanted to let you know that Luna Shores PD is here. I've given them the information I am allowed, but they have questions for you. Are you OK with talking to them now?"

"Yeah, I'd like to get it done with so I can get back into Faith's room. Hopefully they got the guy."

"Hopefully. Follow me then, I'll show you to the waiting area they're in."

Jackie follows her down the hall into a small waiting area with a handful of chairs and a single vending machine. The lights are turned down so the room isn't terribly bright. The vending machine is cascading bright light over the otherwise shadowed chairs.

The two officers stand when Jackie enters. The first one is a heavier set man with dark brown hair. Jackie isn't sure if the smile on his face is his attempt to comfort her or if it always looks like that. The other officer is a female. Her black hair is slicked back in a tight bun. Her expression is more solemn. Jackie decides she already likes the female officer more.

"Hi, you're Jackie Stafford?" The male officer asks, holding out his hand.

Jackie shakes it and answers, "Yes, I am."

The woman officer steps forward and shakes Jackie's hand as she says, "Nice to meet you, Jackie. I'm Officer Carter." She hooks a thumb towards her partner and says, "This is Officer Strickland."

"It's good to meet you both."

"Under the circumstances anyway… We were told that your friend was drugged at Lee's Pub, is that correct?" Officer Carter asks.

"Yes, that is correct."

"Can you tell us everything that you remember?"

"We got to Lee's Pub around nine, we each got a drink. Once those were finished we danced out on the dance floor for a while. I wasn't really watching the clock, so I'm not sure how long exactly. Then when we were thirsty we got another couple of drinks. That one was Faith's pick. It was too sweet for my taste. I drank mine quickly to help get it down, I pulled her back out onto the dance floor.

When we got back to the table Faith absentmindedly grabbed her drink and took a sip. I smacked it out of her hand mid drink. It was a couple of moments later a man approached us with a couple of drinks in his hands that he intended to give us. I not-so-politely told him we didn't want them. He was acting like I hurt his feelings and his intentions were innocent. I'm sure they weren't.

# APTITUDE

When I looked at Faith I could tell something was wrong. Her eyes were glassy and she was pale looking. I helped her up, told the bartender what was going on and brought her here." Jackie gestures to the hospital walls.

"You think it was the gentleman who approached you that did this to your friend?"

"If I was a betting woman, I'd bet everything on it. He was insistent, even after I was rude to him multiple times. He really wanted us to drink whatever he had in those glasses."

"Well, it was very smart of you to refuse." Officer Strickland offers.

Jackie has to refrain from rolling her eyes. His intentions might be good, but no woman in her right mind would have taken anything from that man.

Instead of saying what she's thinking, she offers him a smile and asks, "Did you guys arrest him?"

Officer Carter answers, "The bartender called us as soon as you told her what you thought happened. She was watching the man as he took both the full glasses into the bathroom, only to come out with two entirely empty glasses. We're thinking he must have flushed any 'evidence' down the toilet. The glasses were left on the table you guys were at.

We got there as soon as we could, but he had already left. The dispatcher informed Tracy not to pursue him. He is being treated as a dangerous suspect and we can't risk civilians' lives like that."

"No, I'm glad she didn't go after him."

"Every squad car that's out on patrol right now has a photo of him that was taken from security cameras. Tracy gave us access to the footage. He was extremely cunning, but we were able to spot him slipping something in Faith's drink, and then also in the two he brought to you ladies after you went back to the table."

"That's incredible." Jackie wants to be more excited that this asshole is going to be punished for what he did to her best friend, but the excitement just isn't there knowing he isn't even in custody yet.

Officer Carter puts her hand on Jackie's shoulder. "We're going to get him. Unfortunately what we saw from the footage was that he had a driver pick him up. We're going to follow up with the company to find out where he got dropped off at, so chances of catching him are good, but it's going to take some time."

"I hope so. For Faith, but also for anyone else he could try to do this to in the future. Who knows how many other women he's done this to before now."

"We haven't had any reports like this here recently. Our guess is that he's from out of town." Officer Strickland says.

Jackie fights rolling her eyes once again.

# Chapter 16

# Fortitude

*Noun; strength of mind that enables a person to encounter danger or bear pain or adversity with courage*

Faith knows that she is at the hospital. She can remember Jackie helping her get into the wheel chair. Right now she can feel the bed beneath her supporting her body and the slightly scratchy blankets covering her, but as much as her mind is aware of those things, her body is unwilling to allow her to open her eyes or even move.

She can hear their voices. She can feel their gentle touch when they grasp her hand or rub her arm. She can decipher between who is talking, but she doesn't know where they are exactly. At times, she has wondered if what she is hearing is really happening or if it is all just a dream.

When Andy was checking her vitals she fought so hard to force her body to make any noise, to let them all know she was still here and she was still fighting.

She has never felt more frustration than she's feeling right now. She wants to wake up. She is fighting to do that, but the drug still has too strong a hold on her body.

She felt when her mom was holding her hand. She attempted to squeeze it back, but it was as if her muscles were no longer able to do whatever she wanted them to. She strained to think and tried to visualize in her mind her fingers gripping her mother's, but they still wouldn't move. She couldn't will them to.

It's such a strange feeling to no longer be able to control your body. The movements she was able to make mindlessly only hours before are impossible to her now.

She heard Jackie say that she was going to try to call Jonathan again. *Why hasn't he been answering? It doesn't make sense. If he was simply working late why wouldn't he answer his phone?*

Faith tries to calm her thoughts, she is stressed out enough without thinking of what could possibly be wrong with Jonathan that he isn't answering. She thinks of her parents and Hope, she can hear them now. They're talking amongst themselves while her dad is holding her hand.

She hasn't heard Jackie come back in yet. *Maybe that means she was able to get ahold of Jonathan!*

Someone knocks on the door. It opens and Faith hears a woman say, "Faith's blood work isn't back yet, but with the fluids we're pushing and how great her vital signs are I feel confident enough to say that we're in good shape. I can't say when she'll come to, but hopefully it will be soon."

# APTITUDE

"Great, thank you, Cassie." Faith's mom says.

"I'll be back to check on her shortly. If you need anything just push the call button."

Faith hears the nurse close the door behind her. A few moments later she hears the door open once again. Hoping to hear Jonathan's voice, her heart sinks a little when it turns out to be Jackie.

"Sorry, I was gone longer than I planned."

"Were you able to get ahold of Jonathan yet?" Hope asks

"No. Tom hasn't either. He's going to keep trying. There were two officers here from Luna Shores PD. They were asking me questions about what happened at Lee's Pub."

"Did they get the guy?" Hope asks optimistically.

"Not yet. They have proof that he did it though. They watched him on the security camera footage."

"That's great, isn't it?" Diane asks.

"They think so. I'm worried that he's already long gone. He dumped the drinks he got us in the toilet and then left before the cops got there."

"What a coward." Hope says.

"Something like that, yeah. How's she doing?"

"Pretty much the same. The nurse did come in." Diane updates Jackie on what the nurse just told them.

"Fingers crossed she wakes up soon." Faith feels Jackie's hand on top of hers.

Faith wants to give them all a sign that she's with them. Even if it seems like she is deep asleep, she is actually quite awake. This drug has made her body feel like some sort of prison. It's as if her consciousness is trapped within a body that cannot function.

Her frustration grows and once again she focuses all of her mental energy into just one finger. If she can get her pointer finger to grip Jackie's hand then everyone will be assured that she'll be OK!

She thinks really hard about moving that one finger, just a little, that's all it will take. Focus, Faith, she tells herself. *Focus and move your damn finger. You can do it!*

With eyes wide, Jackie says, "You guys! I think I felt her hand move!"

"Really?" Hope stands and comes over to the edge of the bed. She continues, this time addressing Faith directly. "We're here, Faith. It's alright if you want to sleep for a little bit longer, but we're here for you. You're going to be OK."

Diane and Frank are both on the right side of Faith's bed. Faith feels them rubbing her arm. She focuses as hard as she can once again to try to move that hand this time. The muscle barely twitches. She slowly breathes in deeply and tries again. It takes all of her mental focus, but she manages to squeeze her dad's hand with her one finger.

His face lights up! "I felt her finger move too!" Tears begin streaming down his face, but he doesn't want to let go of Faith in order to wipe them away.

Diane nods her head yes and says, "I felt her muscle in her arm flex when she squeezed your hand!"

"She's trying!" Hope says smiling widely.

# APTITUDE

Just then Faith hears the door open again. She hears swift movement which comes to a stop next to Jackie. Faith feels a larger hand take the place of Jackie's.

Breathing in, Faith smells Jonathan's familiar scent. She feels his warm breath against her cheek as he says, "I'm so sorry I wasn't here sooner." His lips gently kiss hers.

*Now is the time to wake up! Do it! Just open your eyes! It's not hard, you've done it for the past twenty-three years of your life! It'll be just like in the fairy tales! Do it!*

She fights to make another noise. What comes out doesn't even sound like her, it's almost as if her voice is coming from somewhere outside of her body.

Faith hears Jackie filling Jonathan in on what happened at Lee's Pub. She keeps fighting to open her eyes. She takes a tour of her body in her mind. She tries at first to wiggle her toes, the attempt fails. Then she checks in with her calves followed by her knees. Working her way up her body, being aware of every inch of it. Finally she reaches her eyes. They begin to move while her eyes remain closed. It feels like her eyelids are weighted blankets covering them.

She's not sure how she's going to open them. Instead of trying, she focuses on keeping them moving. She hears someone hit the call button for the nurse, letting Cassie know that Faith is starting to move.

Cassie comes in shortly after that and stands at the foot of Faith's bed observing. "You can try to coax her. Let her know you're all here and that she is safe."

Jonathan starts first. "Faith, it's OK. I'm here now. You can wake up!" She can hear the smile in his voice, but there's something else she hears too. She just can't quite put her finger on it.

Then she hears Jackie. "You're safe and the police are going to catch the guy who tried to hurt you."

Faith hears herself groggily say, "Us."

Everyone in the room laughs with relief.

Jackie says, "Yes, that's true. He did try to hurt us both." She pauses for a second and then says, "If he was trying to drug both of us, how was he going to handle getting the two of us out of the bar? That doesn't make sense unless maybe…"

"There was a second guy." Jonathan finishes her sentence before she has the chance. His voice low and serious.

Jackie looks at Jonathan realizing just how much danger they were in. She can see fear in his eyes, which is quickly replaced by anger.

"Who would want to do that to someone they don't even know?" Diane asks with disgust in her voice.

Frank asks, "Was there anything else you can think of that would help figure out who this guy was?"

"I'd never seen him before. He spoke with a southern accent, though. The cops assume he's from out of town. He said his name was Zander."

"Did you say a southern accent?" Hope asks Jackie, then quickly looks at her dad.

"Yeah. Why?"

"Dad, didn't the guy I punched at the café have a southern accent?"

"He did, didn't he?"

"Yeah." Hope looks back at Jackie again, "Did it seem like Faith recognized the guy?"

"No, not at all."

"Hmmm."

"Maybe the two guys were working together. The one who came to the table wasn't the one she would have recognized. That wouldn't have been very smart on their part if it had been." Jonathan says.

"We should have called the cops when that happened." Hope says.

Frank asks, "Jackie, do you know if the cops are still here? I think we need to let them know about the previous incident at the café."

"I'm not sure."

Cassie speaks up. "I'm pretty sure I saw them right before I came in here. I'll go look. You guys stay here with Faith. If I find them, I'll bring them here if that's OK with all of you."

"That would be great. Thank you." Frank says.

Faith finally feels the weight of her eyelids lift the slightest bit. She's not sure if it's enough to allow her to open them, but she tries anyways.

The brightness of the room is an assault to her pupils. With her eyes stinging, she closes them as quickly as she can. She fights to get the word out. "Lights."

Jonathan hits the lighting button on the remote attached to the hospital bed. "There you go. It shouldn't be so bad now."

Faith attempts once again to open her eyes. This time the room is much dimmer. Her eyes still need to adjust, but it isn't as painful at least.

"How are you feeling?" Jonathan asks with concern in his voice.

"Tired." As hard as she tries she's still not able to get more than one word out at a time. She takes a deep breath in through her nose and tries again. "Head…" Another deep breath. "Hurts…"

"I'm sure it does. It's OK now though. You're safe and we're all here."

Faith looks from Jonathan's face to her mom and dad's then to Hope's and Jackie's moving only her eyes. She tries to focus, but her vision is a little blurry. "Thanks," is all she can manage to get out. The screen above her bed begins beeping and Cassie comes running back into the room.

Faith's heart rate has jumped suddenly.

Cassie adjusts the bed to lay her down flatter. "Faith, I'm Cassie, I'm your nurse. I need you to take some deep breaths for me, OK? Can you do that?"

Faith breathes in as deeply as she can. Her heart rate slowly comes back down into the normal range.

"You're OK. We just need to take it easy." Cassie turns to Frank and gestures towards the hallway and Frank follows her out.

# APTITUDE

Officers Carter and Strickland are standing in the hallway waiting for him. Strickland sticks his hand out. "Nice to meet you, Mr. Brandt, I'm Officer Strickland and this is Officer Carter. We heard you might have some helpful information for us."

"Yes. Jackie told us you reviewed the security cameras. Was there a second guy that could have been in on this?"

The officers look at one another. Officer Carter takes a small step forward and speaks in a hushed voice. "We did see that, yes. Why do you ask?"

"Because Jackie was working through it in her mind and realized there had to be someone else. A guy isn't going to drug two women to have to take care of both of them on his own. Then she also mentioned to us that he spoke with a southern accent.

About a month ago we had a man come into our café that we had never seen around here before. He assaulted Faith while she was waitressing. Hope punched him and I kicked him out. We probably should have called you guys then."

"You should have, but hind sight is always twenty/twenty, Mr. Brandt." Officer Carter says reassuringly.

Frank nods, then says, "This new information makes us think that the two men, both with southern accents, could have been working together."

"Thank you for telling us all of this. We'll look into it further and let you know what we find out. Do you by any chance have any footage available of that incident we'd be able to look at? It would help us figure out if it's the same guy."

"I sure do. I don't want to leave my daughter right now, but I'll be at the Café all day tomorrow. You can come in at any point and I'll have it ready for you to view."

"Great. We'll see you tomorrow then."

Frank thanks them and walks back into the room.

There's a little more color in Faith's cheeks now. He places his hand on her foot, gently squeezing he asks, "Are you doing OK, angel?"

"I'm OK, Dad."

"Well, you sound better."

"Jonathan got me some water." Faith looks up lovingly at Jonathan.

Jonathan leans down and says, "I'd do anything for you."

She smiles and takes a deep breath.

Frank moves next to Diane on the right side of Faith's bed. He explains to everyone that he informed the officers of everything and lets them know the officers will be reviewing footage of the incident tomorrow. "They better catch these assholes."

"They will." Hope says suddenly certain.

Jackie says, "I'm sorry I didn't stop you sooner." Faith notices the tears in Jackie's eyes as she finishes the sentence.

"You did everything you could, dear." Diane says reassuringly.

"Everything." Faith says, then continues, "I was so stupid. I don't know what I was thinking. I know better than that."

# APTITUDE

"You were just dancing, you needed something to drink. You didn't know someone was so sinister to want to hurt you." Jackie says.

"I didn't know."

"No, you couldn't have known." Jonathan puts his arms around her trying to comfort her as she begins to sob. Her heart rate jumps once more making the machine over her head beep once again.

Cassie comes back into the room. "Faith, let's try those deep breaths again."

Once again, she breathes deeply and once again her heart rate returns to normal.

"We've got to get this under control if we're going to be able to send you home tonight."

"OK." Faith agrees.

"We also need to get the results of your bloodwork back. I believe the doctor should be receiving those shortly."

Andy gently knocks on the door. "It's time to check her vitals."

Cassie nods and says, "Thank you." Then walks out the door.

Once Andy is finished they enter the information into the computer and excuse themselves.

Jonathan picks Faith's hand up in his bringing it to his lips, he kisses it gently. "I'm so glad that you're OK, Faith. I'm not sure what I would have done if something worse happened to you."

"It's OK. How are you doing?" She asks knowing how much he hates hospitals.

"I'm OK. I was so worried about you, it didn't matter where you were I was going to be there for you."

"I know how much you can't stand this place."

"I'll be fine." He kisses her hand again. "I'm just so thankful you're going to be able to come home tonight."

As soon as the word is out of his mouth the doctor knocks on the door.

"Come in." Faith says.

A tall lanky man with greying hair and a bulbous nose walks into the room. "Hi, Faith. I'm Dr. Westin. I've been waiting for your test results and they're finally in."

"Great."

"It looks as though you were given a relatively new version of a common date rape drug, it's called Somadazapine. It's a benzodiazepine just like Rohypnol. All that is to say, you'll be just fine. There shouldn't be any lasting side effects. You may find yourself more fatigued for the next couple of days, there could be some confusion, especially around everything that has happened tonight. I suggest lots of rest and hydration."

"Thank you, doctor." Faith says, feeling a bit in shock at the amount of information he just hurled at her.

"I'm glad you're awake. I'll get Cassie started on your discharge paperwork."

Faith smiles at him and he turns to leave. She watches Jackie follow him out of the room.

Diane looks at Jonathan, "Are you going to need any help caring for her this weekend? I can stop by if you need."

"I think we'll be OK. Thank you though."

"You don't have to work at all?" She asks.

"No, I'm definitely not going into work after this."

"OK."

"Thank you though, Mom." Faith says. Seeing the vulnerable look in her mom's eyes. Diane isn't used to not being the one to take care of her daughters.

Jackie comes back into the room and everyone looks at her.

She explains that she was asking the doctor some questions about the drug that was used. "This appears to be the first time he's seen it here."

"That's interesting." Frank says.

"It confirms even more so that the men aren't from around here."

"That's true." Frank agrees.

Cassie comes into the room with the finished paperwork. She tells Faith to try to stay calm and pay attention to her heart rate. "Since it's been over an hour since you've had an episode, we feel pretty confident that you shouldn't have another, but there is still a possibility."

Faith is unhooked from all of the monitors. She sits up giving Jonathan a proper hug. Reality sets in of what could have possibly happened and she squeezes him tighter. He doesn't want to hurt her so his hug is extra gentle. Tears are streaming down Faith's cheeks. She's so exhausted she isn't even sure if she can walk to the front doors.

"There's a wheel chair in the hall when you're ready." Cassie tells Faith.

"That's perfect."

"You might be a bit wobbly on your feet. That drug specifically does a number on your muscles."

"The doctor said he's never seen it here before." Jackie states.

"No, not here. I have done some travel nursing and have seen it in other places though. It's scary stuff. You did good bringing her here so quickly."

"Thanks." Jackie says flatly. "I wish it had never happened."

"But it did and you handled the situation the best you possibly could have." Diane smiles reassuringly.

"Exactly." Cassie agrees.

"I'm extremely thankful for your quick thinking." Jonathan offers.

"I am too!" Faith says.

Everyone laughs.

"I'll bring the wheel chair in." Hope says, "I'm sure Faith wants to go home."

Faith looks at Jonathan. "Our bed sounds heavenly right now."

Hope walks out into the hallway to see Andy standing there holding onto the handles of the wheel chair.

"I was just going to bring this in there for Faith."

# APTITUDE

Andy looks up surprised. "Oh, right."

Hope's eyebrows furrow. "Are you OK?" She asks.

"Yeah, I'm OK. I'm glad your sister is doing better now."

"Yeah, me too. That was some scary shit."

"Hey, I um didn't want to do this earlier, but if I don't do it now I think I'm going to regret it for as long as I live."

"I'm intrigued." Hope smiles.

"Well, I know this probably isn't the best time, but I've been thinking about you." They slip their hands in the pockets of their scrubs. "Would you maybe want to grab coffee or dinner sometime?" They ask rocking ever so slightly from toe to heel.

"That would be really nice." Hope feels her cheeks get warm and wonders when the last time was that she felt like this. Somehow she's got a whole stomach full of butterflies that came out of nowhere. They exchange numbers quickly and Andy heads down the hallway smiling.

Hope turns to push the wheel chair into Faith's room only to find Jackie standing there smiling widely. "That was interesting."

"They were very helpful to me when I was in the hospital after my accident."

"Well, hopefully something good can come out of this fiasco."

"Yeah. Maybe."

They all walk out with Faith. Jonathan pushes her in the wheelchair. They take turns hugging her good-bye and expressing their thankfulness that she's OK now.

Faith tells Jonathan when they first get into the car to head home, "Tonight was scary. I don't think I want to go out for my birthday."

"We can figure out something else to do." He says as he pulls out of the parking lot. He glances over at her only to see her eyes are closed.

# Chapter 17

## Lassitude

*Noun; a condition of weariness or debility, fatigue*

With her mind fuzzy, Faith wakes up on Saturday morning in their bed grateful to have Jonathan beside her. He makes her breakfast in bed; pancakes with scrambled eggs and orange juice.

"No mimosas today. I didn't think you would want alcohol."

"Not at all." At the mention of it, her stomach feels queasy.

"How are you feeling?"

"Not great. My head hurts, my stomach hurts, and I feel weak."

"I'll grab you something for your head."

"Thank you, Jonathan."

"Of course." He stands and walks into their bathroom to grab her some Ibuprofen.

As he hands them to her he asks, "How is your memory from last night?"

"It's quite fuzzy now. It's so strange, it all seemed so clear and now it's all lost. I'm not sure where it went."

"That's how those drugs work. That's why they're used for that."

Jonathan realizes the commonalities between what happened to Faith and how he uses a similar drug. No one he has given it to has ever lived to feel it's after effects. He struggles knowing that anything could have happened to Faith last night. Someone hunted her. They felt she was the best target for whatever reason. She isn't a victim though. Their choice proves their incompetence in Jonathan's opinion. He is almost as angry at them for what they did to her as he is for them attempting to use a similar modus operandi.

Faith takes a few bites of her food then sets her fork down. "I'm so sorry, Jonathan. This looks delicious, I'm not sure that I can eat right now."

"It's OK. You have a little something in your stomach. We can try again at lunch time."

"Yeah, maybe." Faith lays back onto her pillow and soon falls back to sleep once again.

When she wakes up the curtains are closed entirely, blocking the sun from coming in. She doesn't see Jonathan anywhere in the room. She sits up letting her eyes adjust a bit more then she hears footsteps coming up the stairs.

"You're awake."

"Just a few moments."

"I brought you some water." Jonathan sets the water bottle down on the nightstand beside her. Then he says, "How are you feeling now?"

"About the same. I'm really groggy and just feel out of it."

"Yeah, I bet. Make sure you drink some water. It will help."

"I have to get up and use the bathroom, but I'm not sure if my legs are strong enough."

"I am here to help. Any way that I can."

Faith sits up in their bed and Jonathan wraps his arms around her helping her to stand. The edges of her vision begin to turn black as her hands begin to tingle. She sits back down taking a deep breath.

"What's wrong?" Jonathan asks concerned.

"I got extremely light headed."

"Well, you haven't stood up since sometime last night."

Faith struggles to remember, but nothing is coming to mind. "Yeah, probably. I can't remember." She looks down. Tears begin to spill over onto her cheeks.

Jonathan squats down so they're eye to eye. "Hey. It's OK, Faith. Everything is alright. You're home now and I've got you. You're safe."

"I know, it's just very scary. It's like I'm in the middle of a nightmare and I can't pinch myself hard enough to wake up from it."

"I know, my love, I know." He puts his arms around her. With every sob that escapes her lips he feels her body tremble inside his embrace. "I wish I had been there to keep you safe. This never would have happened."

Faith takes a deep breath to calm herself. "It's not your fault, Jonathan."

"I know it's not, but I also know I could have prevented it."

"You're such a good man, Jonathan. I'm so lucky."

"I love you so much. The only thing I want to do is take care of you. Seeing you in that hospital bed last night scared the shit out of me." He moves to sit next to her on the bed and places his hand on her thigh.

Faith takes a sip of the water he brought her which makes Jonathan smile.

"Thank you, Jonathan."

"For what?"

"For taking care of me, for bringing me the water, for loving me so much."

He kisses her forehead then says, "Why don't we try getting you up again so you can use the bathroom."

Faith half-heartedly smiles and wipes the tears from her cheeks. "That would be good."

She takes another drink of water and Jonathan stands to help her up. He places his arms around her, steadying her as she stands. This time she's less light headed. She attempts to take a step, but her legs are very wobbly, almost as if they're made of gelatin.

Jonathan supports her weight as she moves slowly across the bedroom. Once they get into the bathroom she uses the counter to help stabilize her as well. Her whole body feels weak and she's extremely thankful Jonathan is there to help her.

"I hope I feel better than this tomorrow. I need to be able to go to school on Monday."

"If you don't feel better you will have to stay home. I'll see if there's any work I can grab from the office and work from home if needed."

"No, I don't want to be a burden."

"Faith, taking care of you isn't a burden."

"I feel like it is. You shouldn't have to take off of work or bring work home to take care of me. I should be capable of taking care of myself."

"Sometimes we all need a little help, Faith. There's nothing wrong with that."

"So you keep telling me."

Jonathan helps her sit down on the toilet. Faith is feeling a little dizzy from the exertion.

Once she's finished, she takes a deep breath and Jonathan helps her up once again.

"I think I should go back to bed."

"I agree." Jonathan smiles at her reassuringly.

"I wanted to see about going downstairs, but I think the bed is best. I'm not strong enough for stairs or even to be that far from the bathroom."

"How is your stomach feeling? I can bring you something to eat."

"It's still quite uneasy."

"I think you should still try to eat something."

"I agree."

"Is there something that sounds good and you think might sit well?"

"Maybe some whole grain toast with strawberry jam?"

"I can do that."

"I know I've said it before, but thank you for taking care of me so well, Jonathan."

"You're welcome, Faith."

She reaches the bed and sits, Jonathan helps lift her legs onto the mattress and she leans back against her pillows.

"Are you comfortable?" Jonathans asks while pulling the blankets back up to cover her.

"Very. Thank you."

"I'll go get you some toast."

"OK. I'll drink more water while you're doing that."

"Perfect." He smiles wide at her and turns to go down stairs.

Jonathan walks into the kitchen, suddenly he grabs the counter, bracing himself as the emotions hit him like a giant wave. The anger and rage is mixed with disappointment and guilt, he hates those men for doing this to Faith, and he feels guilty for doing this to other women. He's frustrated that he can't stop these urges he has. He's furious that these men tried to take what was his. Faith is his, but so is the way he goes about executing his habit.

Feeling all of this at once is not an onslaught he was prepared for. He puts his head in his hands with his elbows on the cold stone of the counter. He tries to take deep breaths and remind himself that Faith is upstairs and she needs him. It's enough to help him refocus.

He stands up straight and takes another deep breath, breathing in slowly and exhaling slowly he begins to feel the sudden emotions dissipate.

Grabbing a plate for the toast he realizes how much his hands are shaking. He grabs a glass from the cupboard, uncorks a bottle of wine, and pours it in the glass. He takes a big swig before he finishes getting the toast ready.

He drinks the last of the wine in the glass before going back upstairs with Faith's toast.

As soon as she sees him she smiles at him. He reciprocates even though his smile is forced, he's glad Faith doesn't notice.

"Thank you!" Faith takes the plate from him and immediately takes a bite of the food. Mid chew she exclaims, "This is really good!"

Jonathan sits down on his side of the bed. "Let's just hope it sits well."

"Yeah. I think I should slow down. I'm hungry because I haven't really eaten, but my stomach is unsettled."

"Slow is still good. As long as it gets in there."

Faith takes another drink of her water and checks her phone. She finds numerous texts and calls from her parents, Faith and Jackie. "I guess I should have updated everyone before now."

"Don't worry, I already did."

"You texted them all?" She asks, surprised.

"Of course I did. I knew they'd be worried about you so I called your parents this morning after you fell back to sleep and let them know how you were doing and I sent texts to both Hope and Jackie."

"That's so sweet of you, Jonathan. Thank you!" Faith feels her eyes begin to sting so she quickly blinks trying to fend off the tears.

"It's not that big of a deal." He shrugs.

"It is to me. I truly appreciate your thoughtfulness."

"You're welcome."

# Chapter 18

# Attitude

Noun; a negative or hostile state of mind

Jonathan's mind is racing. Faith is sound asleep beside him in their bed. She fell asleep early and as much as he should be able to, he can't sleep. He simply cannot let go of what happened to her last night. He's spent the day taking care of Faith, but now lying in bed he's focusing solely on his anger and resentment towards the guys who did this to her.

He begins to feel incredibly antsy, as if there is an electrical current running just under his skin. Staying in bed is no longer an option. Jonathan finds himself in the closet getting dressed in some jeans and a sweatshirt then putting on socks and shoes. He looks back at Faith before he starts down the stairs as quietly as he can. He grabs his keys, walks outside, and gets in his car.

He drives around Luna Shores for at least an hour. What he's looking for is a mystery to him, but something has brought him out here, so he continues to follow his gut. His senses are so heightened that he finds himself more observant of his surroundings, reading every street sign and making a mental note of every car he passes as if any of those things will give him clues. He considers going into Lee's pub to see if the men are there, but how plausible is it that they would go back to the scene of the crime, so to speak.

At various times throughout his hunt he wonders what it is he thinks he might find. He has very little information about these men and what he does have is all that Jackie had given him. The police have very little to go on either.

Then he has an idea and turns his car around making a U-turn at the next light. He's determined to see if the bartender, Tracy, will show him the video. He knows he can't go in there looking like a boyfriend out for revenge, but he's also sure he doesn't want to impersonate an officer.

As he walks into the dimly lit bar he takes in the scene, it isn't very busy for a Saturday night, not like a bar in Caulfield would be anyway. Suddenly remembering that this is where he and Faith first met makes what those men did feel even more like a punch in the gut. He spots Tracy behind the bar, she's pouring an older gentleman a snifter of brandy.

Jonathan walks up to the bar, taking an empty seat. When Tracy approaches him, he orders a beer and tips her generously. He waits until Tracy is a bit less busy to ask her anything. At first, he simply strikes up a conversation then he steers their discussion exactly where he wants it to go.

He mentions that he and Faith met here. Recognition flashes on Tracy's face, but only for a split second. He decides to lean directly into that.

"She was drugged here last night." His voice is low and sad. He looks down at his bottle. "I just don't know how someone can do that to another person."

Tracy nods her head seemingly unsure if she wants to commiserate with him yet or not. "It was an absolutely terrible thing. I'm glad she's OK, though." Tracy gives him a halfhearted smile.

"Thank you. I'm so grateful she is too. Hey, I was wondering if I might be able to watch any video you may have of that? Faith has been really out of it and she can't remember much. I want to help her try to piece things back together the best I can."

Jonathan senses a bit of hesitation, which he expected. It's not typical to allow a customer at any kind of establishment to view the security footage. He's hoping his ploy is successful.

He watches as Tracy looks at a gentleman who is standing by the pool tables with his large muscular arms folded across his chest and white letters across the pocket which reads security on his tight black T-shirt. Jonathan is sure that the added security was implemented because of what happened. Tracy nods to the man and without a word he begins to approach them.

He walks behind the bar, stopping right in front of Tracy. She leans in and whispers something in his ear. He nods and then Tracy says, "Hector will be able to help you."

Surprised Jonathan says, "Thank you so much!" He stands and follows Hector into a back room where the only light is coming from the computer screen. Hector flicks the light on and abruptly closes the door.

He sits at the desk and inputs the password making the screen light up even brighter. Then he opens the security camera program and opens the file from the night before.

Turning to Jonathan he says, "What times are we looking for?"

"I believe they got here around nine and I'm pretty sure they weren't even here two hours. I could be wrong though." He shrugs his shoulders nonchalantly as if this isn't super pressing.

Hector opens the recording and fast-forwards to later in the day.

Suddenly Jonathan says, "Stop!"

Hector does, but looks up at Jonathan surprised.

"I'm sorry. I just see them. There." He says pointing to the screen.

For the next hour and a half of footage Hector and Jonathan watch very carefully. Hector offers to set it at a slow fast-forward in order to make the time go faster, but Jonathan is afraid he will miss something so he declines the offer.

# APTITUDE

When they've finished Jonathan knows exactly what these men look like, what they were wearing, and even what car they got into when they left. He feels sick to his stomach to see the way the men were looking at his girlfriend. He feels his anger and jealousy rising, but he keeps it in check so that he doesn't raise any suspicions.

"Thank you, Hector." Jonathan says, reaching out his hand to shake Hector's.

"You're welcome. I hope it helped."

"More than you know."

Jonathan leaves Lee's pub and follows his instincts to drive to a motel that is on the south side just out of Luna Shores. He pulls into the parking lot of the Rest Easy Motel and parks beside a couple of big rigs.

He walks into the office and suddenly feels even more confident with this endeavor once he sees a blonde haired woman he went to high school with sitting behind the counter. Smiling he approaches and says, "Rose! It's so great to see you! I had no idea you work here!"

Her smile widens. "It's good to see you too! You look as handsome as ever."

"You flatter me, Rose. You haven't changed a bit." In truth, she had, weather it was alcohol or something stronger, he wasn't sure, but she didn't look sober.

Rose begins to blush, smiling even bigger. "Thank you, Jonathan. How can I help you?"

"Well, I was actually wanting to talk to the guys whose semi-trucks are out there. Would you be able to give me their room numbers?"

"They're sharing a room. It's got two queen size beds." Rose says as she holds up two fingers.

"That's great! I'm sure that saves them a bit of money."

"Yeah, they were nice enough. I'd asked them why they didn't want to sleep in their trucks. 'Cause you know that's what most truckers do, they sleep in their trucks."

"That's true. Most of them do that. Did they tell you?"

"They said it was because those beds aren't as comfortable as normal beds so sometimes they like to get motel rooms when they're out on the road for a long stretch."

"That's a good idea."

Rose smacks her forehead suddenly remembering what Jonathan wants. "You wanted their room number!"

"Yup, I sure do." He smiles.

"They're in room one-twenty-eight. It's just straight down the sidewalk that way." She points.

"Great! Thank you so much! It really was wonderful seeing you, Rose."

"You too. You look so good, Jonathan. Do you have a girlfriend?" As soon as the question comes out her eyes go wide and she covers her agape mouth with both hands.

Jonathan chuckles trying to hide his amusement, but failing. "I do yes, that's actually why I'm here." Then he abruptly turns and walks out the door to room one-twenty-eight.

# APTITUDE

He raps on the door hard and hears a shout from inside the room. "Who is it?" The voice demands.

Not sure what to say, Jonathan takes a few steps back and slams his broad shoulder into the door hard. Forcing it open and breaking the frame in the process.

Both men stand, startled. "What the fuck do you think you're doing?" The larger of the two men asks taking too many steps towards Jonathan. He pushes the door closed behind him even though it will no longer latch.

"You fucked with my girlfriend and now you're going to pay." Jonathan announces.

"You must not have passed math class. There's two of us and one of you." The other man says as he begins to approach Jonathan as well.

"I actually like those odds." Jonathan says as he swings at the larger man.

His fist connects with the man's jaw and he hits the floor hard. His head bouncing off the thinly carpeted floor.

The second man lunges at Jonathan. Jonathan lowers himself and lifts the man, flipping him up over his head. Then he slams him onto the hard table behind him.

He straddles the first man, plummeting him with punches to the face. Each strike is drawing more blood, but Jonathan doesn't care. The smell and feel of the sticky crimson liquid is bringing Jonathan even more pleasure.

Suddenly, he notices the second man begin to attempt to stand up. Jonathan switches his focus to him, landing punch after punch on the man's visage. Once he's certain he's broken the guy's nose, he stops.

He's surprised at his restraint. When he's killing the women he's never been out of control, but this is different. He wants to kill these men for entirely different reasons. This isn't an urge he must satisfy, this is a longing to make them pay, to make them regret that they ever stepped foot in Luna Shores and laid eyes on Faith. He knows the police are looking for these two and the likelihood of getting caught while trying to transport both of them to his building in Caulfield is too high for Jonathan to risk it.

If he was able to find these men, the cops will be able to locate them as well. He isn't worried either of them will even think about calling 911 to report any of this since they would essentially be turning themselves in.

He walks into the bathroom, washes his blood covered, sore hands, dries them, and begins to make his way towards the door. As he walks out he says. "Stay the fuck away from my girlfriend. Nothing would bring me more pleasure than killing both of you if you go near her again."

# Chapter 19

## *Definitude*
Noun; precision, definiteness

Faith's fatigue lessened significantly on Sunday and she was able to go to school on Monday. She was still feeling a little uneasy on her feet, but making it through the day was only possible with frequent sitting breaks while making sure to keep herself hydrated and well nourished.

Jonathan is working on plans for Valentine's Day this coming weekend. He wants to surprise Faith, but he needs Michael's help to do it. He calls Michael on his lunch break.

"Hello?"

"Hi Michael, its Jonathan. How are you doing today?"

"I'm great! Everything is on schedule and looking good at the house."

"That's wonderful to hear. I was wondering if I could ask a favor for this weekend. I want to surprise Faith."

"Whatever you need."

"Perfect."

Jonathan went on to explain to Michael everything he was going to need him to do and Michael agreed that he and the crew would have it all done by six on Saturday evening.

On Valentine's morning, Jonathan and Faith eat breakfast in bed, this time with mimosas.

"I have a surprise for us later. You're going to want to bundle up a bit for it."

Faith gives him a look as if to ask 'what do you have up your sleeve now?' "I can do that." She takes a bite of cantaloupe.

"You're not going to ask what we're doing?"

"No. You told me what I need to wear. That's usually why I ask what the surprise is; I need to be dressed appropriately." She reasons.

"That actually makes sense." Jonathan shakes his head fully understanding now.

"You know you don't have to plan surprises for me all the time, right?"

"I know. I enjoy doing it. The best part is seeing your face. I know sometimes you figure them out before-hand, but its fun even when you do."

"I cherish your surprises. All of them."

Jonathan beams at her, pride written all over his face.

They'd agreed prior to today not to exchange gifts. Faith was adamant that they didn't need to spend money right now on gifts when they would be spending quite a lot in the coming months on things for their new house. Jonathan agreed, especially after Faith had expressed her concerns at

Christmas. That doesn't mean he isn't going to do something special for her still.

When they finish breakfast, Jonathan suggests they get in the shower.

"That's a great idea." Faith says with a flirtatious glance over her shoulder at him. She stands, removes her shirt and tosses it on the bed. Jonathan watches her intently as she then removes her pants and underwear and throws them next to her shirt.

Faith saunters into the bathroom with Jonathan watching eagerly as she goes. He can't get out of the bed fast enough. He jumps up, strips down as quickly as he can and follows her.

He finds her already in the shower, all wet and soapy. As she rinses off Jonathan watches the soap as it runs down the small of her back and over her ass cheeks. He runs his fingers gently over her back. She turns to look at him, water droplets falling from her eyelashes.

His hand moves to the back of her neck. He pulls her into him as he steps into the steam filled shower and kisses her deeply. His tongue finding hers immediately. She lets out a soft moan as his other hand grips her ass, lifting her into him. She wraps her legs around him. The water pours over them, gently hitting their skin and running down in between them. The heat from the water adding to the heat between them.

The layer of the steam that has already collected on the glass is wiped off by Jonathan's back as he leans back against it. His strong arms are holding Faith up while he thrusts himself into her.

A moan fills the thick air echoing off of the glass walls they're contained in. It billows out with the steam over the top of the shower walls. Jonathan can tell Faith is close which brings his climax closer.

Faith moans again this time louder and longer. He watches her face intently as bliss takes her over the edge pulling him along with her. Faith rides the wave of her pleasure until her head rests on Jonathan's shoulder with both of them breathing heavily.

Jonathan gently places her down on the wet tile floor. "That was a wonderful way to start the day." He smiles widely.

Faith smirks. "It sure was. If only they could all begin that way." With that she opens the shower door and grabs a towel.

Jonathan stands in the shower watching the woman he loves dry herself and then apply her lotion. He turns the water off and walks over to Faith. He wraps his arms around her and says, "You are so fucking sexy, and that is only one of the reasons I feel like the luckiest man to have you."

Faith beams at him, gives him a quick kiss, and then says, "Thank you, Jonathan. But we're both lucky."

She turns and walks out to go into the closet and find something to wear for the day.

# Chapter 20

# Promptitude

*Noun; the quality or habit of being prompt*

Jonathan pulls his Mercedes into the makeshift driveway at exactly six. It's only been a couple of weeks, but the construction workers have made more progress than he was expecting to be made in that time frame. He glances over to Faith who sits blind folded in the passenger seat. Jonathan smiles to himself.

"Do you have any idea where we are?" He asks her.

"I think I do." Faith smiles mischievously.

"I was trying to trick you by taking detours."

"I thought that's what you were doing." She giggles.

"I guess it didn't work." He says with his voice low.

"It was still a valiant effort."

"Why haven't you taken the blind fold off yet?"

"I thought you'd want to do the honors."

Jonathan slips his fingers under her chin pulling her face into his. He kisses her while he unties the blindfold and pulls it away, freeing her eyes. As he pulls back, he watches as she opens her eyes and a knowing smile fills her face.

"I knew it!"

"I'm going to have to get better at these."

"No. Your surprises are amazing. Just because I know Luna Shores like the back of my hand, even when blind folded, doesn't mean you didn't do an amazing job with the surprise. I haven't seen everything yet."

"That's true. So, let's go then!"

Jonathan rushes to open Faith's door, as soon as he pulls it open Faith hears the hum of a generator and is instantly curious what this man of hers has up his sleeve. She smiles as he grabs her hand.

They walk to the house which seems to be lit up. There are still no windows or doors, but there appears to be a glow coming from within. As they approach the front door, Faith sees that the glow is coming from string lights leading them through the front door into where the kitchen and dining area will be. They walk through and Faith notices there is a table and chairs set up with battery powered flickering candles. The crew must have cleaned up before they left because the place is cleaner than you would expect a construction site to be.

The table is covered in a white table cloth with a rose bouquet sitting in the center along with the candles and wine glasses. There are place settings for a meal before each chair.

"It's beautiful, Jonathan."

"They did an amazing job."

"Who did?" Faith asks curiously.

"Michael and the crew. I told them what I wanted done and they took care of it."

"That's above and beyond." She says surprised.

"It really is!" Jonathan pulls out Faith's chair gesturing for her to sit down.

He goes over to the corner of the room to a cooler and grabs out their food and a bottle of cabernet sauvignon.

Walking back towards the table he says, "Did you know Tollero's delivers?"

"I had no idea."

Jonathan plates their food and says, "I guess it's not something they typically do, but when you explain the entire situation and what you're trying to do, they make an exception, for a nominal fee of course."

"Of course." Faith laughs. Then she notices what Jonathan is putting on her plate. It's the same meal she ordered on their first date. "You remembered?"

"Of course I remembered. The only thing that could make me forget that night with you is Alzheimer's or dementia."

"That's not funny."

"Maybe a little?" He offers. Next, he plates his own food.

Faith smiles realizing that he got the same thing from that night as well.

"The drinks aren't the same, but this is your favorite wine." He holds the bottle the way a waiter would, showing her the label.

"Absolutely perfect!" She beams up at him as he pours the wine into their glasses.

He sets the bottle down on the table and sits in the chair across from Faith. Jonathan raises his glass and says, "Happy Valentine's Day, Faith. I love you!"

"Thank you, Jonathan. This is completely amazing!"

"You deserve it! When I was thinking of what we could do for our first Valentine's Day I knew that I wanted to incorporate our house. I thought it was a perfect time to have our first dinner here."

"It couldn't be more perfect." She smiles, looking around at the ambiance created by the string lights. She never would have thought this construction site could be transformed into something so romantic. An enormous sense of gratefulness washes over her thinking of how much thought he put into this and that tonight will be a lasting memory for them both.

"Michael suggested the battery powered candles." Jonathan says as he gestures to the candles on the table. Then he continues, "Less of a fire hazard."

"That's the last thing we need." Faith chuckles.

"Exactly. I rather like what they've done with the place." He says looking around.

"It's going to be incredible, Jonathan."

# APTITUDE

"The table is set up exactly where the island with the built in bench and table will be."

Faith thinks of all the meals to come to be eaten in this space. She envisions herself serving apples and peanut butter snacks to a small handful of toddlers at the table with a high chair pulled up for the littlest. Her heart swells at the thought. Tears begin to form, but do not fall. She has such high hopes for their future and it all begins in this home.

Reaching across the table for her hand, he asks, "Faith, where'd you go?"

"Eight or so years into the future." She smiles sheepishly.

Jonathan notices the tears that still haven't spilled over. "I'm going to do everything I can to give you all that your heart desires, Faith."

"Thank you, Jonathan. That means so much." She smiles and takes a bite of food.

She loads her fork with a little bit of everything and offers it to Jonathan. He takes it smiling, recalling their first date. He does the same giving it to Faith.

"Should we walk the property when we're done?" Faith asks remembering their walk in the park by the river after their dinner at Tollero's that night as well.

"That's a wonderful idea. It might be a bit chillier tonight though."

"You'll keep me warm." She smiles flirtatiously.

"You know I can."

With the moon lighting their way, Jonathan leads them to a break in the woods along the line of trees. "There's a path this way."

They both turn the flashlights on their phones on and proceed into the woods. The moonlight now being filtered through the overhead tree tops making the path a little harder to see.

"I'm excited to explore our property, but maybe in the daylight would be a better idea." Faith suggests cautiously. She's having second thoughts, but is also worried Jonathan has his heart set on exploring the woods tonight.

"We'll just walk in a little ways. We can go further another time."

His reassurance lessens her second thoughts. "OK, that sounds good."

They walk on, the smell of pine and salt hangs in the air. Faith looks up seeing the stars that fill the sky between the tree tops. Jonathan reaches for her hand as they walk down the trail and Faith squeezes and looks back up so he will see the stars as well.

They stop walking and he raises his eyes to look at what she's seeing, but notices even more so the look of awe on her face as she does. It's as if she's a child watching a magic show for the very first time.

With eyes wide Faith says, "We get to see this whenever we want."

"We're the luckiest two people in Luna Shores."

"The most incredibly lucky." She smiles, still gazing up at the stars. "Our house, this land, all of it is magic and we're lucky to have it all."

"And our love, we can't forget how lucky we are to have that."

"No, we can never forget that. And our future, we're lucky to have such a bright future ahead of us."

They continue walking down the path their flashlights casting deeper shadows all around them. Faith starts to get a little scared imagining what could be just beyond those shadows watching them, following them. She squeezes Jonathan's hand a little tighter.

"Are you doing OK, Faith?"

"Yeah, my imagination is just playing tricks on me."

"It's the dark, right?"

"Yeah."

"Me too, a little, if I'm being honest. Good thing we have flashlights." He moves his all around them through the woods, and down the path farther. Then says, "No lions, tigers, or bears."

"Oh my."

They both begin laughing so hard it echoes through the trees which makes them laugh even harder. Just then, in between their laughter, they hear a twig break and leaves rustle a few feet to the left of them. Jonathan instantly shines his light in the direction the sound came from. There is nothing there. He scans the area around it when he thinks he sees something move, he follows the movement with the flashlight.

Faith is holding her breath, standing behind Jonathan looking around him to try to see what is moving through the darkness in the forest beyond them. Her adrenaline is coursing through her veins so fast it feels like her entire body is buzzing.

"Did you see that?" She whispers.

"What?"

"That, over there. Something moved."

"I didn't see it." Jonathan says in a hushed voice.

"I think we should head back to the house now."

"Yeah, you're probably right."

They begin walking backwards slowly not wanting to take their eyes off of where the noise came from at first. Faith glances behind her so she can see any roots or other trip hazards. Jonathan turns around and passes around her to walk in front of her, never letting go of Faith's hand. She's relieved to have him leading the way out of the woods.

Suddenly, there's another noise that comes from behind them. Turning quickly, Jonathan shines the light back there, but neither of them see anything. Jonathan quickens his step and Faith follows suit. Before they know it, they are both jogging, still hand in hand.

Once they reach the edge of the trees they both hunch over with hands on knees trying to catch their breath and calm themselves down. Their hearts are practically beating out of their chests. They look at one another and begin laughing uncontrollably.

Again, they hear a noise behind them in the woods. They jump, instantly ceasing their laughter, and together they move further away from the tree line. They can hear something coming towards them, they both try to shine their light in the direction the sound is coming from, but neither of them see anything.

The noise is getting closer and closer, they take a few steps back and then a few more. Faith wants to run to the small bit of light spilling through the window opening from the string lights in the house. That feels safer than standing here, but she finds herself frozen.

Jonathan is looking towards the tree line. The brush moves slightly. His curiosity makes him take a step closer. Faith is pulling his arm back trying to keep him from getting closer. She's too afraid to say a word or even make a noise.

All of a sudden, a yellow lab puppy clumsily appears through the brush. The poor thing's hair is dirty and matted and it looks as if it hasn't eaten in at least a week.

"Oh, look at the poor thing!" Faith rushes towards the puppy before Jonathan can do anything to stop her.

She scoops him up in her arms and he happily licks her face. "Let's bring him inside and give him some food. I didn't finish all of mine."

"Faith, I don't think we should be feeding it table scraps."

"He's so hungry though. It won't hurt, just this once."

Jonathan can see he's not going to get his way this time, so he lets it go and follows Faith back to the house.

Faith takes the plate from the table and sits down on the floor in front of the puppy setting it down, he happily laps the food right up. When the plate has been licked clean he clumsily sits down. Faith looks around, not seeing any more food.

As if the puppy realizes there isn't anything more he moves towards Faith and curls up in her lap. Before she knows it he's fallen asleep.

Jonathan watches the two of them and his heart fills. They weren't going to give each other gifts for Valentine's Day, but the house had a different idea.

Faith looks up at him expectantly. "Can we keep him, Jonathan?"

"I think we have to."

"Yeah, I do too!" She can hardly contain her smile! She's so happy!

"What do you want to name it?"

"It's a him." She corrects him. The puppy picks up his head as if he knows they're talking about him.

"OK then, what do you want to name him?"

She looks at the puppy and says "Rufus?" The little dog just looks at her. "No, that's not it." Faith says shaking her head. Next she tries, "Bailey?" The puppy stares blankly still.

"Faith, I'm not sure that's how it works."

"Maybe it doesn't, but it's still a fun game. Do you have any suggestions?"

# APTITUDE

"How about Cooper?"

She looks at the dog again, his light brown eyes looking back into hers. "What do you think about Cooper?" She repeats. He tilts his head as if he's confused by that one. "OK…maybe Zeke?" The puppy licks her face incessantly and Faith laughs. "That's it! Your name is Zeke." The dog continues to lick her face and Faith continues to giggle.

Jonathan can't help but smile at their fortune. "We were just talking about how lucky we are and then this little fella finds us."

"It was meant to be."

"Definitely. I think we should clean up here and head to the store to pick up some supplies for Zeke."

"That's a great idea."

Back at the condo they set up the crate for Zeke in their bedroom; Faith insisted on having it in there. They had gotten a matching collar and leash as well as food and a name tag with Faith's phone number on it from the store.

The next thing Faith did is give Zeke a bath. The water turned brown as she rinsed him, and got even worse when she used the shampoo.

"I think we're going to have to wash you again, buddy." The puppy looks at her expectantly. So, she began to soap him back up again. Suddenly he began to shake sending the lathery bubbles everywhere!

All her and Jonathan, who was watching from the doorway, could do was laugh at the cute puppy's antics. Faith rinsed him again and he shook the water off splashing water all over the place.

Jonathan got Zeke's food and water ready while Faith was toweling him off. By the time she got done he almost looked like a whole new dog. When she brought him downstairs his little puppy paws were sliding all over the floor as he tried to make his way to the food dish by the island. He ate the food so quickly, Faith didn't want to give him more quite yet worried that he was going to over eat and have a tummy ache.

"That's it for right now, OK Zeke?"

As if he understood what she meant he laid down at her feet, quickly falling asleep again.

"We need to take him outside." Jonathan whispers.

"Yeah, and then try to get him to sleep in the crate." Faith whispers back.

"So, we should wake him up then?"

"Probably."

Faith attempts to wake the puppy up, jostling him just a little. Sleepily he opens his eyes and Faith excitedly says, "You want to go outside Zeke? You go potty outside!"

She grabs the leash and collar from the bag putting it around the puppy's neck and then attaches the leash, she leads him towards the door.

He goes potty pretty quickly, Jonathan cleans it up immediately and they head back inside.

"OK, Zeke, its bed time now." Faith carries him up the stairs and helps him get into the crate closing the door behind him. Then her and Jonathan get ready for bed and crawl in under the blankets, snuggling into each other's arms.

"This couldn't have been a more perfect Valentine's Day, Jonathan. Thank you so much!" She kisses him with fervor.

"You're so welcome, Faith. I couldn't have planned finding a puppy, but it kind of works out perfectly. I'm not sure why I hadn't thought of it before now."

"What do you mean?"

"You won't be home alone now, and the new house won't feel quite as empty while I'm at work."

"Oh." Faith says in a melancholy tone.

"What's wrong?"

"I didn't realize my feelings about that situation were so easily fixed with a puppy." Her voice showing her annoyance at his callous words.

"That's not what I meant."

She cuts him off before he can make more excuses and rolls over as she says, "Its fine. Zeke is going to fix the fact that you're never home."

"He won't fix it. I'm still going to try to be home more. It's just for the times I'm not. Faith, please roll back over." He puts his hand on her hip gently pulling, hoping she'll comply.

"I'm tired, Jonathan." She says curtly.

"I don't want you to be upset over something stupid that I said."

"Then maybe you shouldn't have said it."

"I agree, but unfortunately I can't take it back now. I would love to be able to reword it, but you're not being very receptive to my apology."

"You haven't apologized."

He realizes she's right and his frustration with himself grows.

He takes a deep breath and says, "Faith, I am sorry that I said Zeke would be a good solution to you feeling lonely while I'm gone. It's something that has been on my mind since you mentioned how empty the new house is going to feel. I just think having him around will help, plus he's going to be a protective dog. It's a good thing he came into our lives. I think it's for the best."

She does realize that he has a point, but she isn't ready to forgive him entirely for saying it in such an insensitive way. So, she just says, "OK."

"Will you please roll over now?"

Slowly she rolls back towards him, coming face to face. Jonathan places his hand on her cheek. "I love you."

"I love you too."

He smiles half-heartedly at her wishing the end of the night had gone differently. "I can't believe we found a puppy."

"Me either." Faith's face suddenly lights up. She sits up to look at Zeke's crate and sees him curled up in there sleeping soundly on his cushy blue bed. "It's going to be hard to leave him to go to work."

# APTITUDE

"I know, but we're going to have to. He'll be OK in the crate."

"Hopefully eventually he won't have to stay in there."

"I'm sure. Some dogs do enjoy being in a crate though, it simulates a den for them."

"Well if he's more comfortable we can keep it, but I'd rather just have him be free to roam the house."

"It's a little early to know right now."

"That's true."

Faith falls asleep with thoughts of the days, months, and years to come spent with Zeke and all the adventures they'll have with him. She envisions what he'll be like with the kids and how much of an integral part he'll play in all of their lives.

# Chapter 21

## Rectitude

*Noun; moral integrity, righteousness, being correct in judgment or procedure*

The rest of the night with Zeke really opened Faith and Jonathan's eyes to how much work it's going to be to have a puppy. He woke up multiple times whining. Faith wasn't sure if he was hungry or needed to go outside so she tried both, multiple times. Sometimes it seemed to be neither.

Faith was worried about leaving him home alone for Sunday night dinner. So she sent her parents pictures of him and asked their permission to bring their new grand-puppy to dinner. They text back almost immediately saying they can't wait to meet him.

Zeke rides happily in Faith's lap, sleeping half the way and only wakes up when Jonathan parks the car. As soon as they walk in the door with him Frank, Diane, and Hope are all standing there waiting for their turn to pet him.

"You're going to have to get one next, Hope." Faith suggests.

"Not until I have my own house." She leans down and gives Zeke some pets saying, "Aren't you just a cute little fart face!" Zeke immediately starts licking her face.

Faith starts giggling. "Well, I'm glad we already named him." She looks at Jonathan who starts laughing too. Then Faith suddenly remembers Jackie telling her about Andy and Hope setting up a date. "So, have you and Andy gone out yet?"

"We met up and had dinner last night, actually."

"And we're just hearing about this now?" Faith asks, exaggerating her surprise.

"I kind of figured it's no one else's business at this point." Hope says dryly.

"OK, but maybe since we already know about it now you could share a little?"

"I guess." She half rolls her eyes then continues. "Andy took me to a restaurant in Caulfield called The Farmhouse."

"Oh, I've heard of that place!" Diane says excitedly. "It's a little on the fancier side and they have farm to table food."

"Yeah."

"That sounds lovely. Was it as good as its reputation leads us to believe?" Diane asks.

"The food was really great and the atmosphere was laid back! We definitely enjoyed it. You and dad should go sometime."

"I think we will." Frank smiles at Diane, patting her knee. Zeke takes that as a sign that Frank wants to pet him. He pads over to Frank looking up expectantly at him as he sits. "Hi, Zeke! You're such a good boy!" He scratches behind his floppy ears and Zeke's tail goes crazy, wagging back and forth as fast as it can go.

While they eat dinner, Zeke happily sleeps curled up beneath the table at Faith's feet. As she's eating she often peeks below the table cloth just to see his cute cream colored fuzzy little butt.

As Faith helps her mom clean up in the kitchen after dinner, Zeke follows closely behind. Jonathan tries to bring him into the den with him, Hope, and Frank, but Zeke manages to make his way back into the kitchen to find Faith.

Leaving Zeke the next morning was just as difficult as Faith imagined it would be. The whole situation made her wonder if she would have similar feelings leaving her children or if the dread and worry would be even worse then.

When she came home though she found Zeke so excited to see her. There was no sign of him feeling betrayed that she left or that he was ever worried she wouldn't come home. She immediately carries him downstairs, hooks up the leash to his collar, and walks with him outside. When they get back inside she puts a scoop of dry dog food into his blue doggy bowl.

Everything she read online earlier today said starting a routine would help with the transition. Plus, taking him out and feeding him right away when she gets home just makes the most sense. She also knows that the majority of his care lies on her shoulders since Jonathan's schedule is sporadic.

Faith wonders if getting a dog right now is the best idea, but then again it's not like they bought him. Zeke showed up out of the blue and they certainly couldn't just leave him in the woods all alone. He has been a good boy so far, and Faith has already fallen so in love with him. Jonathan seems slightly less attached, but loves Zeke in his own way. However, it is clear to see that Zeke is more drawn to Faith.

After scarfing down the food in his dish, he sleeps on the kitchen floor while Faith makes dinner. Her phone rings making him pick his head up and perk his ears.

"Hello?"

"Hi, is this Faith Brandt?" A female voice asks.

"It is. Who is this?"

"This is Officer Carter. I'm sure you don't remember me, but my partner and I are the ones looking into the incident that happened at Lee's Pub last weekend. We have a couple of men as suspects." The officer lets that statement hang on the line for a moment. When Faith doesn't say anything she continues, "We would like for you to come in and answer some questions for us. We've asked Jackie to come in as well."

Looking at Zeke, Faith says, "Alright." Then exhales heavily trying to relieve some of the dread that just bubbled up. "I'd like to bring my boyfriend, if that's OK."

"Of course! Whatever makes you most comfortable."

"Thank you."

"I know this may be difficult, but there's no pressure. You weren't the only person who saw them that night."

"I appreciate that. I will get in touch with my boyfriend and we'll be in."

"OK, see you then! Bye."

"Bye."

Faith ends the call and immediately dials Jonathan. He answers on the second ring.

"Hi beautiful. Everything OK?"

"Yeah. The police department called and asked for me to come in to answer some questions."

"Oh. Is that really necessary? It seemed like they got a lot of information from both Jackie and the footage at the bar."

"I don't know, Jonathan." She says exasperatedly. "Officer Carter called and asked me to come in. That's all I know. I'd like for you to come with me."

"I can do that. I'll do anything you need, Faith."

"Thank you."

"Let me just finish what I'm working on quickly and then I'll head home. How did Zeke do today?"

"He did really well. And thank you, Jonathan."

"Good. I'll see you in a bit. I love you."

"I love you too."

# APTITUDE

Once Jonathan gets home an hour later they quickly eat dinner, even though Faith barely touches hers. Then Jonathan drives them to the Luna Shores Police Station. Faith's leg is bouncing the whole way there. Jonathan attempts to calm it by placing his hand on her knee, but it does very little to help subside her nerves or the constant motion.

Shortly after they check in with the receptionist, Officer Carter greets them and leads them to a brightly lit conference room with a large oval wood table and numerous black mesh backed office chairs where Officer Strickland and Jackie are already waiting. Jackie stands and hugs Faith as soon as she enters the room.

"How are you doing?" Jackie asks.

"I'm doing OK. How are you doing?"

"I'm OK. We're here, right?" Jackie says, looking around the room.

"Exactly." Faith gives her a sideways glance.

They take their seats at the table and Officer Strickland says, "I think we should begin, the sooner we get this going the sooner you can put this all behind you and go home."

"That would be great, officer." Faith says.

Jonathan reaches for her hand under the table as Officer Strickland says, "We have these photographs; stills from the camera footage at both Lee's Pub and Love's Café."

Faith's expression changes to one of confusion. "What do you mean from Love's Café?" She asks in a slightly demanding tone.

"After some discussion with your father it was brought to our attention that the man at the bar, Zander, may not have been working alone." Nodding towards Jackie, he says, "Jackie informed us that he had a southern accent. When we spoke with your dad, he told us about an incident that happened last month at the Café with a man that also had a southern accent. We now believe these incidents to be connected."

Faith's look of confusion is now replaced with shock. Officer Strickland begins to lay out the photographs taken from the café first, followed by the ones taken at Lee's pub. It's a strange feeling for Faith to see herself in the pictures. Once she gets past that weird feeling she notices that the large man from the café is also in the photographs from Lee's Pub.

"I don't remember seeing him there that night." Faith says. She looks at Jackie with a silent question.

"I can honestly say that I don't think we were being the most observant. We felt safe there." Jackie adds with a small shrug.

"That's true. I obviously felt safe enough to leave my drink unattended and then drink from it." She rolls her eyes at her thoughtless mistake.

Jonathan places his arm around her and says, "Hey, you shouldn't beat yourself up over it." He rubs her back trying to comfort her.

Officer Carter says, "Men who do this sort of thing often times have an ideal victim in mind. They know how easy it is to get distracted when you're having fun and not be as vigilant as you normally would be, especially when alcohol is involved. You have to remember that this wasn't your fault. You were a victim of a terrible thing. It was also very lucky that your friend here," she looks at Jackie then back to Faith, "was there to keep you safe and that she got you to the hospital as quickly as she did."

Faith nods as she fights back tears. "I just wish it never happened."

"We all do. The good thing about this though is that we're going to do everything in our power to get these guys before they have the chance to do it to anyone else, and if the justice system works the way it's supposed to, they'll never be able to do it to anyone else." Officer Carter reassures her.

Faith wipes away her tears and looks back at the photographs splayed out on the table before them. She takes one in her hand from the café then one of that same man at the bar. He was sitting next to the stranger who approached them with the drinks. In the picture you can tell that these men probably knew each other. They are both laughing and are turned slightly toward one another with their drinks on the bar in front of them.

Faith grabs another picture from the pub. Holding in it her hand she notices that she is shaking. Jonathan's hand on her back is giving her some comfort and she's so grateful to have him there.

In this photograph she sees her and Jackie standing right beside the stranger who approached them with the man from the café sitting right on the other side of him.

"I really wasn't paying attention." Tears threaten to fall once again, but she blinks them away before they can.

"It wasn't your fault, Faith." Jonathan says.

"Was there any way that the man from the café would have known you would be out at Lee's Pub that night?" Officer Strickland asks.

"I don't see how he would have. I haven't seen him since what happened at the café."

"OK. How did he seem when he left the café that day?"

"Pissed. My sister had just hit him pretty damn hard and then my dad kicked him out. He wasn't happy about any of that."

"Do you recall seeing this man at the café that day? Officer Strickland asks pointing to Zander in one of the photographs.

She shakes her head. "No. He wasn't there."

"We didn't see any footage of him from the café, but I still needed to ask."

Jonathan asks, "So you think that this man," he points to the man from the café, "planned to more-or-less get revenge on Faith?"

"Yes, but he clearly had help." Officer Carter points to Zander.

"Are you trying to establish premeditation?"

The officers look to one another, then Officer Strickland answers, "We're simply trying to figure out a time line and possible motive."

"The motive is pretty clear, don't you think?" Jackie says looking at the photo of the man on the floor of the café with Hope standing over him holding her hand and a shocked look on Faith's face.

"It is, yes. However, sometimes things that seem clear-cut aren't always. We need to cross our T's and dot our I's to make sure nothing slips through the cracks to allow these men to go free." Officer Carter says.

"I'll do whatever I can to help." Faith says. She looks at Jackie and then at Jonathan. Then she adds, "I don't fully remember that night at the pub though."

"We don't expect you to. We know how those drugs work. Luckily we have Jackie here to help us fill in some of your blank spots." Officer Carter says.

"What else do you need from us?" Jonathan asks.

Officer Carter looks at Faith. "Can you walk us through the night, as best as you can remember it?"

"Sure. Jackie and I got to Lee's Pub around nine. We had a drink, danced, and had another. I believe that's when this photo was from. Then we went back out onto the dance floor and I left my drink unattended at the table we were sitting at."

"Where was that table?" Officer Strickland interrupts.

"It was by the pool table and the bathrooms."

"OK." He writes that down in his little note pad.

Faith continues. "After that song finished we went back to the table, and I grabbed my drink and took a sip through the straw. As soon as I started drinking it Jackie smacked the glass out of my hand, which made a mess and that's when the guy came over. He had two drinks in his hand. I think they were pineapple upside down cakes, which was exactly what we had ordered.

This is where it gets hazy. I remember Jackie telling him we didn't want the drinks," Faith closes her eyes, trying hard to remember the details, "and I remember being glad I was sitting down because I started to not feel right."

"Do you remember leaving the pub?"

"No. I don't remember leaving. I don't remember the drive, and I don't remember being in the hospital."

"OK." Officer Strickland turns to Jackie. "I know we questioned you at the hospital, but is there anything else that you may have remembered after the fact? I understand that night was incredibly stressful."

"Nothing more has really come to mind."

"You didn't happen to also be at the café when that incident occurred?"

"No, I wasn't there."

"Did either of you post on social media that you were going out to Lee's Pub that night? Or did you happen to tell anyone that you'd be there?"

Faith answers first. "I hardly ever post on social media, and I definitely didn't post that. As far as telling anyone, Jonathan is the only person I talked to about it."

Jackie says, "Pretty much the same here. I didn't post anything and my boyfriend, Tom, was the only other person I discussed it with. Our plans were actually pretty last minute."

"Where is Tom tonight?"

"He's at his place." She says with uncertainty. "Why do you ask?"

"We may need to have him come in for questioning, just crossing T's and dotting I's." Officer Strickland says. Then he turns to Jonathan and asks, "Did you talk with anyone about Faith and Jackie's where-a-bouts?"

"No. I didn't see the text from Faith until around dinner time. Tom and I work together at Kansen Corp. He would have been the only one I would have said anything to, but he was already gone for the day."

"Now, you came to the hospital later. Is that correct?"

"Yes, it is."

Officer Strickland looks at Jackie, "Tom did not though?"

"I told him not to."

"What was your reasoning for that?" Officer Strickland prods.

"The room was getting a bit crowded with Faith's family, who deserved to be there. It didn't make sense for him to come." Her tone is slightly defensive. She watches as he writes something else in his little notebook.

Officer Carter begins, "We're just trying to figure out if there was any way for these men to find out where you were, or if it was simply coincidence and they took advantage of the situation."

Jackie feels herself relax a little. She sits back in her chair still slightly annoyed with Officer Strickland's line of questioning.

Faith gives Jackie a reassuring smile. This isn't exactly what she thought it would be either. It's almost as if the officers suspect them of something nefarious. "Are we about done here?" Faith asks.

"Yes, just about." Officer Carter says. "I have one more question."

"OK." Faith nods.

"How are you doing with everything?"

"I'm doing OK. It seems that I feel better every day. It's a scary thing, but nothing really bad happened, aside from the effects of the drugs." She looks over at Jackie. "I know entirely how lucky I am."

# Chapter 22

## Solicitude

*Noun; attentive care and protectiveness*

When Faith and Jonathan get home, Jonathan takes Zeke outside while Faith pours herself a glass of Cabernet and sits down at the island. When Jonathan gets back in the house, he goes up the stairs right away. Faith is fighting the feeling of being alone in all of this when Jonathan promptly comes back downstairs and says, "Follow me."

Faith walks up the stairs following Jonathan with her glass of wine in her hand. He leads her through their bedroom and into the bathroom. The first thing she notices is the scent of lavender with a hint of eucalyptus. Breathing in deeply she allows the aromas to fill her nose, helping to calm her.

Jonathan gestures to the large soaking tub that is full of warm water and dried leaves and flowers. Faith sees the steam billowing from the top of the water. She smiles, thinking how entirely lucky she is.

"Well, are you going to get in?" Jonathan runs his hand through the water creating ripples.

"Are you going to join me?"

"If that's what you want?" Jonathan smiles.

"That is definitely what I want."

Faith sets her glass down beside the bathtub and begins undressing, Jonathan follows her lead watching her with his full attention. When they're both naked, Jonathan steps into the bathtub first leaning against the back, he rests his arms on the sides of the large tub. Faith sits in between his legs and leans into him with her back resting against his torso.

The moment she feels the water's embrace nearly all of her muscles relax. She grabs her glass of wine and takes a sip. Jonathan takes her hair in his hands and moves it over to one side, then gently begins to massage her neck and shoulders.

Faith closes her eyes concentrating on the feeling of his fingers' caress on her skin.

In a soft tone, Jonathan says, "I'm sorry you had to deal with all of that tonight. There should have been a better way."

"It's nothing you need to apologize for. You didn't cause it."

"No, but I can see that it's taking a toll on you."

"It is. The whole situation is, though."

"That's true."

Zeke comes bounding into the bathroom, and attempts to jump into the tub, making a loud thud against the side.

# APTITUDE

Faith's eyes shoot open, just as he attempts it again. Faith and Jonathan's laughter floats on the steam that is filling the bathroom, echoing all around them. Zeke shakes his head and then sits looking expectantly at them. Faith moves her head from side to side and says, "Oh, no you don't."

"You're not coming in here." Jonathan adds in a very serious tone holding his finger up for emphasis.

Zeke keeps staring at them while wagging his tail.

"I hope he didn't get into anything downstairs." Faith says slightly worried.

"Me either. I wasn't even thinking about it when we came up here."

"I wasn't either." She reaches her hand out of the water, over the edge of the tub, and pats the top of Zeke's head leaving it slightly wet. His tail wags even faster. "I guess this is something we're going to have to get used to."

"I didn't realize he knew how to get up the stairs."

"Looks like he's a fast learner!"

"He just wanted to be by you. Do you see the way he looks at you?"

"I think maybe I recognize it." A sly smile spreads across her face as she glances back to look at Jonathan.

"Is that so? From where exactly?"

"From you, silly." She giggles.

Jonathan laughs. "I look at you like a puppy?"

"Sometimes." She shrugs her shoulders.

"No, I look at you like you're the most beautiful woman in the world. Because you are. Zeke looks at you with undying love and devotion."

"And he's only known me a couple of days." Faith thinks a moment, then continues. "Wait, you don't look at me with undying love and devotion?"

"He's got good instincts and of course I do. But I don't look at you like a puppy."

Faith smiles and leans into Jonathan a little more, still stroking Zeke's head. He quickly lays down and falls asleep on the fuzzy grey rug right beside the bathtub.

"Thank you for taking such good care of me, Jonathan. This whole past week has been such a mess. I don't know how I would have gotten through it without you."

"It's my pleasure, Faith. You didn't deserve what happened to you and I'll do anything I can to help you feel better."

"Thank you."

"You're welcome." Jonathan kisses the top of her head. "Those officers just better make sure those two go away for a long time."

"I sure hope so."

Faith closes her eyes allowing the envelopment of the warm water around her body to soak into her muscles relaxing them even further. She takes deep breaths, holding for a moment before releasing it. Then does it again. Soon Jonathan's breathing begins to match hers as he continues rubbing her shoulders.

# Chapter 23

# Inaptitude

### Noun; lack of aptitude

On Friday evening, Faith receives a call from Officer Carter that they had both suspected men in custody. She felt a small sense of relief, but that was swiftly overshadowed by thoughts of a long drawn out trial. As she begins to feel the impending stress of that, her mind wanders.

"What do I have to do now?" She asks Officer Carter.

"Nothing. We'll handle it, and if you need anything or have any questions, feel free to let us know. We'll be in touch if there's something more we need from you."

"They weren't from around here, were they?"

"No, turns out they both drive semis over-the-road. That's part of the reason it took us two weeks to get them. I'm sorry you had to go through all of this, I truly hope knowing we have them brings you some peace."

"Thank you, Officer Carter." She says, not really thinking it's going to bring her much peace at all.

"We appreciate your cooperation with all of this. I know it hasn't been easy. Ultimately they've messed up in a huge way. I don't see how in the world they could get out of this."

"What do you mean they messed up? With what they did to me?"

"That, but also the amount of evidence we were able to acquire from just their trucks alone."

"Well, that is reassuring."

"I was hoping it would be."

"Thank you for calling me and letting me know."

"You're welcome, Faith. If there's anything we can do for you, please let us know."

Shortly after the phone call from Officer Carter, Faith meets Jonathan at the door with a beer in one hand and a glass of wine in the other.

"Are we celebrating something?"

"They got them." She says heavily.

"They did? That's awesome!" He scoops her up in his arms and spins around in excitement.

"It is! I'm happy, but I also know that this is far from the end of it."

"That's true. I'm surprised they informed you."

As they walk into the kitchen, Faith rehashes the conversation her and Officer Carter had just a little bit prior.

"Being truck drivers explains their accents." Jonathan muses.

"Yeah. It was a relief to find out neither of them were from around here."

"I'd be interested to know how the officers caught them."

"I'm sure the whole story will be posted soon."

Faith sits down at the island while Jonathan begins making dinner. She takes a sip of her wine and says, "You're home kind of early for a Friday night."

As he places a pot full of water on the stove top he says, "Yeah, I was able to get everything done that I needed to. It was a slower week than normal."

"Well, I'll try my best not to get used to it, but it is really nice having you home at a decent hour."

Jonathan stops and thinks for a moment, then says, "Maybe I should have taken you out."

"No, I'm happy staying in."

"OK." Jonathan turns back towards the stove and takes a swig of his beer. "Have you thought about what you want to do for your birthday? It's less than a week away now."

"Just by one day." Faith half rolls her eyes. "And no, I haven't. I'd have thought you had an elaborate plan in place already."

"Well, as much as I've thought about it, I wasn't really sure what you'd want to do considering everything that happened two weeks ago."

"Right."

"What do you think of just inviting everyone here?"

"Who's everyone?"

"Whoever you want."

"Yeah, that could be fun."

"We could have the patio set up, it might be a bit chilly, but we can get a couple fires going, between the fire place and the fire pit that should help keep everyone warm. Or we can always have it inside."

"Both sounds lovely." She takes a sip of her wine.

"OK! It's a plan then."

"Is there anyone you want to invite?"

He turns to look at her wiping his hands on the grey towel he's holding. "It's your birthday. Everyone that is invited should be here for you, Faith." He grabs the bottle of wine from the counter and refills her glass. She smiles at him as she grabs it taking another sip. He asks, "What would you like me to make for dinner for the party?"

"Anything you want. You're the one cooking." She glances at him sideways knowing he isn't going to let that pass.

"It's your birthday, Faith. If anyone is picking the food for the party, it's going to be you."

"But what if I don't know what I want."

"You better start thinking about it and decide; relatively quickly since it's a week away now."

"So you've said." She rolls her eyes and purses her lips.

"I didn't think it would hurt to remind you." He winks at her and then starts plating their dishes. "Do you want to sit in here or go into the dining room?"

Faith looks out the wall of windows and notices the setting sun outside. "Let's sit in the dining room."

# APTITUDE

Jonathan grabs both of their plates as Faith leads the way carrying the drinks to their chairs. They enjoy their dinner together with the color filled sky as their backdrop. They talk a little more about the party and decide to have it on the Saturday after her birthday.

While they eat Zeke falls asleep at Faith's feet underneath the table. After they've finished she takes him outside. They all finish their evening snuggled on the couch watching a movie. Jonathan isn't fond of Zeke being on the furniture, but seeing him all cuddled up in Faith's lap quickly changes his mind.

# Chapter 24

## *Gratitude*

*Noun; the state of being grateful, thankfulness*

"Jonathan, I have no idea what to wear." Faith complains as she takes the navy blue dress off that she just put on and hangs it back up on the hanger. She grabs a red one instead, slipping that over her head. Then she walks over to the doorway of their walk-in-closet and sees Jonathan is lying on the bed scrolling on his phone. "Did you hear me?" Her tone laced with annoyance and frustration.

"I did. What you have on looks amazing, but then again, the three before that have as well." Jonathan chuckles.

"That isn't very helpful."

"You don't really need my help though, do you? Faith, you will look stunning in absolutely anything you wear. Besides, it isn't that big of a deal. It's just us, and your closest friends and family. You could wear a potato sack and they wouldn't care. The point I'm trying to get to is that we all love you no matter what you look like, so the dress or outfit, doesn't really matter."

"OK." Faith says curtly as she turns to go back into the closet. Removing the red dress, she grabs a pair oversized black sweatpants and a hoodie and puts them on. Walking right past Jonathan, her head held high, she goes into the bathroom to put on a little makeup and do her hair. Zeke follows behind her, laying down next to her seat in front of the vanity.

Jonathan stands, walks to the doorway of the bathroom and leans against the door jam. "Absolutely gorgeous as always." He smiles, trying hard to hold back a laugh.

Faith laughs loudly. "I didn't mean for this to be funny."

"No? You could have fooled me." Unable to hold it in any longer, his laughter erupts mixing with Faith's melodically.

"What is that supposed to mean?"

"I know I said you could wear anything, and if this," he gestures to her clothes, "is what you want to wear, then that's fine by me, but I think you'd be happier in something else."

"I was just trying your suggestion." She shrugs her shoulders.

"I didn't suggest this, I simply said you could wear anything. If I suggested anything, it was a potato sack."

"Well, we're fresh out of those."

"At this point it's pretty much just a figure of speech anyway."

"True."

"Now, finish getting ready. I'm going to start getting some of the food prepped. By the way, I left something for you on the bed."

"OK." Faith says absentmindedly as she runs the hot straightener through the small section of her long brown hair.

Once she finishes with her hair she walks out, heading for the closet but stops when she sees a box sitting on the bed that hadn't been there when she walked in. For a moment she had forgotten what Jonathan said before he went down to the kitchen. The box quickly reminded her, she sits on the bed and takes it in her hands. She opens the small card and reads.

**Happy Birthday, Faith! I thought you might have a hard time choosing something to wear so I wanted to help make it an easier decision for you.**

**I love you forever,**

**Jonathan**

## P.S. I know we're not buying each other gifts, but this was necessary. (Therefore it's not a gift)

She runs the silky red ribbon through her fingers before giving it a tug. It releases allowing her to lift the top of the box. As she gently folds the tissue paper back she sees emerald green fabric.

Quickly, she changes out of her sweats and into the dress. The fit is perfect, hugging all of her curves. The fabric's sheen showcases them beautifully as well. She glances at the racks of her shoes in the closet and chooses a pair of black wedges. She slips them on and then Faith walks down the stairs.

Jonathan hears the click of her heel on the top step. He turns his head to see her descending. His breath is taken away as he watches her gracefully walk. The sun coming through the wall of windows is reflecting its light perfectly on Faith creating a natural spotlight. The way the dress shines against her skin makes him wish she wasn't wearing it at all.

A smile slowly spreads across his face as Faith approaches him in the kitchen. Zeke follows closely behind her. Jonathan reaches his arms out to her, taking her into them and pulls her body to his.

"You look absolutely amazing." He tells her as he stares into her eyes intensely.

"You picked it out." She kisses his cheek, "Thank you, Jonathan. It's a gorgeous dress."

"You're welcome. You make it gorgeous."

"That was pretty sneaky of you."

"It was just a well-timed surprise."

"Perfectly timed. Just like our first kiss was."

Jonathan pretends to think very hard for a minute and then says, "Mmm, yes. Our first kiss was really well timed, wasn't it?"

"And so many since then." She leans into him. He kisses the top of her head and she pulls back. He turns towards the stove. "What are you making?" Faith asks.

Jonathan points to the spread on the counter and says, "Well, we've got a charcuterie board, a veggie tray with some dill dip, I also made some crab dip and a spinach dip. You already know what we're having for dinner since you picked it."

"Shrimp scampi! I'm so excited!"

"I've got a side salad and garlic bread to go with that as well."

"Sounds delicious! Thank you, Jonathan."

Jonathan glances at the time. "We've got a little over an hour. Is there anything you need me to do?"

"I don't think so. I wouldn't start the fires outside yet."

"That's what I forgot!" Jonathan grabs a stack of blankets from the couch and places them in a basket near the wall of windows. "I don't want to put them outside, this way they'll be warm, but also accessible if someone wants one."

"You're so thoughtful." Faith smiles, feeling very proud to have him as her boyfriend. She sits down at the island.

"I enjoy looking out for those I care about." He walks back over to the counter.

"It shows."

Jonathan smiles thankful that she sees him in this light and glad she enjoys complimenting him.

"Would you like to start with some wine?" He asks her, reaching for glasses in the cupboard.

"You know I would. Thank you, Jonathan."

He grabs a bottle of wine, uncorks it and begins to pour one for her and one for himself. Handing hers to her he then takes a sip. "You know how much I enjoy a glass of wine while cooking."

"I do. Thank you for doing all of this, Jonathan. Throwing a party is a lot of work."

"You're welcome, Faith. You deserve it! Plus, after everything that's happened I didn't really want to take you out to Lee's pub or another bar in Luna Shores."

"Yeah, I'd definitely feel safer with you there, but even then, I'm not sure how comfortable I would feel. I guess what it comes down to is that I just want to have fun for my birthday, and this is the best way to do that given the recent circumstances."

"We've got music, drinks, and in a little while, we'll have good company."

"That is all I need to have a good time." She thinks for a moment and adds, "Not that I need the drinks in order to have a good time, but it doesn't hurt…until the next day."

Her and Jonathan laugh and Jonathan says, "Just wait until you're my age."

"You're not that much older than me."

"It doesn't seem like it, but it's still a four year difference. If you think about it, I was eighteen when you were fourteen."

"Well, that makes it sound way worse."

"Or…I was in eighth grade when you were in fourth."

"That is so bad. I think you can stop now." She chuckles as she takes another sip of her wine.

"I love you, Faith. And you're right, four years is hardly anything."

"I love you, Jonathan. I especially love it when you say 'you're right'." She begins to laugh and Jonathan can't help but watch her in amusement as she throws her head back laughing harder, he joins in as well.

"You're an amazing woman and you make me feel like such a lucky man."

"Thank you, Jonathan." She leans over the counter smiling and Jonathan leans in to kiss her.

# Chapter 25

## *Beatitude*

Noun; a state of utmost bliss

Jackie and Tom are the first to arrive, followed shortly by Faith's parents. Hope shows up a little later and by herself.

"I told you that I wanted you to bring Andy." Faith says as Hope approaches her.

"Forgive me if only a little over a week into seeing each other I'm not so sure I want to subject them to a party with family and friends."

"Are you trying to keep them from us?"

"No. I'm simply protecting them from all of you."

Faith looks at Hope from the corner of her eyes and says, "What you mean is that you're protecting the start of a relationship from the scrutiny of outside eyes and opinions."

"Yes, exactly. You should have been a psychologist instead of a teacher." Hope rolls her eyes.

"I'm still young enough. I could go back to school."

"You'd be making more money."

"That's for sure." Faith pulls her sister in for a hug. "It's good to see you, I'm glad you came, even if you are alone. When you're ready I'd love to meet Andy. Well, officially meet Andy."

"OK. I'll keep it in mind. Also, I forgot to mention, Happy Birthday!"

"Thank you! It was a couple of days ago, and you did say it then."

"Doesn't matter."

Faith laughs, "No, you're right, it doesn't. Should we go outside with everyone else?"

"Are you going to be warm enough in that?" Hope looks Faith up and down.

"Yeah, there's blankets right here. Plus, I've got a sweater." She reaches for the sweater draped over the back of the couch and grabs a blanket on her way out the wall of windows with Zeke in tow.

Hope follows Faith out seeing their parents with Jackie and Tom sitting around the fire pit. "Where's Jonathan?"

Faith looks around, not seeing him she shrugs her shoulders. "Maybe he's upstairs."

Hope sits next to her parents while Faith takes the seat next to Jackie, leaving room on the end for Jonathan to sit when he comes back. Zeke promptly curls up at Faith's feet.

"I'm so glad all of you could come." Faith says as she takes a sip of her wine.

Diane smiles. "We wouldn't have missed it, dear."

"Thanks, Mom." Faith smiles back.

"How have you been feeling?" Diane asks.

"Have they caught the guys?" Frank adds.

"I've been doing pretty good considering. They did catch them both. They found out that they're over-the-road truck drivers, which explains the accents."

"Thank goodness. I was worried they would be long gone after what happened to you."

"I was worried too. It helps to know that they caught them, but I still don't feel as safe as I did prior to all of that happening."

"That's understandable though, honey." Frank says reassuringly.

"I know, but I wish I could go back to how it was before."

"You'll get there." Diane says.

Suddenly, they hear music coming from the built in speakers surrounding the patio and Jonathan walks out smiling. "I knew we were missing something." He says.

Faith smiles at him and says, "It's perfect!"

Jonathan sits down next to her, placing his arm around her. "Are you warm enough?" He asks as he rubs her arm and shoulder.

"I am. Between the fire and the blanket, I'm quite comfortable."

"Good!" He smiles at Faith and then asks everyone, "Is there anything I can get any of you?"

They all shake their heads no except Jackie who says, "Could I get a blanket?"

"Of course!" Jonathan stands and begins to walk towards the condo. Zeke picks his head up to see where he's going then places it back down again.

Jonathan comes back handing the blanket to Jackie. "If anyone gets too cold, we can always go inside."

"It's really not that bad out here." Hope says. Diane and Frank nod in agreement.

Everyone is snacking on the spread Jonathan put out and enjoying their drinks and conversation. Faith feels a sense of wholeness having all of her people here for her to celebrate her birthday. She smiles to herself feeling happy for her blessings.

Jonathan stands, "I've got to go check on dinner. We'll eat that inside."

Faith mouths 'thank you' when Jonathan looks her direction before heading into the condo.

Twenty minutes later he comes back outside to announce that dinner is done. They all shuffle inside. Faith inhales deeply the scent of garlic and shrimp. Her mouth begins to water.

"That smells amazing." Tom says, echoing Faith's thoughts.

"Thanks, man. Faith picked it."

"She chose well."

One by one, they all make their plates and find their seats at the dining room table. Jonathan grabs everyone a fresh round of drinks, placing them in front of each of them.

# APTITUDE

Frank says, "Thank you, Jonathan. For the beer and the meal. You've outdone yourself, son."

"Faith deserves it." He smiles at Frank and then continues. "Speaking of which," he raises his glass. "I'd like to make a toast to honor and celebrate this amazing, beautiful woman that sits beside me. She has brought me more happiness in the last ten months than I've had in the last twenty years. I can't thank her enough for everything she has brought into my life and for the love that she gives me." He looks directly at Faith, then says, "Faith, you are the most incredible woman I've ever met. I'm so grateful to be building a life with you. I hope you have the happiest birthday imaginable." Turning back to address the table he says, "To Faith."

They all respond, "To Faith," and take a drink.

Faith's eyes are threatening to allow the forming tears to fall, but she blinks them away quickly.

When Jonathan sits, Faith says, "Thank you, Jonathan. That was the nicest thing anyone has ever said about me."

"I have a hard time believing that." He grins.

Faith feels her cheeks getting hot and looks down at her plate. Taking her fork in her hand she begins to eat the delicious meal Jonathan made. Her eyes get wide when the shrimp explodes with flavor as she bites into it. She swallows and exclaims, "This is phenomenal, Jonathan! Thank you!"

"You're very welcome, Faith."

There is some conversation during dinner, and at times it seems there are two conversations going at once with a lot of laughter. One between the men, and one between the women.

Shortly after they've finished dinner and Jonathan has put it away, with help from Diane who insisted on helping, Diane and Frank decide to head home.

"Thank you both, so much for coming." Faith says as she gives them each a hug.

"We wouldn't have missed it, sweetheart." Frank says.

"We'll see you both tomorrow night, right?" Diane asks.

"Yes, we'll be there."

"Good! I'll have cake!" Diane smiles broadly.

"You don't have to do that, Mom."

"I definitely do! It's tradition! We don't need to start breaking those now."

"No, I suppose we don't."

Jonathan walks them out to Frank's truck, thanking them both. Diane hugs him extra tight and says, "Thank you for celebrating our girl so well."

"She deserves it, ma'am."

"We know, son. It's just good that you do too." Frank says with a chuckle.

When Jonathan gets back into the condo, he sees Jackie, Hope, and Faith all dancing in the living room, the music is turned up louder since he had walked out the door with her parents.

Tom is sitting at the dining room table, his beer in one hand and his phone in the other. Jonathan grabs another beer for himself and sits down next to Tom.

# APTITUDE

Nodding to the girls he says, "They don't need a bar, or a DJ. Just some drinks and music."

"The drinks here are cheaper."

"I can't argue with that." Jonathan raises his bottle and taps it against Tom's then they both take a drink. "So, how are things going?"

"At work or home?"

"Either one."

"Well, I tried to talk to Jackie about moving in with me and she refused. So, there's that. Work is going well, I suppose. You probably know better than I do how I'm doing on that front."

"As far as work goes, I hear nothing but good things from the higher ups." He says reassuringly. "As far as Jackie goes, I don't think I have any advice. Did she give you a reason?"

"She said that she needs her own space still. She isn't sure when or even if she's going to want us to move in together."

"Well, that doesn't sound very promising."

"No. It sounds like she wants to break up with me."

"Did you ask her about that?"

"I couldn't. I was too afraid of what her answer would be."

"That's understandable. When did all this go down?"

"Last night. I took her out to dinner, it seemed like everything was going really well and then suddenly it wasn't."

"Had you talked about this with her before last night? Was her reaction the same then?"

"We have visited the idea a few times through the past couple of years. This is the first time she made it seem like it might not ever be a possibility."

Lowering his head, Jonathan says, "What a fucking bummer, man. I'm sorry, I wish I had something better to say to you than that."

"It's OK. I get it. I don't even know what to tell myself at this point. How could I expect you to have some amazing words of wisdom for me?" Tom starts mindlessly picking at the label on his beer bottle.

"So, what's your plan?"

"I'm seriously considering breaking up with her before she gets the opportunity."

"Wow. OK. That's not really what I was expecting."

"That's where my mind is." Tom shrugs.

"Do you still love her?"

"I've questioned that a lot in the past twenty-four hours."

"And your conclusion?"

"I do, but not in the same way as I did. If she doesn't see a future with me then what the hell are we even doing?"

"That's true. It sucks that you're going through all of this, though."

"Yeah, thanks, man. I appreciate you listening to me, even though it's depressing as shit. You and Faith seem to be doing well, though."

"We are, and of course I'll listen to you. We all need an ear sometimes."

"Well, if things do go south with Jackie, I hope that you still being with Faith doesn't affect our friendship."

"No way, man. Besides, we'll still have work."

"Thanks. I appreciate that."

"You're welcome. Try not to stress about it. I know that's hard, but you can't do anything right now anyway. I'm somewhat surprised you came with her tonight when you're feeling like this."

"I surprised myself by coming, too. I figured it might help me decide, I also couldn't turn down free beer." He nods tipping the bottle in Jonathan's direction.

"Free beer is hard to pass up." Jonathan takes a drink and turns his gaze to Faith dancing. It reminds him so much of the first time he saw her and how vivacious and captivating she was that night at Lee's pub. A smile slowly spreads as he remembers how he asked her out that night. Then he recalls when they exchanged phone numbers.

It's hard to believe that was only ten months ago, it's also hard to believe that was the beginning of something so amazing and they didn't even know it at the time. Jonathan knew she was special, but he had no clue how entirely special. He also didn't know if she was even going to be able to love him.

Now they're planning a future together, building a home for their someday family. They have a dog that is currently so excited with his mom dancing around he can hardly contain himself. His tail is wagging uncontrollably.

Jonathan watches as Faith grabs Zeke's front paws and lifts him slightly to dance with her. He imagines her holding their children in much the same way, dancing with them.

Tom abruptly interrupts his daydream, "I'm going to grab another. Do you want one?" He gestures towards the bottle in Jonathan's hand.

"Yeah, that would be great. Thanks!"

Tom stands glancing in Jackie's direction. Jonathan sees a look of longing on Tom's face for a split second. When Jackie's eye's meet Tom's the look disappears into something closer to annoyance mixed with pain.

# Chapter 26

## Plenitude

*Noun; the quality or state of being full, completeness*

Hope plops down on the couch when the song ends and takes a long pull from her beer. "I'm so warm! Do you guys want to go outside with me?" She asks Faith and Jackie while practically shouting over the music.

Both nodding in agreement, they grab their blankets as they walk through the sliding wall of windows. Faith stops at the dining room table and gives Jonathan a kiss on her way out.

They sit by the fireplace tucked in the corner better protected from the wind. The moon is shining high above them with a spattering of stars twinkling in the inky blue sky. Jonathan turns on the string lights for them and then sits back down with Tom at the table.

"I'm so glad you guys came tonight!" Faith says exuberantly. Realizing it's not as loud outside and she doesn't have to shout she laughs a little as she lowers her head as if it's going to also lower her voice.

Hope laughs with Faith then says, "I wouldn't have missed it, sister! Not for anything at all."

"Me either. I'm also glad we aren't going out. This is so much better!" Jackie says.

"Right, I agree." Faith says nodding her head enthusiastically.

The music has followed them outside, but isn't nearly as loud. Faith takes a sip from her wine glass. Zeke hops up laying down next to her on the seat, with his head placed perfectly in her lap. She pats the top of his head. He lifts his eyes to look at her making his forehead crinkle and she smiles.

Jackie notices the two of them cuddled up. "He's absolutely adorable, Faith."

"He is, right!"

"And the way you guys found him. It's just perfect!"

"Like it was meant to be."

"Definitely." Jackie smiles.

"Would you ever get a dog?" Hope asks Jackie.

"I've thought about it, but I want to wait a while yet. I'm still in school and renting. Neither of those are really conducive to having a pet that's demanding of your time."

"That's true."

"What about you, Hope?" Faith asks curiously.

"I would, eventually. Like Jackie said, I'm renting and going to school too, but I've always liked dogs."

# APTITUDE

"Mom and Dad never let us get one. Do you think that has something to do with why we both want one?"

"Probably. Their excuse was always the café."

"No matter how much we begged. It's obvious that they like dogs! Did you see the way they acted over Zeke?"

Hope nods her head in agreement.

Jackie scoffs. "Mine couldn't give me enough attention, there was no way they would bring another responsibility into the house."

"It's a good thing we don't have to live with our parents as adults." Hope says remembering how hard it was after her accident.

"The first eighteen years was enough for me." Jackie says in agreement.

Jonathan and Tom join them outside. Jonathan is carrying a fresh bottle of wine. "Mind if we sit with you ladies?" Jonathan asks.

"Not at all. Especially when you come bearing a full bottle of wine!" Faith says smiling.

Jonathan sits beside her with Zeke in between them and sets the bottle on the table. Tom sits down next to Jonathan. "I figured you might need a refill." Jonathan says to Faith.

"What about me, Jonameister. Did you grab a beer for me?" Hope says shaking her empty beer bottle in his direction.

"I'm sorry, Hope. I didn't. I can go in and grab you one if you'd like." Jonathan smiles.

Tom stands. "I got it. Anyone else need anything?"

Jackie doesn't say a word. Tom says, "OK then."

When he comes back out, he opens Hope's beer and hands it to her.

"Thank you, Tom."

"You're welcome."

Jackie looks at Hope smiling widely and says, "So, I heard you and Andy went on a date. How'd that go?"

"It went really well. We had a nice time and have been seeing each other pretty much every day since."

"Good!" Jackie says.

"I'm just glad something positive came out of that whole ordeal." Faith says.

"Me too." Jackie agrees.

"I couldn't have planned it if I wanted to." Hope offers.

"The best things in life happen spontaneously, Hope." Jonathan says.

Hope smiles at him and says, "Some of the worst things happen that way too, Jonameister. Most recently would have been my car accident."

"I know exactly how devastating those can be." Jonathan says lowering his voice.

Faith doesn't like the way this conversation is going. Jonathan shouldn't be thinking about his parent's accident and Hope shouldn't be so negative. "This thing with Andy deserves a little optimism, I think."

"Oh, I know that." Hope takes a swig of her beer. "I am quite optimistic. Everything with them is great so far. It doesn't mean I'm going to ignore everything I've learned from past relationships."

"No, you don't need to do that. You do need to remember that this isn't one of those and that even if there seems to be some similarities, it might not actually be true."

"It sounds like you might be speaking from experience." Hope says in an almost accusing tone.

Faith looks around at everyone sitting at the table. "We've all had bad things happen in past relationships. It's our job to make sure those bad things don't follow us into our new ones, tainting them from the start with our cynicism." She squeezes Jonathan's hand under the table.

"Are you calling me cynical?"

"Do you not think that you are?"

"I think I have a healthy dose which helps keep it all in perspective."

"A healthy dose would be realistic, but not cynical. There is a difference." Faith offers in as gentle a tone as she can muster.

"You may be right." Hope shrugs her shoulders. "This works for me, though."

"Does it really? I feel like it works by keeping everyone at arm's length. I'm not trying to put you on the spot, I would just hate to see you miss out on something amazing because of things from your past."

Hope's tone is very serious. "I'm not going to miss out on this. Andy knows where I stand and is sympathetic of where these feelings stem from. I appreciate your concern, but it's unnecessary, Doubt."

Faith puts her hands up in surrender, "OK. I'm glad to hear that you've had these discussions."

Jackie speaks up. "Sometimes those conversations can be awkward, but they are necessary."

Hope looks at Jackie. "That's very true. We're taking our time, but also both feel like it could be something special."

"That's so great, Hope!" Jackie says.

With a big smile Hope says, "It definitely is."

Tom shifts his weight, takes a drink of his beer, and then gets up and walks inside. Faith looks from Jackie to Jonathan. Jackie shrugs her shoulders and suggests, "Bathroom maybe."

Jonathan sets his beer down on the table and walks into the condo. Faith looks back at Jackie and says, "OK. What's really going on?"

Jackie explains that Tom was adamant about them moving in together and she was simply honest with him about her feelings on the subject.

"Ouch, that had to have hurt." Hope says.

"He didn't take it well, no." Jackie looks down at her hands shaking her head. "I probably should have spoken up sooner. I've been having these feelings for a while."

"I remember you mentioning that a month ago at Mama Garcia's." Hope says.

"I've been putting it off. I'm not sure if it's because I'm not sure or if I don't want things to change yet, or am I

# APTITUDE

procrastinating because I don't want to hurt him? Whatever it is, it's not fair to either of us."

"No, it isn't." Faith says. "But you can't end it here. Not tonight."

"I won't. I'd suggested I just come alone, but he kept saying Jonathan is his friend too. When I pointed out that it was for your birthday it didn't seem to make a difference."

Hope takes a drink of her beer then says, "I think he's torn. He wants to still be with you, but not if you don't want to be with him."

"He's a nice enough guy, it's more that I'm not receiving everything I need to in this relationship. It's all been discussed ad nauseam and nothing has changed. I think I need to pull the Band-Aid off."

"That would probably be best." Faith says as she looks down at Zeke, petting him. She reaches for her wine glass with the other hand.

Jonathan comes back out and sits next to Faith. "What was that about?" She asks.

"He wants to leave. I told him that he was free to do whatever he wanted and that we would make sure Jackie got home safe."

"Thank you, Jonathan." Jackie says with a bit of relief in her voice.

"He loves you. I just don't know if he can be in love with you anymore."

"I get that." Jackie starts running her finger around the rim of her beer bottle. "I'll talk to him tomorrow."

"That's an idea." Faith says trying to sound reassuring, but feeling like she failed miserably.

After a few moments of silence, Jackie says, "I'm sorry guys. I didn't mean for this to darken the evening."

Faith feels bad that Jackie feels responsible. "We know that's not what you meant to happen. Sometimes these things happen at the worst times. We can't do anything to change the timing."

"Not now." Jackie says then swallows down the last of her beer.

Jonathan stands, kisses Faith on the top of the head and says, "I'm going to walk him to his car." Then walks back into the condo.

Jackie smiles at Faith, "You two seem to be doing really well."

"We are. Everything seems to be coming together."

"There haven't been any delays or setbacks with the house?"

"Not at all. If you ever build, I highly recommend Amethyst Bay Construction. They've been awesome to work with!"

Jackie looks at Hope, then back to Faith. "I'm not sure either of us will ever have the opportunity, but we'll keep it in mind."

They all laugh loudly. Hope says, "Speak for yourself." Laughing even harder as she finishes.

Feeling all of the love, Faith says, "Maybe this should become tradition."

# APTITUDE

Jackie laughs, "What? Breaking up with my boyfriend at your birthday party?"

"Well, you haven't done that yet."

"No, that will be for tomorrow." The dread in her voice is very apparent.

"What I meant, was just hanging out at home with you guys. Drinking, dancing, listening to music, and talking. I think it's been perfect. Plus, we literally have nothing to worry about." Faith takes another drink of her wine. Then grabs the bottle Jonathan placed on the table and refills her glass.

"I'm so glad they caught those guys." Hope says, relief flooding through her. "It's been hard on all of us, I can't even imagine what it must have been like for you, Faith."

"Jonathan was extra attentive and caring. It only took a few days to feel normal again…physically at least."

"Yeah, but the emotional and mental aspect of it are just as important." Jackie offers.

"That's true, and I'm dealing with those the best I can. I think the worst of it is the unknown. What did they plan to do with us?"

The question hangs in the air like an anvil waiting to fall into the abyss like on any random Saturday morning cartoon.

# Chapter 27

## Pulchritude

*Noun; beauty, especially a woman's beauty*

In the middle of March the weather begins to warm significantly. There has been little in the way of developments from the arrests. In the past couple of weeks Jonathan has been making it home earlier than before. Faith told him she'd try not to get used to it, but it has been very nice having him there.

Jonathan's twenty-eighth birthday is fast approaching. Faith still isn't feeling comfortable enough to go out, but she wants to do something special for him. She's been thinking of taking him out for dinner and then coming home for drinks.

Having people over would be nice, however, since Jackie broke up with Tom it seems like it would be awkward to have them in the same place, at least for now.

# APTITUDE

"What do you think about driving out to the house tonight after dinner?" Jonathan asks as he puts the steamer full of broccoli on the burner.

"That sounds like a wonderful idea."

"I thought so. It's been a few weeks since we've been out there."

"Do you think we should bring Zeke with us?"

"Will he think we're taking him back and leaving him there?"

Faith looks down at Zeke sleeping on the floor beside her chair at the island. "I don't think so. I'm pretty sure he knows we're his family now."

"Have you ever wondered how he got out there in the first place?"

"Of course I have. I also wonder where his littermates are. I am glad we found him though. Even if he scared the crap out of us."

Jonathan laughs uneasily remembering how creepy it felt being out in the woods hearing the noises Zeke was making when he was following them. "I'm just glad he wasn't a bear or a mountain lion."

"No kidding." Faith laughs imagining what either one of those animals could have done to them out there. She looks down at Zeke again. "He's perfect, Jonathan."

"He is. I can't believe how much he's already grown in just a month!"

"How big do you think he'll get?"

"The vet mentioned he could be over a hundred pounds by the time he's done."

"That's a heavy dog."

"Yes it is."

When he's finished cooking, Jonathan plates their dinner and sits down next to Faith at the island.

Getting a forkful of her chicken Marsala Faith says, "I'd like to bring him with. I think he should see the house with us."

"Then that's what we'll do."

When they've finished eating, Faith takes Zeke outside to make sure he's gone potty before getting in the car. He's been doing well with potty training, but Faith has made sure to take him out regularly.

Jonathan starts the car and Faith gets Zeke in the back seat. She then attempts to sit in the front, but as soon as she opened the front door she sees that Zeke has hopped into her seat. She attempts to push him back into the rear seat, but he is hard to make budge, especially when he keeps licking her face. Jonathan can't help but laugh at the scene.

"OK, alright." She lifts him up slightly, and slides into the seat, setting him back down on her lap.

"You know that you're going to have to get him to stay in the back seat at some point, right? We can't have a hundred pound dog sitting on your lap every time we take him somewhere."

"I'll have to work with him on that."

# APTITUDE

The whole way to the house, Zeke sits up looking out the windows. When they pull into the driveway his tail starts to wag, smacking the center console and Faith in the side. She doesn't have a chance to grab his leash before Jonathan opens her door and he bounds outside happily.

The crew is about done for the day, but Michael is still there supervising clean up. He notices the large yellow puppy running toward him. He crouches down to the ground and yells, "Here, puppy!"

Zeke runs straight to him, giving him kisses and happily receives all of the pets. Faith rushes over to them, grabbing ahold of Zeke's leash.

"Thank you for getting him, Michael."

"I was wondering where he was."

Jonathan and Faith look at one another puzzled. "What do you mean?" Jonathan asks.

"We'd seen him around here a few times, but when we'd try to catch him he'd run back into the woods." Michael explains, pointing towards the woods. "We even tried coaxing him out with some food."

"Really?" Faith says, surprised.

"Yeah. It looks like he knew the two of you were his ticket out of those woods."

"I guess so." Jonathan says. He gestures towards the house and asks, "How's everything going?"

"It's great! Do you guys want to take a look around? These knuckleheads are finishing clean-up for the day. I'm sorry to say it isn't as clean as we had it a month ago." Looking back down at Zeke he says, "But this guy is much cleaner than he was the last time I saw him. I almost didn't recognize him."

"He made it seem like he knew you." Faith said. "We were just saying how we wondered how he got out here."

"I have no idea about that, but like I said, we tried to catch him and he wouldn't come to any of us; always stayed at the edge of the woods. He seems much better now! You guys have clearly been treating him well! What's his name?"

Faith smiles widely, "Zeke."

At the mention of his name he whips his head around to look at Faith. His tail wagging wildly.

"That's a great name! I had a grandpa named Zeke. Well, it was Ezekiel, but everyone called him Zeke." Michael says.

"No kidding?"

Michael shakes his head and holds up his right hand to show his honesty. "C'mon let's go look in the house!"

Michael hands them each hard hats. "Sorry, Zeke, I don't have any puppy sized ones."

Faith and Jonathan follow Michael towards the house with Zeke following them. All of the exterior doors, and windows have been installed. The exterior of the house still has the house wrap on half of it, the other half has the stonework and siding done. The roof has been shingled and as they enter the house they can see that some of the plumbing, electrical and HVAC has been roughed in.

"We'll be able to start insulation and then drywall next week."

"That's exciting!" Faith says happily.

# APTITUDE

Jonathan echo's her thoughts. "This looks fantastic, Michael."

"Well, thank you, but I can't take all of the credit! These guys have been working very hard on this house for all of you."

"We appreciate it so much!" Faith says, getting the idea to bake them some cookies or some other sweet desert.

"Overall, it probably doesn't look too different from the last time you were here, but now you'll be able to see more easily where the fixtures will be in the bathrooms and the kitchen."

They walk around, taking the grand tour with their gregarious guide. Zeke seems extra excited to see more of the house, even more so than he had when they'd found him; although he was starving that night.

Michael's excitement grows as they go down into the basement. The natural light spills in through the wall of windows at the far end where you can walk right out to the side yard.

"This is going to be perfect for entertaining!" Jonathan says enthusiastically.

Faith is suddenly reminded why he insisted on such a big flashy house in the first place. Besides wanting a big family, it's even more-so a status symbol for him. He envisions inviting Kansen Corps higher ups to dinners and parties. Faith understands his drive and need for them to see him in a good light, it just isn't who she is to want to impress people with materialistic things like houses and cars.

She did allow him to buy her a new car for Christmas, but she protested at first. A new car wasn't entirely necessary, but it did give her the opportunity to give her old car to Hope who was in need of something to drive, once she was cleared after her accident on Christmas.

Jonathan looks over at Faith, watching her look around the lower level. The way the sun is shining through the wall of windows highlights her beauty in such a way that his heart swells. Smiling to himself he imagines her taking the children outside to play and teaching them how to swim in the swimming pool that has yet to be installed.

It is such a lovely thought that he doesn't realize Michael and Faith have walked on without him. He catches up quickly walking into the room that will become their gym.

"We'll need to start looking into some equipment for in here; make some decisions on what we want."

"I'd definitely like a treadmill and some free weights."

"We can do that." Jonathan smiles.

They walk around the rest of the lower level finishing up back where they started. Michael takes them through the wall of windows outside to the side yard. They walk around the side of the house where a patio with stairs and a path will be installed to connect it to the back patio.

"We'll work on all of this after the interior is finished. The patio will go in as well as the pool."

He takes them out to the edge of the property, overlooking the bay. "We'll put in the fire pit and a sitting area out here like we discussed."

# APTITUDE

"Perfect!" Faith smiles. She looks at Jonathan and asks, "Can we have some hanging lights out here too?" She looks at Michael and adds, "We have them around the patio at the condo now and they create such great ambiance!"

"We can do anything you want, Faith." Jonathan assures her.

"We have lights and speakers spec'd out by the patio and pool areas too."

"That will be great! Thank you, Michael." Jonathan says.

"Anything we can do to make you guys happy!"

"You've done an incredible job so far!" Faith says.

"Faith, look." Jonathan points at the sky above the bay where the sun is beginning to set, igniting the sky in beautiful oranges and yellows.

"The clouds look like they're on fire!" She says.

"Fire in the sky." Michael states.

"We'll get to see so many of these sunsets. It'll be absolutely incredible. And look!" Jonathan points to a different part of the sky where the moon is just beginning its ascent.

"Absolutely gorgeous." Faith says in awe of the view in front of her. "I can't believe this is ours, forever."

Jonathan walks up behind her and places his arms around her. "Forever." He whispers into her ear.

# Chapter 28

# Magnitude

Noun; the importance, quality, or caliber of something

Faith reaches for the backless black dress she's been thinking of wearing for the past couple of weeks. She didn't buy Jonathan an outfit for tonight, like he did for her, but she figured he is less indecisive than she is and probably wouldn't have any issues finding something to wear for his birthday dinner.

As she finishes getting ready, Jonathan comes up to the bathroom and quickly gets dressed. He fixes his hair and goes back down stairs to wait for Faith.

When she's done she heads down the stairs. Jonathan is sitting on the couch with a glass of wine, waiting for her. A smile spreads across his face as she comes down the steps.

"You look absolutely gorgeous."

"Thank you. You look very handsome."

"Thank you."

## APTITUDE

"It didn't take you long to pick something out." She stands in front of him and he hands her the glass of wine and places his hands on her legs gently pulling her closer to him.

"As soon as I saw what you were wearing, I knew it wouldn't matter what I had on. No one will be looking at me." He looks her up and down. "That dress hugs you perfectly." He runs his hands down her sides, from her waist, over her hips and down to her thighs.

"Thank you." Faith feels her cheeks get warm.

"I can't wait to take it off of you."

She takes a step back from him so he can barely reach her. "You'll have to wait. We have reservations." She holds up one finger for emphasis.

"I'm sure we can be late to them."

"No. We definitely can't be." She shakes her head seriously.

"Where are we going anyway?"

"I rarely get to surprise you. Let me have this one, please."

"OK. I can do that." Jonathan smiles.

"Thank you."

"No problem."

Faith drives into Caulfield and pulls into the parking lot of a restaurant Jonathan has never been to before called Francesco's.

"I hope you want Italian."

"That sounds delicious. I've never been here, but I've heard amazing things!"

"Yeah, me too. I was lucky to get the reservation."

"I can imagine."

They walk through the heavy ornate dark stained wood double doors into an entirely different world it seems. It's as if they have walked into fifteenth century Renaissance Italy. A very detailed mural that would rival the Sistine Chapel is painted on the domed ceiling in the entry way. The hostess desk is marble with columns that go up to the tall ceiling.

The floors are terracotta tile and the walls are covered in marble. The owners really wanted to make this place look authentic.

Once they're seated, the waitress comes and takes their drink order. Jonathan takes Faith's hands in his on top of the table. "Thank you, Faith. This is going to be an amazing night."

"You're welcome. And happy birthday!" She reaches into her purse and takes out a card and a small wrapped package.

"I thought we weren't getting gifts."

She gives him a sideways glance and says, "You bought me the outfit for my birthday."

Jonathan shakes his head, "No. Remember? The note said it wasn't a gift."

"I remember." Faith smiles.

The waitress brings their drinks and asks if they're ready to order.

Jonathan and Faith let go of one another's hands and instead pick up their menus.

"No, I'm sorry. We haven't had a chance to look yet." Jonathan explains.

# APTITUDE

"It's no problem. I can explain things to you a little more if you'd like."

"Sure." Faith says.

"At Francesco's we feature regional Italian cuisine. The region changes seasonally. Currently, we are featuring food from the Tuscany region." She points to the central area of Italy on the map placed on the front of the menu. "Our menu is divided into four courses and you're able to order something from each course. Your selections will be brought out in sequence. On the back of the menu there is more information about the city of Florence including history and the origins of the menu options."

Jonathan looks at Faith surprised by this. "That sounds amazing."

"I'll give you some time to look at the menu. If you have any questions please let me know."

Faith smiles at the kind waitress, "Thank you!"

"You're welcome! I'll be back shortly." The waitress walks away checking in with a nearby table.

Jonathan and Faith both look at the menu trying to figure out their selections for each course.

Faith takes a drink of her Sassicaia. "This all looks so delicious. I'm not sure if I can pick something."

"Luckily, you've got multiple things to pick." Jonathan gives Faith a sarcastic smile.

"That makes it worse!" Faith laughs. "There's too many choices to make."

Jonathan laughs with her. "That is true, but I think I know what I want."

"You know everything you're going to order? Already?"

"Yeah. Do you want me to help you?"

"No, I'll figure it out."

Faith looks down at the menu once more. She notes the options for the antipasti. She chooses the ribollita which is a Tuscan vegetable and bread soup with extra virgin olive oil. Next, she looks at the primi course. She is torn between two options, but ends up deciding on the Penne "Alla Vecchia Bettola" which is pasta quills with tomato cream, and vodka sauce with parmigiana-reggiano.

Faith looks up from her menu to see the waitress walking towards the table. "Are you ready to start?"

Faith wavers, "I've only chosen two things."

"That's perfectly alright. We can get you started and then when you're ready I can take the rest of your order."

"OK."

Jonathan and Faith tell the waitress what they would like to begin with. She finishes writing down their selections on her order pad and then says to Jonathan, "I'll bring you another beer. That was a Dolomiti Rossa, correct?"

"Yes, it was."

"And you would like the same?"

"I would. Thank you." Jonathan takes the last swig of his beer. The waitress grabs the empty glass before she walks away.

# APTITUDE

Looking Faith in the eyes, he takes her hand and says, "Thank you for bringing me here. This place seems quite amazing already."

"We haven't even tasted the food yet."

"No, we haven't." He nods towards a table across from them. "But it does look delicious!"

"It does!"

Before they know it the waitress comes with their appetizers and asks, "Have you had a chance to look at the menu more?"

"I have." Faith smiles. "I'll have the tagliata di manzo con ragu di porcini al romarino and the budino di mou salato. I'm sure I butchered that." She laughs nervously.

The waitress smiles. "That was actually pretty impressive and wonderful selections. And you sir?"

"I'll have the peposo all forncina dell'impruneta and the classico tiramisu, please."

"Also wonderful selections. I'll get these in. Enjoy your appetizers."

"Thank you!"

They both look down at their plates their mouths watering. Jonathan had ordered the chicken-ricotta meatballs with tomato veloute sauce. Grabbing their forks they each take a bite. Jonathan watches as Faith's eyes close savoring the flavor.

Simultaneously they say, "This is delicious!"

When they've finished their appetizers the waitress refreshes their waters. "I'll be back shortly with your pasta course."

"Perfect! Thank you!" Faith says emphatically. She's very excited for her pasta with vodka sauce.

Jonathan smiles at Faith. "I'm really looking forward to this next course."

"What did you order?"

"It's a pasta with duck ragu. It sounded absolutely amazing."

"It does! I was thinking about that one too! I'm glad we got different things though. That way we can try each other's food."

"I love when we do that."

"We did it on our first date too!"

"The best first date ever!"

"Our last first date."

"So happy for that!" Jonathan smiles.

The waitress interrupts their reminiscing with their bowls. Setting each down in front of them, she asks, "Do either of you need refills on your drinks?"

Faith grabs her glass, drinks down the rest of it and says, "Yes, please."

They once again eat and share their food. Faith looks around the restaurant taking it all in. Jonathan watches her in total awe of her beauty and grateful for her positive outlook on life. The fact that she possesses such a sense of wonder and optimism makes him love her even more.

# APTITUDE

Once they finish that course, Faith looks down at the small wrapped package atop the card on the table. Taking a drink of her Sassicaia she gestures towards them and says, "Jonathan, would you like to open your gift now?"

Placing his hand on top of the package he says, "I would like that very much."

He takes the card and opens it first. He smiles to himself as he reads the sweet card Faith chose for him.

Looking up from the card, he says, "Thank you so much Faith." He takes her hand over the table squeezing it gently then brings it to his lips.

Blushing Faith says, "You're welcome, Jonathan. I'm glad you like it."

Taking the box in his hands he begins unwrapping it.

Faith nervously says, "It's nothing big."

"It was supposed to be nothing at all, so I'm glad it isn't big." Unwrapping it entirely reveals a white box. He opens that and pulls out its contents which is covered in tiny bubble wrap.

He unsticks the tape that is folded over keeping its contents contained. As he pulls the item free from the bubble wrap he reveals a three by three picture frame. Placed perfectly within the frame is the picture from their second date at Silverwood State park where Jonathan asked her to be his girlfriend.

"I thought you might put it on your desk at work." Faith says sheepishly with a shrug of her shoulders.

"That's a wonderful idea! I love it Faith! Thank you!" He smiles broadly at her. Realizing this was a big deal for her.

"I'm happy you like it."

"I really do love it!" He looks at it again admiring how good they look together. "We should get professional pictures taken."

"Do you think this one isn't good enough?" She gives him a sideways glance.

His stomach drops and instantly he begins trying to explain. "I didn't mean…"

Faith interrupts him with a laugh. "I was just kidding! I completely agree that we should. Maybe once the house is finished." She offers.

"That sounds like a great idea. We can have the pictures done there. The property would be the perfect backdrop!"

Faith smiles just as the waitress comes with their next course.

"These are timed quite well." Jonathan says.

"I'll let the chef know that you're pleased with everything so far?"

"Yes, please do!" Faith says.

When the waitress comes back a few moments later, she is carrying a freshly opened bottle of Sassicaia and another glass. "Compliments of the Chef." She looks at Jonathan, "And a very happy birthday." She begins pouring the wine for the two of them, topping Faith's glass off.

Jonathan looks at Faith, smiles and tells the waitress, "Thank you."

"That was so kind of you." Faith says surprised at the gesture.

"I hope you enjoy the rest of your meal."

"It has been amazing so far." Jonathan assures her, taking a sip of his wine.

Both Jonathan and Faith begin eating their meals, Faith had ordered beef shin slowly braised in sangiovese with garlic and roasted apple. Jonathan is currently cutting the beef strip steak with procini mushroom ragu that he had ordered, and then he loaded up his fork.

They each took their own bites before offering one to each other, thoroughly excited for the other to enjoy it.

After a few moments and a couple more bites of her food, Faith asks, "What was it that you ordered for desert?"

"I'd thought about the tiramisu as well, but after you ordered that I was glad I went with the sea salt caramel pudding with chocolate ganache."

"That sounds delicious too!"

Jonathan takes another bite of his steak and then says, "You are an amazing woman, Faith. Thank you again for bringing me here."

"You're welcome, Jonathan. I just wanted to make you feel special on your birthday."

"You've definitely accomplished that."

"Good." She smiles, taking another bite of her main dish.

Once they're both finished with their food, the waitress comes and removes their dirty dishes. She then comes back with palate cleansers before returning once again with their desserts.

Jonathan's eyes get huge as he sees both of their plates. His mouth is watering as he tastes his dessert first. While he savors his, he watches as Faith takes the first bite of her tiramisu.

A smile spreads across her face as the flavors hit her taste buds. Jonathan wants to take another taste of his, but he's too content watching her. Once she finishes her initial taste, Jonathan holds out his fork for her to try his dessert.

Faith holds up a finger and grabs her water taking a sip before allowing him to put the forkful in her mouth. She closes her eyes as he slowly pulls the fork through her lips. Jonathan is thoroughly enjoying watching her degust his dessert.

"That is amazing! Want to try my tiramisu?"

"You know I do." Jonathan says smiling.

Faith loads up her fork then reaches across the table and feeds it to him. "That is delicious as well, but I'm still glad I got mine."

"They are both very good. I'm glad I got mine as well, though."

When they've both finished their desserts the waitress brings the check placing it on the table. Faith grabs it before Jonathan has a chance.

"It's your birthday. You're not paying for your birthday dinner." She half rolls her eyes at him.

# APTITUDE

Jonathan crosses his arms defiantly, but then says, "OK, Faith."

Once she settles the check, they both finish their drinks and walk out the ornate large double doors, back into the real world. It feels as though they've stepped through a portal transporting them back to their current lives.

The darkness surrounds them as they walk to the car, with only a few sparse street lights interrupting the shadows around them. The air is thick with dew and exhaust from the numerous cars traveling on Main Street just a couple blocks over where the light pollutes the side street Francesco's calls home.

# Chapter 29

# Amplitude

*Noun; extent of dignity, excellence or splendor*

Once in the car, Faith considers taking Jonathan to a bar for a drink, but decides against it when she feels her anxiety kick in at the thought. She also got the feeling that after their meal he would rather just go home. The fact that the idea of going to a bar is still such a daunting one for her, is concerning. She isn't sure how long it will take for her to get more comfortable with the idea. She's found beating herself up over not being ready yet isn't helpful at all, so now she quickly leans into giving herself grace for her complicated feelings.

During the forty-five minute drive back to the condo, Jonathan talks about how great the food was at Francesco's and mentions that they should go back soon. Faith agrees, it was a wonderful experience all around and she's very happy that he enjoyed it as much as she did.

As soon as they get into the condo, Faith lets Zeke outside and Jonathan opens a bottle of wine and pours them each a glass. When Faith returns Jonathan hands it to her and holds his up and says, "Cheers to the best birthday of my adult life."

Faith feels her stomach lurch at his words with the realization of how drastic of a turn his life took after his parents died. "To your birthday, Jonathan."

Jonathan smiles at her and they both take a sip from their glasses.

Jonathan leans in and kisses Faith, pulling her body against him. Feeling his strength and desire ignites passion within her. Jonathan's hand rubs the bare skin on the small of her back. His touch sends shivers down her spine.

She kisses him harder trying to let him know how good he's making her feel. She reaches up and her fingers find their way intertwined in his hair.

Suddenly, Jonathan places his hands under her ass and lifts her up in his arms. She giggles and then wraps her legs around him forcing her dress up her thighs. Then he walks into the living room and carries her up the stairs.

Once in the bedroom, Jonathan places her on the bed, slipping the straps of her dress down her arms. The dress slips down to Faith's waist. Jonathan continues its removal and Faith steps out of it. He hooks his fingers in the lacey band of her panties and pulls them down over her hips to free them. They fall to her feet and she steps out of those.

Faith reaches for his shirt, earnestly lifting it to bring it over his head and pull it off of him. Then she begins trying to work the button and zipper on his pants. Jonathan holds himself above her so she has the space to undo them. Once they've been undone he stands once again and pulls them and his boxer briefs down in one fell swoop.

Faith's eyes light up at the sight of him naked in front of her. A memory flashes in her mind of the first time she saw him at Lee's pub nearly a year ago. He was fully clothed, but he wore almost the same look he's giving her now. That smile had her from the moment he shared it with her.

Jonathan notices the way she's looking at him, curious he asks, "What are you thinking?"

"Just about the first time we met and how handsome I thought you were." She smiles shyly.

"You thought I was handsome?"

"Incredibly so, yes."

Jonathan smiles to himself as he places himself on top of her once again, this time with nothing between them.

He lowers his lips to hers, gently nibbles and then says, "You've always been the most beautiful woman, Faith. But lying naked in my bed right now, you a+re utterly breathtaking." He thrusts himself into her and she releases a soft moan.

He kisses her hard wishing the ecstasy they're both feeling could last forever. The noises she makes is only making him harder. It's becoming more difficult to hold his splendor back, but he wants to make sure Faith is satisfied as well.

He pulls her with him as he lays down on his back. Faith, now straddling him, looking as beautiful as ever in the pale moonlight coming through the curtains they forgot to close.

She throws her head back, thoroughly enjoying the pleasure he's granting her as her body rocks back and forth on his. He can't wait any longer. The moment Faith feels his ecstasy begin she feels herself follow him into the same euphoria.

Riding the wave of her pleasure she collapses against him when it's over. Jonathan sweetly kisses the top of her head.

"I love you, Faith. Thank you for tonight, for loving me the way you do, and for simply being you. You're an amazing woman and I am so damn lucky to have you."

Sitting up she says, "Thank you, Jonathan. I love you, too! I feel so lucky to have you!"

"I want to tell you something, but I originally thought I'd want it to be a surprise."

Faith's eyes light up. "You're going to tell me a surprise?!" She thinks for a moment and then says, "But it's your birthday, it's a day for surprises for you!" She places her hands gently on his chest tracing her fingers over his bare skin.

"Well, I think it would be best to give you a heads up about it. Plus, you know how much I enjoy spoiling you."

"I'm intrigued." She smiles widely, excited to hear the surprise he's going to divulge.

"I hope you haven't made plans for spring break."

"You're in luck! I haven't made any plans at all."

"I'd like to take you on a vacation."

Her eyes grow wider. "A vacation?!" She exclaims excitedly! "Where to?"

Jonathan revels in her excitement. Wanting to hold off a little bit longer. He asks her, "Do you have any suggestions?"

"Wait? You don't have it planned yet?"

"Oh, I do! I was just wondering if you could guess it."

Faith playfully hits his arm. "That wasn't very nice!"

"Wait…I'm taking you on a trip and I'm not very nice? I don't understand how that's possible."

"You are very nice." She says sweetly as she bats her eyelashes.

Jonathan starts laughing and Faith asks, "Are you going to stop laughing and tell me where we're going?"

Suddenly Zeke bounds up the stairs, jumps on the bed, and lays down next to Jonathan looking proudly up at Faith.

Faith laughs hard and Jonathan tries to push Zeke off the bed. Zeke just thinks he's trying to play so he jumps up, then crouches down with his butt in the air wagging his tail wildly. Faith laughs even harder.

This wasn't the distraction Jonathan was going for when he was trying to draw out answering Faith's question, but he can't help but see the humor in the situation.

Faith asks another question provoked by Zeke's antics. "What are we going to do with him while we're gone?"

"I've already got that settled."

"What did you settle on?"

"Your parents said they would take him."

"Seriously?" She says surprised.

"Yup. It sounded to me like your dad was actually looking forward to it."

Faith smiles, "Good. It'll be good for them."

She scoots off of Jonathan, walks into the closet, grabs a robe and slips it on before taking Zeke downstairs and outside.

When she comes back upstairs with him she tells Jonathan, "Luckily it doesn't appear that he got into anything while we were up here."

"That's good."

Faith puts Zeke in his crate, places her robe back into the closet, and then sits cross legged on the bed beside Jonathan looking very excited. She asks, "So…where are we going?"

Jonathan laughs again, but quickly sees the frustration overtaking her excitement so he answers in a hushed voice, "Napa Valley, California."

"Really?"

Jonathan can't quite tell if that is a good 'really' or a disappointed one so he says, "I know it's not Italy or Bali, but given the amount of time we have I thought it was a fair option."

"It's going to be absolutely wonderful!" She begins bouncing up and down on the bed exuberantly. Then she leans down and hugs him around the neck tightly.

Jonathan smiles at her eagerness. He realizes he should have known she was going to love it. He puts his hand on the back of her head and leads her to his lips and kisses her fiercely.

When Jonathan loosens his grip, Faith pulls back slightly and says, "This is such an amazing surprise, Jonathan."

"I'm so happy you love it!"

"I do!"

"I wanted to do something for us to celebrate our anniversary. With everything going on with the house and just the stress of life right now, I thought it would be nice to get away."

"I am so excited, Jonathan."

Half laughing he says, "I can tell!"

"How did you manage to get off of work?"

Jonathan shrugs his shoulders and explains, "I haven't really taken much time off since I started working there and certainly not since becoming general manager. I'm long over-due to take some time off."

"You know that I completely agree with that!"

"Yes I do!" Jonathan laughs again. He's happy he told her now instead of waiting. Surprises are good, but sometimes it's better to let the person you're surprising be prepared. Besides, it was still a surprise, just not on the day they leave. This way she'll get to live in the excitement until they go.

Again, Faith expresses how excited she is. She lays her head down on Jonathan's shoulder. He reaches up and strokes her silky long hair.

"There will be more surprises while we're there of course." He assures her.

"They're unnecessary, Jonathan."

"You know I don't feel that way."

"I know you don't. But I do."

"And I respect that."

Faith takes a moment and looks past her excitement to realize that maybe now isn't the best time to go. "Don't take this the wrong way, please, but is right now the best time to take a week away?"

"Firstly, I want to hear your concerns, I won't take them the wrong way. Secondly, it's a week and a half. Thirdly, and lastly, I've already talked to Michael about it and he agreed to do a video call while walking through the house so we can stay updated on the progress. And, of course, if there are any issues he'll let us know. I have every confidence in him. Are there any other reasons we shouldn't go?"

Faith contemplates the question for only a moment before responding. "I don't think so."

"You can feel excited again!" He offers.

"I am! When did you plan all of this?"

"Don't tell Mr. Kansen, but I did it while I was at work." He laughs.

Faith laughs as well. "It must be slow."

"It has been a little slower, yes."

"That probably helps with you taking time off too."

Still stroking her hair, Jonathan kisses her forehead.

# Chapter 30

## Magnitude
*Noun; the importance, quality, or caliber of something*

A couple of weeks later Faith finds herself packing for Napa Valley, even more excited than she was when Jonathan initially told her about the trip on the night of his birthday.

As delighted as she is, and as much as she knows Zeke is going to be just fine at her parents', she is still having a tough time with the idea of leaving him for that long. She worries it's going to confuse him, but she also understands there will be times that he can't come with them when they go out of town. Getting him used to the idea of it now is ideal since he's still so young. Plus, they're fortunate that they have someone willing to take care of him so they don't have to send him to boarder.

"Are you doing OK in there?" Jonathan asks as he ascends the stairs to their bedroom.

# APTITUDE

Faith is in the closet grabbing the bikini Jonathan got her for Christmas. "I'm fine. Just packing." She calls out.

As she turns and begins to walk through the doorway, Jonathan is right there. She screams and jumps back. Zeke runs up the stairs barking, ready to protect her.

"It's just me, Faith. It's OK." He says holding up his hands.

Her heart pounding, but feeling silly at the same time, she says, "I can't believe you startled me that much! I didn't realize you were even up here. I thought you called to me from downstairs." Zeke sits at her feet and looks up at her, realizing there is no threat.

"I'm sorry." He gently places his hands on her arms and rubs up and down reassuringly.

"You don't need to apologize. I'm a little jumpy I guess." She smiles sheepishly, feeling embarrassed about her reaction. She reaches down to pet Zeke and says, "That's a good boy, Zekie!" She ruffles his ears and he looks at her lovingly. Faith can feel her heartbeat slow slightly.

Jonathan pats his head as well and agrees, "That is such a good boy, Zeke." He looks at Faith and says, "I knew he was going to be a good protector."

"He really is." Faith smiles sadly, suddenly feeling even guiltier for leaving him behind.

"What's wrong?" Jonathan asks concerned.

"I just feel horribly about leaving him."

"He'll be OK."

"I know he will be. He'll be in great hands. I'm going to miss him so much, though."

"And he's going to miss you too, but it will be fine when we get back. He's going to be so excited to see you, he won't even remember we left."

"You really think so?"

"I do."

Looking down, Jonathan realizes what she has in her hands and says, "I cannot wait to see you in that." He looks her up and down, attempting to picture it in his mind.

"Well, you're going to have to wait until we're in Napa." She flashes him a flirtatious smile and then pushes past him to put the bikini in the luggage.

Jonathan playfully grabs her from behind, pulling her back to him.

"Hey!" She protests laughing.

Zeke pops his head up, not understanding what they're doing.

Faith attempts to get out of his grasp, but it proves futile. Zeke suddenly realizes they're playing and assumes the pounce position.

Jonathan covers Faith's neck and cheeks in quick kisses, playfully kissing her everywhere he can reach. Faith lets out a giggle and stops trying to get away.

"OK, OK!" She says surrendering to his kiss attack.

Jonathan laughs and says, "I'll let you get back to packing now." Then he places one final kiss on the top of her head.

"Thank you." She says facetiously.

# APTITUDE

"Excuse me, ma'am." A tall, lean, salt and pepper haired man in a grey suit says to Faith after he's just accidentally run into her. Faith responds, "Sorry. I didn't mean…" She stops herself because it wasn't her fault and she knows she shouldn't even apologize.

Jonathan takes her hand. "Let's go, our concourse is this way." He leads the way through the busy airport to their gate.

They had dropped Zeke off at Frank and Diane's on their way to the airport. Faith had a very difficult time leaving him. Jonathan had to practically pull her out of the door and into the car.

As they sit, waiting to board, Faith asks, "Do you think it would be weird to video call my parents to see Zeke while we're on vacation?"

"No, I don't think so. If it makes you feel better you can call every day."

"I'd like to do that." She looks down at her hands, still not feeling very positive about leaving him behind.

"Once we get to Napa you'll be so busily distracted you won't feel so bad anymore." Jonathan elbows her playfully.

"Until I see another dog." Faith says in a sad, but serious tone.

The announcement comes over the speaker that they are now boarding. Jonathan and Faith stand and grab their carry-ons then begin to shuffle with the other people waiting to line up. When they board, Faith sits by the window and Jonathan takes the seat next to her.

The flight is cross country with a quick stop in Denver, Colorado for refueling. The time goes by surprisingly quickly since Jonathan had downloaded a series of shows for them to binge to help pass the time.

There is a flurry of activity and people bustling past when they disembark after landing in Oakland, California. Jonathan and Faith rush to get to the baggage claim and then to the car rental desk. They are understandably eager to start their vacation.

The first of many surprises Jonathan has in store includes the vehicle they're renting. He'd reserved a blue Maserati GranTurismo convertible through one of the car rental companies. He wanted to splurge on something sporty and luxurious for their trip, there's no need for it to be practical.

Jonathan watches earnestly as Faith's face lights up when the attendant pulls the car up to the curb in front of them. The driver hops out and starts loading their luggage into the car.

"This is fancy." She muses.

"I wanted something a little special for us."

"It's definitely that!"

The drive to the house that Jonathan rented is absolutely breath taking. It took nearly an hour, and they got to go over the Richmond Bridge which took them over the San Rafael Bay. The water was so vividly blue on both sides of the four mile long bridge. Faith was a little uneasy on the drive, simply because she isn't used to the amount of traffic, and the cars weaving in and out between lanes.

Jonathan chose a very well-appointed house that is nestled on five acres with a working vineyard and a swimming pool with hot tub. There is a game room in the basement complete with pool and an air hockey table.

As they meander down the long gingko tree lined driveway with the top down, Faith peers out at the landscape before her. The rolling hills fold into one another, their tops lined with rows and rows of grape vines. They approach the home and a gasp escapes Faith's lips.

To the left of the driveway they can see that the infinity edge pool is over-looking the valley, just past that are more rolling hills leading into the Napa Mountains. The slightly elevated deck with a large table for outdoor dining is overlooking the same view.

Jonathan pulls the car around to the garage. He steps out and puts the code provided into the keypad, which raises the garage door. He parks the car and Faith practically jumps out excitedly heading for the door. Jonathan grabs their bags and quickly follows her in through the service door into the mudroom which leads into the large bright kitchen. Off of the chef's kitchen is a huge family room with vaulted ceilings and a beautiful stone fireplace. The large windows allow an abundance of light in with sliding glass doors that walk out onto the deck and to the lower pool area.

Continuing on, Faith finds a half bath and a study with shelves lining the walls, completely filled with books in every genre. In the middle of the room are two leather wingback chairs and a large solid wood desk with an office chair.

Faith follows the hallway to the grand entrance, again the ceilings are vaulted and the large solid wood staircase is the focal point of the entire entry. They've done an incredible job of creating a modern vintage vibe throughout the home so far.

Jonathan is having a hard time keeping up with Faith. He decides to leave their bags at the bottom of the stairs and follows as she climbs the steps and explores the bedrooms and bathrooms up there.

Faith turns around in the primary bedroom to face Jonathan who is standing behind her in the doorway and says, "This is absolutely stunning!"

"What I'm looking at is absolutely stunning. I love how excited you get about things. It's like a breath of fresh air."

Faith blushes a bit. "Thank you, Jonathan."

The ceilings in this room are coffered, the large windowed wall has a door in the center leading out to the furnished balcony complete with gas fireplace. In the master bathroom, there is another fireplace at the end of a large soaking tub which is big enough for both of them to fit.

# APTITUDE

There are also double sinks, a vanity, and the walls are entirely covered in tile.

"What do you want to do first?" Jonathan asks.

Faith saunters over wishing there was some way to show Jonathan how appreciative she is of his incredible level of thoughtfulness. She kisses him deeply, grateful they're already in the primary bedroom.

"Might as well start here." She gestures towards the four poster king size bed in the center of the room.

Jonathan needs no further instructions and begins by removing his shirt, then he gently kisses Faith's neck and pulls her sun dress off over her head. She watches as he steps back, undoing his pants. Faith keeps her eyes on him as she makes her way towards the large bed. Jonathan follows her as she unhooks her bra exposing her breasts. Then she tosses her bra on the window bench.

Jonathan picks her up, gently placing her on the elevated bed. He begins by kissing her stomach and running his fingers along the line of her white lace panties. He grabs them and swiftly pulls them down her legs and begins kissing the inside of her thighs moving up slowly.

# Chapter 31

# Splenditude

*Noun; the quality of being splendid*

Hours later, they lay naked together in the large four poster bed with the sun setting just outside their balcony, casting shadows across the room. Jonathan and Faith hold one another not wanting the intimacy of the day to end. The blankets as well as Jonathan's hair are both disheveled.

Suddenly, Faith's stomach grumbles loudly. Jonathan puts his hand on her tummy, rubbing he asks, "I bet you're hungry. I know I am."

"Yeah, we haven't eaten since before boarding in Caulfield."

"Plus, we just worked up quite an appetite." Jonathan smiles recalling the last few hours of pure bliss.

"Yes, we definitely did."

Jonathan unwraps himself from around Faith and walks into the bathroom. Faith enjoys the view. He finds two black silk robes hanging on the back of the door. He brings them into the bedroom, puts one on and holds the other out for Faith to slip into.

"Let's head downstairs and see what they might have in the kitchen. Most of the time the owners will have some sort of welcome basket set out."

They make their way back to the chef's kitchen taking in the Viking appliances and pulling inspiration for their own home. They find the basket on top of the table in the breakfast nook complete with two complimentary bottles of wine from the working vineyard on the property.

Inside the large basket they find a fresh loaf of bread, some crackers, German chocolates, and assorted other candies. Jonathan opens the refrigerator door and finds some cheeses and jams. He takes them out then begins slicing the fresh bread.

"Looks like we'll be having sandwiches." Faith smiles.

"We can always order some food for delivery if this won't be enough. It's at least something to tide us over."

"It's perfect." She says blissfully.

Finding the wine bottle opener, she places it over the bottle uncorking it. She pours the wine into the glasses sitting beside the basket. The aroma hitting her as soon as she begins the pour.

"This is going to be splendid."

"It already has been." Jonathan smiles as he finishes slicing the cheese.

"I meant the wine." She says, slightly blushing she adds, "Yes, it really has been."

They eat the bread and crackers with jam and cheese. Both of them are quite hungry, but this manages to take the edge off. Jonathan orders food from a local restaurant for delivery, but that's going to take over an hour.

"We never did check out the basement." Jonathan realizes audibly.

"We need to do that!"

"Yes, we do!"

Jonathan leads the way down the stairs that don't look like any basement stairs Faith has ever seen before. They appear to be just as grand as the stairs that leads to the second level.

In the fully finished basement they find the pool table and air hockey table in the game room that was mentioned in the listing. What wasn't mentioned was the full bathroom, kitchenette, and large family room complete with a bar and fireplace.

"Do you want to play?" Jonathan asks gesturing towards the air hockey table.

"I'd love to! Air hockey was always one of my favorites!"

Jonathan smiles, "Does that mean I have my work cut out for me?"

"Maybe." Faith raises her eyebrows challenging him.

Jonathan fires up the table and retrieves the puck and the mallets, sending one across the table to Faith and says, "May the best person win."

Faith takes a sip of her wine and then sets it down on the nearby table. Jonathan does the same.

Jonathan serves, sending the puck straight at Faith. She blocks it, quickly sending it gliding back, bouncing off the wall and then towards his goal.

The game goes back and forth, Faith is winning, and then Jonathan, but ultimately Faith takes it. Jonathan is a gracious loser and celebrates with her.

"That was fun!" Faith exclaims.

"It was! We'll have to play again sometime this week! I'll need a rematch."

"You don't want one right now?"

"I'll let you enjoy your win for a while. Besides, I was thinking we should enjoy the warm night air out on that deck."

"That does sound pretty amazing."

They stop in the kitchen once again to refill their glasses with what's left of the first bottle of complimentary wine. Then they sit at the large table on the deck, thoroughly enjoying the view before them. The air is earthy with scents of pine and eucalyptus which adds to the flavor of the wine they are enjoying.

Before they know it, the food they ordered arrives. Jonathan brings it out to the deck with plates and utensils and the last bottle of wine provided. This one has more floral notes, but both are absolutely delicious.

"I think I prefer this one." Faith says plating her food. "Especially with this food." Her eyes grow larger as the steam rises from her plate wafting the delicious scents of the food to her.

"I'm glad you're happy with what I ordered."

"Very pleasantly surprised." Faith looks down at her plate of Nero seafood medley. She takes a forkful into her mouth, the flavors igniting every taste bud on her tongue. Her eyes light up, savoring the food. "I'd say you have to try this, but you got yourself the same thing."

Jonathan smiles, "I thought it sounded so good that we both had to have it."

When they finish dinner, Jonathan cleans up their plates and suggests a dip in the hot tub.

"Aren't we supposed to wait a half hour?"

"I think that's only if you're going into a deeper natural body of water."

Faith gives him a sideways glance as if she doesn't quite believe him. He holds up his hands and says, "Really, we'll be fine to sit in the hot tub, but if you want to wait, we can."

"No, it's fine. I was just picking on you a little." She grins at him.

Jonathan laughs.

# Chapter 32

# Latitude

*Noun; freedom of action or choice*

In the morning, Jonathan and Faith wake slowly to the sun shining through the ample windows. Their night of ecstasy fresh in their minds, which started in the hot tub and moved into the family room, then ultimately upstairs in the primary bedroom once again. Jonathan felt as though he couldn't get enough of Faith, but eventually exhaustion hit and neither of them could fight it any longer.

Jonathan has a full day planned for them, starting with breakfast. They'll need to do some grocery shopping, but he hoped to simply place an order and have them deliver it. He knows that Faith will want to shop for their fruits and vegetables herself so they'll stop at a farmers market Jonathan found while searching the area online.

Faith rolls over, putting her arm across Jonathan's chest. A sleepy smile spreads across her face as she opens her eyes to see Jonathan peering back into hers. "Good Morning."

"Good Morning, beautiful. How did you sleep?" He brushes her arm back and forth with his hand.

"Like a dream."

"I slept well too."

She leans in to gently kiss him. "That's good."

"Yes, we need to be well rested. We have a busy day planned. You'll want to wear comfortable shoes. We're going to be walking a lot."

"OK. Wait…walking like hiking? Or walking like shopping?"

"We won't be hiking today, but that is on the agenda for the trip."

Her face lights up! "I am sure it's going to be beautiful!"

"This whole trip will be."

She leans into him, "It already has been."

They shower together and get ready for their day. Jonathan places the grocery order while Faith finishes getting ready. They go to breakfast and then hit the farmers market before returning with their goods, not wanting to leave the food in the car to spoil.

Luckily the grocery order arrives shortly before they leave once again for a destination unknown to Faith. Even though Jonathan told Faith about going on the trip, he has still managed to keep the particulars such as the car, house, and itinerary a surprise, Faith seemed perfectly content with that.

# APTITUDE

The drive is absolutely beautiful. With the top down the warm wind whips through Faith's long brown hair making her come alive in a way Jonathan has never seen before.

The thought occurs to him that he may need to get a convertible for drives like this at home. He smiles watching her thoroughly enjoy their surroundings. The green valleys covered in trees all the way to the hills beyond them rising out of the ground.

Over the next six hours they visit three vineyards, buying multiple bottles of wine from each. All of their landscapes were incredibly beautiful and the majority of the wines were delicious. There were a handful that Faith expressed a slight indifference to.

As Faith took in the sights throughout the day, Jonathan took in the sight of her. Knowing in his heart there was never a man who loved a woman more.

The day could not have been more perfect which gave Jonathan a sense of longing as he drove them home. The sun setting beyond the hills is the perfect back drop. He simply isn't ready for their first full day to end. He realizes that this trip is going to fly by quicker than he is prepared for.

"Is there something wrong, Jonathan?"

"No, why do you ask?"

"You just seem quiet. We had such a beautiful day!"

"We did." He agrees.

"Then what's wrong?"

"I'm good. Really." Jonathan insists.

"Well, as hard as you try, you won't convince me. I know you too well." Faith persists.

"You're a beautiful, incredible, and stubborn woman, Faith Brandt. I love you for all of those things."

"You forgot determined." She says looking at him through her lashes.

"I could never forget how determined you are. I simply forgot to mention it. But then again I couldn't possibly list every single one of your exhaustive attributes."

"So, tell me what could possibly be wrong when we've had such a perfectly amazing day."

"I am merely coming to terms with how quickly this vacation is going to go. I've thoroughly enjoyed being one another's sole focus."

"I have thoroughly enjoyed being you're sole focus." She reaches for his hand, grasping it, their fingers intertwine and she rubs her thumb on the top of his. She gently squeezes his hand and continues, "This vacation is going to go by too quickly, but that simply means we need to enjoy it while we're here living it. Besides, we'll have more vacations to look forward to."

Jonathan smiles, feeling reassured. "You're absolutely right, Faith."

She beams with pride and in a slightly smart ass tone says, "I know."

Jonathan laughs and Faith joins in, then she says, "Thank you for sharing that with me. You always tell me I need to share my feelings with you so that you can try to help. You need to do the same." She raises an eyebrow.

"I know." He concedes.

Back at the house, Jonathan begins cooking dinner while Faith uncorks one of her favorite finds of the day. It came from the smallest vineyard they visited. She pours her and Jonathan each a glass and walks across the cool tile floor handing Jonathan his wine.

"I knew you were going to pick this one." He says after taking a sip.

She narrows her eyes at him playfully and says, "You know me so well."

"I'm so glad that I do. I cannot imagine how significantly different my life would be if I hadn't met you."

"We would have met eventually, you know."

"Maybe not. Jackie and Tom have broken up. There is no guarantee that we would have met before that ended."

"That is true, but it is possible that we would have met some other way."

"Faith, we've both lived in Luna Shores our entire lives and had never met."

"Not that we remember -"

Jonathan interrupts her abruptly by saying, "I would have remembered meeting you."

"Maybe, maybe not."

"There is no maybe not. I definitely would have. Without a single doubt."

"I don't think it's very plausible that we wouldn't have met before last year." She states firmly. "Things happen in just the way they are meant to."

"Yes they do." He pulls her into him and begins kissing her fiercely feeling refreshed by her positive perspective.

When Jonathan finishes making dinner they once again eat out on the deck at the large table.

"This is going to become our nightly ritual." Faith muses.

"With perfect evening weather, how could we not eat out here? It would be horrendous to sit inside and eat."

"Completely horrendous." Faith agrees, laughing.

Later in the week, Jonathan has reservations for a decadent dinner as a celebration of their anniversary. The restaurant has a beautiful outside seating area he requested. Again, Faith has no idea.

When she was packing, Jonathan made sure she had plenty of appropriate clothes for all of their ventures. He however, did not include their anniversary dinner since he wants to take her shopping for the dress she'll wear.

Their evening ends in the pool playfully swimming together, seeing who can do handstands and hold their breath the longest. They compete to see who can swim the fastest from one end to the other. Jonathan pulls her into him, feeling her wet skin pressed against his body makes his insatiable appetite for Faith awaken once more.

Untying the top of the bikini he bought her for Christmas, he attempts to toss it on one of the poolside reclining chairs, but it lands with a wet splat beside it. Next, he reaches for the ties holding the sides of her bottoms together, pulling them simultaneously he releases them. He tosses the bottoms to the same chair, this time it lands on his target.

Faith slips her fingers beneath the band on Jonathan's swim trunks. She pulls them down as she goes under the water to slip them off his feet. Coming back up she throws them to the same chair Jonathan had been aiming for, the trunks land with a large wet splat on the chair.

Faith lets out a giggle and Jonathan reaches around placing his hands on her ass cheeks, lifting her and pulling her into him. He swims over to the side of the pool, leaning against it, he positions her on top of him.

She lets out a faint moan and begins rocking back and forth. She holds on to the edge of the pool. The faster she moves the more waves she creates. Water is splashing all around them and even in between them as she begins to ride her own wave. As her moans of ecstasy get louder Jonathan is pulled with her over that ledge with zero resistance.

The perfect end to their perfect day.

# Chapter 33

# Solitude

*Noun; the quality or state of being alone, or remote from society, seclusion*

The next day, instead of going out to more vineyards and doing additional sight-seeing, Jonathan and Faith decide to have a lazy day in bed, enjoying one another in every way known to man.

The groceries Jonathan ordered are enough to sustain them for the week, even with the change in itinerary. Jonathan's goal today is to lavish Faith in every kind of pleasure, to ignite every single one of her senses, beginning with breakfast in the bath.

Jonathan ran her a nice hot bath before going down stairs to start on their breakfast. Some of the fresh bread and jam is left over from their first night so he uses that for toast. He also makes some scrambled eggs and bacon then brings one large plate upstairs to Faith who's relaxing in the sumptuous bath.

# APTITUDE

"I can't possibly eat that in here!" Faith says surprised that Jonathan is actually serious.

"You can, and you will." He smiles sweetly at her.

She smiles back a little less sweetly. "I don't like being told what to do." Her tone sounding as if she should have her arms folded in indignation.

Jonathan holds back a chuckle. "I'm not trying to tell you what to do. I just want you to experience something entirely different." He pulls the make-up vanity stool up beside the tub and sits.

Holding the large plate in one hand and a fork in another, Jonathan feeds Faith her breakfast. She smiles at him as he takes a bite himself.

"This is delicious." Faith says after Jonathan gives her another bite.

"I want you to know decadence, to feel the opulence you deserve, Faith."

"I am definitely feeling spoiled, Jonathan." She leans over the side of the tub dripping water on the marble floor beneath them and kisses him.

"That is exactly what I'm going for. This would be better with candles, but I couldn't find any."

"No, I suppose not. The owners would not want this place accidentally burned down."

Jonathan laughs and Faith gives him a look.

"I'm serious. A house fire isn't something to joke about."

"I know, Faith." Jonathan says in a serious tone. "I'm sorry. I shouldn't have laughed." Thinking for a moment he asks, "Have you ever had a house fire?"

"No, I haven't, but Jackie did. It was so horrible to watch her have to go through that. They lost everything. Her parents weren't great caregivers before that, they were even worse after."

"I'm so sorry to hear that. Do they know how it started?"

"We were in first grade I think, so I don't remember or maybe wasn't even told the details." Faith looks down at her hands under the water. "It's not something Jackie talks much about."

"OK. I won't bring it up then."

"Thanks." She smiles up at him.

"Another bite?"

"Please."

He loads the fork with some scrambled eggs and slides it gingerly into her mouth as she parts her lips. The act of feeding someone can be quite sensuous. Jonathan then takes a bite for himself.

Faith looks at the plate and then at Jonathan. She asks, "When are you going to be ready to join me?" She smiles flirtatiously at him.

Standing abruptly Jonathan sets the plate down on the counter and unties his robe. "I'm ready if you are!"

Faith giggles and scoots forward in the bathtub so that Jonathan has space to sit down. "The water is surprisingly still warm."

"We can always let some out and add more hot water when needed." Jonathan says as he steps into the water.

"That's true."

After their sensual bath, Jonathan and Faith have that air hockey rematch he was waiting for. This time Jonathan wins. Faith is also a gracious loser and congratulates him with a kiss. He pulls her into him feeling the silk beneath his hands. He runs them over her curves. She leans in to his ear and whispers, "You're giving me goosebumps."

"I want to give you more than that."

Faith giggles and kisses him harder. She feels his excitement grow against her as their kiss becomes even more passionate. Jonathan scoops her up and walks with her over to the soft brown sofa set against the far wall.

Faith straddles him and says, "You didn't get enough in the bathtub?"

"I could never get enough of you, Faith. Ever."

"Thank you." She leans in and kisses his cheek, then moves to his ear, then down to his neck.

He feels his breath coming quicker and deeper. Having her on top of him is only making him want to take her even more. The thin silk between them is simply adding to Jonathan's arousal.

He gingerly unties her robe revealing her nakedness. She moves her arms to pull them from the robe's sleeves. Then Faith tosses it to the seat next to them. Jonathan adjusts to uncover himself so he can feel her body on top of his.

At lunch time, Jonathan and Faith eat their lunch, a chicken cob salad, out on the deck with their robes back on.

"This has been the best vacation ever." Jonathan says.

"It's been our only vacation." Faith half rolls her eyes.

"So far. We'll have many more."

"They'll all be this amazing?" She asks.

"If I have anything to say about it, of course they will be."

"This life of ours, it's splendidly amazing." Faith says in awe of everything to come for them.

Jonathan places a hand on her knee. "It truly is." He leans into her and kisses her cheek.

Once they finish their lunch they go for a dip in the pool then move into the hot tub.

"This place is absolutely perfect, Jonathan."

"I'm glad you like it."

Faith looks around taking in the view and surrounding vineyard. Sitting beside Jonathan relaxing in the hot tub she can't imagine being anywhere else in the world.

They watch the sunset from the deck as they eat their dinner. This time Jonathan made garlic butter steak bites over whole grain pasta with green beans.

"You definitely spoil me, Jonathan."

"You so deserve it, Faith."

He smiles at her and she feels the same butterflies she did when they first met at Lee's pub when she was trying to order drinks for Jackie and herself. That moment nearly a year ago changed their lives forever.

"So, what's the plan for tomorrow?" Faith asks curiously.

"I was thinking we should try a different place for breakfast."

"OK…"

"Then we should go hike in the Robert Louis Stevenson State Park. There's miles of trails, rock climbing, and we can even hike to the top of Mt. St. Helena!"

"That sounds amazing!"

"We'll need to pack plenty of water and food."

"Definitely."

"Then I think we'll go out to dinner somewhere pretty casual so we don't have to come all the way back here to shower and get ready."

"OK!" Faith can easily imagine the day they'll have tomorrow and she's excited. She's loving the intimacy of today, but getting out and seeing more of the area sounds absolutely incredible.

When they finish eating, they end their day by curling up on the large cushy couch in the family room to snuggle and watch a movie. First though, Faith video calls her parents to talk to Zeke for the first time. She feels a bit guilty about it. They missed the first Sunday dinner in years, so calling now seems like the right thing to do. Hope has already gone home for the night. Diane mentions how strange it was to just be the three of them with Zeke and how she should have made less food, but there are plenty of left overs. Zeke doesn't seem to understand what's happening, but he's excited to hear Faith's voice none-the-less.

Faith doesn't want to keep her parents up too late since she hadn't taken the time difference into account when making the call. She reassures herself that Zeke is doing well and that going on this vacation, and others in the future, means he'll be fine then as well.

She snuggles into Jonathan as he pushes the button to start the movie grateful for the technology that allowed her to see Zeke even with being so far away.

# Chapter 34

# Finitude

### Noun; finite quality or state

"How did you find this place?" Faith asks Jonathan with a smile on her face. She gathers a bite of her meat lover's omelet on her fork then slips it in her mouth.

Jonathan smiles with a hint of pride in his eyes. "I just looked up the best breakfast places in town and this was number one on multiple lists."

The restaurant was quaint and very busy. Faith and Jonathan were lucky to arrive when there was a lull, for people just now coming there is over an hour wait. Faith notices many people choosing to leave after being told that.

"The food is amazing." Faith says after swallowing the bite she just took.

"The service has been really good too!"

Faith takes a sip of her mimosa. "It has been."

The waitress comes to the table and asks Faith, "Would you like another?" motioning towards her mimosa glass.

"I probably shouldn't. We're going hiking."

"Juice then? Or maybe water?"

"I'll have a water. Thank you so much!"

Before Faith knows it the waitress has already returned with a fresh glass of water.

When they've finished their breakfast, Jonathan drives them to the state park. The drive is longer than Faith had thought it would be. She honestly didn't know how long it should take, but was under the assumption it was closer.

The drive is extremely beautiful, however, and Faith knew the hike would be more than worth the time in the car. Jonathan had put the top down and the wind felt exhilarating whipping through her hair. Luckily, she already had it up in a ponytail or it would be quite a mess by the time they got to the park.

She remembers the first hike they went on together, it was at Silverwood State Park, and it was the day Jonathan officially asked her to be his girlfriend. For a split second she allows her mind to wander into thinking he may propose here, but she stops herself before those thoughts can get too far out of hand. Expecting it to happen on New Year's caused her unnecessary feelings of angst and doubt. She doesn't want to put herself through any of that again.

Faith was managing to keep those thoughts at bay surrounding this entire trip. It wasn't easy, but she simply reminded herself of what Jonathan told her when they discussed her feelings about him not asking yet. *They have a lot on their plates and don't need to add more to it.* That's what Jonathan said, and really nothing has changed, so why would she think a proposal would be coming?

Faith doesn't notice Jonathan looking at her, but it snaps her from her thoughts when he asks, "Faith, where did you go?"

"Huh?" She blinks. "Oh, I was just thinking of Silverwood and how nice it would be to take Zeke hiking there. I think he'd love it." *It wasn't a total lie.*

"That is a fantastic idea." Jonathan smiles. "Are we ready?" He asks.

"Yeah, I think so."

Jonathan parks the car in the parking lot off the highway. Then he grabs their backpacks from the trunk. He hands Faith hers as he slips his arms into the straps. Luckily the house had a few more supplies than they had listed. In the mudroom cabinets Jonathan found these backpacks along with flashlights and a first aid kit. Faith made the sandwiches they would be having for lunch and they both filled the packs with the necessary supplies.

After consulting the map, Faith and Jonathan find the trailhead for the Mount Saint Helena peak trail which actually begins with a staircase. Faith couldn't imagine not doing that while they're here. From what she'd looked up at breakfast the views are breathtaking.

The water bottles are making the packs heavier than Faith thought they would be. As they consume them on their hike, they'll squish the bottles down and put them back in their backpacks.

The terrain is a bit more rocky and harder to navigate than Silverwood had been, but Faith and Jonathan both manage just fine. She's simply happy Jonathan had told her to bring the shoes she's wearing. They're nothing special, but they are comfortable for long hikes like this and are pretty good on slightly slippery ground.

The first portion of the trail is nicely shaded. They come across the monument to Robert Louis Stevenson and Faith takes pictures. After the first mile, Jonathan and Faith find themselves no longer surrounded by trees, but instead surrounded by vistas.

They arrive at Bubble Rock and watch a handful of people climb to the top. After that, they hike a bit longer before they reach a clearing and decide this is the perfect place to eat their lunch. Neither of them packed a blanket or anything to sit on, but luckily there are large boulders speckled with manzanita that make great chairs.

While they eat, Jonathan consults the map, showing Faith where they currently are and how much further it is to the peak. They're just below the south peak. The north peak is another couple of miles ahead.

Jonathan points out that in order to get to the south peak they will need to take a side trail. He also mentions that the trail does not circle around so they will have to come back the same way they came up the mountain.

Faith takes in their surroundings. They haven't seen too many other hikers, but they have been passed by mountain bikers going either direction. They've all been very courteous and announce their presence or say hello. It's refreshing to be out here in nature. She's grateful to be here on a weekday since she's certain it's a much busier location on the weekends.

Jonathan takes a swig of his water then nudges Faith. "What are you thinking about?" He asks curiously.

"I'm just grateful to be here with you. This has got to be," she gestures to their surroundings, "one of the most beautiful places on earth."

"I want to show you them all, Faith."

She smiles. "I'm so glad you do!"

"I'm so glad that you're basically game for anything. It makes things easy."

"I just enjoy life. Whatever it may have in store for me is better than the alternative."

Slightly confused Jonathan asks, "What's the alternative?"

"Being dead."

Feeling kind of idiotic for not realizing that's what she was referring to he says, "Oh, duh."

Faith rubs his back reassuringly holding back a giggle.

"You can laugh." Jonathan says, chuckling at himself.

Faith can't hold it in any longer. With his permission she laughs at his momentary absentmindedness.

"It happens to us all sometimes."

"It does and the best thing we can do for ourselves is not take this all too seriously."

"That's so true." She says still laughing a little.

"Are we ready to get to the south peak?"

"Yes!"

They both stand and reposition their packs on their backs. Faith takes one more look around where they were sitting to be sure they don't leave any garbage behind. She finds only crumbs which she brushes off of the rock they were sitting on.

The south peak is easy enough to climb for the both of them. The views are beautiful with the clear blue sky above them and the various shades of green surrounding them. This place looks like heaven on earth to Faith, almost as if there would be gnomes, fairies, and sprites hiding in the large leaves or holes in the trees. If she looks hard enough she may discover the magical forest they inhabit.

"It's pretty cool to imagine that the entire earth was once untouched like this." Jonathan says in awe of what lies before them.

"That is cool to think about. I was just imagining that there would be little magical beings hiding in here."

Jonathan furrows his brow and repeats, "Little magical beings? Like what exactly?"

"Gnomes, and fairies, and sprites."

"That's an interesting thought, Faith." He says slowly.

"Did you enjoy playing pretend when you were a kid?"

Jonathan's voice is low as he says, "I sometimes have a hard time remembering my childhood."

Faith's heart sinks understanding why that could be. Before she can stop herself she asks, "Have you ever thought about going to therapy to help you with any of that stuff?"

# APTITUDE

A mix of surprise and pain flashes on Jonathan's face. Faith instantly regrets asking and is silently scolding herself as he softly says, "You think I need therapy?"

"That isn't what I meant, Jonathan. I'm so sorry if that's how it sounded."

He thinks for a moment and then says, "I think I've done a pretty good job of managing all that happened, considering."

"You have. There are resources out there now that you may not have had access to before that may help you, though."

Jonathan sternly says, "I don't have the time for any of that."

Faith decides this isn't a conversation they should be having right now and simply answers, "OK." And then promptly drops the subject entirely.

They stand on the peak in silence for a few moments before Jonathan sighs heavily and shakes his head as if he's trying to shake thoughts away. Then he says, "Should we go see what the north peak has in store for us?"

"That's a fantastic idea." Faith tries to force a genuine smile, but she can feel that it falls flat.

Jonathan doesn't seem to notice and starts off back down the trail. He slows down and reaches for Faith's hand. He takes another deep breath and runs his fingers through his sandy brown hair.

Normally, Faith absolutely loves it when he does that, but this time the reasoning behind it seems a little more emotional than it typically is and it unintentionally makes her feel guilty for being the reason for it.

In Faith's mind, everyone has something that therapy can help with. The negative connotation that used to be associated with it is lessening all the time, as it should. She feels like she should have known Jonathan wasn't going to be receptive and that it may even possibly make him take pause. She's really wishing she either approached it differently, or hadn't brought it up at all.

Faith reasons that she was caught off guard by what he said. He's never mentioned not being able to remember his childhood to her before.

As they hike on, the trail turns into a main fire road, and the grade gets steeper letting them know they are nearing the summit. Despite Faith's guilt her excitement grows. Maybe she is imagining it, but she feels like Jonathan is becoming more excited as well.

Reaching the summit has them both feeling a huge sense of accomplishment. It isn't every day you climb a mountain figuratively or in actuality.

Standing on an area that seems to jut out, Jonathan places his arms around Faith while standing behind her so that they can both see the vast views in front of them. Faith breathes in the fresh air and tries to locate anything in the distance that would be familiar, but comes up with nothing.

He kisses the top of her head and rests his chin on it.

"I love this." Faith says as she holds his arms that are wrapped around her.

"Me too, Faith."

She worries because there is a hint of pain in his voice still and wonders if she should apologize for what she said.

Jonathan moves, and begins to turn to a different side of the mountain top, then he grabs her hand as he does so that she follows him.

"It's absolutely incredible. Thank you for bringing me here, Jonathan."

"You're welcome, Faith. I'm glad to be here with you. It makes me happy that we can experience things like this together."

"Me too."

They stay at the summit for a little while before venturing back down the trail. The hike back goes faster since they aren't looking at their surroundings quite as much. There are still things that they notice, however, making it a spectacular hike back still.

By the time they reach the stairs that lead back down to the parking area, Jonathan seems to be back to his normal self, almost as if the therapy comment never came out of Faith's mouth.

Jonathan puts the top down once again and drives them to a small barbeque place in a little town nearby.

"This place is definitely casual." Faith says as she takes a drink of her vodka lemonade.

"That's what we were going for, right?"

"It's perfect." She practically shouts over the music.

In truth, the restaurant has some similarities to a bar. As soon as they pulled into the parking lot she felt the unease sink into her stomach. She pushed those feelings away and held Jonathan's hand as they entered.

The interior is brightly lit and the food smells amazing. Faith keeps reminding herself that she's safe, that Jonathan wouldn't let anything happen to her, and that the men who caused this angst are locked away.

"Are you doing OK?" Jonathan asks suddenly.

Faith takes a deep breath. "It's reminding me of a bar a little. I'm doing OK though. I'm excited for the food."

"It's alright." Jonathan takes her hand across the table. "I'm here. No one will hurt you. They'd rather be dead than try." He says, his eyes dark.

Faith smiles feeling reassured with his words. She squeezes his hand. "Thank you, Jonathan."

"Anything for you, Faith." He squeezes back.

Once the food is delivered to the table, Faith finds herself relaxing. Lee's pub has food, but it's mostly just pizza or club sandwiches. Nothing like this.

She looks down at her plate of pulled pork, corn bread, and mac and cheese. Then glances at Jonathan's. He got the brisket. Once he's taken his first bite, he offers some to Faith.

"That is delicious!"

"How's yours?" He asks.

"You want to try?"

"Of course I do." He says it as if she should already know. Faith shares hers with him as well.

# APTITUDE

Dinner was amazing, they sat and had another drink each before heading back to the house. The drive home was different with the sun already set and the dark looming in the trees.

When they pull into the driveway, they see the house is brightly lit making them both feel safer. They haven't spent enough time there yet to know where all of the light switches and things are.

With the exhaustion from the day weighing on them, they go upstairs to the primary bedroom right away.

When Faith walks out of the bathroom, Jonathan is waiting for her with nothing on. He pulls her in tightly, first hugging her, then he leans down to kiss her. Faith feels every ounce of worry leave her body as Jonathan kisses her harder.

He walks her over to the edge of the bed. She sits down and Jonathan begins removing her pants, but they get stuck around her ankles. Faith lets out a giggle and asks, "Would you like some help?"

"No, I can do it." He says stubbornly as he yanks her pants off so forcefully he stumbles back a bit.

Faith giggles again.

Jonathan steadies himself and says, "Is something funny?"

"Yes! You are! You're hilarious!"

"I was definitely going for something other than hilarious."

"Oh yeah? What was that?"

He places himself over her half naked body and replies in a low voice, "Sexy, irresistible, tempting, alluring, or seductive to name a few."

Putting her hands on his cheeks she says, "Oh, my dear, you are all of those things." Then she pulls his face to hers kissing him fiercely.

# Chapter 35

## *Similitude*

*Noun; an imaginative comparison, simile*

They slowly awaken to the soft sound of raindrops hitting the window panes on the door that leads out to the balcony. Jonathan quickly realizes that any plans he had for today will need to either be changed drastically, or saved for a different day.

"Good morning, handsome." He hears Faith say, taking him away from his train of thought.

"Good morning, beautiful." He smiles and then kisses her forehead.

Faith looks out the window. "I guess it's a rainy day in today." She snuggles in closer to him.

"What would you like to do today?"

"This is a great start I think." Faith says running her fingers over his chest.

"What about cuddling on the couch and watching movies all day?"

"Do we have to get dressed?"

"I don't see why we would."

"Then that sounds absolutely perfect."

"How about some breakfast first?"

"That's a great idea."

They both slip on their robes and go down the grand staircase. Jonathan begins making eggs and cinnamon rolls. Faith heads into the study to see if there might be a book that interests her.

"That smells delicious." Faith says with a grin as she walks into the kitchen holding a dark covered book.

"Thank you!" Eyeing the book Jonathan asks, "What do you have there?"

"Just a book. I thought I might read a little. The library in there is kind of crazy! I'd love to have something like that in our office!"

"Consider it done!"

After breakfast, they curl up on the couch in the family room and watch a movie, snuggling under one of the large plush blankets that are kept in a basket next to the fireplace.

When the first movie finishes, Jonathan decides to light the fireplace. With the rain there seems to be a chill in the air today. Jonathan starts another movie, this one a romantic comedy neither of them have seen, but had talked about wanting to see in the theater.

Faith smiles when she sees what he's selected.

"I had heard this was a good one."

"Me too."

"Jackie and Tom saw it when it came out. Before they broke up, obviously."

"What are your thoughts on that? I don't think we've talked about it at all."

"This stays between us?"

"Yes, of course." Jonathan pauses the start of the movie.

"OK then. I think that Tom wasn't giving Jackie what she wanted even after she directly asked for it. If he wanted to keep her he could have." Faith brushes the hair away from her face. "What are your thoughts?"

"I agree with what you're saying, I just wish it didn't have to end for them. They seemed so good together otherwise."

"The way things seem is rarely ever how they actually are."

"That's true."

"I simply want Jackie to be happy. Tom wasn't doing that for her. I'm sure that someday she eventually will find the person who belongs with her."

"Like we have."

"Exactly."

Faith lays her head on Jonathan's shoulder and he takes that as a sign that the conversation is finished. He un-pauses the movie and pulls the blanket up around her shoulders, leaving his arm around her.

At a really funny part of the movie, Jonathan chuckles. He doesn't hear anything from Faith. When he looks down he finds her asleep with her head laying on his chest. He pauses the movie and closes his eyes as well.

Faith slowly opens her eyes, the glow from the fire is the only thing lighting the room. Through the sliding glass doors, comes a bright flash of light igniting the entire space quickly then turning dark as fast as it came. Thunder roars off in the distance bouncing off of the hills surrounding them.

Jonathan blinks and rubs his eyes trying to clear the sleep away.

"How long were we napping?" Faith asks.

Jonathan checks the time on his phone. "A couple of hours."

"That flew by. It's so dark now."

"I think it's just because of the storm."

"Probably."

"Would you like some lunch?"

"I would, yes."

Jonathan gets up and walks into the kitchen to make them sandwiches. Faith turns towards him still sitting on the couch and says, "Did you finish the movie?"

"No." Jonathan chuckles. "I saw you were asleep and decided that was a splendid idea. I paused the movie and took a nap as well."

"We can start it over while we're eating, if you want." Faith suggests.

"Would it be too early to have some wine with the sandwiches?"

"No, not too early at all." Faith says as Jonathan reaches for one of the bottles they brought back from a winery the other day. He opens it, walks to the cabinet and grabs a couple of glasses then pours them each one.

He takes the plate and glass to Faith, setting it down on the coffee table in front of them. Then he goes back to grab his own.

He sits back down next to Faith, placing the blanket back over himself.

"This sandwich is really good. Thank you, Jonathan."

"You're welcome. I'm glad you're enjoying it. It's just a sandwich." Jonathan shrugs his shoulders as he pushes the button to turn the movie back on.

"You make the best food." She smiles at him and then takes another bite of her sandwich.

Faith watches the start of the movie that she's seen already, feeling so cozy and safe in Jonathan's arms. She looks up at him, the features of his face are highlighted perfectly by the glowing firelight. Her heart fills with happiness and pride. Being here with him, on vacation, is more than she hoped for.

With him working so much they've never really gotten this kind of quality time together. When they have a free weekend together it never feels this easy to connect because real life is still just on the outside, waiting to come back in with a vengeance.

Here, though, it's only the two of them. They don't have things they need to get done and the setting is entirely different making it feel as though it's a completely altered life.

There is a nagging feeling of how badly reality will slap her in the face when they return to Luna Shores on Monday, but for now she shoves those feelings way down in hopes they don't try to resurface until they're on the plane home.

She can only hope that their lives will mirror this someday. Possibly when they're in their new home, or maybe after they're retired and the kids are all out of the house. For now, she chooses to cherish this time with Jonathan since all of those things seem so far off in the future right now.

# Chapter 36

# Multitude
*Noun; the state of being many*

The bacon sizzling on the stove fills the air with the aroma, mixing with the coffee Jonathan has brewing, it's bringing back childhood memories for Faith. These two distinct smells were an every Sunday morning thing at home. She smiles to herself as she watches Jonathan cooking breakfast.

She briefly recalls his mention yesterday of not being able to remember much from his childhood. Faith has resolved to not bring up therapy again. As far as she can see, he has done a wonderful job dealing with everything life threw at him at such a young age. He certainly doesn't need to drudge up those feelings from so long ago.

Jonathan turns from the stove and smiles at Faith. She's sitting in the breakfast nook getting the plates and forks set out. She returns his smile. The bright sunlight coming through the large windows fills the room as does the music Jonathan turned on when he started making breakfast.

"Come here, Faith."

She walks over to him. He places his arms around her and begins swaying back and forth.

"Dancing in the kitchen?" She smiles up at him.

"Always. It's as good a place as any."

"Yes it is."

The song finishes and so does the coffee. Faith brings two mugs to the brewer and fills them, adding a bit of sugar and creamer. She hands Jonathan his, then takes a sip of her own. The warm liquid feels smooth and invigorating.

"I'd say coffee is probably tied at the number one spot with wine." Faith says amused.

"Yeah, but one is appropriate at any point in the day, while the other typically is not."

"That's true. Unless it's brunch, then you can have champagne with your orange juice." She giggles.

"Or pineapple juice." Jonathan offers.

"Those were so delicious!" Suddenly remembering the mimosas Jonathan made on New Year's morning. "That was only a little over four months ago, but it feels like so much longer!"

"It really does. That reminds me, we should do a video call with Michael today."

"That's a good idea. What is the plan for today anyway?"

"Well…" Jonathan wants to stall, but at this point he's not sure how to. He turns to the stove and flips the pancakes. "There is something I have planned for tomorrow night that you'll need a new dress for. Rather than feeling rushed to

# APTITUDE

get it done tomorrow before-hand I thought we could go shopping for that today."

Faith's face lights up! "We're going shopping?!"

"Yes, we are."

"Are you also getting something new?"

"I might, but this shopping is more for you."

"I'd like it if we can both try things on."

"OK, but some stores cater to women and won't even have a men's department. I won't try on any dresses." He says with a smirk while shaking his head.

"No, as amusing as that would be, I don't think the sales people would appreciate that."

"Only if it lead to a sale."

"That's true." They both laugh. Faith is having a hard time picturing Jonathan wearing a dress.

After breakfast, they shower together and Faith gets ready while Jonathan looks up some stores for them to shop at.

She runs her fingers through her hair and asks, "You mentioned a dress, is there a budget for this dress?"

"No budget."

"OK, then." She tries to wrangle in her thoughts of all the possibilities this special thing is that he has planned, but fails miserably.

"Do you want there to be a budget?"

"Well, it's only fair if there's no budget for you either then."

"OK. There's no budget for me either." Jonathan smiles at her insistence. She always has a way of getting exactly what she wants. Then again, he is more than happy to give her exactly that.

He has a plan and a rough map of where they'll be heading once Faith emerges from the bathroom ready for the day.

She is wearing navy blue cotton shorts and a short sleeve white shirt. "I wanted something that would be easy to take on and off.

"Very important thing to think about when you know you're going to be trying on clothes."

"It is!" She looks at Jonathan who is wearing his jeans and a button up short sleeve shirt with a pair of brown flip flops.

"Sandals is a good idea." She goes into the closet and finds a comfortable pair that can slip on and off easily. "OK. I think I'm ready now."

"Then let's go." Jonathan smiles and gestures towards the door.

At the first store, Faith tries on three dresses, not loving any of them. There is no men's department, so Jonathan doesn't try anything. The sales people were helpful, but Faith is unsure of what to wear.

She wants to ask more questions for a bit of clarity as to what they'll be doing, but is thinking Jonathan won't want to divulge too much. "Can you give me any hints that might help me pick something out? I feel like I don't know enough about what we're doing or where we're going."

"Well, a sundress would be too casual, but a full length dress would be a little too much. I'd suggest a cocktail dress.

I'll leave the level of sexy up to you." He smiles slightly mischievously.

"The level of sexy? Huh...OK." She giggles at the way he worded it.

On the way to the next store, they video call Michael. He walks them through the house excitedly. Everything has been roughed in and the house is looking even more like a home.

The next couple of stores prove fruitless, so they decide to have lunch and then go to another store which has both men's and women's clothing, but is neither of their styles.

Next, they go to the last store that Jonathan has planned, there are both men's and women's departments, so they venture to the women's area first. Faith picks out four dresses, then they go to the men's department and Jonathan picks out a couple pairs of dress pants and a couple of shirts. He also finds two ties he would like to try with them.

They head into their respective dressing rooms, luckily the store has them directly across from one another. With it being a Wednesday afternoon they aren't very busy which is also nice.

Jonathan comes out of his dressing room and waits for Faith to come out in her first dress. When she emerges the dress doesn't look quite right at the shoulders. She points to the back and asks, "Can you please zip this? I was having a hard time."

"Of course I can!"

Faith turns and Jonathan slowly zips up the dress, admiring his girlfriend's bare back for as many moments as he can. He then leans down and kisses her neck.

Faith steps forward and turns in front of him. He absolutely loves the dress. She pulls him with her over to the mirror to look at themselves.

Leaning back she looks at his ass and says, "Those pants make your ass look amazing."

"That dress fits you perfectly." He smiles admiring her curves.

"It's not too much?" She asks while pulling at it to adjust it.

"Not at all. I think it's perfect."

"You're just tired of shopping." She says with a laugh.

"With you? Never. I could shop with you all day."

"You basically have." She laughs even more.

"That is true. It was a day well spent."

"Lunch was quite delicious as well."

"It should have been. That's where I'd ordered dinner from the very first night we were here." He smiles then asks, "What do you think of this shirt?"

"I really like that color on you."

It's a grey shirt with light blue and purple pin striping. The tie he has on with it is a light purple which enhances that color in the shirt even more.

Her dress is black satin with subtle purple embellishments. The two outfits go quite well together especially with Jonathan's black pants.

# APTITUDE

"I don't think I need to try any more dresses on."

Faith watches Jonathan's face in the mirror as his smile widens. "You look absolutely incredible, Faith. I'm not just saying that. I've had the best day shopping with you."

"So, we have our outfits for tomorrow?"

"Once we check out, yup!"

The sales lady comes up to them. "You both look so stunning! May I ask what you're celebrating?"

"Our first anniversary is coming up." Jonathan says simply.

"Oh! Congratulations!"

"Thank you, we're here on vacation."

"It's beautiful, isn't it?" She asks.

Faith smiles thinking of the wineries and the hike, "It is magical."

"Well, I'm so glad you two came in today! I can get these wrapped up for you if you're ready."

Jonathan responds, "Yes, we'll take these."

Jonathan and Faith both turn to return to their dressing rooms. When they emerge with their new outfits they hand them to the sales woman.

"They'll be waiting for you up front when you're ready." She smiles.

"Thank you." Faith smiles at her.

"Did you want to look at anything else?" Jonathan asks as the sales woman walks away with the merchandise.

"I've got my black wedges that will work with the dress and I think my little black purse will work well. I don't think I need to look at anything else. Do you want to?"

"I've also got shoes, so I'm fine too."

Once they've paid for their new outfits, they head back to the car and Jonathan drives them back to the rental house. Faith can't help, but let her mind wander to what he has instore for them tomorrow.

"What time are we doing whatever it is you have planned tomorrow?" She asks him curiously.

"Well, I don't have anything planned for the majority of the day. That way you can take your time getting ready. We will want to leave the house around six though."

"OK." She assumes they'll be going to dinner. He could have other plans after dinner, though.

When they get back to the house, Jonathan starts making them dinner. He prepares the steaks and gets them on the grill, then he starts getting the veggie kabobs ready.

Faith watches him intently as she sips her wine from the breakfast nook.

"You really like sitting there while I cook, don't you?"

"It's pretty cozy and you look so sexy in there cooking. It's not the island at the condo, but it works nearly as well."

"Do you miss home?"

"I miss Zeke."

"Me too. I'm sure he misses you too. Did you want to video call him? Dinner won't be done for a little bit yet."

"OK, I'll do that." Faith smiles.

She calls her parents via video and sees Zeke bound over to the sound of her voice wagging his tail excitedly.

"How has he been?" She asks Frank and Diane.

Diane smiles, "He's been so good. He's super smart, Faith."

"Yeah, he hasn't had any accidents and even goes to the door when he has to go potty." Frank adds.

"That's awesome." The fact that he's doing that makes her heart swell, but also pains it with the realization of what all she's missing out on.

"How's your vacation so far?" Frank asks excitedly.

"It's been great! We went shopping today. Jonathan has a surprise planned for tomorrow."

"He's always full of surprises." Diane says smiling.

"Yes, he definitely is." Faith smiles back.

Jonathan pokes his head into the frame of the phone screen and waves. "I hear you guys talking about me."

"Nothing bad." Frank says.

"Never anything bad." Diane adds.

Jonathan chuckles. "That's reassuring. How are you guys doing?"

"We're doing great. It's been very nice having Zeke here with us. It's actually made us question if we want to get a dog for ourselves." Frank says.

"Really? Now you're going to get a dog? Hope and I begged all throughout our childhood." Faith says in disbelief.

"Well honey, times were harder then. Now the café is more of a well-oiled machine. Especially with Hope doing the majority of the day to day at this point. It gives us more time to be home taking care of a dog." Diane explains.

"I'm just giving you crap. It's funny though because Hope and I were talking about that on my birthday. I think a dog would be great for you guys."

"We're still mulling it over." Diane says.

Jonathan goes outside to check the steaks on the grill and Faith finishes the call with her parents and Zeke.

The kabobs go on the grill and a few moments later they're eating dinner.

"Are you glad you called them?"

"Yes. It was really good to see them and Zeke. It does make me miss him more, though."

"I can see how that would be."

"Don't get me wrong, I am thoroughly enjoying our vacation and I'm grateful for all of the things you've done and planned to make it all possible."

"Thank you, Faith. I understand that you missing Zeke doesn't mean you wish you weren't here with me."

"Right. I'd hate for you to feel like I don't appreciate any of this."

"I don't feel that way at all."

Faith takes a bite of her delicious steak thinking about how lucky she is.

# Chapter 37

## Plentitude

*Noun; the quality or state of being full, completeness*

Faith and Jonathan enjoy a relaxing morning, going swimming and reveling in the company of one another and the better weather. Faith spends an hour or so getting ready before they have to leave to get to whatever Jonathan has planned for them for the evening.

Jonathan is leaning up against the doorway to the bathroom, he's been watching Faith do her hair and makeup for the past fifteen minutes. A smile spreads across his face. "You're so beautiful, Faith."

"Thank you, Jonathan."

She turns to look at him and returns the smile. She breathes in deeply taking in the sight of him in his black dress pants, shirt and tie. He looks so damn handsome and sexy. For a moment she imagines not going out at all, and just staying in, but is too excited to see what Jonathan has planned to even seriously consider it.

After she finishes her hair and makeup she goes to the closet where the dress is hanging. She takes the black silk robe off and puts the dress on. Jonathan is watching her every move with a dark look in his eyes as if he wants to devour her right here and now. She smiles at the thought and puts her black strappy heals on.

The drive isn't long, and Jonathan doesn't insist on Faith wearing a blind fold. He pulls into the parking lot of a restaurant called Cashmere. Faith is practically bouncing in her seat with excitement.

"Do you know this place?" Jonathan asks.

"No. It looks really nice, though."

"It is. I've had these reservations for four months. They book out pretty far."

"Four months? That's crazy."

"Yeah, but from what I hear, it's completely worth it."

Jonathan pulls up to the valet who opens the door for Faith. They walk into the restaurant taken aback by the old time money feel of the décor. It has a feeling of opulent superiority. The walls are covered entirely in white marble with a rich dark stained wood trim. The table tops are black marble with large round wood bases in the center.

They are seated immediately at a semi-private table outside in the corner of the exterior seating area. The lighting is low creating a feeling of intimacy. Faith looks around at the other couples who are dining here tonight. She almost feels as if she doesn't fit in. They all look overly comfortable with this sophisticated level of quality fine dining, whereas she feels like a fish out of water. She only hopes that it isn't noticeable.

Next, she looks at the menu. The maître d brings them each a goblet filled with ice water. Faith picks it up to take a sip feeling the heaviness of the glass.

"Do you know what you want to order?" Jonathan asks as he considers the menu as well.

"Not yet. Do you?"

"Not yet, but I think I have it narrowed down."

They both continue looking until the waiter comes to take their order.

"We'll take a bottle of the 1974 Robert Mondavi Reserve Cabernet Sauvignon and the masa toro with caviar to start please." Jonathan notices Faith's eyes go wide.

After the waiter walks away Faith leans in over the table and whispers, "Caviar?"

"Have you ever had it before?"

"No. It's extremely expensive."

"I figured there was no better time to try it."

"Wait. You've never had it either?" Faith starts to laugh.

"No. We can try it together." Jonathan says while trying to figure out what she finds so funny.

"What if neither of us likes it?"

"I've always heard good things. I don't see how that would be possible."

"Maybe they just say good things so people who don't know better will pay the money."

"I don't think that's it, Faith." Jonathan laughs at the idea and at how silly she's being.

The waiter brings the bottle of wine, presents it to them, and pours a little in their glasses for them to taste. After Jonathan takes a sip and nods, the waiter continues the pour, then they order their main dish.

Faith clears her throat. "I'll have the A5 Aragawa style Wagyu strip loin please."

Jonathan smiles at her and then says, "I will take the ten ounce Kobe tenderloin."

They both hand the waiter their menus.

Jonathan is half chuckling as he asks Faith, "Are you doing OK?"

"There's a bit of sticker shock looking at that menu."

"We aren't in Luna Shores." He chuckles a little more.

"Not even Caulfield has any restaurants that compare to this."

"No, but we're on vacation, and we are celebrating. What better way to do it than to enjoy an amazing meal?"

"That is true, I suppose."

Raising his glass, Jonathan says, "To us, to our first year of many together. And to our future and all of the incredible things it has in store."

They gently clink their glasses together and then take a sip of the wine.

A few moments later the waiter brings their appetizer. Faith isn't sure what to think, but is open to trying it.

# APTITUDE

Jonathan does the honors and dips the grilled bread in, scooping up a bit of the toro and caviar. He then lets her take the first bite.

The flavors dance well together on her taste buds. She watches Jonathan take his first bite, happy that he ordered this for them to share.

"What do you think?" She asks.

"It's different, but delicious."

"Can't ask for much more than that."

"No, you can't. I'd probably order it again if the opportunity presented itself."

"I'd eat it with you again." She smiles at him feeling grateful for him pushing her out of her comfort zone.

A few moments after they've finished their appetizer and the waiter brings their main entrees.

Both plates look like pieces of art with the steaks as the main focus. It's as if the sautéed mushrooms, truffle mashed potatoes, and jus are simply there only to highlight the cut of meat. Faith and Jonathan are both happy with their choices and take their first bites simultaneously.

"Mmmm." Faith doesn't realize she's just let that come out of her mouth until she sees Jonathan smile at her.

"It's that good, isn't it? Mine too."

"I think they're similar aren't they?"

"Yeah, I really wanted a larger cut which is why I ultimately chose this."

Faith tries the truffle mashed potatoes and is pleasantly surprised by their flavor. They are extra creamy with an almost earthy flavor. "Do you know that I have eaten some of the best meals I've ever had with you?"

"That's surprising considering your mom is an amazing cook."

"Yeah, but it's not like she was making anything like this!"

"That's true. Sometimes, those home cooked meals make these pale in comparison."

"They do. I will say that I missed being at their house on Sunday for dinner."

"I did too. It's so nice how they've all, in their own way, accepted me into the family."

"I was never worried."

Jonathan raises his eye brow. "Not even with Hope?"

"Not really. Maybe just that first dinner." Faith laughs lightly.

"I was worried about getting on Hope's good side."

"Really? I never knew."

"Well, I wasn't trying to show it."

"No, I suppose not. I knew she would ultimately warm up to you."

"I'm glad she has. She's a good sister."

"She is." Faith looks down at her plate while getting her next bite ready on her fork. She thinks about how Hope had knocked the guy out at the café. She was always protective. There was no way to know that that stranger was going to retaliate by trying to drug Faith and do who knows what to her.

# APTITUDE

Jonathan reaches across the table for Faith's hand bringing her out of the memory. "Are you doing OK, Faith?"

"Yeah, I was thinking of Hope."

Jonathan doesn't prod further and they both go back to eating their dinner.

Faith asks, "Do you have anything planned after this?"

The waiter comes to check on them and refill their glasses of wine.

Taking a sip from her glass, she watches Jonathan, expecting an answer. He doesn't say anything so she asks again.

He wavers before saying, "I'm not going to divulge that yet."

"OK." She half rolls her eyes behind her glass of wine as she takes another sip.

"Did you just roll your eyes?"

"I did."

"You know I have a plan, right? What's there to roll your eyes about?"

"Just that we're in the middle of it, and you're not going to tell me. It was more out of amusement than frustration."

"I can accept that."

"That's good. You didn't have too much of a choice." She says with a chuckle.

The waiter comes back to take their empty plates and offer them desert.

"I think we're finished. Thank you, though." Jonathan says.

After he pays, the valet has their car waiting at the front of the restaurant and opens the door for Faith to get in. "Thank you."

As Jonathan drives, Faith soon realizes that they are not headed towards the house. They're going closer to downtown. Next thing she knows, he's pulling the car into a parking spot on the street.

"I hope your feet are OK to walk a bit."

"Yeah, they'll be fine."

"Good. We might be a little over dressed for this next place, but I'm sure it's fine." He waves his hand as if it's no big deal.

They walk hand in hand down the sidewalk towards rows of shops before stopping at an ice cream parlor.

"This is why you didn't want desert?"

"Absolutely." Jonathan smiles.

They walk inside and see the large menu on the wall behind the counter. The entire upper area of the wall is painted with chalk board paint and the menu is written in beautiful colorful handwriting.

Faith chooses a salted caramel cookie dough flavored ice cream in a waffle cone. Jonathan decides on a cinnamon roll flavor also in a waffle cone. The lady behind the counter hands over their cones and they sit next to each other on a bench outside in the courtyard at a small table to enjoy them.

# APTITUDE

"I hope that you're not disappointed with tonight so far." Jonathan says. Faith thinks she hears a bit of trepidation in his voice.

"Not at all. Why would you think that?" Faith asks as gently as she can.

"Well, it's because I know with the vacation and all of the plans and it being our anniversary that you may have thought I was going to propose."

"I'd be lying if I said it never crossed my mind." She reaches her free hand for his. "But I simply reminded myself that nothing has really changed since the last time we talked about it, and that you will propose at some point. Also, that when you do, it will be incredible and magical." She leans into him. "No pressure." She says jokingly.

He smiles and chuckles softly as he takes another lick of his ice cream. "I definitely will make it everything you could ever dream of. It is no pressure because I'm going to be so happy to do that for you!" He says, then kisses her forehead.

# Chapter 38

## Vicissitude

*Noun; the quality or state of being changeable, mutability*

On Friday, they spend the day visiting more vineyards. Jonathan thought that Faith may want to go home early since she had mentioned how weird it was to miss Sunday night dinner at her parents' house. Plus, she would be missing it two weeks in a row, and its Easter. So, he spends time in between tastings trying to find a flight and figuring out logistics for that.

They eat dinner at one of the vineyards where Jonathan explained why he had been looking at his phone so much. He told her that all she had to do was say the word and they would head home late Saturday night and be there in time to celebrate Easter with her family and Zeke.

Her excitement mirrors the level it was when he told her he had a vacation planned for the two of them. He quickly books the flights and arranges for the car to be turned in early. He also lets the host know they would be leaving the house early.

Now so far, Saturday they've been enjoying hanging around the house and walking the grounds outside since they hadn't gotten a chance to do that. After they have lunch, they begin to pack their things up to get ready to go to the airport.

"I know I shouldn't be this excited to go home." Faith starts. "But I am. I miss Zeke and I really didn't love the idea of missing Easter with my family."

Jonathan leans against the massive bed frame at the foot of the bed. "No worries. You can be excited, Faith. Maybe next time I should include you a little bit more when I plan the dates."

"I didn't want to tell you and have you change things and lose money on it."

"If it makes you happy..." He offers. "And besides, we ended up changing our plans and losing money anyway." Jonathan flashes her a snide smile.

Faith smacks his arm playfully. "Hey!"

Rubbing his arm and laughing so hard he can barely get the words out he says, "What? I'm just stating facts!"

Faith smacks his arm again, this time a little less playfully.

Jonathan laughs harder and says, "I didn't realize being honest would get me abused."

"I don't abuse you!"

"Please, don't hit me again." He pretends to recoil. At this point Jonathan is practically howling with laughter.

Faith is having a hard time containing her amusement. She ultimately gives in and begins giggling too. Jonathan smiles and sets his grey sweatpants in the luggage and reaches to embrace her.

"I fucking love you, Faith Brandt."

"I fucking love you, Jonathan Hall."

He kisses the top of her head.

Looking up at him through her lashes, Faith smiles and says, "We need to get packing."

Still holding her tightly against him, he holds a finger up to her lips and says, "Shhh. I know, but this feels too perfect to interrupt."

She lowers her head to his chest, resting it against him, she can hear his heart beat. She closes her eyes, simply enjoying the moment.

Pulling into the driveway of their condo feels like the best feeling in the world to Faith, even though she's exhausted. It's late, or early, depending on how you look at it. Technically it is morning, but since neither of them have really slept it can still be considered night, right?

Being so late, they weren't going to pick up Zeke yet. They decided not to tell Frank and Diane that they're back early. Faith thought it would be a great surprise for them to show up to Easter. She knew they would be more than happy to see them and Diane would have made enough food to feed a couple extra mouths.

They don't even unpack. Jonathan suggests that bed sounds better than anything else and Faith agrees. Unpacking can wait.

When they wake up, it's a little past noon. It doesn't feel like they've slept much at all, but they begin getting ready to head to Faith's parents' house anyway.

Faith is vibrating with excitement as her anticipation to see Zeke grows, she practically runs to Jonathan's car. The short drive to Frank and Diane's seems to take way longer than normal. Faith practically has the car door open before Jonathan has the Mercedes in park.

Frank answers the door with a confused look at first, but recognition and surprise quickly take over. He welcomes them in warmly, then shouts to Diane who's in the kitchen.

"Oh dear, I'm so glad you guys made it back for Easter! It was going to be strange not having you guys here." She embraces Faith and then Jonathan. Faith is scanning the room looking for Zeke.

Zeke comes running up quickly with his tail wagging ferociously shaking his entire body. He stops right in front of Faith, practically jumping up on her.

Faith crouches down and starts to pet him. Zeke incessantly licks her face, getting her long brown hair in his mouth making him lick even more in an attempt to get it out.

"Zekie, I missed you so much!!" She tries to hug his wiggly body with very little success.

Jonathan surprised says, "I think he got bigger since we left!"

Faith takes a look at him for herself and agrees. "He sure has." She looks up to her mom and dad. "It looks like you've been feeding him well!"

Frank smiles proudly. "We did. He was such a good boy!"

Diane nods her head. "He sure was." Zeke looks at her wagging his tail and then turns his attention and his kisses back to Faith.

Jonathan reaches down and pats Zeke's head. "I missed you too Zeke!" Zeke looks at him, his tail still wagging, and cocks his head to one side. Jonathan starts laughing.

Faith stands and looks at Diane. "So, what do you need us to do?"

"Nothing. Nothing at all! I'm just so glad you're here!" She embraces Faith again, hugging her even tighter than before.

"What time is Hope supposed to get here?"

# APTITUDE

"Well, you know her." Frank says. "We told her three, but we'll see when she gets here."

Faith checks the time on her smart watch. "That's not long from now." She looks at Jonathan and asks, "Do you want to hide? We can surprise her too!"

"I don't think Zeke is going to let us hide." He says, looking down at the adorable puppy.

"You're probably right." Faith says as she reaches down to ruffle the hair on the top of Zeke's head.

Hope walks in through the door fifteen minutes later. She shows no amount of surprise what-so-ever, but is happy to see them. It seems as if it never even occurred to her that they were going to miss Easter.

"Hey Doubt, how was Napa Valley?"

"It was incredible! If you ever have the opportunity to go, you definitely should! We hiked and went to so many vineyards, and ate deliciously."

"That sounds amazing. I'm glad you're back. I missed you both last week, but having this guy here helped fill the void." She reaches down and pets Zeke, who hasn't moved from Faith's feet since they got there.

Diane comes out from the kitchen wiping her hands on her white and pink gingham checkered apron. "Dinner is ready." She announces.

"It smells amazing, Diane." Jonathan says smiling. "But then, it always does!"

"That's why you came back early." Frank says jokingly.

"I can't say it wasn't a huge draw!"

As they eat dinner, Faith and Jonathan tell them all stories about their trip. Hope catches them up on everything they missed at last week's dinner and Frank and Diane can't stop talking about how much fun it was to have Zeke stay with them.

"You mentioned during the video call that you guys were thinking of getting a dog. Any idea when you might do that?" Faith asks.

Hope interjects loudly before Frank or Diane can answer. "Wait! What do you mean, you're thinking of getting a dog? We BEGGED you when we were kids!"

Frank begins laughing at Hope's outburst. "I'm sorry, that isn't funny, but..." His words trail off as his laughter grows even more. He attempts to get it under control when Diane speaks up.

"Well dear, it would be easier for us to take care of a dog now. Having Zeke here has shown us that. I am sorry that we weren't able to do it when you guys were younger. I'm sure having a dog would have been an impactful and beneficial addition to your childhood."

"Well, when you put it like that, and apologize, how can I stay upset? Besides, I'll get to come and visit it whenever I want to."

Frank's laughter has finally subsided. "I think it will be good for us. It may even get us out walking more."

"Did you guys take Zeke for walks?" Faith asks.

"We did, a couple of times a day. It seemed easier to do that at times than having the mess in the back yard."

# APTITUDE

"That makes sense."

After they clean up dinner, Diane offers them all pie.

"I've got lemon meringue, banana cream, key lime, and apple."

Hope chuckles, "That's a lot of pies for the five of us. We could ALMOST each have one all to ourselves."

Frank smiles and pats his protruding belly. "No, that just means we'll have left-overs!"

Diane adds, "And you can all take some home."

Frank scowls at her playfully.

Diane begins plating everyone's pie requests and then passes them around the table.

When they're finished with pie, they go into the living room to visit before Hope heads home. When Faith and Jonathan start falling asleep on the couch, they decide that would be the time to head home.

Faith is so happy to be bringing Zeke home with them. She's even happier when they get into bed an hour later. Both of them have the next day off which is good since they need to get back in their routine and catch up on some sleep before their work week begins.

Lying in bed Faith turns towards Jonathan and says, "Vacations are very nice, but our own bed is nice, too."

"It really is." He says sounding as exhausted as he feels.

"I'm not entirely sure if I'm ready for everything to go back to normal though."

"We've got one more day."

Faith snuggles into Jonathan with her head on his shoulder and his arm around her. She breathes in his scent feeling grateful for the time they had in Napa and for being home with Zeke asleep in his crate beside their bed.

# Chapter 39

## Amplitude

*Noun; extent of dignity, excellence or splendor*

The following Saturday, they celebrate Jackie's birthday at Mama Garcia's. Jackie mentioned that Hope should bring Andy as well, but Hope didn't seem too enthused with the idea. So when Hope brings them, Faith and Jackie are both pleasantly surprised.

Faith asks Andy a plethora of questions about being a CNA and what made them want to become that.

"I'm actually still in school. I graduated with my CNA certificate and got a job doing that because I thought it was better to be in the field, but I didn't waste any time starting classes towards my nursing degree."

"That's awesome! Did Hope tell you our mom had thought about becoming a nurse?"

"She had mentioned it, yeah. It's a great profession, as long as you have the heart for it. Even then, having the heart, can sometimes make it harder for you, but it's better for the patient."

"That is so true. I kind of feel like teaching can be like that too, at times."

"I can imagine that it is."

The waitress brings their round of margaritas on a platter on one hand and a pitcher full in the other. Jackie smiles and thanks her.

Andy takes a sip of theirs first. "This is delicious."

"Is it your first time here?" Jackie asks curiously.

"Yeah." They look at Hope and continue, "She had mentioned coming here with you two before and that we should come sometime. I'm glad you invited me. Thank you."

"You're welcome! The more the merrier."

Jackie looks at Faith, "Jonathan was alright with staying home?"

"I didn't really give him the option. I told him it was just us," She gestures to the four of them. "At the request of the birthday girl. He was fine with it especially when I told him we weren't going out for drinks at a bar."

"We don't need a bar to have fun." Jackie shakes her head.

"No, we don't. I think my birthday proved that."

Hope leans over to Andy and reminds them that Jonathan just threw a party at the house for Faith. They nod.

The waitress brings the heavy molcajete filled with guacamole and a heaping wooden bowl of homemade tortilla chips.

# APTITUDE

Hope, Faith, and Jackie watch Andy intently while they take the first bite of the guacamole.

When they're done chewing they finally notice that everyone is looking at them. Wiping the corner of their mouth they ask, "What? Do I have something on my face?" Andy holds the napkin for a moment longer before placing it back in their lap.

Hope places her hand on theirs and gently pushes it down saying, "It's not that. We were all watching you enjoy your first taste of Mama Garcia's guacamole." She looks around to Faith and then Jackie. "I think we all wish we could go back to our first time here."

"She's right." Faith shrugs.

Andy chuckles a little and everyone takes turns grabbing some chips and guac.

Before they know it, the waitress is bringing their food and another pitcher of strawberry margaritas.

When they've finished eating, Jackie invites everyone back to her place for more drinks. Hope and Andy decide to go back to Andy's place, while Faith and Jackie go to hers.

Jackie stands at her slightly ajar front door, completely frozen and unable to move. Faith grabs her by the arm and whisks her back to the garage. They get into the car and lock the doors. Faith quickly calls 9-1-1 to report the break-in.

"Wait. How do we even know that someone broke in? We didn't even go inside."

"Jackie that would be a horrible and completely stupid idea."

"Maybe you're right."

"I am."

Even though it feels like it takes them forever, the Luna Shore's police department shows up a few moments later. The officers enter Jackie's home and search quickly while she and Faith wait outside in the driveway. Jackie over hears them discussing if there is a need to dust the door for finger prints.

A tall handsome officer walks over to Jackie and Faith. "Well, no one is in your home now, ma'am. We also don't think it was any sort of robbery. It doesn't appear that anything was stolen. I'll have you walk through with me so you can let us know if you see anything out of place."

"OK." Jackie says with trepidation in her voice.

Faith puts her hand on Jackie's shoulder. "I can come with you, too."

"I'd appreciate that."

As they walk through the main level of the lower duplex, Faith doesn't see anything out of place.

Jackie stops in front of the antique wooden credenza she has her TV sitting on in the living room. She is staring at the shelves just below it.

Softly she says, "I know who was here. Everything is fine. There's no threat. I'm sorry I wasted your time."

"Are you sure? Whoever it was entered your home without your permission."

# APTITUDE

"I am sure. Thank you, though. I appreciate how quickly you got here. I don't think there will be anything else to worry about from now on."

The officers pack up and head out, but not before they make sure that Jackie is absolutely certain she is OK. She assures them she is and Faith mentions that she plans on staying awhile as well.

After they're gone, Faith asks, "Was it Tom?"

"Sure was." Jackie says as she plops down in her large cushy blue chair across from the TV.

Faith goes into Jackie's kitchen and grabs a bottle of wine and two glasses. She brings them into the living room with her then sets them down on the coffee table. A small smile appears on Jackie's face.

Faith pours each of them a glass of wine. "Do you want to talk about it?"

"He didn't break in. He still had a key." She points to the shelf below the TV. "Do you see it, it's right on top of that stack of books."

"I see it. Did he take anything?"

"I don't think so."

"Why the hell would he wait until tonight to return your key? And leave the door open at that? Talk about making someone feel paranoid!"

"I'm sure he figured I wouldn't be home. I also don't think he left the door ajar on purpose." Jackie gets up, taking her glass of wine with her, and checks the door knob. "It's locked. Something must have kept it from closing."

"Why did he still have a key though? It's been like a month, right?"

"I never even thought about it. He rarely ever used it. I'd actually totally forgotten he had one."

"Well, I'm glad that it turned out to be nothing."

"We should have just come inside when we got here. Obviously everything was fine."

"I've been so on edge lately, I wasn't willing to take any chances."

"I get that. I feel like I wasted those officers' time."

"I don't think they had much else going on. Do you think they needed five of them here?"

"No, that was a bit excessive."

"They thought they were going to have a real case on their hands!"

Burying her head in her hands Jackie says, "Now I feel even worse! I not only wasted their time, but I let them down."

Faith can't contain her laughter.

Jackie picks up her head abruptly. A smirk dancing at the corners of her lips. Then, she too begins laughing so hard she is suddenly afraid she might pee her pants.

"Oh my goodness! I need to stop laughing!" Jackie sits back in the chair trying desperately to hold in her giggles.

Watching her failing attempt makes Faith's laughter grow even more. In between breaths and laughs Faith manages to say, "You…are…making…it…worse." Then erupts in laughter even more. "My…stomach…hurts." She says as she wipes a tear away.

Jackie's laughs get louder. She gives up and lets the laughing fit happen.

Almost simultaneously they both inhale deeply, trying to catch their breath. Which only makes them start laughing once again. When they begin to quiet down a little again, it starts up, and so on and so forth for another few minutes. They go back and forth each one instigating the laughter alternatively.

When they've finally gotten ahold of themselves again, Faith says, "I don't remember the last time I laughed that hard."

"Me either! But it always seems to happen when we're together!"

"It does! I guess you bring it out in me. The funniest part is that I don't even remember what we started laughing about in the first place."

They both begin to giggle again. Then Jackie says, "I can't laugh anymore! My cheeks hurt!"

Faith shakes her head vigorously. "Mine too!"

They both take a deep breath and reach for their wine glasses.

# Chapter 40

## Inquietude
### Noun; disturbed state

Jonathan and Faith are in the shower discussing Sunday night dinner. They'll be heading there in a little while. Frank and Diane have added a dog to their household this week so Faith wanted to make sure to ask if it was still OK to bring Zeke to Sunday dinner. Her parent's thought it would be good for Orpheus to meet him right away.

When the two first meet a few hours later, you would never have known that they hadn't met before. The two puppies play and snuggle and it seems as if they will be lifelong friends. Faith is so happy to see it.

"So, where did you find Orpheus?" Jonathan asks Frank.

"We went to the Humane Society. He had been found a week ago in the Break Water Hills subdivision. No one had claimed him and he wasn't chipped. Yesterday was the first day he was available for adoption, so we made sure to get there first thing."

# APTITUDE

"Well, he's a good looking dog. How old do they think he is? He's a little bit bigger than Zeke."

"They gather he's about a year old. He wasn't fixed when he was found so the Humane Society took care of that."

"I suppose that's something we'll have to look into pretty soon for Zeke."

"There are benefits besides helping to keep the population down. It helps calm them, and keeps them from wanting to run away so much."

"Those are both good things."

Jonathan watches Faith, smiling to himself. She's sitting on the thick grey carpet giving both dogs all of her attention and receiving their undying gratitude and all of the puppy kisses. She's giggling and radiating with happiness which is making every ounce of love he has for her ignite and make its presence known. She looks up and smiles at him and he feels as though his heart could burst right out of his chest.

They sit and eat dinner in the dining room like always. Diane has Faith help bring the food out to the table while Hope grabs everyone something to drink.

"This looks amazing as usual, Diane." Jonathan says as he's eyeing the roast she made with potatoes and carrots along with the perfectly golden browned biscuits. The scents of each mingling together in the air is making his mouth water.

Each of them make a plate and they begin eating with little conversation. Faith takes a few bites of her roast. Moments later she excuses herself to the restroom. She isn't gone for very long so Jonathan isn't too worried.

When she comes back she does look a bit pale, though, so Jonathan asks, "Are you feeling OK?"

"Yeah, it was the weirdest thing. I was fine and then I started eating and a wave of nausea hit me. Now I feel OK, though."

"That is weird." Jonathan says then goes back to eating his meal.

Diane assesses Faith with a look of concern. "Dear, have you eaten yet today?"

"Yeah." She hooks her thumb towards Jonathan and continues. "He made us some breakfast this morning and then we had some chicken and dumpling soup for lunch."

"OK. I was just wondering. Sometimes when our stomachs are empty and we finally get some food in them, they don't always react to that very well."

"It couldn't have been that, Mom."

Hope blurts out, "Maybe you're pregnant." Then she nonchalantly shrugs her shoulders as if what she just said isn't entirely life altering and not a joke.

At the mention of that Jonathan's stomach lurches.

"I doubt it, Despair. Birth control is pretty effective."

"But not one hundred percent." Hope retorts putting a finger in the air.

"Abstinence is the only thing that is." Diane says matter-of-factly.

"Mummy is right." Hope says in a teasing tone.

# APTITUDE

Faith takes a couple slow, deliberate bites of her food. She's clearly testing to see if the nausea will return.

Frank eyes her plate. "You sure you're OK, kiddo? You don't have to keep eating if you're not feeling well."

"I know. I am hungry, though."

Zeke places his chin on her knee under the table and she absent mindedly pets him while Orpheus is laying in his bed in the corner of the living room, just outside the dining room.

After dinner Jonathan and Frank take the dogs outside. The air is starting to warm up a little more and the days are starting to get longer. Flowers and plants are beginning to poke through the dirt emerging from their winter slumber.

The dogs sniff everything it seems as the guys walk them around the block. When they return fifteen minutes later, Faith is looking pale again.

"How are you feeling?" Frank asks.

"I'm not feeling very well." She looks at Jonathan. "I think we should head home. I don't want to get anyone sick and I'd really like to lay down in our bed."

"OK." He places his arm around the small of her back.

They quickly say their goodbyes and head to the car with Zeke in tow. Luckily the drive home goes quickly and Faith makes it without an issue. Jonathan helps her into the condo and straight up the stairs to bed.

After he gets Zeke taken care of, he goes up there to check on her. She is lying in bed, still wearing the clothes she'd had on all day, fast asleep. Jonathan can't help but stare for a moment, taking in her beauty and appreciating how lucky he is to have her.

Ever since she was drugged at Lee's pub, Jonathan's urge hasn't surfaced. Just a few fleeting thoughts that pop in and are gone just as quickly as soon as he thinks about that night.

That's the main reason he's been coming home earlier, especially on Friday nights. He isn't entirely sure why the urges have subsided. If he were to guess, it was because of having to watch the side effects of the drug on Faith, but also the reality that someone tried to do what he does to the woman he loves.

Part of him realizes that if he could keep the urges at bay forever, he would. Another part of him, the more damaged part, knows that that can never happen. He's accepted what he is, even if he wishes it weren't the case.

Being so torn apart, that you feel you have no control over yourself and your choices, is maddening. That's why when Faith mentioned therapy, when they were in Napa, he was hurt and got defensive. There's no way therapy could fix what's broken inside of him. Nothing can. He's tried before.

He closes his eyes and takes a deep breath, brushes Faith's hair from her face, and then goes back downstairs to see what Zeke might be up to.

# Chapter 41

## Lassitude

*Noun; a condition of weariness or debility, fatigue*

Faith insists on going to work Monday morning even though her symptoms haven't subsided. As the week progresses she realizes that she was supposed to have gotten her period last week Friday, which makes her begin to think that Hope may have been right. Before she gets her hopes up, she goes to the drug store and buys a pregnancy test.

Thursday night at dinner seems like as good a time as any to talk to Jonathan about her suspicions. She wants to take the test with him there. Surprising him with an unplanned pregnancy doesn't seem like the best idea to her.

Jonathan came home at his new normal time and got started on dinner right away. Faith has found herself feeling better about their routine with him coming home earlier, which is nice, but it also worries her for when the office gets busier and Jonathan has to start staying late again.

She sits at the kitchen island sipping on ice water. She hasn't had any wine since Saturday because of the nausea. Her nerves are making her stomach hurt even more than it has been. She isn't sure how Jonathan is going to react. She knows that he prefers things planned, but a baby is a blessing no matter if it's planned or not, that is if she's even pregnant.

When they finally sit down to eat, Faith has gone through this conversation in her head about a million times, and yet she still doesn't know how to start it.

Deciding to spit it out, she says, "I think I might be pregnant."

Unfortunately she said it when Jonathan had a mouth full of mashed potatoes which then went flying across the table uncontrollably. Faith laughs nervously.

Jonathan's shock is very apparent on his face when he says, "You what now?" He grabs his napkin, wipes his face first and then attempts to clean his mess off of the table.

"I think I might be pregnant." Faith says quietly, then quickly continues slightly louder. "I was supposed to get my period last Friday, and the nausea, and I've not really been feeling like myself. I'm not sure how to describe it."

"But you haven't taken a test yet, so you don't know for sure, right?"

"No. I haven't taken a test yet. I bought one though, but I wanted to take it together." Faith looks down at her plate. She's barely touched her food.

Jonathan must have noticed because he asks, "Is the nausea that bad?"

"It's a little of that, but I think it's more because of nerves tonight."

"What are you nervous for?"

"I wasn't sure how you were going to react?"

"Well, I'm glad you didn't take the test without me. I think that's something we should find out together. I'm a bit surprised that this could have happened, though. You're so good about taking your birth control."

"I know. I was thinking about it, trying to figure out what might have happened. I may have missed one or two while we were on vacation. I'm sorry Jonathan. I know this isn't in your plan. It's just that our schedule and routine were so off that I must have forgotten."

"Accidents happen, and we don't know anything for sure yet." He places his arm around her shoulder, pulling her into him, he kisses her forehead. With his lips still pressed against them he says, "Why don't we go take the test now? The food can wait. I think the sooner we know, the better."

"OK."

Faith practically jumps up and goes to the stairs. Jonathan and Zeke follow.

There is very little conversation between the two as they wait the allotted time the instructions specify which isn't helping to ease Faith's anxiety. She can only imagine all of the things running through Jonathan's mind.

"Are you doing OK?" Faith finally asks him.

"I'm OK. I'm a little worried if I'm being honest. We have a lot on our plate. I'm not sure that adding a baby right now is the best idea. Plus, I very much wanted us to be married before we became parents."

"I did too. I was thinking of the time line though, we've only got three or so months before we're able to move into the house, babies aren't born for nine months. That gives us time to get a nursery set up."

"It does."

The timer on Jonathan's phone goes off and Faith jumps up and goes into the bathroom to check the test. Jonathan follows her trepidatiously.

She picks the test up in both hands, looking at the little window with the blue words clearly stating "Pregnant". She is mixed with every emotion ever experienced. She is elated, excited, and full of anticipation for what's to come for them, but then dread and worry take over.

Jonathan places both hands on her shoulders looking over her shoulder at the results. She feels him take a deep breath, she takes one as well preparing herself for his reaction.

She spins around and he wraps his arms around her. "I know that this isn't what we planned, and I know that it will be an adjustment, but can you be happy with me?" Her voice betrays her as it cracks at the end of the sentence. She so desperately wanted this whole experience to be under different circumstances.

"I am happy, Faith. I'm just also worried, and most of all scared. I want us to be ready. I wanted to be able to plan all of this."

"I get it. Your five year plan was a very good one, but this little baby," she places her hands on her lower stomach, "had different plans."

"I guess so." Jonathan's smile is faint, but Faith can see it and it gives her hope that there is a part of him that can be happy with her.

"I'll have to make an appointment with my doctor to have it confirmed. Is that something you want to be there for?"

"Would you feel more comfortable with me there?"

"It's not like we'll get the results right away or anything. They'll just do some blood work."

"When do you want to tell people?"

"I think we should wait a bit, definitely not until after we get the results from the doctor."

"OK."

"Are you sure you're OK with this?"

"Well, Faith, I don't really have much of a choice, do I? I'm aware this is as much of a surprise for you, but I've had a little less time to process the idea of it than you have. The moment you thought you could be pregnant you began going through all of the feelings I am right now, except that you didn't have confirmation. At that point, it was still just a 'what if'. Now it's more or less confirmed and I have to adjust everything I thought was going to happen in the next few years. It's a lot."

"I get it. I'm sorry. I wish we could go back and do things differently."

"What would you do differently? Take your birth control like you should have?" The question leaves his lips in an accusing tone.

Faith flinches at his words. Instead of responding she goes into the closet, changes into her pajamas and goes to lay down in bed. Tears are streaming down her cheeks. She is trying to hold it all in, but tonight has been a roller coaster of emotions and she's feeling entirely too drained.

When Jonathan comes to bed an hour later, he attempts to console her. He tries to talk to her, to explain that he didn't mean to say it the way he did. None of that does anything to make her feel better, though. She simply wants to go to sleep and have a do-over tomorrow. Knowing that there is no do-over in the cards, and that sleep won't come with the level her emotions are currently at, she rolls over onto her back.

Jonathan places his hand on her stomach. Faith fights the strong urge to recoil and roll away from him again.

"This baby," he says softly as he begins to rub her stomach, "is going to be so loved by everyone. I'm sorry that I have created such a shitty memory of us finding out you're pregnant. I should have done better. I'm only trying to be honest about my feelings."

Not wanting to respond in anger and make things even worse, Faith waits to say anything. She takes a couple of deep breaths and reminds herself of all of the love she feels for this man, despite what he's done tonight, he's been an amazing partner to her.

"I want to go to sleep and forget this night ever happened."

"I get that, Faith, but I can't fix it if you're sleeping."

"I don't think you can fix it when I'm awake either. I love you, and this will all be fine. I'll call the doctor tomorrow and make an appointment for the blood work."

"This conversation isn't done."

"It is for tonight. I don't have the energy. I appreciate your apology, I really do. I don't think that us talking more right now is going to get us anywhere."

With that, Faith rolls back over taking her stomach out of Jonathan's reach.

# Chapter 42

# Plentitude

*Noun; the quality or state of being full, completeness*

On Friday morning Faith wakes up with a renewed sense of completeness and determination, as well as the morning sickness she's come to accept as her new normal. She has decided to be happy about this pregnancy even if Jonathan can't be.

The phone call to the doctor's office on her way in to school that morning wasn't anything special. There was no excited reaction from the person on the other end of the phone, as Faith had foolishly anticipated. Then again, she reminded herself, that not everyone is looking forward to pregnancy and having children.

The thought brings tears to her eyes. For only a moment she allows herself to think of Jonathan's reaction last night, then she shoves it away and brings her feelings of happiness and excitement back to the forefront where she wants them to stay.

# APTITUDE

After the school day is finished, she goes in to have the lab work done. Again, everyone is simply doing their job. No one asks her if she's excited, no one asks if she wants a boy or a girl. It's as if the baby isn't even a reality yet. Faith contemplates telling Jackie, just so that she can have someone to be excited with her, but she and Jonathan agreed to wait.

The results came through the app less than twelve hours later and then she receives a phone call first thing Monday morning to schedule an appointment with an obstetrician. They were able to get her on the schedule for Friday after school.

Jonathan has attempted to apologize multiple times in the past few days and his demeanor towards Faith and all things having to do with the pregnancy has been positive now. Faith is still wrestling with his accusation, though. Even if he didn't mean for it to come out the way it did, a part of him had to have actually meant it. He was clearly thinking that it was entirely her fault for missing her birth control while they were on vacation, as if pregnancy prevention should only be the responsibility of the woman.

This isn't something she wants to keep holding against him, but she's having a hard time getting past it. She doesn't want him to not express his feelings about the pregnancy, but she also wanted a happy memory to look back on when she thinks of when they first found out. He took that from her and in some ways she's mourning that loss.

Jonathan is already home from work when Faith gets home Monday night. As soon as she opens the door to their condo the smell of roses fills the air.

Jonathan is standing in the entryway with a beautiful large bouquet as she comes through the door.

"I'd like to take you out to dinner if you're feeling up to it." Jonathan offers holding out the bouquet for her to see.

"Jonathan, I am exhausted."

"I fucked up. I know that, Faith. I want to try to make it up to you. I've been trying, but I also need you to allow me to do that."

She takes the roses from him. "And I needed you to respond better to all of this." With that she walks past him and into the kitchen to put the flowers in a vase.

Jonathan follows her. "Please, Faith," he pleads.

She exhales sharply then says, "I'll go to dinner with you. I'd like to change into something more comfortable. We're not going anywhere too nice, right?"

"OK! And no, I was thinking Tollero's." He sits on the couch as Faith heads upstairs to change.

When she comes down the stairs she sees Jonathan sitting on the couch petting Zeke who's sitting right by his feet. She smiles to herself.

"Ready?" Jonathan asks, standing up.

"Yeah, we just have to get Zeke put away."

At Tollero's they order their usual. Jonathan reaches for Faith's hands from across the table.

# APTITUDE

"I am really sorry for the way that I reacted, Faith. There's nothing I can say that is going to fix it. I know that. I also know that I can't go back and change it. I I wish I knew what I can do right now to make you feel better about everything. I've tried apologizing. I've tried being excited about the baby, I've tried talking to you, but I've been met with silence, or if I'm lucky, one or even two word answers."

"I think it's going to take time. Probably consistency too. I didn't expect you to be over-the-moon happy about it. I knew this would be a shock to you. I also knew that this would put a wrench in your five year plan, but I definitely didn't think you'd blame me for it. Maybe I am at fault somewhat, but why is it solely my responsibility to not get pregnant? Why is it on the woman in general in society? Men have just as much of a responsibility in the making of a baby, why are we the only ones who have to do anything to prevent it?"

"I can't answer that, Faith. I see where you're coming from, though. As a society, it is unfair that we put it all on women to shoulder the responsibility of. I fell into that stereo type when I made the stupid comment that I did."

"I thought you were better than that." She looks down at her fork that is pushing pasta around her plate.

"I am." Jonathan protests. "I was scared and in shock, and I reacted poorly. I am so sorry."

"While I appreciate your apologies, they don't really take the pain away." She says matter-of-factly.

"I know." Jonathan's voice low and defeated. He takes a swig of his beer. "I wish it had never happened."

"What? Finding out we're pregnant?"

"No! My dumb mouth." He runs his fingers through his hair. "I wish I knew exactly the right words to say to make you sure of me as a partner and a father to this baby." He looks down towards her stomach as if he can see through the table between them.

"I believe in you, Jonathan. I'm just hurt right now."

"I'm so sorry that I hurt you. I was wondering when you might want to start telling people? I was actually somewhat surprised you didn't mention anything at dinner on Sunday."

"I felt like I would have been forcing you to pretend to be happy about it. I don't want to do that. I have an appointment with the doctor on Friday at three thirty. I think we should wait until after that."

"OK. Whatever you want, Faith."

"Thank you, Jonathan."

"I would like to come with for the appointment."

"OK." Faith says simply.

She's happy to see him trying, and it seems to be helping. She takes a bite of her food. Her stomach has been settling at various times of the day giving her a slight reprieve from the nausea.

Jonathan smiles and asks, "Are you having any other symptoms?"

"Well, my boobs hurt, and I just feel tired."

"Your boobs hurt?"

"Yeah. It's all basically hormonal at this point."

"I guess that makes sense. If there's anything I can help you with, I will. Just let me know."

"I will. Thanks Jonathan." She flashes him a quick half-hearted smile.

"Do you know what the doctor is going to do on Friday?"

"I'm pretty sure they'll listen to the heartbeat and probably order me some vitamins. The person who scheduled me mentioned that I have to go to some pre-natal education with a nurse practitioner, but that will be scheduled on a different day."

"OK. I'm going to try to make it to every appointment. I can't guarantee that I will, but I'm definitely going to try."

"I appreciate that, Jonathan."

"I'm here for you and the baby, Faith. I need you to know that."

"I do. I am positive you're not going to leave us or anything. Honestly, that thought never crossed my mind."

"Good, it shouldn't because it'll never happen."

Faith looks down at her plate and then back up to Jonathan. "Don't use this baby as an excuse to propose any sooner than you would have otherwise."

With a puzzled look on his face, Jonathan asks, "Why do you say that?"

"I don't want you thinking that putting a ring on my finger is going to fix anything. I also don't want a ring if it's because of the baby."

"It was never going to be because of a baby, Faith. I've known I was going to marry you from the moment I first saw you. The only reason I haven't asked yet is, like I said, we have too much on our plate right now. Adding a baby to that plate makes everything else seem miniscule in comparison, but it doesn't change the fact that I want to marry you. I'd never ask you solely because you're pregnant. Besides, I doubt you want to plan a wedding and get married while you're pregnant."

"People do it all the time and there's nothing wrong with it, but you're right. It isn't what I want."

Jonathan lowers his fork to his plate, setting it down with a clink. Then he grabs his glass and takes a swig. Faith grabs her water and drinks as well.

"Is it weird not drinking alcohol?"

"Not really. I don't miss it. I'm trying to do everything right so that this baby is happy and healthy."

"You're such a good mother, Faith, and the baby isn't even born yet."

"I'm only a few weeks. Anything can happen."

"What do you mean anything can happen?" Jonathan asks curiously.

"The statistics say that it's pretty common to have a miscarriage with the first pregnancy."

"I didn't know that."

"I have a feeling you'll be learning a lot through this whole thing." She gives him a sideways glance.

## APTITUDE

"I think you're right." Jonathan chuckles then asks, "How do you know this stuff?"

"I'm not entirely sure. Part of it was simply paying attention in health class. I think having co-workers, friends, and family members who have gotten pregnant also helps to educate us women."

"That makes sense."

Faith is feeling her anger towards Jonathan subside a little. She smiles at his eager questions and is grateful that she agreed to go to dinner. She doesn't want to stay mad at him. She only wishes she could go back in time and create a new, happier memory.

# Chapter 43

# Rectitude

*Noun; moral integrity, righteousness, being correct in judgment or procedure*

The rest of the week seems to go by so slowly, but yet quickly at the same time. The anticipation of her doctor's appointment being the culprit. Faith found herself having a hard time keeping the secret of her pregnancy. She wants to tell her family and Jackie most of all. Telling them would make it seem more real and not something only her and Jonathan talk about.

Jonathan parks next to Faith's Evoque in the school parking lot and waits as patiently as he can for her to come out. He didn't want them to drive separate to the appointment. He wants the time with her beforehand and besides the condo is in the opposite direction of the hospital from Hilltop Elementary.

Faith smiles at him as she approaches his Mercedes and his heart swells. He's so grateful that things have been slowly getting better since dinner on Monday.

# APTITUDE

He hops out quickly and opens her door. "Thank you, Jonathan."

"You're welcome, Faith." When he gets back into the driver's seat he asks, "How was your day?"

"It seemed to take forever! It wasn't the kids fault, of course. I'm sure it was knowing I have the appointment today and all of the unknowns with that."

Jonathan reaches for her hand, he holds it in his and places it atop the shifter. "It was the same for me. I have no idea what to expect, aside from what they show on TV or in movies, but those women are usually a lot more pregnant."

Faith giggles. "That's true. I'm sure it'll be pretty simple today."

"Can they even use that jelly stuff with the joystick looking thing when you're only a few weeks along?"

She laughs again. "I don't think so."

"What do they use then?"

"I'm pretty sure they use an internal one?"

"Internal? What do you mean?"

"Like they use something that goes inside, near the cervix."

Jonathan's eyes get big as he realizes what she's saying and he says, "I'm glad I asked before we got there." Then he laughs nervously.

"You guys have it so easy." She says as she looks back out the windshield.

"I guess we do." He brings her hand to his lips and then rests their hands back on the shifter.

After Jonathan parks, they walk through the large revolving door and stop at the front desk off to the right to get directions. The building is spacious with three story windows in the entryway and is open the entire three stories. The receptionist gives them directions to the Women's Pavilion which requires them to take the glass elevators up to the second floor. They then walk through large swinging wood doors and see another desk to check into directly in front of them with a waiting area on their right that is filled with natural light that's spilling in through the large wall of windows.

When Faith is called to go back to a room, Jonathan stands anxiously and follows her. The CNA has her step on a scale and then have both of them follow into an exam room. They check her blood pressure, blood oxygen levels, and heart rate.

"Everything looks good. Here's the gown to change into." The CNA smiles at her. "Doctor Graves will be in shortly."

"Thank you." Faith says getting up to change out of her clothes. She changes into the drab hospital gown and then sits on the bed and waits.

A few moments later Dr. Graves knocks and walks in with an assistant and a laptop.

He holds his hand out to faith first. "Hi Faith, it's great to meet you, I'm Dr. Graves."

"It's nice to meet you, Dr. Graves. This is my boyfriend, Jonathan Hall."

The doctor and Jonathan shake hands as well then Dr. Graves opens his laptop and looks at the screen as he sits on the rolling stool.

"So it looks like this is your first pregnancy and your first appointment."

"That's correct." Faith answers.

"OK. So what we're going to do is take a listen to the heart beat, we'll see if we can get a look at where baby is at in there, and we'll get a tentative due date for you. Can you tell me when your last period was?"

Faith thinks a moment and then says, "It would have been around March thirty first."

"OK, perfect. Given that timeline you're around six weeks along. What kind of symptoms are you having?"

"Mostly morning sickness. My breasts started feeling sore earlier this week and in just the past day or two my lower stomach feels weird, like pressure or something. It's hard to describe. I've also been peeing a lot!" Faith giggles at the admission.

He chuckles. "All of those are completely normal. Some people don't experience symptoms this early, and others have every symptom."

"Wait, did you say she's six weeks? As in already nearly two months pregnant? How is that possible?" Jonathan asks surprised.

"It's pregnancy math." Dr. Graves says simply, turning to Jonathan. "The weeks are calculated from the first date of the last period, not from conception."

"That doesn't really make sense."

"No, I suppose you're right." Dr. Graves shrugs his shoulders and then says, "I don't make the rules, I just learned them in medical school and follow them." He turns back to Faith and continues. "So, based on that date your tentative due date would be January fifth."

Faith smiles. "A New Year's baby."

"It's quite possible."

Faith looks to Jonathan. "Our birthdays would be January, February and March." She grins at him.

"Yes they would."

"OK. So we're going to try to listen to baby's heart today, sometimes it can be hard to hear at this point in the pregnancy, but we'll see what we can get. We'll do a Pap smear as well. Then we'll have you do some lab work, both blood and urine. Do you have any questions for me at this point?"

Faith shakes her head. "No, I don't think so."

"OK. I'll ask again before we're done today, don't worry."

The assistant begins getting all of the supplies from the drawers as the doctor washes his hands and puts gloves on. Then he instructs Faith to lay back and put her legs in the stirrups. Feeling uncomfortable, Jonathan isn't quite sure where to look or what to do. This is all very foreign to him and quite frankly, a bit surprising.

Faith looks over at him reassuringly as the assistant wheels in the ultrasound machine.

"This one isn't as fancy as the one you'll have done later, but for these appointments it works just fine."

"Do you do an ultrasound at every appointment?"

"Sure do! I believe it helps us keep track of everything a little better. We'll know where your placenta is, the level of amniotic fluid and the position the baby is in when that time comes."

Faith smiles at the thought of the baby growing inside of her getting to be that big.

"Now, you're going to feel some pressure. We'll get the not so fun stuff out of the way first."

Jonathan hears a few clicks and sees the assistant unwrap something and hand it to the doctor. Next thing he knows the doctor is placing it in a tube and sealing it. Then he grabs the wand from the ultrasound machine.

"Are we ready for the best part?" He asks Faith.

"Yes." She says reaching her hand out to Jonathan, motioning for him to come closer to her.

Jonathan stands and walks over to the side of the bed where he takes her hand and can see the screen.

The doctor readjusts the wand and all of a sudden the room is filled with a 'thwump thwump' sound. Jonathan exhales deeply as he fights back tears. Faith is looking up at him with tears in her eyes and a smile on her face. Their eyes lock and he smiles back. Then they both go back to looking at the magic on the monitor.

The doctor points out the small fluid filled sac and does some measurements.

"Looks like we're right on track. There's a strong heart beat at 89 beats per minute. That's a little on the lower side, but shouldn't be anything to worry about." Doctor Graves says as pictures begin printing from the side of the machine.

"How long before we can find out if it's a boy or a girl?" Jonathan asks.

"We may be able to tell as early as fourteen weeks, but typically we know around the eighteen to twenty week mark."

"OK."

"Now, I'm going to send you to the lab to have some tests done. I will see you back here in four weeks, unless something comes up. Stop at the front desk before heading to the lab to have them schedule that as well as the pre-natal education appointment. It was great meeting you two and congratulations!"

"Thank you, Dr. Graves." Faith smiles unable to hide her excitement.

As they walk out of the exam room hand in hand, Jonathan can't help but think about their future. He's feeling better about it's abrupt changes and how his five year plan has shifted. There is now a level of excitement that has replaced the dread and worry that was so prevalent last week.

Faith walks to the scheduling desk. There they take care of getting the next few appointments scheduled. Jonathan and Faith both make note of them in their phone calendars. Next, Faith leads the way to the lab.

# APTITUDE

When the testing is finished, Jonathan drives her back to Hilltop Elementary School.

"Do you have to go back to work?" Faith asks.

Jonathan shakes his head. "Nope. I'm all yours for the rest of the day."

Faith smiles, genuinely happy at his answer. "What should we do?"

"Anything you want."

"I'd love to snuggle on the couch and watch a movie."

"That sounds pretty perfect to me." He pulls his Mercedes into the parking spot next to hers.

While he drives home with Faith following him, he thinks of the sound of the baby's heart beat filling the room. He wished there was a way for them to have recorded that. Pictures are great, but being able to relive that and hear it whenever they please would have been nice.

He glances in his rearview mirror to see Faith still behind him and smiles to himself. The day she came into his life was literally the best thing that's ever happened to him.

# Chapter 44

## Certitude

*Noun; the state of being or feeling certain*

"So when do we want to start telling people? Faith asks as she snuggles into Jonathan Sunday morning. The sunlight is flooding the room. This is the longest they've been able to sleep in since getting Zeke, aside from when they were on vacation.

He pulls her in tighter, then says, "I was thinking about that. I'm somewhat surprised you don't already have a plan of how you want to announce it, but I think we should tell your family at Sunday dinner tonight."

"I do have a few ideas. I think that tonight would work best. Then we can tell them all at the same time."

"Right. You haven't told Jackie yet?"

"We agreed to wait." Faith says matter-of-factly. "Plus, my parents and Hope should find out first."

"I wasn't sure if Jackie fell under the umbrella of everyone."

"We agreed, Jonathan. Everyone falls under the umbrella. You haven't told anyone yet, have you?"

"No. No one in my life would have even come close to being the exception."

"Have you thought about telling your aunt Suz?"

"I've thought about it, but decided that I don't want her to have anything to do with this little one." He places his other hand on top of her lower stomach.

"OK. I won't bring it up again."

"It's OK, Faith. I'm not upset at all. I feel very protective of this baby, and you of course. I never want anything bad to happen to you. I wouldn't know what to do with myself."

"We're all going to be happy and healthy, Jonathan."

"What ideas did you have for the announcement?"

"Well, I know that I don't want to give them a stick I peed on." She laughs.

"No. I don't think that is the best way to tell someone you're pregnant." Jonathan agrees.

"And we don't know if it's a boy or a girl yet."

"No, we don't." He shakes his head.

"So that limits buying an outfit or something. We could go that route, but I think I'd rather give them something they get to keep."

"I like the way you're thinking."

"I'd like to get them a picture frame and put one of the pictures that Dr. Graves printed for us at the appointment. I also want to do something else, I'm just not sure what."

"We can think of something."

"We don't have much time."

"Then I guess we should get up!"

Faith see's Zeke's head pop up in his crate. In an excited voice she says, "Are you ready to get up too, Zeke? Do you want to go outside?"

Zeke's entire body is buzzing with energy and it seems to all be exiting his tail as he wags it back and forth, making a racket when it hits the sides of his crate alternately.

As Faith bends down to let Zeke out, she suddenly exclaims, "I got it!"

"Got what?" Jonathan says from the bathroom with his mouth full of toothpaste foam.

"How we'll tell them! Zeke will do it! I need some of my art supplies."

Faith works diligently nearly until it is time to leave for her parents' house, making a sign that Zeke will wear hanging down from his collar.

Faith is sitting in the passenger seat of Jonathan's Mercedes with her finger entangled in her long dark hair twisting it around in a nervous fidget. Even though she knows there is no need to feel that way since she's sure her parents will welcome becoming grandparents. Although, she isn't entirely sure how Hope is going to react, her desire is that since she was the first one to throw the idea out there, her reaction won't be too bad.

Before getting out of the car, Faith fastens the sign to Zeke's collar. Her heart rate picks up a couple of beats as they walk down the concrete path to the door. Jonathan opens it and they walk through. Frank, Diane, and Hope are all sitting in the living room.

"Perfect." She says to herself.

Smiling at everyone she holds Zeke's leash in one hand and the envelope containing the ultrasound picture in the other. They didn't have time to get a picture frame today, but they can always pick one up a different day.

"Hi, everyone!" Faith says as Orpheus comes bounding up to them, excited to see all three of them. Faith bends down to pet him feeling his soft fur beneath her finger tips. As she stands she says, "Zeke has something to tell you all." She releases her hold on his leash.

Diane calls Zeke to her with a confused look on her face and he beelines straight for her. She looks down as he sits in front of her. She pats his head saying, "Good boy!" Then she notices the sign.

Diane reads it out loud, "Since I've been promoted to big brother, it's my pleasure to announce your promotion to Grandparents."

Tears instantly begin to form and she looks up with surprise and delight at Faith who's vigorously shaking her head yes. Diane and Frank both stand and walk over to Faith embracing her. Blinking hard, tears instantly form in Faith's eyes. Frank shakes Jonathan's hand. "Congratulations, son." Frank pulls him into a tight hug.

"Thank you, sir."

"I can't believe it!" Diane says excitedly, "A grand-child!" She looks down at Faith's lower stomach. "This is the best news!"

Once everyone settles back into the living room, Faith notices Hope smiling. She hadn't gotten up when Frank and Diane did. Faith reaches out handing the envelope to Hope. "Here Despair, we have something for you."

Hope takes the envelope and slides her finger in-between the seal to release its hold and reveal its contents. She pulls out the photograph, turning it to the left, then to the right, then tilting her head. "I have no idea what I'm looking at." She laughs.

"I wouldn't know either if the doctor hadn't explained it." Faith leans into her sister and points at the small spot on the photo. "That is your niece or nephew."

"It doesn't look like much."

"No, not yet, but soon enough."

"Did they give you a due date?"

"Yup!" Faith smiles. "January fifth."

"It seems so far away."

"We found out pretty early. Which is also why the baby doesn't look like much yet."

Hope hugs her sister. "I'm so happy for you guys." Pulling away she holds up the picture. "Thank you for this." She says genuinely.

"You're welcome! You're going to be a great aunt." Faith smiles.

# APTITUDE

"Do you agree Jonomeister?" Hope asks looking at Jonathan.

"Of course I do! You'll be the coolest aunt ever!"

Hope smiles. "That works for me!"

Dinner is filled with conversation about the baby and the pregnancy. Diane throws out a couple of names of relatives from the past as suggestions.

Frank seems to be in awe of the entire situation. "I can't believe my daughter is having a baby." He says. "I'm going to be a grandpa!" He smiles at Diane, then he looks at Faith. "So a couple of weeks ago at dinner…that was the baby?"

"Yup, I've had morning sickness ever since then."

"So, Hope was right!"

Faith nods her head, "Yes, she was."

Hope smiles proudly. "I knew it!"

Faith laughs. "Honestly, I'm surprised that wasn't the first thing out of your mouth."

Jonathan adds. "Me too!"

Diane laughs and says, "Me three."

They all laugh and Diane and Faith begin cleaning up dinner.

While they're in the kitchen Diane asks, "How are you feeling about everything?"

"I'm excited! Obviously it's not exactly how we planned things, but it's still a good thing."

"Babies are always a blessing and this one will be lucky to have you two as their parents."

"Thanks, Mom."

"You're welcome, dear."

On the drive home Jonathan says, "That went really well."

"It did!"

"How do you feel?" He asks.

"Like it's totally real now." Faith smiles.

With his eyebrows pinched together Jonathan asks, "You didn't feel that way before?"

"A little, even more so after the doctor's appointment, but telling everyone solidified it that much more."

"I agree."

"How are you feeling about all of it?"

"I'm glad we told them. They were all very excited for us and for themselves."

"It was great to see."

"Even Hope was happy." Jonathan says surprised.

"Right!"

"I was worried she was going to be jealous or something."

"I was too. Especially because of some of the comments she's been making when we talk about the house and stuff. I think it has more to do with how she feels about where she is in her own life. I'm sure having Andy has helped." Faith explains.

"It seems to have. I'd like to meet them. When do you think Hope will have them over for Sunday dinner?"

"I'm not sure. Jackie and I met them at dinner for Jackie's birthday, but Hope didn't seem too keen on bringing them around the family quite yet. I can't say that I blame her."

"You brought me around relatively early."

# APTITUDE

"I didn't have much of a choice since I couldn't walk on my own." Faith gives Jonathan a sideways glance.

"That's true. I wasn't complaining. It was kind of nice not having a long time to think about and build up meeting your parents. Although, a warning that your sister was going to be the one that was hardest on me would have been nice." Jonathan chuckles.

As Faith brushes her hair before bed, she thinks back over everything that happened throughout the day. Telling her parents had made the baby seem so much more real. Waiting two and a half more months, at least, to find out the sex of the baby is going to be difficult though.

She has the urge to begin buying things now. She has already started looking at furniture for the nursery and looking at inspiration for the décor. Not knowing the gender is making it difficult to come to a decision.

She hasn't shown Jonathan anything she's found yet since there's still an inkling of fear in the back of her mind that he isn't as excited about the baby as she is. She can clearly see that he is more excited now than he was when they first found out, but she is having a hard time getting his initial reaction out of her thoughts.

Faith looks up from the mirror with luke warm water dripping from her face, all of her makeup is washed away. She brings up the image of her mom's face as she read the sign that hung around Zeke's neck in her mind. She smiles to herself as the warmth from that thought washes over her bringing her a sense of peace and gratefulness for her family.

# Chapter 45

# Decrepitude

*Noun; the quality or state of being dilapidated, run-down*

Faith's eyes open suddenly, the dark of their bedroom surrounding her. The only light she sees is coming from the bathroom. She holds her stomach and hunches over in pain, unable to get out of bed. This feels like the worst cramps she has ever had. Her chest tightens as she realizes that this can't be good.

She reaches over and attempts to shake Jonathan awake. A few moments later he sleepily asks, "Is there something wrong?"

"I think so. I don't know." She says exasperatedly.

It's been a week and a half since her appointment with Dr. Graves and a week since her pre-natal education appointment. Her lab work had come back normal. She isn't sure what exactly is happening, but she doesn't want to allow herself to even think of the worst, but she's finding that nearly impossible.

Jonathan jumps out of bed and comes to her side. Kneeling down he asks, "What can I do? How can I help you?" His tone is desperate.

"I'm not sure. Maybe help me get to the bathroom?"

Jonathan gently scoops her up into his arms and carries her into the bathroom. "What do you think is going on?" He asks eagerly.

Faith buries her head in his shoulder. "I can't say it." Her tears make a wet spot on his T-shirt. "I feel like I have extremely bad cramps."

"And that isn't normal?"

"No. Not that I've ever heard of."

She feels the cold tile on the bottom of her bare feet as he sets her down then she reaches down to raise the toilet seat cover. As she sits down she grabs a wad of toilet paper, using it to wipe she sees what she feared most. Blood.

Tears are streaming down her cheeks. She asks Jonathan to grab her cell phone from her night stand. She pulls her pajama pants up and moves carefully to sit on the vanity stool.

At the pre-natal education appointment she was given a number to call at any time if something like this happened. Scrolling through the saved phone numbers in her contact list, she selects 'Women's Pavilion 24Hr Help-line' and hits the call button. She puts the phone on speaker and a woman answers on the second ring.

"Women's Pavilion help line, Maureen speaking, how can I help you this morning?"

Faith takes a deep breath trying to hold back her sobs as the words come out, "I think I'm having a miscarriage."

The woman says, "Oh, dear. I know it's scary, but everything is going to be OK. Take a deep breath and try to explain to me what has made you think that."

Faith does as she is instructed, she breathes in deeply and feels the cold soothing air rush in through her nostrils. Then she finds herself telling the woman about how she woke up and the blood on the toilet paper.

"There are a couple of things that could cause that. Let me pull up your chart and see if we can narrow it down to anything else. We'll need you to come in for lab work and an ultrasound to rule it out completely, though."

Faith looks at the time on her phone screen. It's three in the morning. "How early can I come in for that?"

"I will set you up with a seven o'clock appointment, if that works for you?"

"You can get me in that soon?"

"Of course we can. We would never want you to have to wait that long for something like this."

"Thank you so much." Faith says with tears still running down her cheeks.

"It looks like you're nearly eight weeks along. It's actually quite common to have some light spotting anytime between the four and eight week mark. Sometimes our bodies aren't sure about missing our periods."

Faith sniffles trying to fully comprehend what the woman on the other end of the phone is saying. She wants so desperately to believe it, but finds herself asking, "Is it normal to feel horrible cramps too?"

"Cramps can be normal, yes. Horrible ones are definitely a cause for concern, though. I'm going to send a message to Dr. Graves and let him know that you'll be in for lab work and an ultrasound this morning."

Faith hears the woman's fingers clicking against the keyboard on her computer. She doesn't feel like anything has been narrowed down at all. She feels her frustration level rise and despair take hold of her emotions.

Jonathan stands beside her rubbing her back, clearly wishing he could help her.

"What can I do, Faith?"

"I'm not sure, Jonathan."

The woman on the phone says, "I've got you scheduled and have sent the message to Dr. Graves. Is there anything else I can do for you right now?"

"I don't think so, Maureen. Thank you for your help."

"You're welcome. I'm very sorry that you are going through this, I truly hope that everything is normal."

"Thank you."

Faith pushes the end call button and slumps over on the stool. Jonathan kneels down to be eye level with her. He pulls her into him attempting to comfort her. Her tears making a new wet spot on the other shoulder of his T-shirt.

She pulls her face away and says, "I'm so sorry!"

"What are you apologizing for, Faith?"

She shrugs her hanging shoulders. "I don't know. For everything…for getting pregnant, for getting mad at you for not being excited and then when you finally are, we're going to lose the baby." She inhales sharply unable to get enough oxygen to keep the sobs from coming. A loud wail fills the bathroom as her shoulders shake with every sob.

Jonathan holds her tighter to him. "Faith, you have nothing to apologize for. Nothing at all." He tells her softly.

"I'm getting your shirt all wet." She sobs even harder at the realization. "I can't do anything right, not even carry your baby."

"Faith, we aren't even sure what's going on yet."

"I know, Jonathan. I know that I'm miscarrying. I feel it. You couldn't possibly understand what I'm feeling."

He pats her back, trying to reassure her. "You're right, I don't know. I simply want to think positively. In moments like this, it's all we can do, and I believe it helps."

"I can't bring myself to think happy thoughts right now." The words come out broken. She inhales quickly in an attempt to regain some semblance of composure.

"We don't know anything for sure yet." He says in his most comforting tone.

"Don't you get it? I do know, Jonathan. That's what I'm saying." Her voice is full of anger and frustration.

She feels his body stiffen right before he pulls himself away from her. "I'm sorry, Faith. I'm not saying I don't believe you. I just don't want to."

"You think I do?" She accuses him. "Of course I don't! I don't want to go on fooling myself until the tests come back and prove that I'm right."

"OK, Faith. We can do it that way. What do you want me to do for you? I can make you some breakfast if you'd like?"

"I can't eat right now." She practically spits each word out.

"OK, that's understandable. Then can I get you some water, maybe?"

She feels her anger subside and then says, "That would actually be very nice. Thank you." She lowers her head to her hands and says, "I'm sorry, Jonathan. I shouldn't be taking this out on you."

"Faith, you can take it out on me. Not because it's my fault, but if it helps you deal with it, then I'm more than OK with it."

"It's not fair to you."

"This isn't fair to you either. I'd do anything to help you feel better."

"But I shouldn't be making you feel worse."

Jonathan shrugs his shoulders, "It's OK, Faith. I'm fine." One corner of his mouth turns up.

Faith can't bring herself to smile even the slightest at him. His understanding only makes her feel guiltier, but she is grateful for it.

"Thank you, Jonathan. You're more understanding than I deserve."

"That's untrue. You deserve it all." He pulls her back into him and Faith's tears return with a vengeance.

A few hours later, Faith is wearing another hospital gown as the ultrasound tech preps the wand for her ultrasound. Her heart is pounding in anticipation of what she may see on the small black screen in front of her.

The nausea she feels is hard to discern if it is morning sickness or anxiety. She tries to take deep cleansing breaths, but they don't seem to help.

The tech must have noticed. "Are you doing OK, Faith?"

"I'm worried about what we're going to find."

"I understand. I'm going to apologize right away because I'm not going to be able to let you see anything. The radiologist is going to have to review the ultrasound before we can give you any definitive answers."

Jonathan speaks up before Faith gets a chance to. "What do you mean? We aren't actually going to find anything out even though we're here right now?"

"That's correct. We don't want to run the risk of giving you false information. Your provider may also review the images and make a diagnosis at which time he will be in contact with you."

Faith feels any semblance of calm she had leave her body entirely. She accepts what the tech is saying indignantly. "It would have been nice if Maureen had mentioned that at three o'clock this morning when I called."

"I agree that she definitely should have told you this would take some time. I'm sorry. I can make a note of it so that it doesn't happen again."

"Please. I'd rather not have any other women have to go through what I am right now. It's like mental and emotional warfare here." Gesturing for emphasis, she swipes her hand from her chest to her head.

"I understand. Whenever you're ready, we'll begin. Please put your feet in the stirrups."

The internal ultrasound only takes twenty minutes, but each second seems to tick by slower than the one before it. There is no talking and the tech makes no facial expressions as to give away anything. There is no heartbeat for them to hear. The excitement from the first ultrasound has been replaced by fear and anguish.

Faith feels the tears begin once again. She allows them to run down to the pillow case beneath her head, wishing the end of them would be in sight, but she has no hope for that now.

When the tech has finished she hands Faith some paper towel to use to clean herself up and says, "You may notice some blood after this procedure, which is completely normal."

"It has been today, at least." Faith says.

"My suggestion is to give yourself some grace today, but also try to keep yourself busy. It can help the wait not be quite so bad."

"Thank you." Faith and Jonathan say at the same time.

They walk out of the Women's Pavilion into the overcast cool morning air. Both of them are feeling defeated and hopeless.

"Why don't we go get some breakfast?" Jonathan suggests.

"I don't really want to be in public right now, and I certainly don't want to go to the café." The sobs begin once again. "How am I going to tell my parents? They were so excited!"

"Faith, you're not letting them down. You have no control over this." Jonathan stops walking making Faith stop as well. He grabs her by the shoulders and then lifts her chin up to look him in the eyes. "This isn't your fault." He says emphatically.

# Chapter 46

## Attitude

*Noun; a negative or hostile state of mind*

As rain begins to fall, Faith looks out the wall of windows past their patio and to the bay, each raindrop making a splat atop the water. Faith's phone rings, its Doctor Graves asking her to come back into the office to go over the results, which instantly confirms that her strong knowing was entirely accurate. Staring out at the drab sky, watching the rain pelt the water she begins crying once again before hanging up the phone.

Jonathan drives them back to the Women's Pavilion for the second time today. Faith feels the stark difference between their first appointment with Doctor Graves and this one. The waiting room suddenly feels darker and less cheery, maybe it has something to do with the grey dreary day outside, but Faith believes it has more to do with her state of mind.

Jonathan tries to be supportive as they sit in the waiting room. Faith is still mentally reprimanding herself for how she treated him early this morning. He's been incredible over the past few hours that actually feel as though they consisted of an entire lifetime.

When she's called back by the CNA, Faith and Jonathan both stand reluctantly and follow them. They pass the numerous exam rooms on either side of the hallway and come to a small conference room in the back. Faith figures this to be another bad sign.

"Dr. Graves will be with you shortly Ms. Brandt."

"Thank you." Faith says softly.

Jonathan sits beside Faith, instantly taking her hand in his. "Whatever he tells us, Faith, we will get through this together. I'm here for you, OK?"

"OK."

"I know that you are believing the worst right now, but it will all be OK. If we have lost the baby then we'll be sad for a bit, but we can always try again, as soon as you feel ready."

"OK." Faith can't seem to bring herself to say anything else. Jonathan must have taken the hint that she isn't in the mood to talk because he stops speaking.

Dr. Graves knocks softly on the conference room door and enters. His demeanor is less jovial than it had been just a week and a half ago.

"Good afternoon, Faith, Jonathan. I'm so sorry to have to bring you in like this. I wish there was a different way for us to be able to do this. I got the message from the help line this morning and I've reviewed the tests that were performed first thing." His voice cracks as he says, "I'm so sorry to inform you that this pregnancy is no longer viable. During the ultrasound there was no heart beat detected. There was also no change in the measurements from the first ultrasound, which tells me that this was inevitable. I am so sorry." His eyes and voice are both soft and Faith is pretty sure she sees tears forming in them, or maybe they are just her own tears creating an optical illusion.

Her breathing is shallow and her tears flow down her cheeks uncontrollably. Jonathan squeezes her hand.

Faith tries to take a deep breath and asks, "What do we do now?"

"Well, there are a couple of options. Typically our bodies are efficient at naturally taking care of this, that's called expectant management. However, sometimes they need assistance. If that's the case, then we start with one of two things. There is a medication which you can take first that will help your body pass any remaining tissue, or if need be we will do dilation and curettage, where we go in through your cervix and remove any remnants."

"I don't want to do that." Faith's voice is barely audible.

"I understand. We will wait to make that decision. What I can do is give you a prescription for the medication. You can choose to take it whenever you please, the only side effects will be cramping and bleeding. You've already been experiencing those which leads me to believe that your body may not need any intervention at all. I will have a nurse come in and schedule you for a two week follow up.

We'll check to make sure there are no remnants left that could lead to infection, at that time."

"So we just wait?" Jonathan asks.

"Yes, unfortunately. I'm sorry, I wish there was a better way to do this, as I said." Doctor Graves looks at Faith with kindness in his eyes. "Faith, you should know that there's nothing you could have done to prevent this. These things just happen, they are quite common in early pregnancy, especially if it's a woman's first."

"Is there cause for concern of future pregnancies?" Jonathan asks. Faith looks at him slightly shocked at the question.

"Not at this time. As I said, this is quite common. If there are recurring miscarriages then there are additional steps we can take once we get there, but with a vibrant young couple, such as yourselves, I typically don't see infertility issues. I certainly wouldn't be able to identify them from a singular miscarriage."

"OK, Doctor. Thank you."

"You're welcome."

Infertility had never even crossed Faith's mind, but it had obviously been on Jonathan's enough for him to ask Doctor Graves about it.

"Do you two have any further questions?"

Jonathan looks at Faith and then says, "I don't think so."

"I am going to step out now and send the nurse in to schedule that follow up. Please, take as much time as you need when we're all finished here. There's no rush. I'm so sorry for your loss." He reaches for Faith's hand then Jonathan's.

He closes the door behind him and the nurse knocks shortly after. She comes in with a laptop in her hands.

"Is there anything I can get you guys? Some water, maybe?"

"That would be good." Faith says softly.

"I'll be right back."

She comes back in with two bottles of water and hands one to each of them.

"I'm sure Doctor Graves went over everything with you two, but if there are any questions I can answer or if you're confused about anything, please let me know." She opens the laptop screen and signs in, then continues, "We need to schedule you for a follow up in two weeks. Is there a day or time that works best?"

Faith looks at Jonathan who says, "After three would be great."

"We have a four o'clock on Wednesday, June ninth. Will that work?"

"That sounds good. Thank you." Jonathan says.

"What happens if there's still remaining tissue when we come back in two weeks?"

"I see Doctor Graves has sent the prescription to the pharmacy for you. So, if you've already taken the medication, then we will have to schedule a D&C. Doctor Graves did make it seem like he was confident that your body was already well underway with taking care of it."

"OK." Faith says. *My body was supposed to take care of my baby.*

"Do you have any other questions?" The nurse asks.

"No, thank you." Jonathan says.

"I am so sorry for your loss. If you have any other questions or if there's anything else we can do for you, simply give us a call." With that she closes her laptop and leaves the room, closing the door behind her.

The room is silent as Faith's pain filled sobs fill the air. All Jonathan can do is wrap his arms around her as her shoulders shudder with every weep.

"I don't know how this could have happened." She wails. "I did everything I was supposed to do. I quit drinking. I am a good person. We would have been great parents."

"You heard the doctor, Faith. It wasn't your fault. These things just happen."

With tear filled eyes she looks up at Jonathan. "Why did you ask him about infertility? Do you think there's something wrong with me?"

"No. I never said that." He shakes his head. "I thought you might be worried about that is all. I was trying to ease your mind, not make things worse." He runs his fingers through his sandy brown hair.

"I wasn't even thinking of that." Her cries become louder once again.

"I'm sorry, Faith. I was trying to help."

Faith puts her head on top of her arms on the table and cries. She doesn't hold back. She cries for the loss of her baby and how this one will always be hanging over her head when she gets pregnant again. She cries for all of the hope she once felt, she cries for how crushing the news is going to be for her parents and Hope. She cries for not being able to share this with Jackie and wishing that she'll be understanding. She cries for January fifth, this coming year and all of them to come, knowing what stark reminder that day will always be.

On the way home, Faith watches Jonathan as he drives and she wonders if he's even sad. She wants him to cry like she is so that she knows how he's feeling. She knows that this has obviously hurt him too, on some level. It seems like the only reason he's feeling any pain is more because of how upset she is than it is over the loss of their baby.

Jonathan's hand is holding hers on top of the shifter like he normally does. She feels his thumb rubbing the top of her hand, almost absent mindedly. Tears haven't stopped streaming down her face, but the sobs have subsided. There is a heavy emptiness that fills her chest now. She isn't sure if it can ever be filled again.

"I need to figure out how I'm going to tell my parents and Hope."

"What about Jackie?"

"I didn't even get to tell her about the pregnancy. We never got a moment to ourselves and I didn't think sending her a text was the best way to do it."

"Do you want to go over to your parents' house tonight?"

"That's probably the best idea. They're going to take one look at me and know right away."

"That will make it easier, though, won't it?"

"No. They'll look at me with sorrow and pity. It's going to be so hard." She wipes the tears away from her puffy eyes with annoyance.

"Life requires us to do hard things sometimes."

"Life can shove it, for all I care."

"It'll get easier, Faith. I know it doesn't seem like it right now, but it will."

Later that evening, all of Faith's worries were true. Her parents' knew something was up as soon as they came to the door. It isn't like Faith and Jonathan to just stop by, but Faith knew if she made it a point to ask if they could come over they would know and be anxious about it for hours and she wanted to spare them that.

Diane instantly embraces Faith as she walks in. Tears pooling in the corner of Diane's eyes.

"I'm sorry, Mommy."

"You don't have to apologize, dear. You haven't done anything wrong."

"You were so looking forward to being a grandma."

"It's OK, darling. Shh." Diane rubs Faith's back in an attempt to console her. "I know we can't do anything to make you feel better, but we're here for you, dear. Anything you need."

"Thank you, Mom."

Frank rubs Faith's shoulder. "It's going to be OK, peanut. Everything is going to be OK."

"It doesn't feel like it, Daddy."

"No, I suppose it doesn't, but eventually it will. Eventually it will." He repeats.

Jonathan stands with his arms crossed watching the interaction. Frank takes a step back and embraces Jonathan. "I'm sorry, son. I'm sure this isn't easy on you either."

"I'm most worried about Faith."

"Of course you are, but you still shouldn't gloss over your own feelings. They don't need to be shoved to the side. They're important too."

"It doesn't feel appropriate, sir."

"That's because you were never given permission to feel your feelings before. I'm giving you that now. Mourn with her. You don't have to be a rock all the time. Sometimes your partner needs you to connect with them in the same emotional place they are. It doesn't make you weak. It actually means you are stronger than you thought."

With that Frank backs up and signals for Diane to do the same. They walk hand in hand to the living room and sit beside each other still holding hands, both in tears.

Jonathan takes Faith in his strong embrace. She feels his chest shake beneath her head and realizes that he too is crying. The comfort that she feels in this moment is so overwhelming she can't help but cry harder.

"I'm so sorry, Jonathan."

"It's not your fault, Faith. I could never think it was your fault." With tears streaming he lifts her chin, sniffles and kisses her gently on the forehead. With his lips still pressed against it he says softly, "Never."

They both try to wipe away their tears as they walk into the living room to sit with Diane and Frank. Diane offers them the box of tissue.

"Thank you." Jonathan says.

Diane looks at Faith. "If you'd like, we can tell Hope."

"I really think I should do it."

"If that's the way you feel. We just wanted to try to alleviate some of the pressure."

"It helps knowing that you are all so supportive and understanding. Thank you."

"You're welcome, Faith. Of course we would be. This is a tragedy, but it's also fairly common."

"Do you know anyone who's lost a baby this early?"

"Quite a few people actually, dear. Why, your aunt Julie had one with her very first."

"Really? I didn't know that."

"No, you wouldn't have, you weren't even born yet."

"It took them eight years to even try again?" Faith asks astounded.

# APTITUDE

"Yeah, I don't remember the exact reasoning. I don't think there were any issues beyond the first."

"No one ever talked about it after?"

"Not really. I think once you're cousin Matthew was born, they wanted to focus on him. I do remember that me being pregnant with you and then Hope was very hard on Julie." Diane glances at Frank. "She was happy for us, but you could tell it pained her to see the attention we were getting and the excitement around the baby with each pregnancy."

"I could see how that would be a normal reaction."

"No one blamed her. Goodness, no!" Diane exclaims.

Frank adds. "We also felt guilty when we had no reason to."

"I remember that her doctor told her that sometimes these things just happen. It's difficult to accept, especially when you were so excited about it, but life is going to go on, and you'll move on as well. I know it doesn't feel like it, but there will be other things to be excited about and eventually other pregnancies and babies."

"Thanks, Mom."

"You're welcome, dear."

"I think we're going to get going. Do you know when Hope normally gets home? I can always text her."

Diane checks her watch. "She should be home now."

"OK." Faith looks at Jonathan. "We'll head over there now then."

Jonathan nods his head and they both stand. Faith walks over to Diane who stands and hugs her. Frank follows suit.

As they pull up to Hope's apartment, Faith feels the queasiness from earlier return. Jonathan opens her door for her and they walk up the walkway hand in hand.

Faith rings the bell and Hope opens the door a few moments later.

"Hi guys. What's up?" Realization flashes on her face as she takes in the sight of Faith's tear filled puffy eyes. "Come in, come in."

She leads the way into her living room and asks, "What's wrong, Faith?"

"We lost the baby today, Hope."

"Oh no, I'm so sorry." Hope leans in to hug her sister. "This sucks."

With a slight chuckle she says, "No kidding."

"Are you in pain? Well…like physical pain?"

"I have had the worst cramps I've ever had in my life pretty much all day."

"Is there anything they can give you?"

"I've been alternating acetaminophen and ibuprofen, but it isn't helping much."

"Is there anything I can do to help?"

"I don't think so. Are you doing OK?"

"I'm sad, I was very much looking forward to being an aunt, but there will be other opportunities, right?"

"We'll try again at some point. I'm not sure when that will be, though. Did you know that Aunt Julie had a miscarriage?" Hope shakes her head. "Yeah. Mom and dad just told me tonight. I guess it was before we were born."

"That's crazy. I'm surprised no one ever talked about it."

"That's what I said."

Faith and Hope talk a bit more before Hope asks if they'd like to stay for dinner.

"I think I'd like to just go home, but thank you so much for offering. It's been a really long day and I want to have a little something to eat, snuggle my dog, and go to bed."

"No problem. Faith, if you need anything, reach out. I'm always here for you."

"Thank you, Hope. I love you." She says as she hugs her sister.

"I love you too, Faith and I'm so sorry you're going through this."

"Thank you."

# Chapter 47

## Lentitude
### Noun; slowness, sluggishness

The next two weeks drag on. Jonathan is able to go to Faith's follow up appointment with her, which she is so grateful for. Doctor Graves performs the ultrasound this time, which is also a relief since he talks her through the entire procedure and tells her what he is or in this case, isn't seeing.

There is no remaining tissue from the pregnancy. Faith is so happy to be able to look to the future again. The past two weeks have been hell for her mentally and emotionally.

After the appointment, Jonathan drives them to the house which is only a few weeks from being entirely finished. The driveway, pool, and patio were just finished on Monday and Faith is looking forward to seeing them done.

Michael greets them gregariously as they step out of Jonathan's SUV. "Welcome home you two!"

Jonathan smiles, shaking his hand. "Thank you, sir. How are things going?"

# APTITUDE

"We're right on schedule to hand over the keys to you, tentatively, on July second."

"July second?" Faith asks surprised.

"Yes, the second. We're working on installing flooring, countertops and doing the exterior grading this week. We'll have the final inspection three weeks from today."

"I can't believe it's coming up so soon." Faith says. She turns to Jonathan. "I guess we should start packing!" She catches herself feeling more excited than she has in the past couple of weeks and is instantly hit by a wave of guilt.

Michael takes them through the home so that they can clearly see that it is only the finishing touches needed yet. There are no sinks, faucets, or toilets installed. Michael explains that will all be done next week then goes back to supervising the subcontractors.

Jonathan is obviously impressed with the workmanship as he walks through since he keeps commenting on how amazing everything looks.

Outside on the patio, Faith turns to Jonathan. "Do you remember when all of this was just a rendering on Stephen's computer screen?" She spins around taking it all in. "I can't believe it's nearly finished and we'll be moving in soon. Like, less than a month soon!"

Jonathan smiles gratefully at her. "I think we should start planning a double party, if you're up for it."

"A double party?"

"Yeah, housewarming and Fourth of July."

Faith smiles. "I'll be up for it. It'll be fun and maybe even exactly what we need."

"You don't think it'll be too much between planning that, packing, and moving?"

"No, especially not with school being out now. It'll help keep me busy."

"I suppose it will. Maybe you can get Jackie to help you."

"I think she's got a couple more weeks of classes for her master's before they go on break, but I'll ask."

Jonathan gestures towards the house, which from the outside looks like it may be finished on the inside. "This makes me want to camp in the yard and watch the entire process."

"I bet. It took so long to get to this point, but we're incredibly close now. It's hard to believe."

"It is. I'm glad to see you get a little bit of the spark back in your eye."

Faith smiles half-heartedly. "Me too, Jonathan."

"It's OK to be happy, you know."

"I'm not sure that I do. It doesn't always feel OK. I find myself feeling guilty out of the blue."

"There's no reason to feel guilty, Faith."

"Of course there is. Our baby died, they died inside of me, when I was supposed to keep it alive and help it grow."

"Faith, it wasn't your fault and you deserve to still be happy." He grips Faith's shoulders gently. "We both deserve to be happy."

# APTITUDE

Faith looks down at her feet as she kicks a rock that was underfoot. "I'm trying Jonathan. Being here," She looks up at the house, "is helping."

"Good. And planning the party will help?"

"I believe it will, yes."

"If it gets to be too much, I need you to let me know."

"I will, Jonathan."

Jonathan takes her hand and leads her to the area overlooking Amethyst Bay. It's nearly sunset. They stand watching the colors change in the sky.

Before they know it, the dark is settling in and the construction crew has all gone home. Faith turns to look at their new home standing tall against the dark sky. There is no glow coming from within like there had been on Valentine's Day, but it still looks like something out of a painting.

"How did we get so lucky, Jonathan?"

"What do you mean, Faith?"

"We have the perfect home, the closest thing I've ever known to a perfect relationship. It obviously wasn't lucky to miscarry our first child, but in every other aspect we are blessed beyond measure."

"We really are. I don't think there's only one reason. I also don't think we should overthink it. We need to simply be grateful for all of the good we have in our lives."

"You're right, Jonathan."

Jonathan moves to stand behind her, wrapping his arms around her. "I can't even begin to explain to you how grateful I am to have you. This adventure we're on is only just beginning, Faith. We've got a lifetime of happy memories to make together."

"A lifetime of all kinds of memories, Jonathan. They won't all be happy."

"If I have anything to do with it I'll try for ninety percent."

"That's a lofty goal, but I'm along for the ride." She smiles.

Before heading home to the condo, they stop at a store and pick up some boxes and tape for packing. While Jonathan makes dinner, Faith gets to work packing knick-knacks and non-essential things.

Jonathan chuckles. "If you get it all done now, there won't be anything to keep you busy for the next three weeks."

"Well, I've got a party to plan yet."

He holds his hands up, one still holding a spatula. "You're right."

She smiles lovingly at him as she runs a strip of tape across the top of a box and writes 'knick-knacks', 'Living room' on the lid and the side with a black marker.

# Chapter 48

## Splenditude

*Noun; the quality of being splendid*

Michael greets Faith and Jonathan at the entrance to their freshly finished home. He holds out the two keys for them to take. Jonathan gestures to the door. "Go ahead, Faith."

She slides the key through the slot and turns, hearing the mechanism inside give way. Then Jonathan scoops her up in his arms and carries her over the threshold.

Michael is laughing as he follows them through the double doors. "You two love birds deserve this beautiful home! It was an honor and a pleasure working on it for you!" A tear forms on his lower lash line, threatening to fall. He swipes it away before it gets the chance.

"You've done a marvelous job, Michael. We couldn't be happier." Faith assures him.

He clutches his chest. "Thank you, Faith. That means the world to me! Now I'll get out of your hair and let the movers get in here."

"You and your family will be coming to the party on the fourth right?" Faith asks eagerly.

"We wouldn't miss it!" Michael smiles his huge gregarious smile and closes the front door behind him.

The movers arrive a short time later with their truck full of Faith's things from storage. The second load they bring is everything from the condo.

Faith stands in their spacious living room, which has suddenly been filled with boxes lining the wall that has the fireplace on it, looking at the space she asks Jonathan, "How in the world are we going to get this place ready for the party in two days?"

Jonathan takes a deep breath and says, "We've got this. No one will expect the house to be fully unpacked. I think we start in the kitchen. We'll need to have that organized first. Besides we still have furniture we need to pick out."

"Remind me, why didn't we order that ahead of time again?"

"We felt like we needed to be in the space with it finished before we could decide on what we wanted."

"Right. Well, now I'm feeling like it's going to look funny with discombobulated furniture that doesn't go together."

"Faith, no one is going to care about the furniture. It's OK. There's no need to stress."

Faith scoffs. "I'm surprised to hear you say that. Mr. Kansen is coming." She places her hands on her hips for emphasis.

# APTITUDE

"I know. I'm the one that personally put the invite on his desk."

"And you're not worried about what he might think?"

"Not in the least. Like I said, everyone who's coming knows that we're getting the keys just two days before the party. They won't be expecting perfection. Besides, the party is going to be mostly outside anyways." Jonathan shrugs his shoulders.

"That's true."

He takes her by the arm, "So let's go get started in the kitchen."

She pauses, making him stop in his tracks. "Do you think we should hide some of these boxes somehow?"

"Well, considering part of a housewarming party will be a tour of said house, I don't see where we can hide them."

"Good point." She says as they walk into the kitchen and start opening boxes. "I'm glad I donated most of my kitchen things. It's going to make this so much easier." She states as she grabs a handful of utensils from the box in front of her.

She turns with the utensils in her hand, staring at the cabinets in front of her. She looks at Jonathan and starts laughing. "I have no idea where I'm going with these."

"Me either, but you looked so confident!" He begins to laugh as well.

He locates the drawer organizer for the utensils in one of the boxes and they continue unpacking, trying to set up the kitchen in a way that makes the most sense in hopes that for the party they will be able to remember where they put everything."

"Maybe the Fourth of July was a bit ambitious for a party." Jonathan admits.

"I'm glad you're realizing that." Faith chuckles.

"I still say everything will be fine, we just could have saved ourselves a bit of stress if we had done a party later in the month."

"Well, we can't change it now." Faith says matter-of-factly as she grabs another box and cuts it open.

The next two days goes by in a flurry of unpacking and breaking down boxes. Zeke has been very intrigued with living in the new house. Faith often wonders if he's confused about their living situation, but it seems as though he's entirely content.

They bring Zeke to the parade on Main Street this year. Hope and Andy are there as well as Jackie and Faith's parents. When the parade concludes Jonathan and Faith go back to the house to finish getting everything ready. They had started setting up early that morning. Diane and Frank follow shortly after to give them a hand as well. Jackie stops off at the liquor store to pick up a couple bottles of wine as a house warming gift first.

# APTITUDE

Faith waits until Andy and Hope get there to take everyone on the first official tour. Jonathan follows as he watches Faith light up talking about their new home.

Frank stands next to Jonathan, "This is a hell of a home, son. Nice job. It is incredibly beautiful."

"Faith picked everything out."

"You've done an incredible job of giving her everything she could ever want."

"That's my job, sir."

Frank pats Jonathan's back as they move along the tour with Faith as their guide.

Diane is mostly speechless throughout with the exception of repeating "Oh my" at nearly every turn.

Hope seems genuinely happy for them despite her previous envy filled quips. Andy makes a remark to Hope towards the end of the walk-thru that it seems a little like overkill. They weren't trying to be rude, just state that something this large isn't for them.

Jackie has a smile plastered on her face the entire time. When they've returned to the kitchen and it's only her and Faith, she says, "I am incredibly happy for you. No one deserves a beautiful home like this more than you do."

"Thank you! That means so much! We…well, really, I was worried about how we were going to get this place together in time for the party, but I think its fine. It's not perfect, but that's OK. We did just get the keys." Faith grabs a spoon to put into the veggie dip in the middle of the tray full of a variety of vegetables.

"It looks amazing! You've gotten so much accomplished in such a short time! How are you doing with everything?"

"I'm doing OK. Being here, having so much to get done helps to keep me busy and keeps my mind off of everything."

"That's good. If you need anything, I'm here for you."

"I do know that, without a doubt. Thank you, Jackie. I'm sorry I hadn't told you. I should have made the effort a bit more."

"You don't need to apologize. It was a hectic time with getting things ready for the end of the school year. I don't know about your class, but my students were absolutely out of control by the last day!"

"I don't think the class matters. It happens every year." Faith says as she opens one of the bottles of wine Jackie brought and pours them each a glass. "Thank you for this, it was very thoughtful."

"I could have done better, honestly. Things have been a little crazy with school, but I've only got one more year and I'll have my masters!"

"We're going to have to celebrate! What do you have in mind?"

"I'm thinking a vacation or something." She laughs.

"Seriously! We should! Where would you want to go?"

"Anywhere with a beach. Well, it's got to be warm too, not just have a beach."

"OK! We've got one year to plan a girl's vacation on the beach!"

# APTITUDE

"Nothing too expensive. I've got student loans I'll have to start paying."

"We can figure out a budget to stay within."

With that they grab their glasses and the hors d'oeuvres trays to take outside to the tables they have set up on the patio.

"This pool area is so pretty. It almost doesn't even look like a pool with all the rocks and landscaping." Frank says.

"There's lights too!" Jonathan says excitedly.

More guests begin showing up and Jonathan and Faith take turns giving the tours. When Mr. Kansen arrives they both take him around the house, showing him every room and all three levels.

"You two are going to have to hurry up and get married and start making babies to fill some of these bedrooms."

Faith's heart sinks, but she tries to hide it knowing that he didn't know what they just went through weeks before. She excuses herself to the kitchen and fills her glass of wine to the top.

Hope see's the look on her sister's face from the patio and goes inside as quickly as she can, leaving Andy with Jackie.

"What's going on? Who do I need to beat up?"

"No one. It was just a comment Mr. Kansen made unknowingly. I'll be OK." She takes a sip of her wine and fights back tears.

Hope moves to hug her, but then thinks twice. "I want to give you a hug, but I don't want to make you cry more."

"Thank you. I don't want to be crying at all."

"I know." Hope looks down at the beer bottle in her hand. "Do you want to come outside with me? We can go see Andy and Jackie. I'm sure mom and dad are out there too."

"Yeah, some fresh air sounds good right about now."

As the sky starts to change colors with the setting sun, Faith sits snuggled in Jonathan's lap on the Adirondack chairs that were a house warming gift from Kansen Corp which sit around the fire pit overlooking Amethyst Bay. Zeke lays down beside them. There's music playing softly from the outdoor speakers Michael had installed for them and the string lights hang surrounding the paver patio adding to the ambiance.

The fireworks will be starting within an hour and everyone is eagerly waiting.

The entire day has been so fun, with only a few minor hiccups. Faith kept busy with hostess duties and still got to enjoy the party with Jonathan's help. The turnout was better than they expected.

Jonathan kisses Faith on the cheek. "How's this for our first fourth of July in our forever home?"

"I think we need to do this every year."

"Yes! I love making new traditions with you! It's perfect having so many friends and family members around to celebrate. This has been such a great day!"

"It definitely has. We can only have one house warming party, though."

"That's true."

# APTITUDE

The fireworks in Sol Port begin a few minutes before Luna Shores begins setting off theirs. When they are both being set off simultaneously the sky is filled with flashing colors and numerous thunderous bangs and booms that fill the air.

A little while later, both finales are incredibly loud and bright, Luna Shores' ends right after Sol Port's.

"I've never been able to watch two firework shows at once." Mr. Kansen comments after all of the booms have ended.

"You'll have to come back next year to experience it again then!" Jonathan says.

"I think I'll have to do just that."

Shortly after the shows are done and most of the smoke from the fireworks have cleared from the sky everyone begins going home.

Hope, Andy, and Jackie stay to help them clean up even though both Faith and Jonathan tell them it's unnecessary.

Faith is more than happy to accept their help though. Her body is still recovering from the loss of the pregnancy and she still hasn't quite gotten her energy back. She's most exhausted at the end of the day and today has been a lot for her.

The warm water rushes over her hands as she rinses the dishes she's loading into the dishwasher. "Today went by very quickly."

"It did, but everything was good! I think everyone had a fantastic time and I know they all loved the food." Diane says.

"Well, of course they did since you made most of it, Mom!" Faith says with a laugh. Diane smiles at her and Faith continues, "We appreciate it very much. I know it was a lot of work, but it took so much off of our shoulders."

"I'll work in this kitchen any day!" Diane says as she looks around the room.

"It's pretty amazing isn't it?" Jonathan says. "Faith picked out all of the finishes and this booth style table built into the massive island was all her idea!"

"It is beautiful!" Frank gushes.

Faith feels her cheeks getting hot. "Thanks, Dad. It was a lot of fun, somewhat stressful, but definitely fun."

Diane smiles at her. "When will you start looking for furniture?"

"Very soon." Jonathan says. "We wanted to wait, but now I feel like I can't wait any longer." He chuckles.

"We should get going." Frank says as he and Diane walk towards the door. "Orpheus probably needs to go out."

"You should have brought him with you." Faith suggests.

"We thought about it, but with everything going on and people coming and going we thought it best to leave him home. Maybe next time."

"Sounds good!" Faith smiles and hugs her parents.

Jonathan opens the giant double doors to let them out and hugs them both as they leave. "Thank you for everything you helped with. It was a huge relief with everything else going on."

"That's what we're here for, son." Frank says.

Once everything is cleaned up, Hope, Andy, and Jackie also head out, leaving Faith, Jonathan, and Zeke to collapse on the couch in exhaustion.

Jonathan places his arm around Faith and says, "This party today was exactly why I wanted this house. Not that the condo wasn't enough, but this house is so much more."

"I know that it's more of a status symbol for you."

"It is, but it's also our home and a symbol of our love and our life together. It's an incredible home. I couldn't have known when I was nine, living with aunt Suz completely heart broken and miserable, that I could ever possibly be here with you." He squeezes her hand.

"I never thought this was possible either." She looks around the massive family room with the large stone fireplace as the focal point and imagines it with the new furniture they'll be shopping for soon.

"Thank you, Faith. I'm happy to be on this journey with you." He pulls her head towards him and kisses the top of her head.

"This journey is going to be absolutely incredible, Jonathan."

"There's so much more to come, Faith."

Faith snuggles against him, fighting to keep her eyes open. Grateful for the day and for their new home. Jonathan will be putting his condo up for sale once they have cleaners come in to do a deep clean. Then their new chapter can officially begin in their new home.

# Chapter 49

## Turpitude
*Noun; a vile or depraved act*

Ever since the miscarriage Jonathan's urges have come back full force. He's been trying to do everything he can to keep them under wraps, from reminding himself of past kills, to remembering what it was like when Faith was drugged. None of it is working. He's found himself making excuses to "work late" again, explaining to Faith that work has picked up again.

It's the Friday following the Fourth of July and house warming party. Jonathan finds himself sitting in the parking lot of the Blue Rooster. He's breathing deeply with sweat beads dotting his forehead. Feeling so torn apart, he annoyingly swipes the back of his hand across his forehead and opens the door of the Lexus that he keeps just for nights like this.

He hears the crunch of gravel beneath his feet which makes him walk quicker, feeling as if he's being followed.

His heart rate quickens as he opens the door and is hit with the sound of loud music and the smell of stale beer.

Almost immediately a wave of nausea hits him as he walks to the bar to sit down. The pretty brunette bartender approaches him wearing a soft smile.

"I'll take a water for now. Thanks." He gets the words out as quickly as he can.

She returns with the water and asks, "Are you feeling OK?"

"I'm alright, thanks for asking." He takes a drink from the neon green straw.

"If you need anything else, just let me know."

"I will." He usually doesn't like bringing attention to himself while he's hunting. That's the last thing he wants to do.

A few moments later just as he's decided he should leave a woman walks in that stops him in his tracks. He watches as she walks over to the end of the bar and takes a seat in the corner. He takes a deep breath, knowing that his plan is back on track.

He smiles at the bartender and drinks down the rest of his water, the sweat running down the glass still in his hand as she approaches.

"Can I get you something else now?"

"Yes, I'll take a rum and coke. Thank you."

"Coming right up." She mixes his drink and brings it back quickly. Jonathan tips well and the bartender smiles seductively at him.

His attention turns to the woman at the end of the bar. He watches her without her noticing for quite some time. It doesn't appear that she's waiting for anyone. She orders a long island iced tea. She's definitely here to drink away some kind of heartbreak.

As he takes a closer look, her shoulders are slightly slumped and her eyes are puffy. She's been crying. She drinks the first one quickly. Jonathan takes a sip from his glass and motions for the bartender.

"What would you like? Same thing?"

He holds up his half full glass. "Actually, I'd like to send her a drink." He points towards the woman.

"Oh, OK." Dejection in her voice. "I can get that for her."

"Thank you. It looks like she needs it."

The smile reappears on the bartender's face. "It really does."

Ten minutes after the bartender delivers the drink to her, she walks slowly up to Jonathan seeming quite unsure of herself. Jonathan doesn't seem to know of her presence until he feels her tap his shoulder.

As he turns, the woman instantly moves in for a kiss. This is going to be easier than he could have hoped for.

Getting home to their new house late that night Jonathan has a new sense of guilt as he enters the bedroom seeing Faith asleep in bed. How can he fight these urges? He resolves to try harder. Faith deserves better.

He showers in the full bathroom in the basement. When they initially sat down with Stephen to plan this home he hadn't thought that much about the usefulness of having this available to him. Now he realizes how convenient it is that he doesn't have to worry about waking Faith up.

When he's done showering he sits in the family room in the basement on the couch from Faith's old house. Sitting on this couch, remembering being in her house for the first time when he picked her up for their first date. He recalls how nervous and excited he was that night. He suddenly feels overwhelmed with thankfulness for that time, which has led to this point in their lives, this amazing level of perfection that he never could have imagined prior.

In this time of reflection, Jonathan begins to make a plan, one more immediate than his five year plan, and one much sooner to feel its gratification.

# Chapter 50

## Altitude
Noun; a high level

The following two weeks were filled with unpacking and organizing. They went furniture shopping, and picked out quite a few new pieces including new bedroom furniture. Jonathan has been home earlier again which Faith is incredibly grateful for. She had been worried when he told her things were picking back up, but it seems to have been short lived.

Faith wakes up Saturday morning to light pouring into their bedroom from the large windows. They must have forgotten to close the shades last night. Jonathan's arm is holding her tightly against him, and she can hear the soft snore of Zeke in his crate.

The furniture won't be here for another week, but Faith is already envisioning where she'll position it and how each piece will look in its respective room.

Jonathan begins to stir beside her, pulling her in even closer. He buries his face in the crook of her neck and begins gently kissing it. Faith slowly pulls away. He's been completely patient with her and allowing her to take as long as she needs, but she is still worried. She fears that she hasn't healed fully yet, but possibly even more so that she'll get pregnant again.

She kisses him quickly hoping to not give him any false hope. He seems to take the hint since he goes back to snuggling.

"Good morning, beautiful." He says softly.

"Good morning. How did you sleep?"

"It was pretty good." Blinking his eyes he says, "It's really bright in here when the shades don't get closed."

"It's because we insisted on these big windows." Faith giggles then she hears Zeke moving around in his crate.

Jonathan leans up onto his arm and looks at Faith lovingly. He smiles and says, "I can't wait any longer. I've got a surprise planned for us today. Zeke can come too."

Faith's face lights up. "A surprise? What should I wear?"

"Comfortable shoes for walking, probably shorts and a tank top since it's going to be pretty warm today."

"OK!"

"I'm going to get up and make some breakfast."

"Do you want some help?"

"No. You go ahead and get yourself ready."

"OK."

Even though Jonathan didn't give her much to go off of, she quickly gets dressed and puts her long hair up in a ponytail. She takes a little more time with her makeup yet still keeps it simple.

When she goes into the kitchen to see him cooking on their Viking range, her heart fills. Zeke follows her in there happily.

"What'cha cooking?" Faith asks.

"Some scrambled eggs and bacon."

"Well it smells delicious. Even Zeke thinks so." She looks down at him and starts laughing as he sits there with his tail wagging.

"He's gotten so big these past few months."

"He really has. I'd guess he has to be almost fully grown."

"Possibly. Although he could probably still grow a bit. He's not quite a year old yet."

"So what's this surprise you have planned for us?" She asks nonchalantly as Jonathan places a full coffee mug on the island for her.

"I'm not going to tell you that." He tells her.

"What about a clue?"

"No clues beyond what to wear! Which I have to say, you've chosen well." He admires her figure in her tight shorts and tank top. "You always look amazing though, Faith."

"Thank you, Jonathan." She says blushing.

After breakfast Faith and Zeke eagerly wait in the car as Jonathan grabs something last minute from inside the house. Once he comes back, He loads something into the back of the SUV. Faith couldn't clearly see what it was, but it has definitely piqued her curiosity.

Then Jonathan gets into the driver's seat, shifts into reverse, and backs out of their attached three car garage. He has Faith close her eyes, but the drive won't take long at all.

He pulls into the familiar driveway and up to the line before the attendant's booth to purchase a pass. Jonathan tells Faith to open her eyes. Suddenly, her vision is filled with green, browns, and yellows. As her eyes adjust to the bright sun light the trees lining the driveway become clearer.

Her face lights up! "Silverwood State Park!"

"I wanted to recreate our second date, even though it's not an anniversary or anything."

"I love the idea! I love even more so that Zeke gets to be a part of it!"

Jonathan pulls up to the window of the booth and purchases the day parking pass and asks for a map which she hands him. He drives further down the driveway to the parking area at the trailhead that looks familiar to Faith and parks.

When they get out of the car, Faith takes the leash and holds onto Zeke who's ready to go and sniffing everything. Jonathan grabs a backpack from the back end.

They begin their hike hand in hand. A short way past the trailhead they come to the lookout tower.

Jonathan gestures to the stairs. "Are we ready for this?"

"I am. I'm not so sure about this guy." She nods towards Zeke and they both laugh and begin the ascent up the wide wooden stairs.

Faith has the leash in one hand and holds onto the wooden rail with the other suddenly feeling more winded than she thinks she should be.

They stop at the second platform, which helps the stairs wind up the tower, to get a quick breather. Faith mentions, "We didn't have to stop the first time we did this."

"We can blame it on Zeke." Zeke looks at Jonathan suddenly with his head cocked to one side in confusion. Faith laughs.

"It doesn't matter if we have to stop, as long as we don't quite climbing." She says.

"That's true."

They begin up the stairs again, this time reaching the top without stopping again. Reaching the big platform Faith raises both arms, accidentally yanking on Zeke's leash.

Jonathan wraps his arms around her and Faith feels both of their heavy breathing come into rhythm together.

"I love you so much, Faith."

"I love you so much too, Jonathan. This was a great idea."

"We haven't even gotten started! Are you hungry? I packed us a picnic. It's not time for sunset, but it is lunch time."

"A picnic? That's so sweet! Yes I'm hungry!"

Jonathan swings the backpack off of his shoulders and unzips it. He sets it down on the wooden planks beneath his feet and grabs the blanket out. He spreads that and Faith sits while Jonathan grabs out water bottles for them as well as Zeke's collapsible water dish, which he fills right away.

Then he begins handing Faith the food to set out for them to begin eating. Jonathan sits beside her and leans in for a quick kiss. She leans in to him and says, "Thank you for being so thoughtful, Jonathan. I'm an incredibly lucky woman."

Jonathan smiles and simply replies, "You're so welcome, Faith."

He pulls out a couple of plastic wine cups and a bottle of Cabernet Sauvignon and pours them each some.

"Wine?" She smiles at him surprised.

"Well, I thought we might want to celebrate."

"What are we celebrating?"

Just as the last syllable of the question leaves her lips, Jonathan shifts to one knee and turns to her with a small box in his hand. He lifts the lid open to reveal a large diamond ring sparkling back at her. She inhales sharply as she covers her mouth with her hands.

"Faith Victoria Brandt, you are the best thing that has ever happened to me. Our life together has become something out of a dream, something that I always wanted, but couldn't bring myself to fully believe I would ever have. I would be honored to have you by my side as my partner forever. Will you be my wife?"

Ecstatic she answers "Yes! Of course I will, yes!"

# APTITUDE

Jonathan slips the ring onto her ring finger and Faith reaches instantly for his face to pull him closer to her. They kiss as if they are the only two people in the world. Happy tears begin to stream down Faith's cheeks. She welcomes the warm wet trail they leave.

When they finish kissing, Jonathan asks, "Did you know?"

"I had no clue. None. I wasn't even thinking that you would be doing this today."

"Good! I really wanted it to be a complete surprise."

Faith admires the ring as it sparkles brilliantly in the sunshine. Jonathan gently wipes the tears from her face.

"Did you ask my parents?"

"I did, yes, when you were in the bathroom at Sunday dinner."

"I had no idea. My parents didn't let on to anything either."

"They assured me they would keep the secret. Hope and Andy did too."

"They knew too?"

"Yup, and I talked to Jackie about it as well."

"Seriously? Everyone knew and kept it from me?"

"Yes, because they all knew how much you would want it to be a surprise. You have an amazing group of people in your corner, Faith."

"I know. I'm so lucky to have them, but you, my love, are the most important one. Thank you for asking me to be your wife." She holds her hand up once again, "I can't believe this ring." Her eyes open wide.

"I've visited a couple of jewelry stores looking for the perfect ring. Then I realized I needed to design my own with the help of a jeweler of course."

"You designed this?" She says shocked by the news.

"Yeah, you deserve the absolute best, Faith. The jeweler at Riteger's helped me, but I picked every diamond in the setting."

"It is breathtaking Jonathan."

"Does it fit well enough? It seemed to be OK when I put it on."

"It's perfect."

"Good! I was guessing at your size."

"You did amazing, Jonathan. Thank you for all of the work you put into this!"

"You deserve it! We should probably start eating so we can get on with our hike!"

Faith laughs. "Well, when you start the hike like this it makes it kind of hard to just move on."

"We can take as much time as you want."

"You asked me to be your girlfriend in this park."

"I know. I was thinking about waiting until we got to the first waterfall's deck, but I wanted to do it up here, with this view." He gestures to the expanse of woods and little buildings in the distance standing tall against the bay, even further out.

"This is perfect, Jonathan. Absolutely perfect." She feels tears begin to form once again. She glances at the massive elegant ring on her finger. "I wasn't expecting this at all today."

"That was the point." Jonathan smiles with pride filling his face.

"I'm so happy. Two months ago I wasn't sure that I would ever be able to feel happiness like this again." Tears begin to fall and she reaches for Jonathan, embracing him. "Thank you for everything you do for me. I am so damn lucky."

"You're very welcome, Faith. I'm so happy to do anything to make your life better."

She releases him and they finish eating the picnic that Jonathan made for them while Zeke watches expectantly.

The rest of the hike turns into a blur as Faith is feeling every emotion. She wants to call her family and Jackie, but since they all already know, it doesn't feel like it needs to be done immediately.

As they approach the final waterfall Jonathan says, "I had thought about using Zeke to ask you, but there was no way I was going to find a way to attach the ring to him without you noticing it.

"Plus, I would have been worried about it getting lost!"

"That too."

The path is getting steeper, which indicates to them that the waterfall is getting closer. The sound of the water plummeting the river below fills the air. Faith takes Jonathan's hand and starts running for the platform, feeling exhilarated by everything from the proposal to the fresh air and trees surrounding them.

When they reach the deck Faith raises her hands and Jonathan can't help, but laugh. "You forgot the 'Woohoo'."

Faith laughs too. "You just did it!"

Zeke looks up at her excited about running with her and panting. Jonathan takes his collapsible dish out again and fills it up. Zeke gladly laps up the water.

Jonathan puts his arm around Faith as they watch the mist come off of the waterfall.

Faith takes her phone out and spins around. Jonathan takes it from her and she turns her body towards him with her left hand on his chest, showing off her new ring, he snaps an updated picture of them. The photo shows up on the screen before he hands the phone back to her and Faith sees how huge her smile is and how much the ring is sparkling on her finger.

"I might need that one for my desk now, too." Jonathan says genuinely.

"That's a wonderful idea!"

They turn once again to take in the picturesque scene. Jonathan pulls her into him and kisses her hard. She returns his passion tenfold trying to convey how happy he's made her. His hand moves to the small of her back, pressing gently she feels his body against hers. When Jonathan pulls back Faith asks, "Are we going to go to dinner at Catch of the Bay after this?"

"How did you know?"

# APTITUDE

"Lucky guess, I suppose." She smiles slyly at him.

When they're nearly back to the trailhead, they pass the overlook and Faith glances up at the place that will forever hold a piece of her heart and a small but extremely significant piece of their story.

"We're going to have to come here more often now, you know." She tells Jonathan as they reach the start of the trail.

"We'll have to get a state park sticker then."

"Agreed."

During the drive to Catch of the Bay, Faith sends the picture of them to her parents, Hope, and Jackie with the exciting news. For some reason telling people something as huge as this makes it feel so much more real, but then again the ring on her finger makes it feel very real all on its own.

# Chapter 51

## Pulchritude

*Noun; beauty, especially a woman's beauty*

They take their seats at the same table on the back deck at Catch of the Bay that they sat at on their second date. The sun is just beginning to set. The sky looks as though an artist has painted it with all of the warm colors in their palate. Zeke lays down under the table, exhausted from their hike.

The waitress brings them menus and asks if they're ready to order drinks. Faith orders then she excuses herself to the bathroom.

When she comes back Jonathan has a smile plastered on his face. "What are you smiling about?" She asks curiously.

"I absolutely love watching you walk towards me with that ring on your finger, knowing that you agreed to be my wife. It's the best feeling in the world."

She smiles back at him feeling as if her life couldn't be more perfect in this moment.

She takes her seat noticing the drinks have already been delivered. A few moments later, the waitress comes back with food. Faith looks at her plate, then at Jonathan. "You ordered me the same thing that I got the first time we were here."

"Yes, I did. I hope that was OK."

"It's perfect."

"Do you know what I remember most about our first visit here?"

"What's that?" Faith says as she dips a fry in some ketchup and eats it.

"The conversation we had about how my parents died and how much it changed my life. While we talked about such a traumatic life experience, you were gentle, caring, and thoughtful. You asked appropriate questions, but at the same time you did it in a way that didn't make me feel worse." Jonathan reaches for Faith's hand. "It really made me feel like we connected on a deeper level that day."

"We definitely did. It made me feel like I was getting a genuine glimpse into who you are and a little bit about what has shaped you into the man that you have become."

"You're such an incredible woman, Faith. Thank you for being my partner, and now my fiancé."

"I am so beyond happy to be, Jonathan."

They both smile and look down at their plates realizing they've barely eaten.

"You know, this happens a lot." Jonathan says with a chuckle.

"It does." With that, they both begin to eat their dinner.

A few moments later Jonathan excuses himself to the restroom. A little while after Jonathan returns the waitress approaches the table and presents them with a bottle of Riesling. "The manager would like to offer you this complimentary bottle as congratulations on your engagement. We're so happy you chose us to celebrate such a happy occasion."

Faith smiles widely. "Thank you so much!"

The waitress pours the wine for them leaving the bottle in the ice bucket beside the table.

"Did you say something to them?"

"I had called them last week."

"Seriously? Did you make sure Zeke was able to come with us? I thought it was weird that no one said anything about us bringing the dog."

"Yup." He smiles, his face full of pride. "You deserve the best, Faith. I'm trying to give you that." He lifts his glass and continues, "To us, to our engagement and marriage. To our future and our life together. I love you more than I'll ever be able to fully express, but I will spend every day trying to show you."

"Thank you, Jonathan."

They clink their glasses together and both take a sip. The sun setting over the bay creates the perfect backdrop and ending for the most perfect day.

Once they finish eating Jonathan asks, "What would you like to do now?"

# APTITUDE

"We should probably head home." Faith glances under the table. "Someone is tuckered out."

Jonathan looks at Zeke who is passed out at Faith's feet using the base of the table as a pillow.

"What do you want to do at home?"

With a seductive look in her eyes she says, "I think you know."

Jonathan stands up immediately taking his wallet out of his back pocket and places cash on the table.

Faith just giggles and says "I guess we're ready then." She reaches down to gently wake Zeke up.

The drive home doesn't take long. Jonathan may have been going a bit above the speed limit. Zeke goes potty quickly and goes straight to his crate.

When Faith comes back into the kitchen she sees Jonathan leaning against the large island. He motions for her to come to him.

He wraps his arms around her, pulling her into him placing his lips against hers. He slips his tongue between them, finding hers. Faith's breathing picks up as she feels her desire grow.

When Jonathan pulls back, he asks, "Do we want to go to the bedroom?"

Faith looks over to the couch in the family room. "I think there is fine." She says softly.

Jonathan places his hands under her ass and lifts her up carrying her over to the couch. He sits down with her on top of him. She leans down to kiss him, her pony tail moving to one side.

When she pulls away again, she stands and begins to undress. Jonathan watches her with an intense focus. With each article of clothing she removes, his smile gets bigger and his excitement more evident. Before she goes back to sitting on top of him she reaches down to unbutton his pants as he removes his shirt. He lifts his hips making it easier for her to pull them down.

Once they're off Jonathan pulls her down on top of him and kisses her fiercely as their bodies collide in a mix of passion, love, and desire.

# Chapter 52

## Inquietude
Noun; disturbed state

> *Present Day*

Jackie drives them to a little mom and pop place on the outside of Caulfield for breakfast. She figured there wouldn't be any one who would recognize Faith there. Jackie pulls into the pot-hole filled parking lot and Faith smiles.

"I've never been here. Have you?"

"No, but I thought it was a good idea to avoid anyone who might recognize you."

"It looks so quaint."

"From what I saw online, it kind of reminded me of the Café."

"I can see that."

As they enter the restaurant they're hit with a sense of nostalgia. The décor replicates the look of an old fifties diner. There's black and white checkered tiles on the floor and red and white vinyl on the booths and chairs. The quintessential look of any café of that time.

After they sit at a table, Jackie mentions, "You were pretty quiet on the drive here. Something on your mind that you want to talk about?"

"I was just thinking about the past, the first miscarriage, when the house was first built, and how he proposed."

"I know that it is hard for you with everything going on, but do you think that reminiscing about the past is the best thing to do right now?"

"I'm not so sure, but I know that I can't help it. In some ways it feels cathartic and in others it feels like I'm putting myself through hell all over again. For what, I'm not entirely sure."

"That's the part I'm worried about."

"Me too. Some days I wish there was a pill or something that I could take that would make me forget everything, but then again, I don't think I want to forget it all."

"I can't blame you for that."

Faith looks down at her hands that are wrapped around the cold glass of ice water, she stares at the engagement ring and wedding band still there. "I miss him, Jackie."

"I can imagine that you feel a plethora of emotions towards him right now."

"So many emotions." Faith gently shakes her head back and forth.

# APTITUDE

"At what point do you think that you'll be able to begin putting yourself first?"

"I've been trying. It's difficult." Faith leans in and lowers her voice when she says, "I don't want to believe that he's guilty. The love I have for him won't allow me to believe that."

"Not that I'm suggesting this, because I'm not. I'm curious if going to see him would help. Maybe seeing him in jail will make things seem that much more real for you."

Faith takes a deep breath as the image of the swat team hunting him down runs through her mind. "Nothing will make it more real for me than his arrest already has. The way they entered our property and home." She attempts to shake the image from her mind then continues. "It was like something out of a crime movie. It felt so violating."

"I can't even imagine what that must have been like for you, Faith. I'm so sorry."

"You have nothing to apologize for. No one knew what he was doing except him. He hid it from everyone."

"Have you wondered about that at all?"

"What?"

"Why he did it. Obviously we know why he hid it."

"I have some thoughts, but there's no way of knowing for sure."

"They should scan his brain. That would give us some answers."

"It would definitely be interesting to see."

"That should be a mandatory thing for violent criminals." Jackie points her finger for emphasis. "And they should be able to admit it as evidence."

"I think you might be on to something."

The waitress greets them, "I'm so sorry I didn't see y'all come in or I would have shimmied over here sooner! What can I get y'all?"

Faith looks down at the menu and orders the eggs benedict with hash browns and some orange juice. Jackie orders the Denver omelet with a side of fruit and apple juice to drink.

As they hand the menus to the waitress they both say, "Thank you." Simultaneously.

"You ladies are so welcome. I'll be right back with your juices and your food should be up shortly."

Jackie looks at Faith. "I'm very sorry. I want to help take your mind off of all of this and now that's all we're talking about."

"It's OK. Like I said, it can be cathartic in its own way."

The waitress returns with their juice and both women take a sip.

"Not to talk shop, but how are the kids in your class doing?"

"They've been my saving grace in all of this, honestly. They're the reason I get up in the morning. Well, them and Zeke of course."

"Glad to hear it. I strongly believe that we all need something worthwhile to look forward to."

# APTITUDE

"They definitely provide that. That's one of the reasons I was so desperate to keep my job. I would have nothing left if I didn't have that small semblance of normalcy."

"Well, you don't have anything else to worry about on that front. No one is taking your job from you if I have anything to say about it."

"You're a good friend, Jackie. Thank you. I'm not sure what I would do if I didn't have all of you in my corner."

"You'll never have to find out."

After breakfast, Jackie drives into Caulfield. "I was thinking we could go shopping. The outlet mall isn't too far from here."

"That's a great idea."

"Shopping therapy is always a great idea."

When they're finished shopping Jackie drives back to Faith's house. Zeke is eagerly waiting for them to come through the door. Faith bends down to give him ear scratches before going into the family room to set down her bags.

"You found some really nice pieces!"

"I did! It'll be a breath of fresh to wear somethings Jonathan has never laid eyes on before as weird as that might sound."

"It doesn't sound weird. It sounds like you're moving on." Jackie smiles.

"Not as quickly as I feel like I should be."

"Everything happens in the timing that is necessary, which isn't usually the timing we would prefer."

"I get that. It feels so drawn out. Like when will I get closure? After the trial? How long is that going to take? It all seems so far off."

"You shouldn't pressure yourself to feel a certain way if you're not ready."

"I know. I'm not trying to." Faith says as she pulls a new shirt from the bag. "It seems like everyone has some idea of what I should be doing. I honestly have no clue what I should be doing or feeling for that matter. It's all foreign to me. I've never been through this and I don't know anyone who has, so I have no point of reference for how to handle any of it either."

"You don't have to have all of the answers. I can stay as long as you need me to. You don't have to be alone right now."

"I'm not. I have Zeke." At the mention of his name he pads over to Faith and sniffs at the bags she set down on the couch.

"I know you have Zeke, but it isn't the same. Hope has Andy and her own responsibilities and your parents have the café so they can't really come and stay here. I don't have anything that requires my attention and if it helps having me here then I want to do what I can to help you."

"I appreciate that, Jackie. I truly do, I just don't know if that's going to help me. I think it will for a little bit, but long term, I need to be able to get back on my own two feet."

"So I stay for a week. I'm not trying to force my presence on you."

"OK. A week, and then we can go from there. I don't feel like you're trying to force yourself on me. I appreciate you so much."

Faith goes into the kitchen, grabs a glass and fills it with water then takes a sip.

"I'm going to run back to my house and pick up a few more things really quickly. You're OK here? Or do you want to come with me?"

"I'll stay here, thank you though." Faith feigns a smile.

After she walks Jackie out, she sits on the couch going through all of the clothing pieces she purchased that afternoon. She hadn't told Jackie, but she had thought about looking for something to wear to Jonathan's trial.

Once she realized that by the time the trial comes around she may not even want to go she started looking for practically a whole new wardrobe to replace her existing one.

Clothes have the power to make a woman feel entirely different and Faith wants that desperately. In the back of her mind she has also been thinking of cutting her hair, but she has come to the conclusion that doing something so rash could possibly end in a whole lot of regret.

Zeke lays down by Faith's feet as she pulls each piece out of the bags and removes the tags. When she's finished with that she carries them into their bedroom. She has an intrusive thought of cleaning out Jonathan's closet and putting all of his clothing, shoes, and watches in the fire pit and setting it ablaze, instead she closes the door to his closet and spins on her heels to face the door of her own closet. She opens it and assesses the amount of clothes she has. She knows she won't get rid of everything, but there is at least a few boxes worth that she will give away to the women's shelter in Caulfield.

It doesn't fix what Jonathan did by any stretch of the imagination, and it won't give Faith peace of mind, but it is, at the very least, a place to start.

She begins by removing things from hangers and then tosses them into a pile on the bed. Next, she puts her new clothes on the hangers she just cleared. When she's finished hanging everything up, she takes a step back and looks at her refreshed closet feeling empowered.

*I might have to do this to the rest of the house too.*

She sits down on the navy blue velvet bench in her closet and takes her phone out of her pocket. She starts looking for new bedding and utensils to order. Yes, this is exactly what she needs. The house could use a refresh, anyway.

Next, she finds herself creating mood boards for every room in the house including new paint colors and furniture.

If Jackie is going to be here for a week, she can help Faith refresh this place in whatever free time they may have. Faith knows this is going to take longer than a week, though. Having such a big project to plan and work towards is exact-

# APTITUDE

ly what she needs and maybe it will help the house feel a bit less tainted. Much like the new clothes are hopefully going to make her feel less tainted by the evil that is Jonathan Hall.

Please consider leaving a review at your retailer of choice to help other readers find books they'll love!

# Bonus Content

I truly hope you enjoyed Aptitude!! Click the link below to access the first three chapters of **Beatitude**– the next book in The Dark in the Light Series. You'll be asked to enter your email address which will automatically include you as part of our Virtual Vacation Lovers community, that way you can hear all about the incredible things J.S. Wik has coming up!
https://dl.bookfunnel.com/a59ohqc4ic

# Newsletter Sign up

If you would like to be part of our Virtual Vacation Lovers community, and hear all about the incredible things J.S. Wik has coming up, simply go to the website below to sign up!
(You'll even get a free eBook out of it as a thank you!)

https://www.jswik.com

# Also By J.S. Wik

You can scan or click depending on which format you're reading.

https://linktr.ee/JSWik

# About the Author

J.S. Wik lives in Wisconsin with her incredible husband, their amazing children and numerous pets of various species. When she isn't writing, you'll most likely find her out in the garden, or curled up on the couch with a good book, or possibly with a paintbrush in hand and a colorful canvas in front of her.

www.ingramcontent.com/pod-product-compliance
Lightning Source LLC
LaVergne TN
LVHW040035080526
838202LV00045B/3353